AFTER *Rain* FALLS

RIVER OF RAIN DUET
BOOK II

CE RICCI

Editing: Amy Briggs
Proofreading: Samantha Blessley and Zainab M.
Cover Design: Kate Farlow with Y'all. That Graphic

For anyone who has fought for love. Gone to war for it.

Whether you won or lost, at the very least…

You loved.

"Some rise by sin, and some by virtue fall."

- William Shakespeare

Measure For Measure

Theme Song:

Already Numb — Dayseeker

Playlist:

Another Life — Motionless In White
Give Me A Sign — Breaking Benjamin
The Black And White — The Band CAMINO
In Between — Beartooth
You & Me — Memphis May Fire
My Heart I Surrender — I Prevail
Do You Love Me? — Escape The Fate
Secrets — Slaves
Sleeptalk — Dayseeker
Follow You — Bring Me The Horizon
Power Over Me — Dermot Kennedy
Liquid Confidence (Nothing To Lose) — You Me At Six
Bitter — Citizen Soldier
Save Yourself — My Darkest Days
Disease — Beartooth
Killing Me Slowly — Bad Wolves
Fallout — Marianas Trench
Rome — Dermot Kennedy
Burial Plot — Dayseeker
What Hurts The Most — State of Mine
Through It All — From Ashes to New
The Stages of Grief — Awaken I Am
Crawling Back to You — Daughtry
Last Stand — Adelitas Way
Stay With Me — You Me At Six
Teardrops — Bring Me The Horizon
Pet Names — I The Mighty
Until the Day I Die — Story Of The Year
The Reason — Hoobastank

Listen to the playlist on Spotify

Preface

First, I want to let everyone know **this is book TWO** in the River of Rain Duet. If you haven't read book one, *Follow the River*, I highly suggest you pick that one up first because you'll be extremely lost if you don't!

Second, to all of you here for the second half of River and Rain's story, thank you. For loving them enough to come back for more. For all the love and support you've thrown my way in spades. I never imagined these two touching as many people as they have, and I hope they continue to resonate with everyone who reads them.

By now, you guys should've realized this story is raw. Real life things, ones that aren't always easy to swallow, happen to both of them. By each other's hand or by outside forces. It's not an easy love story where boy meets boy and they fall in love and live happily ever after with their two adopted kids and a house with a picket fence. Some characters might be lucky enough to have their story told without the drama, the angst, the heartache. So, if you're coming in hopeful this story is going to be less painful than the first, I'm sorry to disappoint you.

They aren't perfect. They hurt each other as much as they love each other. **They make mistakes.** They're going to do things that make you angry, happy, sad, and probably everything in between. But to me, it makes sense because that's how *real love* works in all of our lives. So if I'm doing my best to make them as real as possible, shouldn't their relationship be too?

For a list of triggers, please visit my website.
www.authorcericci.com/content-warnings/

ONE

Rain

I think I'm gonna be sick.

My knuckles clamp to the point of pain around the steering wheel of my Wrangler as I punch the gas. I'm desperate to get off this tarmac. Out of this city.

Away from him, even when he's the one person I should be running toward.

River.

The look on his face...decimated doesn't even begin to describe. I wouldn't be able to put it into words if it didn't match the feeling in my chest when I turned to find him standing there, not twenty yards from me.

Chasing after me like we're in some fucking rom-com.

But doesn't he know by now? This is nothing but a goddamn horror story.

I shouldn't have been surprised he followed me here. I saw

him in the gym when I passed by, lifting with Garrett. If I'm being honest, it's why I went in to talk to Coach about my lifting schedule changing at that particular time.

I knew he'd be there...and the masochist in me was dying to see him.

Especially after all the shit I said to him yesterday. All the lies that dropped out of my mouth, burning like acid with each word. And so to see him here, after all of it...it gutted me.

Because I know River. Probably better than I know myself. So, I know what was running through his mind when he got in his car and followed me here. What he wanted to do.

He was here to fight for me. For us.

Even when I gave him nothing left to fight for.

"Dude?" a voice startles me from my passenger seat, making me remember I'm not alone, no matter how much it might feel that way.

I glance over at Roman, the man who used to be my best friend, the person who held my entire life in the palm of his hand...and for the life of me, I don't understand how I ever compared River to him.

For a while, I thought they were so similar, what with the cocky, smartass comments and the happy-go-lucky vibes they radiate. Shit, I was even convinced my feelings for River were because the feelings I harbored for Roman still lingered on the surface of my barely beating heart.

But I see now...it isn't true.

"Yeah?" I ask, clearing my throat as I focus back on the road.

"I asked you who he was," Roman says, his brows furrowing over his dark eyes.

The keeper of my existence.

"No one," I reply, but the words catch in my throat inconveniently. As if my body is rejecting the notion that River is anything less than my everything.

Roman lets out a smoky chuckle, slightly deeper than the one I remember. "Can't bullshit a bullshitter, Rain. You know this."

My jaw ticks at my nickname coming from his lips, my heart feeling like someone is crushing it in their fist. And I almost laugh at the irony of this perverse situation I've found myself in. I hated River calling me Rain for so long because, yeah, I was convinced he and Roman were two of a kind. They seemed so similar, it felt like allowing River to call me Rain was a betrayal to Roman.

Because the name...I thought it would only ever belong on Roman's lips.

So as disgusting as it is, a part of me thought if I let River call me that, I was attempting to *replace* Roman with River. I'd let myself be in my most genuine form with someone who would remind me of the guy I thought I was in love with for years.

But now, when I've figured it out and realized the truth? I can't stand the sound of it from anyone else except River.

Even from Roman himself. It just doesn't feel right, not anymore.

Because in the cold light of day, if I had to choose, I know who it would be. I wouldn't have to think twice.

It's River.

Every star in the night sky would have to burn out before it isn't River.

And maybe even then, my mind replays his words from two nights ago.

And Jesus Christ, was it only two nights ago when I last slept with his body curled up next to mine for the last time? It feels like it's been a lifetime, not less than forty-eight hours.

"He's just a teammate," I grumble, my eyes hardening as I glare at him. It's a look which screams *don't fucking push me right now.*

And because he isn't River...he doesn't push.

They're nothing alike.

"Whatever you say." He lets out a laugh, turning his attention out the passenger window to watch the streets of Boulder come back into view.

Part of me can't believe he's actually here. In Colorado. In my car.

God, all of me can't believe he answered the phone when I called, let alone agreed to come help me with this shitty situation I've found myself in with Ted, the media, and just...life. After the way I treated him for the past few years—like he didn't fucking exist—I'm surprised he would be willing.

But that's just Roman for you and some things never change.

"Thank you," I say, working the words out past the knot lodged in my throat.

His eyes, a dark green hazel, come back to focus on mine and I find confusion in them. "I haven't done anything to earn a thank you."

"You came here to help me. I think it merits more than enough thanks, considering."

Roman lets out a sigh, shaking his head while pressing his index and middle fingers to his temple, elbow resting on the door. "I don't know how much help I can be, man. Not without bringing the entire crew in to deal with this disaster you call your family. But I'm certainly gonna try."

His mention of my family causes my spine to stiffen.

Don't fucking remind me.

Those two assholes, Ted and my mother, are the reason I'm driving away from the one person I care most about. Just to protect him.

I groan, letting my head fall back to hit the seat, loathing that I've found myself in this kind of situation. "I don't want to get you into shit, man. I know you're risking a lot by being here when you're supposed to be off...training or whatever it is you do these days."

Roman shrugs, flashing me a smirk I know well. I've always thought smiling was a good look on him, and it really does seem like not a damn thing has changed about the guy in four years. "Don't sweat it. I knew what I was signing up for by taking a contract outside the Enclave." His eyes move over my face like he's memorizing it, causing a sting to shoot up my chest. "It's just good to see you."

Swallowing harshly, I give him the most convincing smile I can muster. Which isn't much at all, what with my heart being left on the tarmac of the airport and my ex-best friend sitting in the passenger seat beside me, ready to help take down my evil, sadistic stepfather.

And here I thought I would have a normal semester of college for once.

Roman returns my smile, but I can tell by the look in his eyes he knows it's false. Even still, he doesn't say anything or call me out. Like always.

And my mind immediately moves back to Doctor Fulton and our conversation about Roman and River only a few short months ago.

Goddammit.

River.

A war is waging inside me, part of me begging to turn the car around and go back to him. Tell him everything, including that I love him and I'm so fucking sorry for saying what I did yesterday.

But the other part of me latches on to what Roman said. About needing to bring the rest of his crew in. About the disaster that is my family.

I can't bring River into that shit. Ask him to blindly trust me because, what? Because I love him?

That's insane.

"So, what's first on the agenda? I'm assuming you want to get this ball rolling as soon as possible? Take down this asshole for good so life can go back to normal?" Roman asks, breaking me from my thoughts as he reaches over to turn the dial on the radio.

I shake my head and glance at his hand before looking back at the road. "I don't even know where to start, but yeah. I guess a plan would be useful."

Leaning back in his seat after settling on a station, he sighs. "Well, I guess the first thing I need to know is if he's been in contact with you at all since the whole investigation started this fall."

My eyes flash to his as the last time I heard from Ted runs through my mind.

The night in Portland when he told me to come home for Thanksgiving.

Where I got fucked up and hallucinated Deacon dead on a coffee table, and going to the bathroom and fucking the—*shit,* and then hallucinating *Roman* in there with me.

Clearing my throat, I flick my eyes back to the road ahead. "A few months back, not long before Thanksgiving."

"And did he know you were in Boulder yet? Know where to find you?"

My jaw ticks, unease spreading through my body. "I don't know if he was aware of me switching schools, but I wasn't in Boulder when it happened." Licking my lips, I keep my eyes straight ahead as I bite the words out. "I was in Portland, actually. After the loss against the Ducks."

It's fine, Rain. You can be in the same state as Roman. It doesn't mean he saw you fuck a random cleat chaser in a club bathroom.

But when I find the balls to glance back at Roman, I find him staring at me in surprise.

"What?" I question, swallowing roughly.

"You were in Portland, and you didn't think to look me up?" He doesn't come off as angry, simply lifting a brow in amusement.

I clear my throat, avoiding his penetrating gaze once more. "I didn't really have a chance to, uh, go do anything. Late game, and we flew out early the next morning," I lie.

He would have said something if he were there that night. Right?

Roman gives me an easy smile, flashing two rows of perfect white teeth before settling back into his seat. "I'm just fucking with you. Relax."

Relax. Right. I can relax easy enough.

It's not like I have a step-father who is rampaging and probably looking for a million ways to make me disappear from the world, and a best friend who I haven't seen in years sitting beside me to help me try to take him down, and a man I'm in love with whose heart I probably just shattered, and —

"Rain," Roman calls, halting the rampant thoughts in my brain. "I said *relax*, not put a Hulk grip on the goddamn steering wheel."

Checking my hands, I see them white-knuckled on the wheel

to the point if I squeezed any harder, I'd break...something. Whether it be the wheel or a bone in my hand, it's a toss-up.

Shaking my head, I loosen my hands, attempting to let the small amount of relief I feel by his presence flood my system. Except, it doesn't work. I'm too wired, both mentally and emotionally. "Sorry. I'm trying."

"Hey," Ro cocks his head, turning in his seat slightly to face me. "It's gonna be fine. I've got your back."

My words catch in my throat at the sincerity of his voice. It's unexpected, really. Just like him agreeing to come here. I was a shit friend the last night we saw each other, and I'd deserve so much worse than just a cold shoulder from him.

Letting out a long sigh, I nod. "I know, Ro."

He lifts a brow skeptically. "*Do* you?"

I let out a strained laugh, knowing he's picking up on every ounce of anxiety I'm feeling right now, just like he would when we were kids.

This is the person you trusted most in the world at one point in your life. The person you told everything to. The person you called to get you out of this shit-storm you're about to face.

It's Roman, for fuck's sake.

When my mind begins to settle after a couple minutes, I rub my temple and glance at him to find him waiting patiently, like the rock he's always been for me.

"I *do* know, man. I'm just..."

"Flustered," he supplies with a nod. "I get it. I don't blame you. It's a lot to take in on its own without tossing me *and* my connections into the mix. Especially after everything that happened…" He trails off, eyes flashing out the window, settling on the passing city. I catch sight of his hands running up and down his legs, anxious and very un-Roman like.

An uncomfortable silence settles between us, and it's a feeling I'm not used to when it comes to our relationship. At least, the one we had four years ago.

"I want to apologize for the night in the pool," he says softly after a while, still watching the city fly by. "Before I left. I never meant for it to fuck with our friendship. I just…" I watch his throat work to swallow before he rubs his thumb over his jaw and looks back at me, his complexion pale enough for me to be slightly worried he might pass out. "I hope you can forgive me."

The gravel in his voice and regret in his eyes speak volumes.

Roman has never been the kind of person to apologize easily, to feel regret. He's not an overly emotional person, at least in the sense of outwardly sharing and being open about them. He's always happy and charming and fun to be around, but when it comes to *actual feelings*, he's just about as clueless as I am.

Yet another difference between him and River.

Shaking free of the thoughts, because I know they'll get me absolutely nowhere but back at the airport at a neck-breaking speed, I give Roman a soft smile.

"There's nothing to forgive," I tell him, and surprisingly, I mean every single word.

But how can I hold something from our past against him now, years later, when he dropped everything to help me? Even *I'm* not that big of a self-important asshole.

"It's water under the bridge."

His face visibly regains two shades of color as he exhales, giving me a smile. "Thank fuck 'cause I've missed my best friend."

I smirk, shaking my head. "Missed you too, RoRo," I say with a chuckle, using his sister's favorite nickname for him.

He reaches over and shoves my shoulder playfully, the way he used to do when I had issues with returning any semblance of affection. "Say it like you mean it, fucker. I just flew halfway across the world in the dead of night for you." He laughs, running his fingers through his hair. "I even packed *jeans* and *sweatpants* in a *duffel bag* as fast as I could. No suits in sight."

That earns him a full-blown grin, knowing the asshole is only ever comfortable in dress clothes; the kind of weirdo he is. He'd sleep in a three-piece suit if it wouldn't wrinkle it to hell.

"And I bet it just about killed you."

He sighs, shaking his head. "Not as much as leaving the Lambo at the airport where anything could happen to it." His eyes flash to mine briefly before he quirks a brow. "You do know you're buying me a new one if I go back to find a scratch on it, right?"

I roll my eyes, shoving his shoulder. "Fat fucking chance. You're richer than God, you can buy a new one yourself. Or have it flown back here."

"There's a grand idea, though, I'm not rich. My *father* is rich," he points out, cocking his head slightly.

"You do realize that's literally something *only* rich people say?" I scoff, but a smile plays at the edge of my lips. He just shakes his head and gives me his megawatt grin known for getting him out of anything.

And for a split second, it's like it used to be. Old times when life was simple and we were just Roman and Rain, inseparable best friends who had each other's backs above anyone else.

Before a heated, drunken kiss, full of anxiety and fear of the unknown fucked it up. Before all this bullshit with Ted came to a head, painting me with the label of a victim. Before we went *four fucking years* without contact because we're both too stubborn for our own good.

Before I went to that cabin and fell in love with River.

And there he is again.

Goddamn, I need to be able to go more than five minutes without thinking about him or I will drive myself off a cliff just to make sure my brain physically *can't* form a single thought ever again.

It feels like he's ingrained himself into every single cell of not only my brain, but also my skin, my bones, my…heart and I can't do anything but think, breathe, and fucking *yearn* for him since last night.

It's exhausting.

As if on cue, the familiar beat of Beartooth's "Disease" begins playing through the speakers of my Jeep. Biting the inside of my cheek so hard it bleeds, I jam my finger on the dial to silence the radio as quickly as possible.

Except it doesn't matter, because the ache in my chest only intensifies.

Because I'll never be able to hear a damn Beartooth song without thinking of River and his tapping fingers and the songs in his mind ever again.

Fucking hell.

He should've tattooed his name across every available inch of my skin in exchange for my sanity because in the end, I'll never be anything but his. Until my dying day, I'll belong to River Lennox.

And for some godforsaken reason, the idea alone of branding myself with his name has the hair on my arms standing on end. As idiotic as it might be, I want it on me.

Forever claiming me.

"You sure you're all good, man?" Ro asks, a slight sense of unease in his voice

No, I'm going fucking insane.

Scrubbing a hand over my face, I let out an exasperated sigh before glancing at him quickly. "I'll be fine. Just stressed." I grunt out the lie, tapping against the wheel, desperate to talk myself out of the dumbest idea I've ever had.

Except, I don't care how dumb it is.

Last night was hell without him there with me. I couldn't even sleep, knowing what was to come today and all the days ahead of us. *Not* knowing how long it would be before I could make an effort to explain everything to him so he'll forgive me.

If he'll forgive me. Because I know there's a massive chance he won't.

And the thought alone makes the idea of having his name on my skin even more enticing. At least that way I would carry a piece of him with me to my grave. Which is *something* if I can't have *him*.

So, when a strip mall with a sign glaring the word TATTOO at me in bright neon letters comes into view, I take it as a sign from Jesus himself.

Fuck it.

"We'll start planning as soon as we make a pit stop.

TWO
Roman

Part of me is still in shock I'm here. Not just in the US after spending the last two months in Asia for what's supposed to be my final part of training. But *here*, in Colorado.

In Rain's apartment, sitting on his goddamn bed like the last *four years* of silence never happened. Pretending he didn't toss me out the window the night before I moved to Oregon.

The night I put my heart on the line and effectively ruined the one good thing in my life that wasn't related to me by blood or obligation.

So yeah, it might not have been the brightest move I'd ever made, kissing him when I knew I was leaving. *Especially* when I knew he was...confused, to say the least. With everything that happened to him, I didn't blame the guy for not understanding what he wanted. And like the supportive best friend I was, I did my best to help him however I could.

Even when I could see the way I'd catch him looking at me

randomly. With a spark in his eyes, speaking so much more of lust than it did friendship.

Still, I wouldn't do anything about it. Wouldn't touch him. Didn't dare toe the line of our friendship because misreading his signals would've been the end of our friendship entirely. I know it to be true now more than ever.

But my last night in Philly, I decided I was done waiting and made the move I was desperate to make for years. I was sick of pussyfooting around my feelings for him, the feelings I've had for him since...forever.

Since we were kids.

I had to know. I just had to know for sure, before I was shipped off to fulfill my duty as an heir to a legacy, lasting hundreds of years. Before I moved across said goddamn country, where my life would become nothing but a string of monotonous training, historical education, and all the shit that comes with being part of a secret society. Not that I ever fucking asked to be part of this bullshit in the first place.

It's just what happens when you're thrust into something like the Enclave because of ancestry and birthright alone.

I was in a shit place that night four years ago, knowing where my life was about to take me. I didn't want to leave, I was going out of my mind trying to figure a way for me to stay.

Or better yet, for him to come with me. Even though I knew both of those ideas were impossible in anything other than theory, no matter how hard I still try to convince myself otherwise.

So, as selfish and shitty as it might have been, I kissed him.

Fuck, I more than kissed him. I had my hand down his trunks, my fist around his cock, and…he fucking loved it. He was right there with me. Felt everything I did. The lust, the desire, the uncontrollable attraction.

And for a split second, I thought he was finally mine, if only for a night.

Until he wasn't.

"I only have the couch for you to sleep on," Rain tells me, pulling me from my thoughts before they can drown me in regret and longing. I glance up from my spot on the edge of his bed to see him standing in the doorway, shoulder leaning against the frame.

He looks good—really fucking good—after all these years. Different, but still the same.

Still muscular, athletic, and downright oozing with sex appeal due to all the intricate artwork on his body. But increasingly so.

Yet somehow, he's more. I don't know how or why, but it's something about him that's grown.

More composed in his presence. More confident and self-assured. More himself.

Whatever it is, whatever's caused it, I hope he keeps it up. The level of balance he radiates now, it's a good look on him. Even if his poise slipped fractionally when he saw his teammate on the tarmac.

I don't know what the story is there—and there clearly is one—but at this point, I don't have it in me to care. I'm here and that's what matters. Against all odds.

"Whatever is fine. You sure you're cool with me crashing here?" I ask him, raising a brow. My eyes travel to his right wrist, to one of the few places his sleeve of Celtic tattoos don't reach, and see the single word he had inked into his skin this afternoon beneath the clear plastic shit the artist put over it to protect it.

Abhainn.

While I watched the artist press the ink and needle into his skin, I googled the word, curious why this was more important than starting to devise a plan against Ted, only to find out it was the Gaelic word for river.

Why the hell he wanted that particular body of water tattooed, specifically in Gaelic, I haven't the slightest idea. Probably something to do with his dad would be my best guess. But with knowing Rain as long as I have, I've learned when to push and when to let things slide. Pointing out we had more pressing matters to attend to was definitely the latter.

"Yeah, it's not an issue. I can pick up an air mattress if that'd be better, though," Rain tells me, still leaning against the frame.

I smirk. "What, you aren't gonna let me sleep in your bed with you like we used to when we were kids? Head to foot because it's not gay that way?"

I expect him to laugh it off with me, but the way he winces at my words makes me uneasy.

Shit.

I grimace, noting he might have accepted my apology for those years ago, but things clearly are still strained between us. "Bad joke or tough crowd?"

Rain's eyes have a dangerous fire in them as he shakes his head, and smiles, though it once again feels forced. "Nah, man. Just might take a second to adjust to the…banter."

It shouldn't hurt, the way he says it. Of course, shit's still gonna be awkward between us, even if we did sort of clear the air in the Jeep on the way back into town from the airport. But it's a razorblade to the chest to hear him still be uneasy with me when we used to be inseparable.

Guess it just proves there are some things the foundation of a friendship can't withstand without making some sort of crack.

I shrug and fake a smile, though I think it's far more convincing than his because he seems to relax a hair the second he sees it. "No worries. We're good, though?"

Please say yes and make me less of a fool for flying halfway around the world in less than twenty-four hours for you.

Better yet, please say yes so I feel like less of a goddamn idiot for harboring feelings that I should've set free the moment you turned me down in the pool.

"Yeah." He laughs softly, turning to leave. "I promise, we're solid. I honestly can't thank you enough for actually being here."

I bite the inside of my cheek as he exits the room before spewing off something stupid like *nowhere else I'd rather be* because if I'm not careful, he's sure to kick me the fuck out as quick as he called me.

Hell.

I still can't believe he called me.

Out of everyone in the world, he called *me*.

No, he *needed* me. He fucking *sobbed* those three words into the phone the second I picked up. Before I could even speak a damn word.

After *four years*.

How the fuck was I supposed to say no?

"What's wrong?" I ask, wiping the sweat from my brow and taking a seat on the sparring mat. Giving my trainer the hand signal for just a minute, I pull my legs up into my chest and wait for a response.

"Ro..." he chokes out my name, and I can hear the agony in his voice.

Swallowing roughly, I whisper his name. Just his name.

"I... need your help. Ted...he's — "

My vision immediately fades to black as he recounts the details the news has been sharing about the building FBI case against Senator Anders. The raid on the therapist. The tapes, hidden for years only to be turned over by his mother.

And then all of it came to a head today when the FBI released his name to the press after confirmation of the tapes landing in their possession.

By the end, Rain's breathing heavily and struggling to keep it together until I faintly hear a woman's voice in the background.

"Is there someone with you right now?" The words come out with more bite than I intend, jealousy flaring through me, but thankfully, I don't think he noticed.

"My therapist," he answers gruffly. "She's the one who showed me the news clip."

My mind is reeling that he'd even consider going to see a therapist again, seeing as it's what caused half of this issue in the first place, but that's a question for another time.

"What do you need from me, Rain? What can I do?"

Fuck, am I really about to drop everything to run to his side? My legacy, my training, my dedication to family and country?

But the second he asks me to come to Colorado and help him plan his next move, I know there's no use fighting it. The hold he has over me. The one he's had since we were nothing more than boys, too young to know a damn thing about love.

"I'll be there tomorrow," I tell him without hesitation.

Because I will be. I'll do anything for the people I care about, the people I love.

Even when I shouldn't...like right now.

"Are you sure?" The anxiety in his voice is palpable; I can feel it running through my own veins the moment I hear it. "I mean, I'm sure you're busy with...whatever you're doing these days. I just know your connections could –"

"I'm fucking sure," I insist confidently, feeling anything but. I could get myself into some seriously deep shit, pulling out of training when I'm only months away from becoming an apprentice.

But...I have to go to him. In my mind, I don't have any other option.

I rise to my feet and grab my bag from against the wall. Glancing over to my trainer, I give him a wave, letting him know we're done for the night.

Perks of being his boss, I suppose.

I jog out into the night to the door of my Lamborghini in the parking lot, the only piece of home I brought with me for my time here, not saying a word. When I toss my bag inside, still on the line with Rain, I finally speak since he, too, has fallen silent.

"I'll text you when the jet's an hour out from Boulder. Just meet me at the airport and we'll go from there," I tell him, throwing the car into drive as I start barreling toward my apartment.

A sigh full of relief sounds from the other side of the line. "Thank you, Ro."

My throat constricts with his gratitude, knowing I'm partially to blame for him having to make this call in the first place. Because I couldn't stand up for him, or for myself, when we were teenagers and fight for what I thought we both wanted.

Each other.

Or even when we overheard meetings between Ted and my father as boys, discussing an under-the-table Enclave contract, strictly between the two of them. I never stood up and spoke my mind, knowing it was against the code we were taught to live by.

What kind of legacy does that make me?

Especially now, as I'm about to take a page out of Father's book and run a private contract behind my brothers' backs.

"I'll see you soon," I whisper into the phone. I'm desperate to stay on the line with him and keep hearing his voice, but knowing I have preparations to make, I disconnect the call before he has a chance to respond.

Turning my attention back to the road, I dial the pilot we have on payroll, thankful I had the foresight to bring him with me while I completed this last bit of my training in Thailand.

I speed back into the city from the training center after ordering him to have the jet ready within the hour, only stopping to grab the essentials from my apartment and bolting back to my car to head for the airport.

This is stupid, I know it is. Reckless and dangerous on so many accounts, and not just for the supersonic speeds I'm pushing my Lambo to as I race through the dimly lit streets at close to one in the morning.

No one has to know, *I remind myself.* Everyone knows you're over here. They won't be looking for you, least of all expect you to be in *Colorado* of all places.

Those thoughts ease my mind slightly, and I begin ticking all the boxes, making sure there won't be any loose ends left to untangle.

My trainer is under my employment, as each Enclave legacy is allowed to hire one in their preferred method of self-defense; mine being Muay Thai. I know he won't say jack to anyone unless I allow it. Even to Father.

The rest of the legacies are back in Oregon, either completing courses or staying at the Estate.

Father is in D.C., per usual. The rest of the elders, also at their respective posts, depending where in the world they're needed. The closest being Moscow, thousands of miles from here.

This is going to work. It'll be fine.

And I'm truly convinced of that until I get to the airport and park my car, only to remember the GPS tracker on it. A safety precaution, they said while installing it back in Oregon the minute I set foot on the Estate property four years ago.

Fuck.

At this point, I don't have any other choice but to leave it here and pray they don't notice it sitting at the airport for God knows how long. But even as I think it, I know I'm screwed.

"Are we ready to take off?" I ask the pilot as I run up the steps of the jet, bag in hand.

"Yes, sir. Just waiting for the okay from air traffic controls. Please take a seat. If luck is on our side, we'll be in the air in less than five minutes."

Luck.

I could almost laugh, knowing it's the one thing I need, but I doubt I'll fucking have. Not in this situation.

They'll figure it out. They'll know I've left.

Abandoned my training. Putting something — someone — before my duties and obligations. Risking some of our secrets to be brought to light.

And for a split second, I don't care. It feels worth it.

Because this is about more than that. It's life and death and protecting those you love.

Because I feel...free. Almost as if I'm running away from them *as much as I'm running* to him.

And I allow myself one minute to believe that's even an option.

THREE

Rain

It's been weeks.

Almost a month since Roman got here and we're still sitting at square one.

No progress has been made in our efforts to find Ted, which means no progress has been made in getting my life back to...*fuck.* Some semblance of normal, if you could call it that.

All my life consists of now is bouncing between dealing with the FBI agent who I meet with weekly, doing my own investigating on the side with Roman, weight training, and school. Although, the last one has taken a bit of a backseat lately.

Oops.

Oh, and how could I forget avoiding the media?

That's been fucking wonderful. Having cameras shoved in my goddamn face whenever I leave my apartment, attempting to get the inside scoop on this case, my thoughts on Ted, the truth behind what happened to me, whatthefuckever it might be that they're looking for. They're snakes in the grass, the lot of them, just waiting to strike whenever they find most convenient.

And it pisses me off.

Thankfully, they've died down more recently as Ted's whereabouts remain a mystery.

That's why I'm heading to a local bar on a Friday night with Roman. Because if I'm stuck in my fishbowl of a one-bedroom apartment for another night with Ro stewing in the semi-awkwardness still lingering between us, I think I'll probably lose my mind.

To be clear, it's not awkward because of harbored feelings or anything. On the contrary, Roman just makes me think of River and the broken expression on his face at the airport every time I look at him.

Which only serves to break my heart even more, if it's possible.

I slam my Jeep door shut, walk around to the front to the entrance of the bar, and wait a moment for Roman to get off the phone.

He's been talking to *his guys* a lot, the others he thinks can help us out with this Ted situation. Not that he's asked for their help. He said he'd rather keep this "off the books" for as long as he can, whatever that means.

A few minutes later, Roman gives me a grin as he slips through the bar in front of me, looking like the cat who ate the goddamn canary, not saying a single word.

He hasn't told me a lot about his time with those guys, the *Enclave,* as they're called. At least from what I recall from our childhood. And our conversation in the car a few weeks back.

As if my life isn't enough of a shitshow already, go figure, my best friend would be involved in a fucking secret society. Still, I know only the surface of the power and clout they hold. I've seen it firsthand. Hell, it's yet another reason why I'm in this shitty situation in the first place.

Shaking my head, I follow him through the threshold of the bar. But I'm not more than two steps in the door when I feel *him.*

His presence is one I've become so attuned to, it's easier to feel than the wind on my skin or the heat of the sun.

River.

He's here. In this bar.

I haven't seen him since the day I left him at the airport, and I wasn't really planning on having to see him tonight. Preferring the *out-of-sight, out-of-mind* approach. Not that it fucking works, what with seeing his name on my wrist every day.

When I'm not thinking about Ted and how to get out from under his thumb, it's River who occupies my every waking thought. My nightmares too.

Ever since we got back from the cabin, the reoccurring nightmare where *I* am raping *River* has been plaguing my mind every goddamn night. I don't even dream about Deacon's death anymore, and *rarely* do I dream about the things Ted did to me.

It's only River. *Always* River.

So, despite the fact that I know he's here, I keep my path aimed for the bar because right now, I need a drink. To drown my sorrows. To forget. To do *anything* other than think about my shitty as hell situation.

And more than that? I'm a fucking masochist who wants nothing more than to be in River's presence—to feel him near me—at least for a little while. Even if it kills me.

Ro and I order our drinks, a whiskey neat for him, beer for me, before he settles against the bar and starts talking my goddamn ear off in the annoying way he's been doing ever since he got here.

God, why am I such a fucking dick?

I should be grateful he's here and willing to help me, not irritated with him for wanting to talk and catch up on what we've missed in each other's lives over the past few years. But honestly, I'm getting tired of it. It's not as if I haven't heard everything he's had to say for almost the past *month* when I've seen him for a majority of my waking hours.

Taking a swig of my beer, I nod and answer when needed in response to Roman's jabbering, but he must realize I don't really feel like talking because he turns and starts chatting with a girl seated next to us at the bar.

Good ole Roman, never pushing me off the cliff.

I swear that's all I think about when he and I have a conversation. The way Doctor Fulton spelled shit out for me even when she wasn't supposed to, since it's against literally every therapist rule there is.

Because, uh...hello, gaslighting.

I just wish I would've put that shit together *before* I found out she was employed by my mother. Hindsight, I guess.

The hair on the back of my neck stands on end when I'm in the middle of another drink of my beer and I hear the distinct sound of River's laugh. Goosebumps rise over my skin and I almost spit my fucking beer out all over the bar.

I should be the one making him laugh right now. Not

pretending he doesn't exist, even as the buzz in my veins alerts me of his proximity, making it damn near impossible to forget.

I don't look up, though. I don't give in to the temptation, no matter how strong it is. Because I know the second I do…there's a very real possibility I'll cave. And I'll run over to him and claim him as mine for the entire fucking world to see.

And I *can't* do that. Because someone is bound to see. Because even though the media hasn't been harassing me as much the last few days compared to when the news broke, they're still around. If they don't see, someone will. If not this time, then the next, and then soon enough, word will spread, and people will know. And that thought, while it should terrify me because of what it means for my *sexuality*, is the least of my worries.

No, people can't know, because if *people* find out, it means *Ted* can find out.

He can't find out about River.

So, even though I haven't so much as seen a glimpse of the man I'm in love with since the day at the tarmac, I grit my teeth and stay strong.

Roman, on the other hand, is staring in the direction I feel the heat flares coming from. His brows furrow as he looks toward River, confusion contorting his face, making the urge to look even stronger.

Biting his lip, his attention dances between me and River over my shoulder before settling on me. "You want to head back to your place? Grab a pizza or something? Just hang out?"

"We've been just *hanging out* for weeks now," I growl, glaring at him. "We've been trapped in my goddamn apartment to hide from the vultures, and I'm going insane. Worse than being trapped in the fucking cabin the first ten days."

He cocks his head. "What are you talking about? What cabin?"

As if the mention of hell on Earth was a calling card, it's in that moment I feel it. His eyes on me, burning through my skin, searing into my very soul.

And like the weak sonofabitch I am, I cave at his attention.

Spinning around, my eyes lock immediately on River across the bar, and to my horror, he's got his arm wrapped around Abbi's shoulder in a way that sets my blood to a boil.

Jealousy rears its ugly head because in my mind, he's still mine. He will always be mine and only *ever* mine.

So, why the fuck does she look so comfortable in his embrace?

I scan them, cataloging every inch of the scene and committing it to memory to playback when I feel the need to torture myself some more before I allow our gazes to collide.

All the air inside my lungs is stolen the moment they do.

Because as sexy and perfect as I think he is…he looks rough. Like he hasn't been sleeping well, eating enough, whatever it might be.

In short, he looks like I fucking feel. Like shit.

But it doesn't stop him from raising a brow and smirking at me before lifting his beer bottle to his lips for a pull.

My eyes latch on to the way his throat moves, his Adam's apple bobbing with every swallow. I remember what it was like to kiss and lick and suck on it like it was only yesterday when I had the right to do so.

Taking a deep breath and meeting his stare again, I find those gorgeous eyes...empty.

Hollow, even.

You did that to him, my brain reminds me. *This is what you wanted. To make him think you don't give a fuck about him.*

I know it's what I wanted. I just never thought he'd believe it.

A hand on my shoulder snaps me back to reality. The firm grip causes me to turn and see Roman, his hard stare plastered to me.

"Your teammate looks like he wants to kill you. Are you sure you're good with being here?"

I just nod once, fighting the urge to glance back at River as the music changes to some shitty country song. Roman sighs and shakes his head, looking at River while speaking to me. "Is his issue with the shit on the news, you think?"

Nope, his issue is I'm a fucking jackass and treated him like he was a meaningless fuck when he's the only thing I give a damn about anymore.

"Nah, we got into some shit last season is all. Probably still pissed about it," I lie, the words slipping off my tongue all too easily.

Roman's brows lift. "Is this the guy you punched on the field during a game and got ejected for it? Your QB?"

Does everyone *know about that?*

I wince, recalling the final game a few months ago when I punched River for calling me out on my shit. A shitty move I never had the chance to apologize for, amongst so many other things.

"Yeah, that's him. I guess, Lennox just isn't over my right hook yet."

Or the broken heart I left him with.

"Lennox? That's the guy's name?"

Gritting my teeth, I rub my thumb over the new tattoo on my wrist absently. "No, his name is River. Lennox is his last name."

Roman laughs, momentarily eyeing my hand. "No wonder

you decked him. Bunch of fucking hippies out here with their nature-named kids. The same thing happens out in Oregon." He shrugs, meeting my eyes. "Anyone with a name like that is just asking to get hit."

Anger bubbles up in me because *fuck him* for being a prick right now. Picking on River's *name?* What the hell? This isn't the Roman I grew up with, and this most definitely isn't the conversation I need to be having right now.

"Oh really? Then why is it you've called me *Rain* since we were eight?"

He just smirks at me, biting his lip. "You should know by now you're special. Always the exception to the rule."

Then he checks me out, his eyes scanning my body *right here in the middle of the goddamn bar.* And it does abso-fucking-lutely nothing, except make me even more pissed than I already am.

"Fuck off, Ro. Don't look at me like that," I snap, grabbing my beer off the bar counter before leaning against it, turning back to meet River's eyes again.

Except, he's not there when I look. Which wouldn't be the end of the world...if Abbi wasn't *also* missing.

Shit, did he leave with her? Is he taking her home?

Is he fucking *her now?*

Each and every ounce of panic and insecurity rises in my chest, and I hear a strangled choke come from my throat as I attempt to breathe steadily.

No, no, no. River doesn't look at her that way. He's not the type to move on so quickly. It's fine. He probably just took her out for air or she went to the bathroom or literally anything *else.*

But I still scan the bar, searching for him, needing my overactive imagination to be put to rest. It doesn't matter we aren't together or I told him all those shitty things. It doesn't matter we haven't seen or spoken to each other since the day we arrived home from Vail.

None of it fucking matters.

He's still mine, just like I'll always be his.

There's nothing happening with her.

The song flips again, this time to something a little slower than the previous, which isn't really fitting for a bar setting like this. It's...alternative, almost.

And the voice of the singer...it's so familiar, I swear I know it.

It takes a moment, but suddenly it clicks into place because I've heard it once before. Recently, in fact.

Up in Vail at the cabin.

The band, You Me at Six, is one of River's favorites.

"Liquid Confidence" is the title, which always gave me a good laugh when it came on.

But I'm not laughing now because as the first chorus rings though the bar, I know what this is.

A message.

From River.

Don't ask me how or why I know, I just fucking do. Deep in my soul, I know he's telling me the song in his head right now, the song I'm always dying to know but no longer have the right to ask for.

My throat goes dry as I search for him around the bar in vain, the lyrics flooding over my skin like an acidic tidal wave.

Telling me I have nothing to lose except for… well, us.

Panic rises in my chest as I frantically search for him, desperate to have his teal eyes lock with mine. Make an attempt to explain myself. Tell him I'm so fucking *sorry* for everything I did, what I said. Even though I know I can't tell him those things.

I know I shouldn't show my cards, let him see I still care. My mind was certain weeks ago a clean break would be best for us, and I know that still rings true now. If I could keep my distance, get this shit sorted out…*then* I could crawl on my hands and knees back to him and *beg him* and whoever might listen to take me back.

As my eyes flick over the area near one of those modern style jukeboxes and then back to where he was standing with Abbi moments ago, I'm terrified he's snuck out without my notice.

But the hum in my blood along with the heat on my skin lets me know he's here.

He's still here and he's got his eyes on me, even if I can't see him.

And when the second verse about love hurting more than you can dream of starts to lead into the chorus once again, I swear to fucking God, it takes every ounce of my willpower not to scream.

Godmotherfuckingdammit.

I hate the honesty in the lyrics, the truth behind each of them. Because at this moment, I *feel* them.

All I want right now as I stand in this bar, searching and praying to find his eyes, is to not be in love with him. To be able to walk and talk and fucking breathe every day without feeling like the weight of the world is sitting on my chest.

I just want the pain to end, the misery and agony of trying to live without him, gone.

And Jesus, I can't even begin to acknowledge the fact that by playing this song, he's admitting to being in love with me too.

Because if I let myself think too much about it, I'm doomed.

My mission to take Ted down, my quest to keep River safe and out of the crossfire…will fall apart the moment I let myself *feel* the love pouring out of him. I won't be able to stop myself from claiming him, right here and now for the entire world to see.

And I can't do that.

I can't bring him into the fold on this. If he knew what was happening, where this is leading, he'd just be in harm's way. That's why I cooked up this scheme to begin with.

I could have told him the truth from the very beginning, sure. Then, River being River — the world's most perfectly annoying and frustrating man he is — would tell me *we can be careful. We can play it safe, just to be sure nothing bad happens.*

Except I know River. Well enough to realize if shit started to go sideways, he would be on the frontlines in an instant. He'd be right by my side instead of staying behind, no matter if I begged him to.

Because he doesn't fucking listen.

And *that*, in this particular instance, could get him killed.

So, despite the need coursing through my body and the anguish plaguing my mind, I force my eyes closed. Take a deep breath. Count to ten. Remember the pros and cons of why it has to be this way, even if it causes my mind to run in circles.

I mentally coach myself to open my eyes and walk out of this bar without a backward glance. Like he means nothing to me.

It's the only way to guarantee he'll stay alive.

Except when I finally do manage to calm my erratic heart enough to school my features and open my eyes…I find him.

He's back where he was when I first saw him. Across the bar, his arm still wrapped around Abbi, like he never left. She's busy chattering to a guy and girl nearby, moving her arms animatedly with every word.

But River's watching me.

His head tilts to the side, zoning in on me before flashing his attention over my shoulder, where Roman is chatting with the bartender. Then with a smirk, he does something I never saw coming.

He grabs the back of Abbi's head, turning it and planting a kiss on her lips for me to watch. And watch, I fucking do. I watch as his hands tangle in her hair, his lips moving over hers. I watch as he takes her bottom lip between his teeth, tugging before releasing it with a smile.

I see red as every piece of my soul is shoved through a woodchipper at the sight of his smile aimed at anyone but me.

God, I need to hit something. Fuck, maybe even *kill* something.

My past. My fucking stepfather. This bitch with her lips glued to River's and her fingers laced in his hair.

I want to put all of it six feet under at this moment.

When he pulls away after far too long for my comfort, licking his lips before aiming a smirk at me, I see a glassy sheen in his eyes through the rage in mine. I can't seem to place it as sadness or drunkenness, but either way, it doesn't make me any less pissed off.

Because I have no clue what the stunt was.

Putting on a show? Revenge? Laying claim?

I just don't. Fucking. Know.

I quickly down the contents of my beer in an attempt to numb the pain stabbing me with every beat of my heart. When it's gone,

I slam the empty bottle on the bar and meet his eyes again.

The wicked glint in them is new, something that I never thought I'd see. It speaks only of animosity and hatred.

I know this because it's the way *I* used to look at *him.*

Biting his lip, he smiles at me before opening his mouth to speak. At first I think it's to someone, maybe Abbi, but the way no one turns to look at him and how his eyes never leave me, I know the words are meant for me.

It's only then that I realize…

We are an example of…

Fuck me.

I watch as those perfect, kiss swollen lips mouth the words to me over and over in time with the song. Telling me he loves me without saying the words. But more importantly, that he wishes he didn't.

His gaze never leaves mine, not for a single second.

Not when he grabs her hand in his. Not when he whispers in her ear as the song comes to an end.

Not even when he slams the rest of his beer before setting it on the table to his left.

No, he watches me until the moment he passes by me, hand-in-hand with Abbi, and walks right out the goddamn door.

FOUR

River

The cool air of February in Colorado sends a shiver down my spine, the wind whipping around me as the door to the bar slams closed. I've got Abbi in tow, her hand locked firmly in my vice grip as I search the crowded parking lot for my car, desperation crawling through me.

I have to get out of here.

Even in my slightly drunken state, I know I need to get as far away from Rain and *Roman fucking Mitchell* as quickly as possible.

I've been doing my best to mentally prepare myself for this moment, seeing them together for the first time, for weeks now. But honestly, nothing prepared me for the utter dropkicking I would take the second I felt him walk into the bar, only to turn and see them standing there. Together.

Trying *not* to think about Rain kissing and touching and fucking anyone other than me, it's been a constant battle. And for the most part, I've been successful in pushing away the thoughts, causing me any amount of anger or sorrow.

But tonight, that all changed.

It only took a split second for every plausible and awful idea of the two of them to flood my mind and instantly drive me to damn near insanity. Every intimate moment they probably share raced to the front of my mind and before I knew it, I let my guard slip.

I let myself be reckless.

Not that I've been a saint since I've been back, getting drunk more often than not, skipping weightlifting, sleeping in class.

Frankly, I'm just barely hanging on, hoping someone or something is able to either pull me away from the waves or push me completely under. At this rate, I don't care which one it is. I only know I'm tired of living in this state of limbo in every aspect of my life.

Stuck in a rut of monotony, unable to break free.

My hand lands on the door of my Rover and I yank the handle, slipping into the driver's seat while Abbi slides into the passenger seat beside me.

Abbi. Fuck.

She's been nothing but kind, and a massive distraction, ever since classes resumed after staying up in Vail. Not in a sexual way, but just as a friend. Dropping by to study with me, calling me to grab lunch at the dining hall or meet for coffee.

Hell, she even took me with her when she got her industrial pierced, daring me to get something done myself. I know she said it as a joke, but little did she know I'd actually follow through on her little wager.

It might be daily, honestly, that she'll text or check in or ask me to hang out, thinking it might serve as some sort of distraction from whatever has been eating me up inside. Because it's obvious to everyone around me who's known me for more than five minutes, I haven't been myself. Far fucking from it.

So, of course, in true River self-destructive fashion, what do I do to make myself feel better?

I take advantage of her kindness and use it as an opportunity to seek revenge, thinking it would taste so sweet to have Rain sitting there, seeing me with someone else too.

And then I take it a step too far and kiss her, like I have the fucking right.

The second my lips landed on hers inside the bar though, I knew it was the wrong move. It took everything inside me not to rip away from her and wipe my mouth free from the lipstick or gloss or whatever the hell she's wearing.

But I didn't.

I did the exact opposite, in fact.

I pulled her closer and bit her lip and made it known to the entire fucking place, whoever was looking my way, she was coming home with me tonight.

Especially to Rain.

Because revenge and jealousy are a pair of bitches and they have a way of bringing out the worst in anyone. Finding the pieces everyone on this planet wants to keep hidden, but being the masters at pulling them out into the light and showcasing them for all to see.

Thankfully, Abbi didn't seem to mind or notice my intention, so I've got that goin' for me at the very least.

Glancing to my right, I find her staring directly at me as I throw the car in reverse.

I feel my cheeks heat as she continues to stare at me while I drive us toward her sorority house. I can only imagine what she's thinking. I've done such a good job about letting her know we're friends, then I go and pull that shit?

I'm such a fucking asshole.

She doesn't speak until I pull up outside, the house surprisingly dark for a weekend night. There must be a frat party instead.

"River?" she says softly after I put my car in park.

I look over to see her biting her lip and looking at me through her lashes. But not in that coy way girls do. She almost seems… nervous? Which is something she *never* is around me.

God, I really am an asshole.

Rubbing my forehead, I let out a sigh. "Abbi, I—"

I don't get anything else out besides that before she launches herself at me and her tongue is in my mouth. It flicks against the bar now running through mine, still a little tender from being a newer piercing, and I realize she was playing coy after all.

Shit, shit, shit. This can't happen.

Putting my hands on the side of her face, I pull back and extract myself from her as gently as I can. Before I can say anything though, she grins at me and licks her lips.

"I have to say, I wasn't sure about you getting your tongue done when I asked you to go with me to get my industrial. But I definitely see the appeal now."

I do my best not to roll my eyes because it definitely wasn't meant to be for her benefit. Or anyone's, for that matter. Just something for *me*.

But it seems Abbi wants to continue surprising me tonight, both with her bluntness as well as her spontaneity. Because now her hands are unbuckling my belt and unzipping my jeans, and *Jesus fucking Christ*, her tongue is on the tip of my cock before I can think. My hips buck on reflex, my dick taking notice of the attention she's paying to it by thickening rapidly.

And I know I'm going to hell for not stopping her the second she wraps her mouth around my length, taking in the first few inches.

Fuck, fuck, fuck.

"Abbi," I groan her name, perfectly aware I need to put a stop to this. But…it feels good. Not just her mouth, but to have someone…fucking *want me.* And after seeing *them* together, I don't care where that want comes from. I just need to drown myself in it, if only for a minute. Just until I can have one blissful moment where I don't remember the people whose love and attention I crave most are the ones unwilling to give it to me.

My hips lift of their own accord, meeting her mouth in a few shallow thrusts, letting my mind get lost in the pleasure. It's not until she gags slightly when I'm hitting the back of her throat that I realize how *wrong* this is.

Grabbing her shoulder, I push her roughly off me and hurry to tuck myself back in my jeans. Which is difficult to do while buzzed, half-cocked, and sitting down.

"What's wrong?" she whispers, as I finally manage to at least get the zipper of my jeans in place and rebutton them. Glancing over, I see drunken tears in her eyes and I immediately feel like shit for this entire thing.

Kissing her, letting *this* happen, only to reject her in the shittiest way possible.

And the feeling only intensifies the second, "I'm in love with someone else," blurts past my lips in a wondrous display of word vomit.

I don't know if it comes out because I'm trying to convince *myself* even more why this is wrong or because I feel like I owe her an explanation. But either way, the words have their intended effect because she blinks and nods in understanding.

"I see," she murmurs, tucking a piece of hair behind her ear. The tears in her eyes start to well slightly, and dammit, I feel like the worst person in the world.

"Abs, I'm so sorry. I didn't..." I trail off because my head is spinning slightly from the alcohol and the insanely tight fit in my pants. "I just can't."

"It's fine, River. You don't owe—"

"But I *do*," I insist. *Shit, how do I put this?* "It's...fuck, this sounds terrible, but it's not you, it's me. It really is, because you know how much I care about you. I'm not in a good place and I *know* that. I just don't want to drag you down with me."

She looks up at me from under her lashes, and quirks her lips into confused frown that quickly morphs into anger. "You don't need to patronize me like a child with your bullshit lines. I'm a big girl and can handle myself."

I'm taken aback so much, she's out of the car in a flash before I have the chance to explain more. She even slams the door closed behind her, probably wishing my head was in the way. With a sigh, I watch her quickly move toward the house and I can tell by her posture she's feeling everything from embarrassed to ridiculously pissed.

I'm about to start the vehicle again when she's at the bottom of the steps leading to the house when she stops, turns around and storms back up to my car.

What the…?

Ripping the door open, this time on the driver's side, she scowls at me. "And next time you want to make someone else jealous, do us both a favor and don't use me. We wouldn't want the line of the friend-zone to get blurred."

My brows shoot to my hairline as she slams the door in my face before I have a chance to get a word in edgewise.

I take my own turn slamming doors later, this one to my apartment, and immediately heading to the fridge to grab something else to drink.

Fuck me.

What was I thinking, letting Abbi get that far? A quick fuck or blowjob or *whatever* isn't going to fix this. At this rate, nothing short of a full lobotomy is going to erase the pain of seeing *them* together.

Again.

Yanking open the door like it's wronged me, I glance inside to only find a six pack of beer. Which isn't nearly enough alcohol to make me forget.

Making the snap decision to make the most of this shitty as hell situation I've found myself in, I pull out my phone and dial Elliott.

"What's up, Len? Aren't you out at the bars?" he answers on

the second ring.

"Change of plans," I grumble into the receiver. "You and Drew get your asses to my place stat. Bring something stronger than beer." I pause for a moment before adding, "And some weed."

I hang up, tossing my phone on the counter and get to work on downing the six beers in my fridge. Popping the top off one of the bottles of Blue Moon, I let the cool liquid pour down my throat in a few short gulps as desperation overwhelms me.

For some sort of buzz to flow through my veins again. For a few minutes of peace from my thoughts that never cease to send me over the edge.

To forget the pain and the heartache that comes with loving Ciaráin Grady.

Forty minutes and five beers later, Elliott opens the door with Drew right behind him. Both of them look pissed the fuck off, meaning they must've gotten into another goddamn fight sometime before they got here.

Whatever. They can just get drunk with me and forget about it.

Elliott holds up a bottle of Jack, a glint of mischief in his blue eyes, and I'm in front of him in an instant. Grabbing the bottle by the neck, I rip off the plastic and cap before taking a swig. The whiskey burns my tongue and throat on the way down, settling warmly in my stomach, and it makes me feel slightly better.

"Jesus, Len. Grab a damn glass, why don't ya?" Drew laughs as he makes his way into the apartment, tossing a few joints on the counter before he heads to the fridge with a twenty-four pack of beer. He opens a cabinet and pulls out three shot glasses, sliding them to his brother across the island.

"Pour 'em," E motions to the glasses, lined up in a row on the counter.

Not wasting a second, I pour all three to the brim, setting the bottle on the counter a little harder than necessary. I don't bother waiting for them, just lift one to my mouth and down it as quick as I can, loving the numbing sting the alcohol leaves behind inside me.

It's almost enough to ease the ache in my chest.

Glancing up at Elliott, then over to Drew, I motion to the other two shots on the counter with my hand. But Elliott shakes his head and nods at the remaining alcohol.

"All you, man. I'm not looking to get shitfaced tonight. Got places to be later."

Drew scoffs at that, and I swear I hear him say *to go get laid* not-so-subtly under his breath, earning a glare from E.

I grab the two shots off the counter and toss them back with ease before glaring at my friends. "Can you two work your shit out on your own or do you need adult supervision? Because I have my own fucking problems right now without adding yours to the mix."

Drew rolls his eyes and picks up a joint from the counter, lighting it and taking a drag. "What crawled up your ass and died?"

I snort out an ironic laugh, but it feels hollow. "Finally coming to your senses and wanna find out for yourself?"

"Because I haven't heard that one from you before," Drew deadpans before handing me the joint.

I take a couple hits, pulling the smoke into my lungs like it's the oxygen I need to breathe. At this point, I wouldn't be surprised if it was because it's the only thing that seems to even slightly numb the pain.

But tonight…I know it won't be enough. Even the mixture of the weed and all the booze in the world won't be enough.

Doesn't mean I won't fucking try.

"What's going on with you, man?" Drew finally asks sometime later, after I've downed what must be at least ten shots of whiskey and smoked half a blunt.

I'm good and buzzed and damn near close to fucking forgetting, so I just shrug his question off and take a swig of Jack straight from the bottle, glancing between them. "I just wanted to say fuck it and get lit. Is that a crime now?"

I watch as the twins share a look, doing that irritating as hell thing where they have a conversation with just their eyes. More than likely about me, which I can't stand even more. "Speak, assholes. I'm right fucking here." The words come out slightly slurred, even to my own ears, but the look on their faces tells me they understood just fine.

Okay, not that *fucked up, I guess,* I think as I take another gulp of whiskey.

Elliott lets out a sigh and scratches the top of his head. "Look, Len. You've been off ever since you got back from the cabin with Gra—"

"Don't say his fucking name," I snap, bringing the bottle back to my lips yet again, yearning for the burn of the liquor.

"That's fuckin' it," Drew growls, attempting to grab the neck of the bottle in my hands and yank it from my grasp. It takes a lot of effort, but I manage to keep my hold on it and pull it to my chest. Glaring down at me, his lip curls back in a sneer. "You're drinking that shit like a fish out of water. And it tells me you need to stop doing whateverthefuck this is — this goddamn *pity party* — and start talking. Right. Fuckin'. Now."

Rage and resentment bubble inside me as I glare at two of my best friends who seem to be staging some sort of intervention right now. "There's nothing to say. He and I, we're enemies. End of."

Elliott tips his head to the side, narrowing his eyes on me. "Rewind and try again, jackass. With the truth this time. Because we saw T and his girl when he was back, and he had a lot to say about *his* time up in Vail. *And* who he saw while he was there."

Without thinking, I rise from the couch, dropping the bottle onto the cushions and shove Elliott in the chest as hard as I possibly can in my fucked up state. My nostrils flare, fury whipping off me in fiery lashes. "What the fuck did Taylor tell you?"

Elliott quirks a brow, crossing his arms over his broad chest, refusing to speak. My eyes fly to Drew, begging for an answer, but Drew just shakes his head, sadness filling his eyes.

"What the fuck do you *know?*" I scream, turning and hurling the half empty liquor bottle across the room, where it smashes against the wall. Shattering on impact.

I watch it for a moment, lost in the thousands of pieces splintered and strewn across the floor, mirroring the state of my heart. The amber liquid streaking down the beige wall, matching the tears begging to stream down my face.

And I want to feel nothing. Except I feel fucking *everything*.

Dropping to my knees, I shift so my ass in on the ground and back is against the island between the living room and kitchen. My entire being floods with every single emotion I've been holding in since the day Rain left me standing on the tarmac like a goddamn idiot. Each one fills me to the brink, threatening to spill from my eyes in an endless cascade of grief and sorrow.

Pulling my knees to my chest, I rest my elbows on them and bury my face in my hands, not willing to let the twins see me like this.

Pull yourself together, Lennox. He's not fucking worth it.

They're words I've chanted to myself on repeat, and I thought they were starting to sink in. Become true and I was starting to be...I don't know, better? Less torn apart about losing the only person I've ever loved.

But that's the thing about lying to yourself. No matter how much you beg and wish and plead the words to be true, it doesn't mean it will manifest in your reality.

"Fuck, Riv." Elliott sighs pulling me from my thoughts. "Did he...do something to you? While you guys were trapped out there?"

I huff out a laugh laced with misery and self-loathing before glancing up at my friends from the floor. The grimace marring my face feels as broken as my heart and the words rip from my vocal chords in a harsh whisper. "You mean something other than make me fall in love with him?"

Drew's eyes pop wide, but Elliott just stares at me, not looking surprised in the least. He squats before me and leans forward, grabbing my chin to keep his eyes locked on mine. "What. Happened?"

I push his hand off my face, a growl working its way out of my throat. "It doesn't matter. It's over and done with."

"Clearly," Drew retorts, rolling his eyes, motioning to me and my drunken mess.

"What do you want me to say?" I shout, my fingers slipping into my hair gripping the strands to the point of pain. "You want me to tell you I was sent to that damn cabin with my nemesis, and somewhere along the way, I made the mistake of falling into bed with him? Because I did! I was an idiot, and I fucked up, giving him everything he needed to win whatever war was between us!" The words crawl out of my throat, ripping from it in a choked cry that sounds more like it came from a caged animal than me. My hands slide from my hair and my head hits the island behind me, shaking back and forth as a strained scoff passes my lips. "Little did I know the real casualty in this battle would be my heart when I fell in love with him too."

Water wells in the corners of my eyes again, quickly overtaking them to the point where my friends' forms blur behind the tears. I try like hell not to let them spill over, I swear I do. Because I won't cry for him. He might've bent me to the point that I'm unrecognizable, but I won't let him break me.

My eyes must not get the memo though, since they allow a few tears to fall down my cheeks. I wipe them away quickly with the back of my hand, looking up at my best friends to find them shell-shocked. They've only ever seen me cry once, years ago.

The night my father walked out, taking his conditional love with him.

A strangled whimper slips from my lips, as Taylor's words, every one of them, ring in my head from the night in Vail.

My best friend, who reads people better than I can read a book…even he was fooled.

And instantly I have the need to tell him how wrong he was.

"Call Taylor," I plead, the sound echoing in the silence surrounding us as I do my best to keep my shit together before my anguish consumes me entirely.

I won't let him break me.

But how the fuck do you survive your heart being ripped from your chest and thrown into a blender? Your lungs being popped, deflated and then flooded with poison? Your brain being transfixed on every smell, kiss, touch, taste you shared with the person who owns every inch of your being, only to now live every single day of your life without them?

The answer is simple.

You fucking don't.

My head finds its way back to my hands again, and I vaguely hear the sound of Elliott speaking to his brother in hushed tones. I can't make out what's being said, not that it matters, and then the conversation turns one-sided as E talks to T on the phone.

I don't know how long I sit there, dazed and confused and just fucking existing in the mess Rain left me in. My heart throbs, desperate to find it's other half or be ripped from my chest entirely and at this point, I don't care which it is.

I just want the pain to stop.

"Len," my nickname, spoken by Drew this time, brings my gaze to collide with his. It's then I see Elliott holding out my cellphone to me, clearly wanting me to take it. My fingers tremble as I wrap them around the device, bringing it to my ear as my other hand wipes away the tears staining my cheeks.

"T?" I whisper into the phone.

"Riv, what's going on?" my best friend's voice floats through the speaker, soft and concerned. "Elliott said you're drunk out of your mind and throwing shit across the room." He pauses, before asking the question I dread hearing. "Are you okay?"

And with that stupid fucking question, I fracture more.

A choked noise, something between a gasp and a sob, slips from my throat as more tears break the levee containing them.

Because no, I'm not okay. I'm the furthest thing from *okay*. I'm holding on by a thread, acting stupidly on impulse, and I'm just not myself anymore. I don't think I have been for a while now.

"River, shh. Breathe," Taylor soothes from the other end of the phone, but it only makes my body quake more.

"Is it me?" I choke out the words, giving traction to the thoughts that have been plaguing me for years, only to be given new life in the last few weeks. "Am I the reason everyone always leaves?"

"What are you talking about, River? No one is leaving, and no, it's not your fault. Where is this coming from?"

I swallow down the bile in my throat. "Everyone leaves me, T. My dad. You. And now…" The word, *his name*, doesn't make it from my lips.

"First, fuck your dad. He doesn't know what he's missing," Taylor insists, which earns him a drunken snort from me. "I'm serious. And I didn't *leave* you. I just went to *college* in a different state."

I wince, knowing him being across the country has nothing to do with me, but it doesn't take away the pain of missing him at a time like this. "That's fine and dandy, man. But I fucking *need* you *here*."

Taylor is silent on the other line, letting each gasp and hiccup escaping from my mouth echo through the phone and the silence of the apartment. It's only after I manage to calm down enough to talk as coherently as possible that he speaks.

"Tell me what he did," he murmurs from the other end.

"Because the pain I can feel you in all the way from here can only be from heartbreak."

The blurred form of my two other friends move, settling themselves on the ground on either side of me while I speak.

"You were wrong, T. You were so fucking wrong," I choke out, wiping the tears from my eyes that have long since flown freely. "We were never going to end up on the same side of the line."

"What? Riv, I *saw* the way he was looking at you. He's head over heels for you, man."

I shake my head, refusing to believe Taylor could be so blind. But I guess he and I were both fooled into thinking I meant a damn thing to Rain.

"I'm nothing to him. Nothing more than a toy to play with to pass the time while we were stuck up in that damn cabin. And play with me, he did." I laugh softly, but it's hollow. "He played the part so fucking well, even *you* thought it was real."

I swallow roughly and say the one thing I've attempted to deny for the last few weeks.

"I love him, T," I whisper the words to my best friend on the other line. "I opened myself up to the idea, and I fell. Hard and fast and all at once, and I couldn't stop myself."

And I couldn't, even if I wanted to try. Because falling for Rain was like breathing.

Instinctual. Ingrained in my DNA.

Automatic.

Hell, if you asked me to tell you the moment I knew I loved him, I'd tell you it was when I held his sketchpad in my hand, seeing the way he captured every inch of me from mere memory.

But if I'm being honest? He swept the rug out from under me the first time I heard his laugh, genuine and smoky. The sound was more addictive than any drug, and I instantly knew I wanted to hear it every day for the rest of my life. In hindsight, it was at that moment I should have realized I was never going to get out of Coach's cabin with my heart intact.

"Put me on speaker." Taylor sighs, and I obey immediately, setting the phone on my knees.

My jaw ticks as I sit in silence with E and Drew, waiting for Taylor to say something. Literally anything to make me feel slightly less miserable.

Elliott grips my shoulder in his palm right before Taylor goes on to talk, "Riv, all of us know you're the kind of person to love and care so fucking deep, it consumes you. You have the biggest heart of all of us, and that's not a bad thing."

I scoff. "Really? Cause it sure fucking feels like a bad thing."

"It's not," Elliott insists, backing T up. "No one is invincible when it comes to heartbreak, Len. Not even you."

"It's not that I thought I'd be any different. Like I couldn't feel it," I mumble. "I already have, just in a different form than the bullshit with my dad." Running my tongue back and forth over my teeth and tapping my fingers against my knee, I feel my buzz start to weigh me down more.

"Are you gonna be okay, man?" Drew asks from my left.

I sigh, glance at him, then his twin, letting my head roll against the island behind me. "Yeah, I will. You know me, just gotta be dramatic first."

"Don't downplay your pain," Taylor snaps through the

speaker, his voice the harshest it's been all night. "You have to fucking feel it, otherwise you're never going to heal."

"I'll feel it tomorrow," I tell him. Closing my eyes, I let out a deep breath. "I just want tonight, guys. One night without having to fucking feel miserable. One night where I can just pretend my heart hasn't been ripped out of my chest and stomped on like a doormat." Opening my eyes, I roll my head again to look at Drew, then back to Elliott. "Please, just let me have tonight."

I watch as E looks past me to his brother, having a moment of twin telepathy before he nods and his blue eyes latch onto mine again. "We can give you tonight. Right, T?"

Taylor is silent on the line for a good minute, but then he lets out a relenting sigh. "Tonight only. But I swear to fucking God, River, you need to go talk to someone instead of keeping this shit bottled up. Maybe think about taking your medication again. So, call your therapist *tomorrow*. And you better not do anything stupid that you'll regret in the morning."

I scoff, but it comes out more like a hiccup. "When do I ever do anything stupid?"

Drew rolls his eyes and gives me the look he gives any of us when he thinks he's the big brain of the group and we're all a bunch of morons. "You mean besides deciding to get your fucking tongue pierced right when you got back from break?"

"You did *what?*" Taylor practically screeches from the phone, causing me to wince.

"I've always wanted to," I grumble in defense of my slightly rash move, but it's the truth. The only reason I hadn't *years ago* was because it went against everything my parents thought was proper for the son who had to look and act and *be perfect* at every turn. Hell, my father was pissed enough about the ink *tainting* my skin. I didn't need to add to the list of things he despises about me.

But after all the bullshit went down with Rain, I decided I was sick of living for anyone else but me. Tired of living my life subjected to the wishes of others. Except then and even now, it's not an act of rebellion for me.

Quite the opposite.

It's all about the pain. The jewelry and ink are just souvenirs.

I really am a fucking masochist.

Elliott raises a brow in suspicion at me when I don't add anything else to my statement, so I shrug. "I'm deadass serious. I just thought it was time I did what I wanted for a change."

Taylor sighs, and I can practically see him rolling his eyes and shaking his head at me. "Okay, well, then don't make this shit a habit. And don't do anything *else* stupid."

"Swear it, T," I tell him before hanging up, reaching to set my phone on the counter above me.

It's only when I stand up with the help of the twins, extremely unsteady on my feet, and Drew leads me to the couch that I realize there's exactly a zero percent chance I'll be keeping the promise I just made to my best friend.

FIVE
Rain

My gloved hands slam into the punching bag with a steady rhythm, the beat of "Through It All" by From Ashes to New pounding in my ears from my headphones while I work out my aggression. With each smack of my gloves on the bag, I feel the pieces of anger and frustration melting away, leaving me nothing more than a sweating, panting mess.

I'm breaking about ten rules in my scholarship agreement with CU by doing this, but I needed to let this shit out in a way that was productive. So yeah, I took the liberty of installing a punching bag in the corner of my living room, suspended from one of the metal beams running the length of the open ceilings.

It's a fuckton more convenient than going to a gym too. Especially with all the people watching my every move. The media might've slowed their roll, but the FBI agent assigned to the case against Ted is still in touch regularly.

And of course, Roman.

I swear, he's been watching me like a goddamn hawk since he got here, but it's almost become a level of obsession ever since the bar the other night. Like he's worried I'll just disappear and slip into Ted's clutches at any fucking moment or something.

Shaking my head, I continue to land punches on the bag, drowning myself in sweat and heavy alternative rock. But when the song moves into the next song on my playlist, Beartooth's "In Between", my focus slips again, and my mind instantly lands on River.

If I'm honest with myself, my thoughts haven't been off him after seeing him two nights ago at the bar. But even before that, he was never far from front and center in my brain.

Still pounding into the bag, I let the music fuel the bitterness I feel from seeing him kiss Abbi. I know it was a power play, a way to get me to react. Hell, I was so close to giving in and doing just that, despite knowing it was exactly what he wanted.

River can be easier to read than one of the books I never see him without. He's in tune with his emotions, feels them more deeply than any other person I've met. Cares and loves with his whole heart the way not many people do anymore.

It's one of the reasons I fell for him, harder and faster than I could have imagined.

But feeling so hard also leaves him vulnerable and open, letting anyone see exactly what is going through his brain. Just like the other night, I could *see* the anger radiating from him. Not just feel it as his eyes bore into me from across the bar.

So, I know he was retaliating against me, looking for a way to lash out and hurt me the way I hurt him. And hell, if he didn't succeed. It was a knife to the heart to see his arm around her, his lips where they didn't fucking belong.

Yet his act of defiance proves why I know to my core he's fucking *it* for me. No one else in this world makes *me* feel the way he does. Whether the emotions he pulls from within me are volatile or loving, that's another matter entirely. But whichever it might be at the moment, it always seems to fit.

Nothing and no one balances me the way he does, makes me content to just *exist* in this shitty world where people rape and abuse and murder others. Even when we are at each other's throats.

Because at the end of the day, *he* makes all the bad worth it.

The door to my apartment slams shut loud enough to hear over my music, causing me to break my concentration. As I look up, I find Roman taking off his peacoat and dress shoes he went out to buy earlier this week. Guess he couldn't live without the suits any longer. Or at least *dress slacks* and *button-downs.*

I shudder because *fuck* wearing that shit when you don't need to.

"Hey," I say, pulling my headphones off.

Ro turns and glances at me, doing a double-take when he catches me sweating and shirtless, wearing a pair of boxing gloves. His brows quirk. "You good?"

Panting slightly, I nod. "Yeah. Needed to let off some steam. You good?"

Running his teeth over his lip, he nods too. "Yeah."

But the way he fiddles with the button on the cuff of his dress shirt tells another tale. It's his nervous tick, his tell...playing with the buttons. Or cufflinks, if he has those on. It's the only one he's ever had, and very few people notice it.

But being his best friend, I did. I once joked about getting him one of those fidget spinners to give him something to occupy his mind and his hands when he was feeling anxious instead.

But now, all it does is remind me of River's tapping.

"You wanna box?" I ask, peeling the gloves off my hands and tossing them to the ground. "I can show you —"

His smirk and cocked brow has me cutting off abruptly. "I know how to box, Rain. Have you forgotten what I'm trained for?"

Right. Enclave training. For your insane secret society.

I grin. "All right then, *suit.* Why don't you show me your stuff if you're so well versed?"

A low chuckle comes from him as he crosses the room, unbuttoning his shirt along the way and throwing it on the back of the couch.

He's filled out quite a bit since the last time I saw him without a shirt, which was the night in the pool before he left. He's still smaller than I am, but he's put on muscle and clearly worked hard for it, looking more like a baseball player kind of toned than a runner like he used to be.

And still completely clean of tattoos.

I raise a brow when he goes to his bag and switches out of his dress pants into a pair of shorts, showcasing the sculpted planes of his back as he bends over. "I see you took my advice and finally started to work out."

He laughs again and glances up at me. "Something like that."

Tossing him a second set of gloves, he straps them on and steps up to the bag. He looks at it for a minute, almost in a way of studying, and I can't help but laugh.

"You have to *hit it*, Ro."

He quirks his lips. "I'm not used to throwing punches at something that doesn't hit back."

Rolling the thought over in my head for a whole two seconds, I throw my headphones onto the couch and push it and the coffee table out of the way to make a little more room for us.

If he wants a sparring partner, I'm not about to object. I could use someone who can hit back right now. Take out my rage on him instead of the bag.

"You sure about this?" he questions.

Strapping my gloves back on, I look him over. He always radiates confidence, but right now, he looks nothing but predatory, his eyes following my every movement as I position myself across from him.

"Yeah. Just no head or face. Ready when you are," I tell him with a smirk. He doesn't have a fucking chance, seeing as I've been boxing for years. "I'll make sure I go easy on—"

He lands his first punch directly to my diaphragm before I can even finish the sentence. Air whooshes from my mouth, and I gasp from a bent over position, glancing up at him in disbelief.

A slight tilt of his head is all he gives me. "You were saying?"

Biting my lip and rolling my eyes, I rise back up and get into position, ready for whatever he throws at me.

We go round after round for twenty minutes, and I'm able to dodge and block most of the punches he throws now that I'm ready. Sweat drips down from both our faces, and I'm thoroughly impressed with his skill level, considering he was never interested in boxing when I took it up. And he's much better than average.

Hell, even with my training, I have a hard time landing a couple good ones to his ribs as we continue to circle each other.

When I do manage to connect, they don't stop him. The bloodthirsty glint in his eyes only grows and intensifies as he watches me move, waiting to strike. It's a look I've never seen on him before.

It's so distracting when I go to make a move, it's all he needs to see an opening to land a blow. Except, instead of landing a hit I left myself wide open for, I'm grabbed around the waist, in the air, and then my back is smacking onto the ground below, my eyes closing in pain as all the oxygen leaves my body on impact.

I cough repeatedly and open my eyes, finding Roman hovering over me, his eyes searching my face as he slowly removes his glove from behind my head. And while I might be pissed he just fucking *manhandled* me like a rag doll and my ego is seriously bruised, I'm grateful he had enough forethought to keep me from being concussed.

"That was—" I gasp, my eyes hard on him, "—not legal."

He smiles, but his eyes are still filled with worry. "You good?" he asks gently. "I didn't actually hurt you, did I?"

"My pride, maybe," I cough some more and try to sit up. "But other than that, no."

Some of his panic dissipates as he helps me into a seated position, his hand on my shoulder to keep me steady, still directly in front of me. We're both still breathing pretty hard, me more so than him, and I search his face.

What kind of training are you doing *with them?*

"You cheated," I tell him with an accusatory tone rather than ask questions I'm not sure I want the answers to.

His eyes dart from mine to my lips and back again. Clearing

his throat doesn't seem to help because his words are still filled with gravel when he whispers, "You know I've never been one to fight fair."

I know better than anyone.

It's only after that thought I realize how close we are, his mouth only a few inches from mine. I don't miss the same predatory glint in his eye as he learns forward slightly, and I swallow as he inches closer and closer.

Much too close for comfort.

"Ro—" I start but the blaring ring of my cell startles us both, dumping a bucket of much needed cold water over us.

"You should get that," he says, his eyes now glued to the floor.

Ripping off the boxing gloves on the way, I scramble to my phone. Glancing down, I see a number I don't recognize and a chill rushes over me. And somehow I just *know*.

"*Roman*," I snap, his head jerking in my direction just as I motion him over to join me. Clearing my throat, I hit the accept button and close my eyes. "Hello?"

An emotionless voice I haven't heard in years chills me to the bone with only four words from the other line.

"How's my *good boy*?"

My jaw ticks and I take a deep breath, allowing my eyes to open and meet Roman's questioning gaze. I give him a nod in confirmation and he scrambles for his phone across the room in an instant.

"What do you want, *Ted*?" I growl into the receiver.

His menacing chuckle fills my ears. "Is that any way to greet the person whose life you're in the process of ruining?"

"You did that on your own, you sick piece of shit," I seethe as Roman returns to my side, pulling up the app one of his guys had created. It has software and coding in it that allows him to track another phone's location simply by pairing it with mine and tracing the number of the incoming call.

Pulling my phone away from my ear, I put Ted on speaker and let Roman do his thing.

"No, you see, that's where I think you've gotten confused. Too many hits on the football field and the like. Because we had a *deal*, Ciaráin."

The way he says my name, spitting it out like a curse, sends ice through my veins.

"Is it a deal if I'm not given a choice?"

"You made your choice by getting involved with *delinquents* your last year of high school when those twins left you behind."

Roman's eyes snap to mine, asking questions I don't want to give the answers to, but I ignore him, gripping the granite counter of the island. I do my best to remember the ground is still beneath my feet and not the other way around, but it's difficult when I feel like I'm being buried alive beneath all my skeletons.

"What do you want, Ted? We can make another deal."

I watch Roman start pairing our phones and while I'm desperate to get off the line with this asshole, I know I need to keep him talking in time to trace his call.

"We're past the point of making deals. I'm here, and I'm watching from the shadows, waiting for the chance to take from you what you took from me."

My mind is spinning, trying to make sense of the words he's speaking. But I'm more confused than ever as I watch the bar on

Roman's phone load while he traces the call location. "You're fucking kidding, right? *You* want to talk about taking from someone else?" I yell in disbelief. "I didn't take *anything* from you!"

"You took *my life* as I knew it," he says, low and venomous and in perfect control. Always in perfect control. "You took my power, my money, my connections. By opening that vile little mouth of yours, you destroyed *everything*." The words ring through the phone on a violent snarl only capable of coming from the worst kind of monster. "It's time, I do the same for you."

The line disconnects immediately and I slam my fist onto the counter, closing my eyes and counting back from fifty as I focus on my breathing.

"Did you trace it?" I ask, my voice resonating shattered glass.

"No, but it doesn't matter," Roman says with a sigh. I open my eyes, my gaze colliding with his. "You heard him. He's here. And I have no doubt it's the truth if he's looking for revenge."

Letting out a long exhale, I rest my elbows on the counter, allowing the cool stone sink into my skin. My head finds my hands, and I run my fingers through my hair.

I know he's right. Ted's here. Somewhere, *anywhere*. Which isn't unexpected, but it certainly sets me more on edge than before.

"It'll be fine," he continues, though I'm not sure if he's trying to convince me or himself right now. "If worse comes to worst, I'll call in back-up. We'll figure it out, man. I promise."

Turning my head, I let my eyes meet his hazel ones and nod solemnly, knowing Roman's almost always true to his word. "Okay."

I head into the kitchen and grab two glasses and the bottle of Jameson since Roman will drink just about any kind of whiskey he can get his hands on and pour each of us a glass. And do we ever need a fucking drink after what just happened. He takes a seat on the barstool on the other side of the island, and I join him, sliding his glass over.

We sit like that in silence, and for once it's comfortable to have it settle between us, even after he looked like he was going to kiss me again earlier. We just drink and don't say a damn word, letting our thoughts spin.

"We do have another problem though," he says after a while, and I stiffen. Because this is about to go one of two ways, and I have a feeling I won't like either option.

"And what's that?" I say, taking a swig and keeping my eyes trained straight ahead on the kitchen cabinets.

"He mentioned a deal…" he says, trailing off, and I release a breath because while I have no desire to speak of this, I'd prefer to avoid the almost-kiss more. I glance over at him and raise a brow, giving him the okay to continue.

"What happened after I left?"

Taking a deep breath, I sigh and refill my glass of whiskey. Because to tell this tale? I'm gonna fucking need it.

Winter in Colorado isn't a joke. You'd think it's the snow or the cold but it's the constant bipolar bullshit it pulls. Yesterday it was almost sixty-five. In *February*. And today, it's freezing and the wind is whipping around me to the point I feel like Dorothy about to be swept up in a tornado and taken to Oz.

Shit, I think I'd prefer it at this point.

That's the thought running through my mind two days after the call with Ted when I see River bundled up in the jacket and beanie I recognize from the cabin.

He hasn't seen me, and I should just leave it that way. Let him go about his day and keep my distance. Let him move on, try to heal from what I did. But seeing him this past weekend at the bar with Abbi…kissing her? Fuck, it feels like I've already lost him.

And it's that feeling that has me calling his name, though from his lack of response, it's been drowned out by the wind.

"River!" I call out again, jogging in his direction a little too quickly not to draw the attention of other students passing by in direction of their classes. Probably because the entire campus knows I decked him in the middle of a playoff game.

Whatever, let them stare.

He keeps walking like he didn't hear me again, but this time, the rigid set of his spine gives him away. It's only when my hand lands on his shoulder he finally acknowledges me with a scowl.

"Ciaráin," he says dryly as he yanks away from my grasp. "What do you need?"

He speaks in such a way, so emotionless and detached, I swear I'm talking to a robot. Not the River that practically *bubbles* with life. That's when I notice the light purple crescents under his eyes and the puffy redness to them.

He still looks like he hasn't slept in days. Maybe longer.

"I, uh," I stutter, being caught off-guard by his haphazard appearance not much different from the one he had at the bar. "I just wanted to check in, I guess."

His eyes roll. "Why bother? Don't you have someone new to

be *checking in with.*" There's an obvious growl in his voice and his teeth peek out in a snarl as he says, "Or should I say someone *old.* Seeing as you two have quite the history."

I frown, though I knew to expect the jealousy from him with Roman's arrival. I'd counted on it even, as a sure way for River to keep his distance. It was yet another benefit of having Roman come here in the first place.

In addition to his connections with the Enclave, he provides the perfect beard. Roman's presence would not only make River *believe* the lies I spewed to him that day in my apartment, but they would also keep Ted preoccupied, looking for ways to use *Roman* against me rather than River.

Which is a chance I'm willing to take, knowing Roman is trained well enough that he could take care of himself, should the need arise.

River on the other hand?

I shake the thoughts free, not allowing my mind to go there.

"So, you know who—"

"Yes I fucking *know,* Rain." He scoffs and shoves his hands into his jacket pockets, shifting his weight to his heels. "How do you think I put all the pieces together and ended up at your apartment the day we got back from Vail? I found *his* Facebook and there was a photo of you, his father, him, and Ted all together at some gala. Coincidence? I think not."

I'd always wondered how River had come to the correct conclusions, both the day he came to my apartment with his knowledge of Ted and then at the airport, when the devastation on his face painted a clear enough picture to all of us there.

He knew it was Roman who got off the plane.

"Riv—"

"Honestly, I shouldn't even be surprised you called him. After what you told me about your *friendship,* it seems only fitting you'd want to have him back in your life now that you know dick is something you actually enjoy."

My eyes sink shut and I take a deep breath, counting to ten. Because I don't want to snap on him, I really fucking don't. Not when every bit of the rage he's aiming my way is well deserved.

Doesn't mean it doesn't hurt.

Opening my eyes, I pin him with a hard glare. "You know what they say about someone who assumes?"

He scowls. "So, you're telling me I'm wrong? Completely off-base?"

I don't answer, just stare at him. Because what can I say? I'm stuck between the proverbial rock and hard place, and at this rate, I'm going to drive myself insane trying to keep my lies straight while playing the most dangerous chess game of my life.

He scoffs, breaking our silent battle of wills. "Fitting you'd shut down when shit you don't wanna share comes up. You haven't changed one fucking bit." His jaw ticks as he swallows, walls visibly forming around him. "Just tell me this. Did you fuck him yet?"

"No," I reply quickly before I can stop myself. It comes out like a reflex, in hopes to silence his line of thinking as soon as possible. Even though I should let him think what he wants. That's the goal after all, right? So, I have no idea why the next words slip from my lips. "I don't want him. Not like that."

His eyes roll, and I instantly know he doesn't believe me. "Then why is he still here? If you don't want him, why *invite him* here not even a day after we get back?"

"Because I *need* him, Abhainn. I need the help only he can give me."

I regret the words the moment I say them, seeing the pained look cross his face, a piece of his wall crumbling. And I know what he's thinking. That he wasn't enough, to help or to trust with the secrets and skeletons piled in the back of my closet. So I had to find someone else who was.

Only it couldn't be further from the truth.

"I see," he says, rolling his shoulders. "Then I guess I should let you get back to him, yeah? The person you *really* need? Because fuck if I'm going to stand here and fool myself into thinking *I* could have been that person for another minute." He shakes his head, his lips forming a thin line. "I should have believed you when you told me us screwing around together wouldn't change anything for you."

He goes to walk away, even makes it a couple steps before he halts, turns around, and cocks his head. "Actually, wait. One more thing. Since he's here, are you like…*out* now? Am I going to see the two of you walking around campus hand-in-hand, making out against the wall of buildings? Or are you planning to stay a closeted gay your entire life?"

My molars grind together because the last thing I'd *ever* do is parade Roman around in front of him, even if I *was* interested in rekindling any sort of feelings I once had for him. I might be an asshole, but I don't want to inflict more pain on River.

Not anything more than absolutely necessary, that is.

"I'm not *closeted*," I hiss.

Another eye roll. "Keep telling yourself that, but it doesn't change the truth. You can't handle knowing you're gay. Or bi or whatever the hell you are. The label doesn't matter, honestly. What matters is you can't accept who you are at your fucking core."

He steps back up to me, getting in my face, our noses brushing from being so close. And I swear I stop breathing altogether.

"That's why you fucked all those girls for the past how many years? To convince yourself you're something you're not? You wanted to fuck the gay out of you and get your dick on straight, right, baby?"

My eyes narrow, seeing right through his attempt at pissing me off and pushing my buttons. But just because I know what he's doing doesn't mean I'm immune to the trick. Mostly because he's right. That's *exactly* what I'd hoped to do for years.

"Is that what you want to hear?" I glance around our surroundings, thankful to see the quad has a minimal amount of people crossing through it. I might not be ashamed of my sexuality anymore, but I don't want to announce it for all of campus to hear either. I deserve to cross that bridge whenever I get there, just like anyone else.

"I want the *truth*," he snarls, and my chest aches at the emphasis he puts on the word I can't seem to give him. Not entirely, at least.

But I can give him this.

"Then yeah, River, I didn't want to be gay. I was worried all the shit he did to me somehow fucked me up enough to make me think this is what I wanted. So, I slept with girl after girl in hopes maybe one of them would spark an interest or yearning enough to…how did you put it? Get my *dick on straight*."

His eyes heat with equal amounts of rage and sorrow at my

honesty. They bore into me as he steps away from me again. The pit in my chest only grows at the distance he placed between us. There's a flash of guilt that crosses his face, and the way he grimaces before it disappears gives me enough courage to keep speaking.

"Deep down, I know that isn't the way this works. *He* couldn't turn me gay just like I couldn't turn *myself* straight. And it was foolish and asinine for me to attempt to live that way. But I refused to accept it."

His eyes narrow on me, his features morphing into skepticism. "Then why go through all the trouble if you knew it was in vain? What's the point of setting yourself up for disappointment in the end?"

I cock my head, incredulous. "Do you really not get it? He already took so much from me. All the power was in his hands and I just didn't want to give him the satisfaction of turning me into this person I had no desire to become."

There's a fire in his eyes that wasn't there a minute ago, and I understand it perfectly. I have it too, every single time we're in this close of proximity to each other. The bone-deep *need* to make the past disappear. To take away the pain and hurt and replace it with something better.

But he just tamps it down, scoffing and shaking his head.

"So *this* is who you chose to be instead? A coward and a fucking fraud."

Biting my tongue, I glance down at the ground. Because I feel like both, and I hate when he can peer right into my soul to find the things I don't want him to see.

"I don't *want* to be either of those things, Abhainn. You—"

"Don't fucking call me that." His glare is penetrating and definitive as I watch him shut down right before my eyes. "In fact, don't fucking call me anything. I have nothing left to say to you."

I don't even bother trying to chase after him when he walks away this time.

SIX

River

I slept for shit last night, the sixth night in a row.

Ever since I saw Rain at the bar with *Roman fucking Mitchell*, sleep has been evading me more and more often, even with the help of the weed I keep supplied at all times. Between that and refilling my Xanax prescription, despite not needing to take a single one for *months* before now, I should be fine and dandy.

That's the whole point of drugs, right? To make you feel better? To calm you down? To do their damn job and make life a little bit easier? More manageable?

I thought so too.

Except they don't work.

Hell, I've been taking an extra Xanax before bed the past couple nights, thinking an anti-anxiety prescription might be enough to, I don't know, *lessen my anxiety* and enable me to get more than a couple hours of shut eye. But nothing seems to calm my mind or erase the images of them together running through my thoughts.

And goddammit, all he does is occupy my mind, whether I want him to or not.

I'm doing my best, trying to let him move on, be happy with his best friend since he was eight. The first man to ever kiss him, and probably, touch him too.

No, Ted motherfucking Anders was the first.

My chest clenches at the thought, and now images of all the vile things Ted did to Rain come rushing into the forefront of my brain. It's too late to keep them out, they just begin to drown me, as if I wasn't already being pulled under without the burden of knowing his pain.

I let out a sigh, rubbing my temples in an attempt to look like something other than the half-living corpse I feel like. Because that's just it.

I feel fucking dead. Inside and out.

Completely and utterly numb.

And if I'm being completely honest, I hate myself for it. I'm not this person I've become in the past few weeks. Not by a long shot.

Moody, irritable, and downright irrational.

Sleeping in class, showing up late to practice.

Not going to either at all…

Something, apparently, not just my friends and teammates have noticed. Coach Scott even pulled me into his office this morning when I showed up in the weight room, hung-over and almost an hour late.

But hey, at least I showed up.

"River, talk to me," he implored, staring at me from behind his desk

while I sat across from him in silence. "You haven't been the same since you came back from Vail. Hell, if I knew sending you out there would've pushed you into a downward spiral, I never would've done it."

I didn't bother responding, just gave him a blank look, lacking the energy to hash out my feelings all over again. Which is all too much about the one person I never should have let anywhere near my heart.

And like he knew I was thinking of Rain, he magically chose to bring him into the conversation when I remained quiet.

"Do I need to bring Grady in here and get the full story about what's going on?"

"No." The word slipped out of my mouth so quick, I didn't even have the chance to stop it. And then they just kept falling. "I'm good. I swear. I'll be on top of it more. Taylor already yelled at me about it."

Thankfully, Coach just nodded. "He's got the right idea. Get your head on straight, kid. I need you to stay focused on school and ball." *He searched my face for a minute before his expression softened. "But please. Come to me if you need anything. You know I'm in your corner."*

I didn't waste any time getting the hell out of there after that. Before he could bring up Rain or the fucking cabin again.

I think the only silver lining of all of this is I haven't actually *had to* cross paths with Rain yet this semester, save for him seeking me out earlier this week after the one fluke night at the bar last weekend. The same night I left with Abbi for the sole purpose of pissing him off, but ended up biting off more than I could chew when she wanted in my pants.

I'm just grateful I wasn't too gone to stop it, before we crossed out of the "friend-zone" entirely. Abbi might be the best friend I have at college, at least of the female persuasion, so letting her finally get her mouth on me after *years* of insisting we were only ever going to be friends wasn't a smart move on my part.

So, she has every right to be pissed at me.

I've never been one to lead a girl on and I feel like scum for doing that. I wouldn't blame her for never speaking to me again, honestly, with how I left things. Even though that's the last thing I want, I'm not exactly in the market of losing any more people that are important in my life.

I haven't seen her since and while it doesn't sit well with me, I'm not really sure what to say to her without completely messing it up somehow. Because with my mental state recently, I know I'll only make it worse.

"Riv?" a familiar feminine voice calls, pulling me from my trancelike state.

Crap. Think of the devil and she shall appear.

I halt in my tracks and debate how I want to proceed. Because, while I don't want to lose her, it's like I just said, I'm not exactly in a chipper mood, certainly not enough to deal with her right now either.

She doesn't give me much of an option though, because she pulls me to the side of the hallway and spins me to face her. Her expression is guarded, big brown eyes look up at me under dark lashes with a tangible amount of vulnerability.

And I hate it. That I've managed to hurt or disappoint yet another person in my life that I care for.

"Hey, Abs," I say, giving her something I could only describe as a mixture of a smile and a grimace. "What's up?"

She adjusts her stance, shifting her weight from foot to foot as she bites her lip. "I was hoping we could have a second to talk, maybe?"

Damn, I can't do this right now.

I try to think up an excuse, but I can tell she needs *something* from me right now. Especially with how she slammed the door in my face the other night. So, as much as I'm dreading this conversation, it needs to happen.

I sigh and pull her deeper into the less busy hall. "Okay, look. This is going to sound really awful, but what happened in my car the other night…"

"River, please don't brush it off as a mistake," she whispers, her eyes pleading.

Goddammit, but it was…

Groaning internally, I take her face in my hands and stare into those big brown eyes that, nine times out of ten, make me extremely happy. "Abs, listen. I've never wanted to lead you on. What I said is the truth, there's someone else. It's why nothing *should* have happened the other ni—"

I'm cut off by the sound of her phone ringing, and honestly, I'm grateful.

She glances down at the name on the screen and frowns before looking up at me. "I feel like an ass for dragging you over here now because I actually really need to answer this."

I smile and thank my lucky stars. "Go ahead. Just know I'm really fucking sorry. And we'll talk soon, okay?" I say it, but I secretly hope we can just go back and pretend it never happened. It was maybe a two-minute blowjob max, from what my buzzed mind can recall, and I just want to erase it from both our minds, and go back to our friendship being completely platonic. Even though it's unfair as hell for me to think that, since I'm the one who crossed the line first.

Either way, I'm just glad we don't have to hash things out right this second.

She nods. "I'm holding you to that, Lennox," she says, standing on her tip-toes and placing a kiss on my cheek. As she accepts the call and turns to head further down the less populated hallway, I hear her faintly speak into the phone as she moves away from me.

I let out a sigh once she turns the corner, finally able to breathe a bit, but the feeling of salvation is cut short the moment a violent grip on my arm causes me to jump, and before I have the chance to see who it is, I'm being tugged around the corner and through a door to what seems to be a janitor's closet.

Yet once I'm closed inside the dark room with my assailant, I immediately know who it is.

His scent, like mint and winter and my own personal downfall, is one that's ingrained in my memory, imprinted on my very soul after the time we spent together in the cabin.

Rain.

He's no longer touching me, but even in the darkness, I'm aware of his presence. The room isn't much larger than a telephone booth, so there's only a few feet separating us.

Those few feet, they're my saving grace.

This is the closest to him I've been since the cabin. I was careful earlier this week in the quad, making sure to keep enough space between us that I wouldn't end up doing something stupid. But right now, his nearness is suffocating, and I feel my walls already beginning to crumble.

"I know it's you," I murmur in a low tone, finally breaking the silence between us before it consumes me entirely. Feigning boredom in my voice, I glare at him in the darkness, knowing full well he can feel it, even if he can't see it. "What do you want, Rain? What could you possibly want from me now?"

"Abhainn," he breathes, stepping up into my personal space. His hands find my face, cupping my jaw in his palms, and it takes every ounce of my willpower not to lean into his touch. "What is going on with you?"

Is he kidding me right now?

"What's going on with me? What the fuck is going on with you?" I seethe, pushing him in the chest, effectively breaking his hold on me. "Shit hits the fan, and when I want to be there for you, you shut me out and tell me I'm nothing to you. But then you see me with Abbi yet again, and what, you get jealous? Which is it, Rain? This hot and cold shit is getting fucking old."

"Damn right I'm jealous," he growls, pulling me in from the back of my neck to press his forehead to mine. "I hated seeing her hands on you, your arm around her. Your hands on her fucking *face* just now and then the other night with your lips on hers, and just…*fuck*. Your body is mine. *You* are—"

"Shut up. Just shut. The fuck. Up," I cut him off, my nostrils flaring. "You don't get to have a claim on me, not anymore. I'm not yours. I wanted to be, but you made damn sure to push me out." I bite my lip, then roll the ball of my piercing between my teeth, enjoying the hint of pain it brings.

"River, please." He releases a sigh before rubbing the tip of his nose against mine. "I swear, I'm just trying to keep you safe."

My teeth grind together at his admission. "From what? You give me half answers which only leads to more questions. And as your secrets just keep piling up and with the shit that's revealed, it gets harder for me to trust anything that comes out of your damn mouth. So why should I trust this?"

He pulls back, and I feel the way he's looking at me. "I know. Fuck, *I know*."

I bite the inside of my cheek, melting with how his words sear my heart without permission as I yank on the chain to turn the light on, meeting his amber gaze. "If you know, then stop looking at me like you want me. Not when you've made it abundantly clear that you don't. Just put me out of my misery once and for all, and let me move on."

It's half plea, half demand, and all desperation.

The emotion behind his eyes doesn't lessen though, driving me fucking mad. Filling me with so many unchecked feelings, my fingers are shaking against his chest as I hold his stare.

Because I won't back down. Not this time.

I feel his fingers weave their way through my hair and the struggle coursing through his body. I know, because I feel it, too. We're both tired. Of fighting each other, of fighting this intoxicating desire that overwhelms us every single time we're in a room together.

And just like every other time since the first in the cabin, we lose.

His mouth is on mine in an instant, before I can protest against it. Because I know I fucking should. Each time I grant him control, he never fails to use it to shred my already mangled heart.

Still, I find myself kissing him back with fervor, like a man dying of thirst, and he's the water I need to survive.

His tongue pries my lips apart and the moment the tip of his hits my piercing, a low rumble rises from deep within his chest. Twirling and twisting the ball with his tongue, his grip on my hair tightens.

"That's new," he pants before moving his mouth across my jaw, his whispered words brushing against my skin. "I love it. It feels amazing against my tongue, so I can only imagine it'll be divine running along my cock."

The comment gives me pause.

No fucking way am I giving him that pleasure. Not now. Never again.

"Too bad you'll never find out," I breathe, moving my hands to my jeans, quickly moving to release myself from their confines. From the intake of breath, I can tell that he has a comeback at the ready, so I shut him up with a blistering kiss, the ball of my piercing teasing his tongue some more.

I might be insane, but the words tumble from my mouth without any thought other than needing to get him out of my system in some way. "Now get on your fucking knees," I growl, shoving my pants and underwear down past my ass and pressing on his shoulder to force him down in front of me.

He doesn't put up much of a fight at the sight of my cock bobbing between us. Sinking to a knee at the pressure of my hand, his warm palm wraps around my length, thick and ready, giving me a few gentle strokes before his tongue snakes out to lap at the crown.

A moan escapes me as guilt pricks the back of my brain, knowing another mouth has been there not more than a week ago.

No. Fuck that.

Knowing what I do about Rain, there's no way *Roman* and he haven't done far more than Abbi and I did the other night. He basically admitted he was in love with the guy, and vice versa. I'd have to be delusional to think nothing has happened between them in the weeks we've been apart.

Images of them together flood my mind, Roman's hands drifting across his firm body, and a tidal wave of rage pulls me under, drowning me in despair.

My cock might want you, but he isn't the one in charge. Even if he was, all he wants is that tight ass and warm mouth. But the thing is, he can get that just about anywhere.

Fuck me. I'm nothing to him. He's said as much.

It's time for him to know what that feels like.

The velvety warmth of Rain's mouth surrounds my dick, and before the angel on my shoulder can talk me out of it, I jerk my hips forward, forcing my cock in deeper. My tip hits the back of his throat, causing him to gag slightly. His hands fly to my hips, the blunt ends of his fingers digging into my exposed ass.

I piston my hips in quick, dominating movements, working my cock deeper into his mouth and throat. He swallows around me, a clenching feeling gripping my length. My fingers latch onto the door on either side of me and I adjust our placement. With his back and head pushed against the wall behind him, I press my palms against the drywall and start fucking his mouth with zero finesse or care in the world.

Because fuck him if he thinks he has any say. That he has the right to claim and control me when he does nothing but shred my heart.

Slamming into him again and again, I revel in the noises coming from him. His ragged breathing through his nose, the moans that vibrate around my shaft, sending bolts of pleasure straight to my balls.

"This is what it was like for me that first time, Rain. In the shower. Are you enjoying yourself?" I continue thrusting into his mouth. Our eyes lock on each other instinctively, and pleasure ripples through my body at the sight of him on his knees below me.

"What was that? You can't talk past my cock? It's so deep down your throat you can't fucking breathe? Now imagine this multiplied by a hundred. Because what you fucking did to me was at least that much worse." I continue to taunt him, my fingers gripping the deep brown strands of hair on the top of his head as I force my cock as far down his throat as I can.

I hate myself even as the words come from my mouth, but I can't stop them. I need him to get it. To feel it. To fucking *understand.*

His amber eyes never leave mine as his head bangs against the wall, and when I see a couple tears leak from them, I almost come on the spot.

"But you needed a taste of this, to get it through your fucking head. This is what it was like to be treated like shit."

I hate the way you made me feel.

Thrust.

"To give a piece of trust to someone, only to have it ripped away."

I hate that you have this hold over me. I hate that I don't fight it.

Thrust.

"To be degraded and humiliated by someone you thought cared about you."

I hate that you did this to me. I hate that I let you.

Thrust.

"To share the deepest parts of yourself, only to be taken for granted."

I hate that despite it all, I still fucking love you.

Thrust.

I bare my teeth and snarl out the words meant to cut him deepest. "How's it fucking feel? Not just to be used like this, but to hate yourself for loving it. How's it fucking taste, baby? Knowing your mouth wasn't the last one to be wrapped around my cock."

His eyes close as tears freely flow from the corners of them, and I know they're not only from me fucking his face anymore, though that's how they started. It's the venom I'm spewing at him, the taunts and jabs causing his emotions to crack his facade.

To break him.

Just like he broke me.

And I don't even have the fucks to give within me to feel the guilt I know I should. Not when the torment he caused me has carved doubt and inadequacy into every inch of my mind, body, and soul.

Those are the scars he left me with, and I'm not sure they'll ever fully heal.

I feel my balls tighten, shooting a zap of pleasure up my spine just as Rain's throat practically swallows my cock whole. The sensation causes me to erupt, my release spraying from me like a fire hose on full blast.

But Rain doesn't let it phase him.

He continues to suck and lick, working every last drop of cum from my body before he finally releases me. The moisture in his eyes is still present as he stares up at me with those fucking amber orbs that have entrapped every piece of my being.

Reaching down, I brush my thumb under his eye, collecting the liquid pooling there on the pad. The action brings me back to the day in the locker room. The first time I ever got my hands and mouth on him. The tiny spec of his cum resting on my finger.

Lifting my thumb to my mouth, I lick the teardrop resting there. The saltiness sweeps over my tongue, burning like acid a thousand times worse than his tears outside the shed after the first time we kissed.

Stop thinking about the cabin. It wasn't real. This is reality now.

But it doesn't stop the ache in my chest as I stare down at him, looking damn near as wrecked as I feel. Remorse covers his face as he slumps back against the wall, his entire body coursing with anguish and calamity.

"There was a point in my life when I thought your cum was the sweetest thing I'd ever tasted." I grind the words out, desperate to gain control over the war inside me. Giving in to my desire to kiss and hold and fucking *love him* is the last thing I can do right now. "But I was wrong, baby. I think I prefer the taste of your tears."

My jaw pulses with the need to hit something, the anger building inside me for allowing this to happen boiling the blood in my veins. The rapidly changing emotions running through me are sending me spiraling more than I was the other night at the bar, or after at my apartment.

Rain swallows before tucking my softening cock back into my pants and fixing me up, like what just happened in here between us was nothing more than a figment of my imagination. And when he doesn't say anything for a full five minutes, just leans back against the wall from his place on the ground and stares up at me, I can't take it.

"You were right all along, it seems. We're better off as enemies." I let out a humorless laugh. "Turns out hate doesn't even begin to describe what I feel for you," I tell him, repeating the words he once spoke to me all those months ago, fully aware of what they turn me into.

A liar, just like him.

Because what I feel for him? It's the furthest thing from hate.

Whatever word is stronger than love, that's what I feel for him.

He is the object of my obsession, the gravity for my orbit, every star in the night sky, reminding me that I'm not alone.

He's the center of my goddamn universe.

And I just broke him.

So no, the person I hate…it's not Rain. Not even close.

The real person I hate is myself.

SEVEN

River

"R iver?" my mom's voice calls from down the stairs of my childhood home.

Shit, so I'm not crazy. I did just hear the garage door open.

I quickly finish rifling through the medicine cabinet of my sister's bathroom upstairs, stashing the ten or so pills I grabbed from her prescription in a baggie in my jacket pocket. Shutting the cabinet door as softly as I can, I call out to my mother before flushing the toilet and washing my hands because, let's be real, I'm paranoid I'm about to get caught stealing my sister's ADHD medicine.

Borrowing. Not stealing, I try to tell myself. Except I know I'm full of shit.

Closing the door behind me, I head downstairs to my mother, who wasn't supposed to be home from work for another hour. Hence why I decided to go on my little scavenging trip *now* when

I thought the house would be empty with her working and my sister still at school for cheer practice.

"Why're you home from work already?" I call, rounding the corner to the kitchen, expecting to find her in there because I swear she's *always* in the kitchen. And she is, not to my surprise.

But the last thing I expect to find is my mother *and* father standing at the kitchen island in what appears to be a deep and heated discussion. One which they both halt the second they see me standing in the doorway.

"Everything okay?" I ask slowly, anxiety prickling the back of my neck, the pills burning a hole in my pocket.

My mother gives me a nervous smile and my father... well, he just glares at me. It's the first time I've seen him since Thanksgiving, having been avoiding this house like the fucking plague in case he decided to stop by unexpectedly.

Clearly, my intuition was right.

"Nothing, honey. Your father and I were just discussing Willow's graduation gift." My mother smiles, but I can tell it's forced.

I'm not about to push my luck, though. "Oh, okay. Well I was just grabbing something, so I won't keep you guys."

"Why don't you stay for dinner?" she asks, quirking her head in what I can tell is a plea. "Willow is going to be out with some friends at a movie. I'd love to have the company and take some time to catch up with you."

I swallow roughly, hating to deny her anything when at least she tries. "Actually —"

"We'd both love to stay for dinner, Kathleen," my father says, inviting himself to join while pinning me with a hard stare, daring me to disagree. "It would be good for the three of us to catch up, what with River spending all of winter break up in Vail serving his...*sentence.* We can spend some time as a family."

Funny, Dad. We haven't been a family since you decided to up and leave us because I won't conform to your rules.

Giving Mom my best fake smile, I nod. "Yeah, Mom, I'd love to stay. Do you want help with anything?"

Shaking her head, she sets her purse on the island and starts to pull ingredients for enchiladas from the pantry. "I've got it handled, sweetie. You can just watch TV or something. Did you bring any schoolwork? I'm sure you have midterms coming up."

I do, but I most definitely didn't bring schoolwork with me. Not like I'm planning to let that information slip in front of Dad.

"Nah, I'll just go hang out in my room. Clean it or...whatever," I say, heading back toward the stairs.

But of course, the second I'm out of the kitchen, a hand that can only belong to my father grips my bicep and drags me through the living room and toward the room that used to be his office.

He pushes me through the door and follows me in, shutting the door with a click and leaning back against it.

"Explain yourself," he demands, his tone hard and accusatory.

My brows furrow. "What would you like me to explain, *Dad*? What have I done to offend you this time? Other than be in your presence?"

To his credit, he doesn't so much as quirk a brow at my abnormal response. I've never challenged him in my life except for the night I told him I wouldn't pretend to be something I'm not. But I can tell he's surprised because he takes a moment to reply.

"Where is your head? Getting ejected from the game that could take your team to a National Championship? Serving a suspension for the entire winter break so you miss the holiday with your family? And *now* I hear from your mother that Coach Scott called and is concerned with your academic performance?"

My heart drops to my stomach.

Fuck, I mean I know Coach has raised his concerns to me recently about my missing classes and lifting sessions. I never thought he'd go to Mom about it though. But seeing as they've known each other forever…I shouldn't really be surprised.

"That's why you're here. Not Willow's graduation gift."

His scowl deepens as he crosses his arms over his chest. "Yes. Your mother called me when she saw it was you who disarmed the alarm to get into the house, and we both rushed over here to catch you before you left."

I roll my eyes and scoff. "So what, I'm not getting a perfect GPA right now and suddenly it calls for an intervention?"

"It wouldn't need to be an intervention if in addition to that, Coach Scott didn't tell her you failed the random drug test." *Shit, I forgot about that.* "Which, of course, I didn't believe. But I could tell you've been smoking weed the second you walked into the kitchen. Your eyes are bloodshot to hell, and you reek." He sneers at me as he spews off all my downfalls like they're crimes, disgust evident in his tone. And that's what it is after all.

You're disgusting. That's what he said at Thanksgiving, right?

Shaking my head, I do my best not to wince as I smile at him. "Go fuck yourself. You don't know shit. Why would you, when you haven't been an active parent in my life for *years?*"

"Don't you dare speak to me that way," he seethes, glaring down at me.

"What are you gonna do about it? Huh?" I taunt, my rage bubbling to the point of bursting. "I'm an adult. I'm fucking *free* of your tyranny, Dad. And I sure as hell hope Willow manages to get as far away from you as soon as she can so you don't screw her up just as much as you have me."

"No son of mine—"

"I'm not your *son!*" I yell, getting in his face. "I'm *not* your son. Not anymore. *You* made sure of that! Or don't you remember practically disowning me for not living up to your standard because I'm *bisexual?*"

"River Christian—"

"No!" I shout again before lowering my voice. "You don't get to belittle me. You don't get to make me feel inferior to you for being true to who I am. And you *certainly* don't get to come in here and suddenly try to parent me after *years* when *you're* the one who chose to leave in the first place!"

He stares at me, a stoic expression on his face. I flinch as he raises his hand to put some distance between us, pushing against my shoulder for some room. His eyes remain emotionless as he seemingly inventories my each and every feature, probably cataloging each and every thing he despises.

Too emotional. Too lazy. Too fucking gay.

Swallowing roughly, I look up at him and utter the word *move.*

He doesn't. Just continues to glare at me.

Hardening my gaze, I snarl and grip the doorknob behind him. "Move, or *I* will move you."

"Get your shit together, River," he growls, removing my hand from the door and opening it himself. Pushing past him, I head up the stairs, hearing him call out behind me to make sure I'm down in thirty minutes for dinner.

Fuck you, you piece of trash.

So in a true act of rebellion, I dig out a blunt from my stash in my dresser to hotbox in the bathroom for forty-five minutes before returning downstairs for dinner.

Dinner is delicious, though the company is absolute fucking garbage to say the least. Dad managed to sink his talons into Mom while I was upstairs, apparently turning her against me as well. Of course she's still taking cues from him, even after he left her—left all three of us.

I love her, but shit, at what point do you put the happiness of your own children on the line for someone who *left you because* you stood up for your kids? Does that even make any sense? How does that set a good example to me and Willow?

It just goes to show parents, while they have the opportunity to shape us into amazing people, they also have to power to irrevocably fuck us up with as little as a few words or actions. Or in this case, lack thereof.

Yet what really gets me is when she sits there and asks me *what's going on with you?* And I have to smile and say *nothing* because I can't bring myself to break her goddamn heart like *he* did.

So, while I enjoy the fuck out of the enchiladas to curb my munchies, I also get to endure the most painfully awkward dinner of my life. Almost an entire hour lecture about keeping my head on straight, putting my grades and my athletics before partying and making sure I keep the *right company.*

That comment was from Dad, and I know it's a thousand percent aimed at Rain. Little does he know, he doesn't have to worry about it anymore because Rain doesn't fucking want me either.

I'm just thankful I'm high outta my mind so the hurled insults and judgment from them both brushes off better. That, and the gin and tonic I made myself at the wet bar. Cue my father's disapproving look for that one.

Shocking, I know.

Once I've had enough of their shit and my glass is empty, I sigh. "I need to go, Mom. I'm supposed to meet some friends to..." I glance at my dad, measuring my words. "...*study.* You know, with midterms coming up."

Not true at all, of course. I have no plans, but I certainly have no intention of staying here longer than necessary with Satan and his...ex-wife. Shit, right now, I'm just glad I parked on the curb so I'm not blocked in with no means of escape.

"Okay, sweetie." Mom smiles and rises from her chair when I do. She rounds the table to give me a hug, which I return because she's my fucking mom. Of course, I don't miss the way she sniffs my shirt as I hug her or how she squeezes me a little tighter. "We just want what's best for you, River. We love you."

Tears well in my eyes but I tamp them down. *How I wish I could believe you, Mom.*

"I know," I whisper back instead before releasing her. "I love you too."

Stepping back, I head for the door as I hear my father say he's leaving too after thanking Mom for dinner.

I slip into my shoes and jacket quickly, hoping to escape before another confrontation happens, but no surprise here, luck isn't ever on my side these days.

He grabs my arm as I step onto the porch, the cool wind whipping around us both as I look up at the green eyes that only ever look at me with revulsion these days.

"Your attention seeking stops here, River. It's done. Quit smoking. Stop skipping class and lifting. Get things back in order, or you're going to suffer the consequences."

Dude, fuck you and the high horse you rode in on.

I raise my brow and smile. "What are you gonna do, *Daddy?* Ground me? Take my car away? Tell me I can't see my friends?" Yeah, it might be childish to antagonize him. But I'm anything but a child. If he wanted to be a parent, he had the chance. As far as I'm concerned, that ship has long since sailed.

Tongue-in-cheek, he shakes his head at me, dismay written all over his features. "I truly can't understand how you've turned into such a disappointment."

I scoff, thankful as hell for the buzz in my brain because I might take a page from Rain's book and actually fucking deck him if I wasn't. Yet the buzz doesn't take away from the way these words always manage to disarm me. The single word, it constantly rings through my head. Always in his voice.

Disappointment.

I feel the grimace on my face as I stare into his eyes and for the life of me, I just don't understand what I did to deserve this.

"If you want to find the disappointment in the family, look in the damn mirror, Dad," I tell him, the words thick in my throat. "Because I might not be the son you asked for, but you sure as hell aren't the father I wanted either."

I trip over my own feet as I stagger out to my Rover, sliding in the driver's seat and throwing the car into drive. I peel off the curb from outside the house, not a goddamn clue where I'm heading because my mind is in a million places at once, and I can't seem to form a coherent thought other than *run* from that fucking house.

My inability to function properly is partially from the high, yes, and mixing weed and alcohol was the worst best idea I've ever had. But that isn't what makes it so I can't walk or see or think straight.

No. I have the mental and emotional abuse of not just my father, but now my mother as well to thank for this.

I can't believe for the first time in fucking *years* they were on the same side of an argument pertaining to me. They decided to put their differences aside and gang up on me, *now* of all times, and I just…can't.

I can't with *any of it.*

Family. Friends. School. Football.

Life.

Because I know I'm spiraling. I feel it in my core like an impending midnight storm, ready to consume the night sky in crashes of thunder and bolts of lightning. I feel it all coming to a head and I know soon enough there won't be anything I can do to stop it. I'm drowning beneath the sorrow and the grief and the self-loathing, all searching for a way to devour every atom of my being. And all the oxygen is being sucked out of the atmosphere.

Because I'm trapped.

By *them* holding me down in an attempt to paint me into the perfect portrait of someone they want me to be because they couldn't stomach not being able to force me into a mold I will never be able to conform to.

It's not who I am, and I can't fucking change that. More importantly, I shouldn't have to. Yet for some godforsaken reason, no one seems to give a shit.

Not one goddamn person.

But how can I expect anyone else to show any semblance of care when the people who are supposed to love me at every step and are the ones to turn their backs on me the quickest?

No one. Fucking. Cares.

About me. My happiness. My life.

My successes and accomplishments are weighed and measured at every turn, and no matter how hard I try, no matter how much effort and heart I put into *everything* I do, it's never enough.

For them, it never will be.

When they look at me, all they see is their son who could have been perfect. He could've been the shining star of their world, the sun the planets revolve around, the child they bragged to their friends or coworkers about, the one that *made something* of themselves and made the family proud.

If only he were *straight.*

What a disappointment.

So, I know this is it. What rock bottom looks, feels, sounds, smells, and tastes like.

It looks like all your dreams being doused in gasoline and set ablaze by those you love the most. It feels like the most intense heat, burning hotter than the sun with anger and disdain radiating in licks and flashes of fire. It sounds like the cracking and breaking of your very soul. The foundation of who you are being unable to defy gravity any longer when the embers become too heavy before it collapses around you in shambles. It smells like smoke to the point you can't fucking breathe anymore without suffocating.

And it tastes like salt and embers. From the ashes sticking to the tears streaming down your face as you watch your world, everything you've ever worked for, go up in smithereens.

Without a single clue how to stop it.

But why stop it? Why save something that isn't worth saving? Because all I want is to scream, cry, and break down.

So…that's what I do.

A violent scream rips from my throat, so loud I'm sure the glass of my windows will shatter as I pound my fists against the steering wheel repeatedly. I use it like a punching bag, hitting it until I'm sure my hands will bruise as I release the anguish inside me. Tears are streaming from my eyes, coating my cheeks and lips and neck with every salty drop cascading down my face.

Whipping my hat from my head into the passenger seat, I yank on my hair with my free hand, desperate for the thoughts in my mind to stop moving and spinning and circling me around and around again. But it doesn't stop, so I tug at the strands hard enough that a few pieces come out of my skull when I tear my fingers away again.

The pain in my head, my hand, my vocal chords, it's all joining together in one giant blur of fucking agony. But it's not enough. Rather than taking away from the ache in my chest, it only magnifies it.

I'm starting to think it won't ever be enough until I cut my losses and burn the rest of the fucking world down with me.

Because someone else needs to feel the misery wreaking havoc on every cell in my body to the point where I'd rather be dead. God, I could just press my foot down on the gas a little harder and run this red light. Jerk the wheel into oncoming traffic this very moment. Drive up into the mountains and into the guardrail, praying it fails.

The possibilities are endless now, when I'm to the point where I'd rather give up the fight and let them win. Bury me in the goddamn ground and leave me there to rot.

Because what is the fucking point?

I'm broken, down to the point where I'm unrecognizable to even myself.

Shattered and fractured beyond repair, shards of me chipping away with every person I ever trusted that decided to get up and walk out of my life, not a goodbye or backward glance in sight.

All the king's horses and all the king's men will never put me back together again.

I know it. They know.

Even *Rain* knows it, now more than ever after what happened in the broom closet.

But what I really want? I want to scream at them, at Rain, to anyone who will listen until my voice is gone and my lungs give out. Shout and curse and rant and fucking *make them hear* every word I have to say.

I hurt all the time. I'm sick of being angry, and depressed, and scared, and broken, and betrayed by every fucking person in my life.

Yet I can't force them to be receptive of my emotions and insecurities. In the end, they're all fickle things, emotions. They drive humans to do the most asinine shit, and for what? For why? Why do we need them in the first place when they just cause one disaster after another? All they do is feed insecurity to the point where you're a mess that can't function without the help of some sort of vice to numb the emotions you don't want to feel.

And for me, that emotion is love.

All I want — no, all I fucking *need* – is someone to love me back the way I should be loved. The way I crave. Love me the way *I* willingly love others, without qualms or questions.

With my entire heart. My mind, body, and soul.

I love with every goddamn inch of who I am. And I know I deserve nothing less in return.

Yet my life would be so much simpler if I could numb the pesky emotion altogether. In reality, I should just be alone and say fuck *romance* and *love* because it seems the universe thinks that's all I deserve. But the cold, hard truth is…I already *am* alone.

So fucking alone, and the silence is deafening. Even in a crowd of people, I feel it.

Alone. Abandoned. Forgotten.

Numb.

I let out a sigh of resignation.

How can emptiness feel so heavy?

The question pulls me back to reality somehow, allowing me to realize I'm no longer driving. I'm pulled over on a curb on a random street. Except it's not random at all. Not when I see the orange Jeep Wrangler under the eerie glow of the streetlight.

My eyes flash up and to the right, finding myself at the last place on Earth I should be.

Why the fuck did I end up driving here? I want to be alone. Seeking him out, showing up at his apartment unannounced is the exact opposite of being alone.

Still, I find myself opening the door to my SUV and slipping out in the cool dark of night, heading up the snowy walkway to his building.

It's stupid. It's so fucking stupid I can't even begin to list the reasons why I should turn my ass around and go home, to the bar, literally *anywhere else.* But as I've said before, something about Ciaráin Grady turns me into a blithering idiot.

Before I know it, I'm inside the building and standing in front of his apartment door, ragged breaths escaping my lips. I don't even stop to think, just pound my fist on the door.

I hear movement inside, but no answer.

"Rain!" I yell, slamming my hand again and again, desperation clawing at me.

I need to see him.

I need to see him.

I need him.

"Rain, please open the fuc —" I'm cut off when the door opens.

But instead of Rain standing there, it's *Roman fucking Mitchell.* In nothing but a towel.

I bite my lip and shake my head at his audacity to answer the door basically naked to an apartment he doesn't actually live in. But then I hear the shower still running in the background, and instantly a piece of me dies inside.

"Can I help you?" Roman says, leaning against the door frame, a smug smile playing on his lips. But fuck if I'll let him get to me. In my bones I knew the likelihood of them being together now was high, even if I wasn't prepared to see the aftermath of it firsthand.

So, I square my shoulders and harden my eyes as I give him a wicked smile in return. Because surviving this moment fucking depends on it.

The number one rule of self-preservation: detach from what destroys you.

EIGHT
Rain

I swear I hear the door to my apartment closing as I'm in the middle of my shower, leaving me wondering where the hell Roman is going now. Because the guy is constantly in and out like my apartment is a never-stopping revolving door.

While it's been more convenient to have him stay with me, because we both feel Ted isn't about to make any insane moves with him around, I also just want my own space back. Some alone time is what I've been craving more than anything. Freedom to go where I want, when I want. I feel like a goddamn prisoner on house arrest, and my "cellmate" is the only person who manages to set me on edge just as much as Ted does.

Damn, I sound like an ungrateful ass.

About ten minutes later, I'm slipping into a pair of sweats and a long sleeve shirt, heading out of the bathroom to find Roman. Padding down to the kitchen, I'm surprised to find Roman standing there, still in just his towel.

My forehead creases. "Did you just go outside in February… like *that?*"

Roman gives me a look, raising his brow, as if to say *are you stupid* while grabbing a pair of boxers and jeans from his bag and walks behind the island to slide into them.

"I didn't go anywhere. Someone came to the door before I had time to get dressed. And then I got distracted by some texts."

Immediately, my skin tingles as worry washes over me. "Was it…" I let the name hang in the air, not knowing if I want to know the answer. If it was Ted, either on his phone, or worse, at the door.

Thankfully, Roman understands and shakes his head. "Nah, it wasn't him. It was River, actually."

My eyes widen. "Texting you?"

Roman cocks his head. "No, the text was from Kaede. River was at the *door*," he says slowly, enunciating the words like I'm a fucking imbecile.

To be fair, River being at the door would make more sense.

"Did he say what he wanted?"

Roman shakes his head again. "Nope, but I'm assuming it was to talk to you. He seemed out of sorts, to say the least."

Biting my tongue to keep from snapping his head off, I sigh. "Why did he leave?"

Shrug. "Beats the hell out of me."

"Did you invite him in?"

"This isn't my apartment to invite him into. So, no, I didn't."

My molars grinds, and I swear to God, I'm about to lose my ever-loving mind. "Roman, what happened? I know he wouldn't just *leave*. He came for a fucking reason."

Another shrug. "He didn't say."

"Motherfucking…" I mutter under my breath, pinching the bridge of my nose. "Tell me the conversation. Verbatim, please."

Roman leans on the island. "Dude, it's probably nothing. Just call him and—"

"Roman," I growl out his name. "The conversation. Now."

Rolling his eyes, he rests his chin in his hands, giving me the most bored expression any person could manage. "He was pounding on the door and yelling your name. I opened the door and asked him what I could do for him. He asked if you were here. I said yes, you were in the shower. He asked if I could let you know he stopped by. I said yes. He said thanks and left. The end." Roman cocks his head and gives me his signature asshole smirk. "Was that good enough for you or should I reenact it as well? With or without props?"

"Dick," I grumble, heading back toward my room to switch into a pair of jeans.

Of course, Roman follows.

"What're you doing?" he asks as I button the jeans and dig a hoodie out of my closet.

"Going to River's."

I glance up in time to see him make that face people make when they taste something sour. "Why? Just call him?"

Sighing in frustration, I pin him with a glare. "Not that I owe you an explanation, but if it was important enough for him to show up here and ask to see me, even when he and I aren't on speaking terms? It means it's important enough for me to go knocking on his door too."

He laughs. "If it was so important, he would have asked to come in and just waited. Seriously, man. Why does this guy have your damn boxers in a wedgie? Just call him before you go barging over there late at night without notice."

I mull it over in my head and decide there's no harm in calling him first. Dialing his number, I wait for him to pick up, my stomach in knots. But he doesn't answer, the line picking up his voicemail instead.

I hang up and dial again, only to get the same result.

Okay, he could still be driving.

Thirty minutes, seven call attempts, and twenty unanswered texts later, I'm pacing the apartment as the worst thoughts run through my mind. Mostly that he crashed his car somehow between here and his apartment. Which, to be fair, I only barely remember where it is from Coach dropping him off first when we came back from Vail.

But I know it's not thirty minutes from here.

One final call attempt that leads me to voicemail, and I'm officially in full out panic mode.

Pocketing my phone and rushing to the door, keys and wallet in hand, Roman calls out to me from the couch. "Are you actually going over there right now? It's like ten-thirty at night. He could be sleeping for all you know."

My eyes narrow on Roman. "Why are you so intent on me not going to see him?"

He sighs. "Look, man. I don't actually give a shit what you do here. But River..." He trails off, searching my face for a minute before continuing. "Look, obviously I don't know the guy. But I do know what fucked up looks like when I see it. And he most definitely was.

I don't know if it was drunk or stoned, maybe both? Either way, it might just be better for you to go see what was up in the morning."

Stoned? Drunk?

"Why are you just mentioning this now?" I growl, my fingers gripping the door handle so tight, I might just break the damn thing off entirely.

"You asked for the conversation, not how he—"

"Roman!" I roar, pushing off the door before rushing up to him. Grabbing the collar of his shirt, I yank him from his seat and pull him up to me. My nose brushes against his as I hiss out the next words. "These are people's *lives* at stake here. When I ask for details, I need them *all. Especially* where River's concerned."

A smirk dances on his lips. "Just a teammate, huh?"

"Roman," I warn, my eyes hard and voice menacingly low.

His eyes flash between mine, then down to my mouth. It's just for half a second, but I catch it, and it makes my blood fucking boil.

No.

Licking his lips, he nods as his gaze connects with mine again. "Yes sir," he says sarcastically.

I release my hold on his shirt, pushing him away from me and take a step back to the door. And that's when the thought, the worst one I could possibly have, hits me.

What if Ted saw him come here? Heard him pounding on the door and asking for me?

What if Ted took him?

It doesn't take me more than fifteen seconds to be pulling my Jeep onto the street, headed in the direction of the only person I'd slay my demons for.

NINE

River

Pounding on my door pulls me from the haze my mind was wandering in for a brief moment. But then I roll to my side on the couch and stare at my television.

Whoever is here can go fuck themselves.

Especially if it's Drew or E, back here not more than half an hour later in an attempt to *cheer me up* from running into *Roman fucking Mitchell* with another twelve pack and a couple joints.

Seeing as I'm not in the mood for company, I'll gladly take what they have to offer before kicking them out of my apartment. *Again.*

Because I drank six of those beers already and smoked an entire joint, so I think it's about time for a restock if the boys are willingly supplying. But from the way the pounding continues, it's not Drew or E. They would just let themselves in with the key I gave them freshman year. The key they used to get in before I got back earlier tonight.

I swear to God if it's Abbi here again to talk about that night in my car, I might shit a motherfucking brick. We already sorted out our shit. Moved on.

"Go away!" I call, refusing to move from my spot on the couch. In all honesty, I might be too fucking high to move.

"River, open the fucking door!" a voice shouts from the other side, pausing the pounding for a moment. It's a voice I recognize well, deep and smoky that slides over me like well-aged whiskey.

Rain.

What is he doing here?

Sliding off the couch with a groan, I make my way to the door, pulling it open harshly to find Rain on the other side looking like…well, a goddamn snack.

He's in jeans and sweatshirt beneath his jacket, a knit cap on his head, but somehow he looks like he just stepped out of a magazine.

And for the fucking life of me, I don't get it.

Why him?

Why did I have to fall in love with the one person who wasn't willing to love me back?

"What do you want, Ciaráin?" I ask, using his full name.

I don't miss his wince, but whether it be from me calling him Ciaráin or my tone of voice, I couldn't say.

Rain rubs the back of his neck, worrying his bottom lip with his teeth to the point I think he might gnaw the damn thing off. "Do you care if I come in for a minute?"

If you come in, I don't think I'm strong enough to make you leave if you asked to stay.

"Yeah, sure," I clear my throat and step out of the way, allowing him into my apartment.

Awkwardness fills the air as he strides in uneasily, like a toddler on roller skates. I watch him through my fog, taking in the disaster that is my apartment.

There are pizza boxes and beer cans and bottles littering every available surface in my kitchen, and don't even get me started on the living room. Piles of clothes are strewn about, and whether they are dirty or clean laundry I never put away, I couldn't say.

It's not normally like this. I'm the opposite of messy, at least on my good days. I guess I just ran out of fucks to give.

By the look on his face, Rain's coming to the same conclusion. His brows furrow as he glances around the space before looking down at the coffee table where the remnants of my blunt are lying there for the world to see. "Have you been smoking weed?"

I shrug. "We're in the off season. Not a big deal."

His brow hitches up. "Not a big deal? River, you told me up at the ca—"

"Don't fucking say it," I growl, slipping past him to grab the second joint off the table to shove it in my pocket.

The last thing I need to think about is the cabin and everything that happened there. It's already seared into my mind, every minute of every goddamn day. It doesn't matter if we were still enemies or not, I remember every fucking thing that happened there.

Every kiss. Laugh. Smile. Touch.

The way his body feels, tastes, smells.

Everything.

Rain sighs and shakes his head, taking a seat on the couch.

"Look, Riv. I just came by to see if everything is good, okay? Roman said—"

I scoff. "Oh, yeah? *Roman* said what, exactly?"

Try sounding a little less insecure next time, jackass.

Rain cocks his head and looks at me, his face contorted with confusion. "He just said you stopped by while I was in the shower. I wanted to come make sure you were good, that's all."

I'd be better if my entire life wasn't going down the shitter. But it seems the only person I want to talk about it with is you and you smashed my heart into a million fucking pieces.

But yeah, I'm fan-fucking-tastic.

"I'm fine, you can leave now," I say flatly, attempting to sound bored when I'm anything but.

Please don't leave me. Not again.

Rain rises to his feet, to do as I asked, I'm assuming. But instead of heading for the door, he just steps into my personal space, getting inches from me.

His scent and presence, it intoxicates me more than any drug or alcohol ever could in an instant, leaving me weak and helpless.

"You don't have to be a dick because of what hap—"

"Where is this coming from?" I cut him off.

His brows meet in the center, clearly taken aback by my outburst. "What the hell has gotten into you?"

"Like you care, *Ciaráin*," I sneer his name, misery wracking every fiber of my being. I hate being this close and not touching him. I hate knowing what it's like to have him, only to...not.

Rain's jaw ticks and he shakes his head, giving me a hardened glare. "Don't play games with me, Abhainn. Not when you know you can't win them."

"Don't I fucking know it," I snap, unable to keep the affliction from my voice. "You made it perfectly clear you'll do whatever it takes to get what you want."

Including use me to work your shit out, only to run to Roman fucking Mitchell *the moment we get back from Vail.*

An unamused laugh escapes him as he steps back, crossing his arms over his chest. "And what is it that I want, River? Since you seem to have it all figured out?"

I grimace, my blood boiling with suppressed tension as I bite out the words. "That's the thing, Ciaráin. I don't even think you know. That's why you're here, right? *Roman* isn't satisfying you, so you come running to me?"

I hate the dash of hope I hear in my voice. Because hope—that he might come to his senses, choose me, and we could live happily ever after—it's nothing more than a futile fight against cancer.

Because there's nothing to be left behind after the cancer consumes every cell in its path.

Rain licks his lips before glaring at me again. "Why don't you say what's really on your mind, Riv. Beating around the bush isn't you."

I scoff in disbelief. "And you know who I am? *Really?* Because I highly doubt it. I don't recognize *myself* anymore and you…" I trail off, looking him up and down before settling my gaze on him. "Fuck, you really aren't the person I thought you were."

"You want to play this fucking game now? This is who I am!" he yells, stabbing a finger in his own chest. "So you need to take it or leave it, because I'm not changing for anyone. Not even you."

The words, they rip from his throat on a battle cry and even in my haze, I can hear the anxiety in them. I'm not so far gone I can't see the fear in his eyes.

Baby, just let me in.

But I know he can't. Or he won't. Whichever it might be, it doesn't matter.

I grit my teeth and snarl out the words, letting them fly off my tongue with a vengeance, "I'm not asking you to change who you are, I'm asking you to just tell me who that is! That's all I ever wanted!"

I feel the anguish on my face as I do my best to keep my shit together. He doesn't get to see me broken. He doesn't get to make me weak.

But still, my voice…it cracks the second I go to speak again. "I can't keep spinning in circles on this merry-go-round with you. Sooner or later I have to get off or it's gonna tear me apart from the inside out."

Rain's chest rises and falls rapidly, his nostrils flaring at my words. But the fury on his face doesn't meet his eyes. In them, I only see sadness and pity.

He pities me. Perfect.

"Fuck this," I mumble, clearing my throat and spinning to head over to the door. "You can leave. I don't want you here."

Just as I go to open the door, Rain's hand slams against it, keeping it in place, and before I can blink, my back is pushed against the wood and Rain's mouth is on mine.

Oh God, this is bad.

But it doesn't matter because my hands are in his hair, locking him in place as my tongue instantly finds its mate. He groans the second the ball of my piercing glides against his tongue, his fingers clutching the back of my neck in efforts to control our speed and rhythm.

And like the lovesick fool I am, I eat it up. I take every ounce of attention and desire he has to give me because something is better than nothing at all.

I'm losing my goddamn mind.

"It seems you've forgotten, so allow me to remind you, Abhainn," he growls against my lips, nipping the bottom one between his teeth. "When it comes to us, you're not the liar."

Before I can object or even think about what he's implying, his mouth is on mine again. His tongue takes greedy pulls of mine, playing with the bar that runs through it while his hands slide all over my abs, chest, and back beneath my shirt.

I'm on fire, burning up with the soft, gentle touch of his fingers on my skin. It's sending me down into a raging inferno I know I won't come back from.

My hands move to his head, flicking the hat off it before ripping off his jacket like it offended me by being on his body in the first place. I quickly yank his sweatshirt over his head in a frenzy while his fingers slide into my sweats, pushing them and my underwear down in one fell swoop. Stepping out of them, I wrench away enough to whip my shirt over my head.

"Bedroom," I pant against his lips, the clink of his belt drowning out my erratic heartbeat. My mouth is quick to mold back to his, allowing my tongue to fuck his mouth like it's the last thing it will ever do.

And goddammit, it just might be because living without him

is killing me slowly.

Because I need him. All of him. Right here, right now. No matter how dangerous it will be to my already shattered heart. After all, he can't break it more than he already has.

No, no, no! River, what are you doing? That's the high talking!

But I don't care. I *really* fucking don't.

I just need to feel the way I felt up at the cabin. The passion and desire and need that flowed between us with the heat of molten lava. Just one more time, I need to feel and touch and taste every inch of him.

One. Last. Time.

"I didn't come here for sex, mo grá," he utters against my lips, stumbling back with me toward my bedroom.

His hand cups the back of my neck, our mouths fusing together down to the cell. My fingers find the knob of the door, pushing it open while my other palm grinds against the ridge of his erection behind his boxer-briefs.

Pushing him down and back on my bed, I discard his last stitch of clothing before climbing on top of him, bracing my forearms on either side of his head. "I'm not surprised, I'm sure you're getting plenty of it with *Roman* in town." His name feels like poison on my tongue, constricting my airway as my mind once again flashes with images of them together.

My eyes meet his, only the glow of the moonlight allowing me to read his features. And what I see there...the guilt...I don't fucking like it.

Not like you've been a saint, letting Abbi try to suck you off, my treacherous brain reminds me.

My tongue licks across his lips in a wicked caress. "Tell me, baby. Do you let him inside your body the way you let me?"

Torment flashes in his eyes for a single, brief moment before his hand is on my throat. It's not as tight a grip like he would use before. But it's harsh enough to get my heart racing faster than it already is.

"Shut up, River," he growls, rolling us so he's on top, pressing me into the mattress by my throat.

The asshole in me comes out to play when the drugs are running through my system, so I smirk up at him and trail a single finger down his cock, from tip to base. It jumps slightly at my touch, making my grin widen. "Now why would I do that?"

Rain leans down, eyes searching my face with a devious smile. "Because the only word I want to hear from your lips is my name while I fuck you."

I don't have time to protest before he fuses his mouth to mine in a bruising kiss. One laced with lust and broken promises and mangled hearts. It shreds the last thin strand of sanity I was grasping onto, leaving me in a free-fall that is sure to destroy me entirely.

"Get me the lube, mo grá," Rain demands, pulling away from me breathlessly. "Not being inside you is killing me."

The Pavlovian dog I am, I roll to my side beneath him and reach into my nightstand, pulling out a condom and the bottle of lube. Rain winces when he sees the condom, holding it like it contains the plague after handing it to him.

"Do I need this?" he asks, rolling his teeth over his bottom lip

Licking my lips, I sigh, bringing my eyes up to meet his. "I don't know, baby. You tell me."

The look of pain on his face sends a bolt of agony into my

stomach, making it roll with nausea. If he…God, just the thought makes me sick.

No, no, no. Don't fucking say it. Don't —

"My dick hasn't been inside anyone else since you, Abhainn. So no, I don't think we need it," he utters before tossing the foil packet to the side, leaning forward to press his lips to mine tenderly in a soft kiss.

And the declaration, it makes my heart swell, at least for a brief moment.

Until I realize, even through the haze clouding my brain...he never said he hasn't *been with* anyone else. I don't have long to latch onto that and let my mind run rampant, though. Because the next words out of his mouth ruin me entirely.

"But we both know you can't say the same."

My entire world slips out from under me, leaving me spiraling. My intestines tangle themselves in knots, and all the air in my lungs has managed to disappear in a flash. And it only gets worse when he leans back and I see the grief etched onto his perfect, handsome face.

You did that. You made him feel that, my brain tells me, and for the fucking life of me, I would do *anything* in this moment to take it away.

Even something as stupid as giving him my body again.

"It was less than two minutes and I didn't even finish," the words slip from my lips on a strangled whisper. Burrowing my fingers into his hair, I reel him back in and anchor his mouth to mine. "I was hurting, seeing you with him after all this time. And I made a mistake."

But my words, they do nothing to erase the tension on his face while I kiss him.

I'm so sorry, baby.

My breath hitches in my throat, and I choke on pain and misery and regret.

Of loving him. Of losing him.

Of not being enough.

He pulls back without a word and slides his body between my legs, flipping open the bottle of lube and coating his bare cock. My heart rate picks up at the sight. Even through the fog in my mind, I know how much pleasure he's about to give me.

And I want it. *Need it.*

Even if I'm left in nothing but shambles when he's gone come morning.

Leaning over me, Rain aligns our dicks before taking them both in his hand. The lube allows them to slide effortlessly together and the feel of being with him like this again might kill me.

Everything about him kills me.

He's nothing but a walking, talking massacre for my heart.

"I don't blame you," he murmurs, jacking us both with leisurely tugs that have me desperate to come already. "I'm not mad, Abhainn. I have no right to be mad when we aren't together."

His words, the honesty in them and the detached tone of his voice…it numbs me more than any booze or pills or weed ever could.

"Because you don't *want me*," I wince, hating the need in my own tone as he continues to work us in tandem.

At least not the way I want you. Not the way I need you.

Without you, it's impossible to breathe.

Rain leans over me, placing his weight on a single forearm

beside my head while he still stokes us together. His mouth presses soft, gentle kisses I didn't know him to be capable of on my jaw, my cheek, my lips.

"I wouldn't be here if I didn't want you." He sighs, nuzzling his nose against mine. "But you have to understand, I was never supposed to get attached to you."

Placing another kiss on my lips, this one more insistent, he releases his hold on our lengths, and pulls me up into a seated position. Still between my legs, he reaches for the bottle again while keeping his eyes on mine.

"Flip over. On all fours," he mutters, flicking open the cap to add more lube to his cock.

The haze in my mind allows his request to be granted, my body moving to my hands and knees, though the rational part of me is still screaming at me to stop this before I can't take it back.

It doesn't matter, though. I want this.

Him.

Because I didn't know the last night in the cabin would be the *last time*. Not for sure. So I'm choosing to feed my addiction for him again, this final time.

Just one more hit.

I feel Rain's body over mine again, hovering there, but not touching. The heat of his skin radiates off him and onto me, causing goosebumps to raise on every inch of my flesh.

His mouth trails softly against the muscles of my back and shoulders, not in kisses, but in a featherlight graze of his lips. "But I did, mo grá. I got attached when I said I wouldn't."

I feel his cock then, slick with lube, at my crease, and every piece of the addict in me is craving him to slide inside me where he belongs. And the second he presses his hips forward, just the head slipping in, my entire body ignites in lust and desire.

A groan sounds out in the silence of the room, but I couldn't tell you if it was me, him, or both of us.

I just know that as he starts working himself deeper inside me for the first time in what feels like a lifetime, I feel complete.

And that's so, so wrong.

"I don't know if I was more afraid to leave you behind for good or to have to see you again, each and every day," he whispers against my skin, sliding in another inch, then another, until his pelvis is flush with my ass. "Having you close, but still so far. Always there, just barely out of reach."

Rain pistons his hips, slipping in and out with ease, building the most exquisite pressure inside me. One hand grips my waist, the other trailing lightly down my spine in a wicked caress that lights my nerve endings on fire.

His hand reaches around my neck to grasp the front of my throat lightly in his palm. Using his grip to pull me up so I'm only on my knees, his forearm rests against my chest to anchor me against him. The angle he's put me in causes him to rub against my prostate with each steady thrust, forcing a low moan to claw out from deep within my chest.

"I didn't mean to hurt you," he pants softly against the back of my neck. "I never wanted that, Abhainn. You have to believe me."

I grimace from the passion behind his words, the agony I hear in them. I know they're true, but all that does is cause me more pain.

Pain for *him*, even when he was the one who left *me* heartbroken.

"You didn't hurt me," I whisper, turning my head to find his mouth. A lone tear slips down my cheek, hidden by darkness as I utter the most honest words I've ever spoken against his lips, "You *destroyed* me."

He moves his mouth and presses a kiss to my shoulder, rolling his hips to hit the place inside me only he can light up. "I'm sorry. I'm so, so sorry," he breathes against my skin. "Let me show you how much I wish I had the power to put you back together."

Every piece of my soul is screaming at me to tell him *you do, you fucking idiot. If you would just love me back.* But I keep my mouth shut, knowing he doesn't deserve those words from me. Not when he was careless enough with my heart once already.

Instead, I grip the wrist of his hand that is around my throat with both hands and yank it down so I can move freely. Arching my neck, I wrap one hand around his neck and pull his head toward me.

"I'm not some fucking *puppet* you can control," I growl against his lips the moment before they crash against mine in a fury of passion and lust. My tongue is in his mouth, tangling with his in an erotic dance.

One of Rain's hands reaches around, gripping my cock and tugging on it and squeezing on every upstroke, the other moving up to cup the side of my face. It's tender and loving, and it makes me feel like someone is shoving a steak knife directly into my heart.

I love you, and it's killing me.

But rather than let him know. Rather than say the fucking words I will never dare speak first, I open my mouth and let out the most wicked thing I can manage.

His own words, aimed back at him.

"I don't *need* you, Rain. I'm not some fucking pet project you can sit here and try to fix. A broken toy you can put back together, piece by piece."

Rain's lips freeze against mine, his hips stuttering in their thrust and his hand working my cock falters before he stops both movements completely. He pulls back enough to meet my eyes in the dim light, a flash of hurt in his own.

"You think you're the only one who remembers the words we've said to each other?" he whispers, his fingers sliding into my hair. "Because you're not, mo grá. Not by a long shot."

Rain pulls from my body quickly before flipping me to my back, the movement startling me. Crawling back between my legs, slips his cock back inside me with one, smooth thrust that makes my toes curl in pleasure, and a moan escapes my lips.

"Your words, they run through my mind the way your songs play in your head. Constantly on repeat. The way I'm sure one is playing right now."

He's right.

"The Black and White" by The Band CAMINO.

Rain grinds his hips into me, his mouth speaking against the skin of my neck and throat. "I didn't understand it before, but I do now. Because that's how it's been every single day since we left that cabin. Your words are all I hear."

Rain begins pumping his hips in long, slow thrusts, letting the pure passion pour out of him as he takes control of my body. My hands fly to his hair and grip it tightly, desperate to hold onto it like it's the grasp to some semblance of my sanity.

"*'You're not immune to me, no matter how much you wish you were,'* he repeats the words from outside the store in Vail, his breath wafting over the skin of my collarbone. His mouth moves up to mine, kissing me roughly, slipping his tongue inside to fuck my mouth in tandem with the way his body is fucking me.

Nibbling at my lip, he tugs one softly between his teeth as his hand reaches between us, grasping my cock again, working and stroking my shaft in time with his unrelenting thrusts. *"'I promise I will always be your safe place for as long as you need one.'"*

My heart clenches at that one, knowing it was when he let me inside his own body for the very first time when I said those words to him. The night that could easily be marked as the single most perfect moment of my life. When he trusted me and opened up to me.

When he gave me his pain and let me fucking heal him.

Rain's pace begins to quicken as he leans back and grabs my hips, fucking me with the power and dominance that I've grown addicted to in such a short period of time. I crave it, honestly. I don't know if I could even choose which scenario I love more; me inside him or him inside me.

My eyes lock onto the rippling of his abs in the moonlight, my fingers reaching out to touch them. Like he's mine to touch.

"'You have me. You will always have me. Until every star in the night sky burns out,'" he pants, locking his whiskey irises on my own. *"'And maybe even then.'"*

That's all it takes for the fog of my high lifting from my brain, allowing me to see this for what it truly is.

Unbridled, untamed passion.

Every unspoken word between us poured out in sweat and pants and pleasure, just like the last night at the cabin. It's what fucking heaven feels like. And goddammit, I wish it didn't feel this good. That I had some sort of self-preservation when it comes to him.

Because I know now…this moment, those words? They'll be my undoing.

Because hearing the things I said to him out of nothing but love and happiness…it's fucking dangerous. It's the kind of thing where I can see myself falling harder and more deeply in love with him.

Because he fucking *remembers* the words I said, even if I wasn't aware they came from the deepest parts of my soul, desperate to connect with his own.

And in this moment, with him deep inside me, bringing me to the brink of ecstasy with his body, I feel what I felt in that goddamn cabin.

Worshipped. Cherished.

Loved.

"I'm there, Abhainn," he tells me, shifting my hips so the head of his cock rubs against that tiny button inside me with every thrust, sending sparks shooting up my spine.

His hand works me harder, faster, and the sensation of his passion, his desire, just him…it overwhelms me, and I can't stop myself from spilling out my release. My cum coats his hand, but it doesn't stop him from jacking me until he pulls himself free from my body, moving to his hand instead.

I watch as he strokes himself through his orgasm, his cum coating my abs and chest with my own.

And then, once he's milked every last drop of cum from his cock, he collapses down to his forearms on either side of my head. With his forehead pressed to mine and our sweat mixing together, I feel it again.

Loved.

But I know it's just my mind playing tricks on me.

Because he doesn't love me.

He loved my attention and my generosity. He loved the words I willingly spoke, the speck of hope I could give him in the darkness of his past. He loved the affection I gave him, the pleasure my body made his feel.

He never loved *me.*

But, oh God, how I love him…

"As terrifying as it is," he breathes against my lips, his voice ragged and drained, "I know in my soul I'll always have a weak spot for you. Fuck, River. I'd leave the entire world behind for you." He presses a kiss against my mouth, just a soft simple peck, before pulling away entirely.

And goddamn him for making this feel like love right now.

Because. It's. Not.

He doesn't love you, River.

Rain sits up from over my body, looking down at the mess coating my stomach. Licking his lips, his first two fingers trailing through the sticky cum, swirling and mixing it together like he would with his paintings.

And that just makes me think of the goddamn sex painting we made, the way I smeared our cum together on him. Marking and claiming him as mine, even if he didn't know it.

But he doesn't want to be yours.

Lifting his hand from the mess, he looks at the cum dripping from his fingers before placing the middle one in his mouth, sucking it clean. His eyes flash up to ensnare mine, watching my reaction to an act I'd never place on him.

And when he's done, he takes it a step further. He lifts that same hand to my face, running his index finger over my bottom lip. Coating it with a thin sheen of our cum.

His eyes stay locked on mine until my tongue flicks out, licking it on impulse. His gaze tracks the movement until I swallow, the salty tang of our mixed essence just about tears me in two.

We stay locked in a stare down, our chests still heaving slightly until he opens his mouth to speak again.

"And that's how I know this isn't over between us," he tells me, something like hope flickering over his face.

My stomach rolls as my chest constricts. "Why?" I barely whisper the word because I'm fucking horrified of his answer. Terrified that my heartache has only just begun.

But Rain just leans into me again, slipping his tongue inside my mouth without protest. It still tastes like our heady releases as it mates with mine. They tangle together to the point where I'm already getting hard again, ready for a second round.

But his response finally comes after he pulls away, flicking my piercing with his tongue one final time.

"People only obsess over each other when things between them are left unfinished."

TEN

Rain

Sunlight streaming into the room wakes me and I'm disoriented momentarily as I groan and rub the sleep from my eyes. Expecting to find myself in my bed and in my apartment, I'm slightly startled to realize I'm not in my room. Or my bed.

Or alone, because there is a warm, muscled arm resting across my stomach.

Glancing over, I find River still sleeping, looking a lot more at peace in his dreams than he was last night when I showed up.

Last night.

Fuck me. I hadn't intended to show up here unannounced like some sort of booty call. I wasn't looking to get laid, just to make sure he was okay after finding out he came by my apartment. In fact, falling into bed with River is the last thing that should've happened last night.

But it *did.*

And I don't have it in me to regret any second of it. Even the moments when I could feel every ounce of his pain and emotional turmoil radiating off his body like it was my own. Knowing he fights me, this, *us,* because *I* put doubt in his mind.

Yet having him, even if it rips us both apart in every way imaginable, it's better than the alternative. God, last night was one of the few nights since the cabin where I've slept without those goddamn nightmares.

The simple fact is...I need him. I don't think there will ever be a moment in my life from this point forward where I don't. I'm just a fucking idiot for not realizing it sooner.

Lifting his arm gently, I slide out from beside him and slip back into my underwear, desperate for coffee even though all I really want is to pull him tighter against me and never let go.

Padding to the kitchen, I glance around his apartment, rubbing my wrist absently where his name is inked in my skin, and take in the disaster surrounding me that doesn't fit River. Not by a long shot, seeing as he always kept his room clean at the cabin. I was the one who was a mess.

I hate knowing I have to be playing a part in it.

Grabbing my clothes from near the door, I quickly redress while I wait for the coffee to brew, but the mess just doesn't sit right with me. Careful not to make too much noise and wake him, I pile beer bottles and pizza boxes in the garbage and toss his clothes into a basket sitting near the corner of the couch.

Once the room looks slightly less like a disaster, I set to looking through his fridge, hoping there might be something in there for breakfast. I'm not much of a cook, but I can do omelets easily enough.

Except, the only thing in his fridge is beer. Otherwise it's completely empty.

My stomach rolls, knowing something is seriously fucking wrong with River because there's no way he lives like this regularly when he was the complete opposite at the cabin.

Maybe he was right. Maybe you don't really know him at all.

Shaking the thought from my head because I fucking refuse to believe it, I focus back on the coffee just as I hear the door to his bedroom creak open. Filling two mugs from the cabinet with coffee, I turn around to find River in the opening of the hallway. He's dressed in only a pair of basketball shorts hanging low on his hips in that tantalizing as hell way and a sleepy look in his eyes as he runs his hand through his unruly hair.

"Morning," I say, setting a mug down on the counter and sliding it over to him.

River squints at me, rubbing the sleep from his eyes before picking up the coffee and taking a sip. My eyes fixate on the way he licks his lips before taking a sip of the bitter liquid, then the way his throat works to swallow. The light hickey I left where his shoulder and neck meet is slightly visible from here, making me smile.

Things might not be sunshine and fucking rainbows between us right now, but he let me in again. I still can't believe it, honestly. Even after the vile shit we both have done and said. Even knowing we have a mountain to climb in order to make things right between us.

He still opened the door, let me inside his apartment. And then his body.

I haven't lost him entirely. Even if I can't act on it right now, there's still hope.

Except the way he won't look at me, it sends another little zap of paranoia to my stomach.

His eyes flick up to mine. "Thanks for the coffee."

Thanks for the coffee?

I just stare at him, dumbfounded, for a minute, attempting to figure out how he is trying to play this. A casual hook-up? Friends with benefits?

The greatest night of my fucking life?

Because *Jesus* there was no other way to describe it. The term *making love,* while as cringeworthy as it is…it fits. It seems to be the *only* way to describe what we did last night.

I gave him everything I had. Loved him with my body, my mind, my soul.

The only thing I didn't do was speak the words. But because I *can't,* not because I don't feel them with each fiber of my being. Because even though I want to try to make this work between us, knowing there's no way that I can keep myself from him anymore, I still want to keep him safe. Protect the thing — the *person* — I love most.

Clearing my throat, I try to shrug off the unease that's building inside me. "So listen. Last night—"

"—was a mistake, I know." River cuts me off.

My chest constricts so tight, I think my heart actually just stopped. Because that's the exact opposite of what I was thinking. Coming here was foolish and irrational and impulsive, knowing Ted could be lurking around any corner.

But a *mistake?*

No, not at all. Right now, all I feel is torn between what I want to do — which is take River right back to bed and say screw all the things keeping us apart — and what I should do. Which is to agree with him and write this off as a single night where we couldn't stop ourselves from falling into old habits.

Only, I don't know what path to take.

"Abhainn, it — " I start, but I don't make it past there.

River lets out a sigh, wincing as he massages his temple with his index and middle fingers. A flash of annoyance and...regret crosses his face before he schools his features entirely. "Look, you should just go."

"Wait, Riv — "

"Leave, Ciaráin," he snarls the words, the sound ripping from his throat with bitter indifference. "I don't fucking want you here."

It's a knife to the stomach, hearing and seeing the disinterest contaminating the space between us. I should be thankful. He's giving me an out. Making the choice for me by asking me to leave.

I don't blame him. I'd have to be blind and fucking stupid to not understand why he wants me gone. I wouldn't want me here either. Yet all it does is add to the sting of knowing things are never going to be simple when it comes to us.

Setting my mug on the counter, I bite my lip and continue to debate my options. Leave or stay. Fight or flight.

Love or hate.

The funniest part is, the second he said to leave, I knew I was about to follow the path of want over should. But from the look in his eyes and the scowl on his face, I know it's pointless. He means the words he just growled out and doesn't want to hear what I have to say.

"Okay, I'll go," I tell him, nodding calmly, even though I'm anything but. I feel like the world is slipping right through my fingertips with every step I take towards the door.

This is wrong, my brain screams at me, and for once, it's on the same page with my heart.

But I do what he asks anyway, slipping my shoes and coat on, not looking him in the eye the entire time. I feel him watching me, though. Every inch of my skin is on fire beneath the layers of clothing from his gaze.

He doesn't say anything, and this time it's my gut telling me I need to do or say something before I walk out of here, leaving him to stew in whatever the hell mood he's in.

Facing the door, my fingers wrapped around the knob, I let out a sigh.

Don't look back. You won't leave if you do.

So instead I open the door, mumbling under my breath as I step through the threshold. "It wasn't a mistake, mo grá. No moment with you ever could be."

———

I barely remember the drive back to my apartment; I'm so out of sorts. All I can think about is the past twenty-four hours and what they mean for us. It's the pain written all over River's face this morning…and in his body language, his *kiss,* last night cuts me deeper with every passing second.

And I hate it. Because I know he's not blind. I *know* he should be able to comprehend what I was trying to show him, not with words alone, but actions too. I also know under any other circumstance, I would've been successful.

He's not *letting* himself believe it. That's how badly I've hurt him. To the point where he's given up hope for us.

Shaking my head, I reach for the handle of my apartment door and find it unlocked, meaning Roman is here.

Great. Just what I want. To come home to an interrogation from my best friend about why I spent the night at my — at River's — *apartment when I'm supposed to be staying away from him at all costs.*

Wonderful.

I turn and close the door behind me the second I enter, pressing my forehead into the cool surface and try to figure out how this all got so fucked up.

"Rain?" Roman calls, and I groan.

Here we go.

"Yeah?" I say, spinning and expecting to see him literally anywhere but at the kitchen island with a fucking *whiskey* in hand before noon, slumped over a barstool with a large manila envelope in front of him.

What the fuck?

Heading directly toward him, I grab a stool and pull it out to sit. He slides it over to me without looking up, taking a sip of his drink.

Fuck, is he drunk already?

"How long have you been drinking?"

He swallows roughly, glancing over at me before taking another drink. Then he stares straight ahead at the wall of cabinets for a good minute before he decides to respond.

"Haven't stopped since you left last night."

Double fuck.

Exhaling, I reach over and grab the glass he's holding,

meeting his eyes before I slide it from his grip. Thankfully, he doesn't fight me on it, just holds my eyes, an immense amount of anguish floating through them.

I've never seen him this way, so damn broken and just… lost, almost.

My eyes move to the envelope, latching onto the handwriting on the outside. It's just my name, but it's written in a neat all-caps handwriting I could pick out of a line-up as Ted's.

"How did you get this?"

Rolling his tongue over his teeth, Roman says, "Someone knocked on the door this morning. When I went to answer, it was taped to the door."

I groan, not liking this news one bit.

Ted knows where I am, but we still have no idea where he is or what his plans are. But whatever the latter might be, I'm willing to bet it has something to do with the contents of this envelope.

"Have you opened it?" I ask, pulling it over to me.

"Yeah," he whispers, his head sinking into his hands. "And I've already called back-up."

Chills shoot down my spine as I slowly open it, pulling out a stack of those giant glossy photos you always see in the movies. And I've got to hand it to Ted, he's always had a flare for the theatrics.

"There's a note on the back of the last one," Roman mutters as he stands, albeit a bit unsteadily, and grabs his glass again before heading to the couch. He flops onto the surface, the amber liquid sloshing over the edge and onto the floor and himself. Not that I care, I'm more worried he's so drunk I'll need to get his damn stomach pumped or something.

Looking down at the top photograph, I find a zoomed in image of Roman and I walking out of the bar the night River kissed Abbi. Which, while the fact he's stalking us isn't completely unprecedented, it's setting me on edge.

The next image is from Vail. The day River and I went snowboarding. It's of us, Taylor, and Siena around a table at dinner after the day on the mountain. Then the next picture is just Siena and I hugging and laughing in the lodge, looking…well, a little cozier than we probably should.

My heart rate kicks up, thinking there might be some damning images of River and I here. That Ted might've caught something between us. But I'm almost *positive* no one would have been able to find us out on the mountains. That'd be next to impossible with how large the resort is.

I try to wrack my mind for any displays of affection I might've shown him and only come up with one when he walked up behind me watching the newscast about Ted himself. But besides that I didn't. Right?

We ran into Siena and Taylor not soon after and then went back out onto the mountain.

Fuck, fuck, fuck, did I fuck this up before it even started if he's been following me since Vail?

I flip to the next photo, anxiety wracking my body as I prepare for the worst. Images of River and I kissing. In public, or worse, up at the cabin.

Did he follow us up there?

I breathe a bit when I notice the last picture is none of those things, just an image of Roman and I entering my apartment building together, arms wrapped around each other because I was literally *carrying* his drunk ass back home from the bar the same night the first picture was from.

I'll admit, had I not known the context of this one, I'd automatically go to a place that's completely off-base. One that says these two guys are about to head inside and hook-up.

Which, we didn't. Or haven't.

But Ted doesn't know that.

Flipping it over, I find Ted's neat scrawl written on the back.

Both twins, Ciaráin? You couldn't decide which family member with power you wanted at your beck and call, so you went for both? Well, while you might have the next generation of Enclave under your spell and in your bed, you have to remember I have the ones with <u>real</u> power under <u>my</u> thumb. Enough power to take you down, put you away, make you disappear. The possibilities are endless, my good boy. It would do you well to remember that.

My eyes snap closed as I process his message.

The ones with real power under his thumb?

I remember a few meetings between Ted and Roman's father when we were kids. That's how I found out about the Enclave in the first place, when Roman and I stumbled across a meeting between them outside Senator Mitchell's office while we were playing at their house.

After that, Roman told me more than I ever imagined. Nothing crazy in depth, seeing as we were only nine and ten at the time. He probably didn't know much more than I did at that point. But he did tell me about this crazy secret society his family was part of and that one day, he'd be in charge of it, just like his dad. He sounded so *proud* of it too.

As I glance over at his now passed-out form on the couch, I wonder what happened to make it all go sideways. Because from the sound of Ted's note, Roman's here on his own without the rest of them knowing. Including his father.

And replaying the day I picked him up at the airport, I feel like my suspicion is confirmed that he's acting on his own right now.

Shit.

Slipping the photos back into the envelope, I debate calling the FBI agent assigned to the case and give him these. He told me to contact him if I ever had any new information about Ted, his whereabouts, literally anything that might be useful.

The only issue is…these images are more damning to Roman and his family than they are to Ted. They don't give any real information, unlike the phone call from a few weeks back which I *did* report.

The only thing I can do now is wait for Roman to weigh in on this decision. I'll let him sleep for a few hours and we can figure it out together. Because this bit of evidence is far bigger than just the case against Ted for what he did to me all those years ago.

And now Roman's bringing in *back-up*. Which can only mean the rest of the guys in his generation of Enclave, if I had to guess. Meaning this entire situation is about to get a whole lot messier if more and more people are being made aware of the truth.

Scrubbing my hand over my face, I groan.

When did every move I make in life become part of a goddamn chess game?

And more importantly, how the hell do I make it through without being forced into a checkmate?

ELEVEN

Rain

It's been three days since the morning River kicked me out of his apartment, and I'm starting to get antsy. So antsy, I've had to go running and to the gym and do literally *anything* to keep me from going back to his apartment.

Thankfully, Roman's been gone; where, I couldn't say. He mentioned something about going up in the mountains to get their local Enclave house outside Boulder ready. While I've been grateful for his help and for him getting everyone on board to fix this mess with Ted, I need some space from him. So I'm more than happy to let him do whatever the hell he does in their fucking secret society to make this nightmare go away.

Jesus Christ, why couldn't I just be a normal person with normal problems?

Pounding on my door startles me from my thoughts, but I

don't have a chance to move from my bedroom before I hear a voice shouting over the pounding.

"Open the fuck up, Rain!"

River?

Scrambling out of the room, I rush over to the door and yank it open to reveal River in all his sexy, pissed off glory.

"We need to talk," he says sharply, not giving me a chance to speak and not at all the greeting I was expecting.

"Okay," I say slowly, watching him like a caged animal. "Do you want to come in?"

"Probably would be best if I didn't," he growls, turning to head back down the hall, retreating to the entry door.

Grabbing my shoes and a jacket, I follow after him like a goddamn lost puppy, finding him on the front lawn, pacing through the dead grass that's still damp from the melted snow.

Taking a seat on the stoop, I watch him move back and forth to the point I think he might catch the ground on fire. "What's going on, Abhainn?"

He halts in place, those ocean eyes snapping to mine. "Why did you come over the other night?"

My brows furrow. "I told you, to make sure you were okay. And clearly from the looks of it and the way you're acting, you're not."

"But why, Rain? Why are you acting like you care all of a sudden?"

It's because I actually do care. I just can't fucking tell you that.

I rise from my spot on the step, taking a step towards him. "Look, Riv. You're clearly not yourself lately, and I just want to make sure—"

Wrong. Thing. To. Say.

"For the love of God, Rain! Just shut up!" he screams, rage radiating from him in waves I can feel from here. "You don't get to come to my apartment, demanding answers and acting like you give a shit about me and fuck me like no time has passed. Not when you're the one who ended things!"

River storms up to me, getting in my face. The fact that he's right here, close enough to touch, yet so far away…it has me in fucking shambles.

"You don't have a clue how bad it's been. What this has been like to just see you here, on campus. Knowing what it is like to touch you, be with you, only to be forced to live without you again. Not being able to do a damn thing about it."

My eyes widen in shock.

How the hell can he be this blind? How can he not see that this is hurting me just as much as it is him?

Ice licks through my veins as I answer him, incredulous. "I don't know? *I don't know?*"

"No, Rain. You don't have a goddamn clue! You're too busy fucking around with *Roman* to spare me a glance! Until the other night, that is." He works to swallow back his anger, shaking his head. "Don't think I didn't catch how carefully you spoke your words, either. You said you hadn't fucked anyone, but baby, is *Roman* fucking *you?*"

My jaw ticks at the mention of Roman. Because while what River wants to know isn't true, I can't tell him that. But had I known the issue Roman's presence would have caused, growing the rift between us, I would have tried any other way to deal with my past first.

Adding Roman to the mix complicated things so much more than I ever intended.

So, *even if* I had always planned to crawl back to River and beg for his forgiveness—for another chance to be everything I know we can be—I have to play the part of the asshole right now. The photos from Ted are reason enough.

I *need* him to think I don't want him. To *keep him safe*. Fully knowing it could destroy what is possibly a forever kind of love.

Frustration continues to flare within me and I sigh, not liking where I have to go from here. Because the question he wants an answer to is the one thing I can't address. And I'm so tired of hurting him by trying to keep my lies straight.

"What is it you want from me, River? Because you say one thing then act another to the point I honestly can't figure it out anymore!"

River takes off his snapback and runs his fingers through his hair before replacing it. "Don't you fucking dare throw this on me. Not when *you're* the one playing hot and cold. Telling me I'm nothing to you, but then telling me no moment with me is a mistake? What the fuck *is that*, Rain?"

He doesn't give me any time to answer or even formulate a response to him *hearing* what I muttered the other morning when I left. Words he was never meant to hear until this was all over.

It doesn't matter, though; I see his control slipping by the second and he continues to lay into me. "*Goddammit,* I just want you to be honest with yourself. With the world. With me. Tell me who you are. What you're hiding. Your deepest, darkest secrets. Because I want them." His eyes, so blue I drown, lock on mine and I can see the plea behind them. "Trust me like you'd started in that godforsaken cabin. Fucking *share your life* with me."

Guilt floods me, tightening the noose I can feel around my throat. "I can't. Abhainn. Babe. I just. Fucking. *Can't.*" My voice cracks on the last word of my choked out response.

He shakes his head and tosses his hands in the air, turning away. "You're such a coward," he mumbles the words under his breath, but I still manage to catch them. At this point, I don't have it in me to be angry about his insinuation.

He's right. I'm a coward.

I'm fucking scared. Petrified.

That this bullshit with my step-father will get him killed.

That I have to let him in completely, let him see the worst pieces of myself and hope he still wants me.

That I won't be able to love him the way he deserves. Why would I be able to love him with every piece of me? Before him, it had been years since I even felt a glimmer of that emotion.

And still, I *know* this is love, even if it hasn't been said aloud. And he must feel it too. Nothing else would cause this level of agony wreaking havoc on our minds and bodies.

River turns back and shakes his head again. "You remember that day outside the store, up in Vail? You screamed in my face, trying to convince me and yourself that this" — he uses his finger to motion between us — "wasn't going to be some *Brokeback Mountain* type shit." He lets out a scoff, followed by a resigned sigh. Fire flickers behind his eyes, showing his rage was tamped down, but still not under control. "Well, guess what, baby? It's too damn late. We're already there. And if you aren't careful? If you can't *let me in*? You're going to wind up as alone as Ennis fucking Del Mar."

River turns away from me again, his hands clasped together on the back of his head, just above the brim of his hat. The set of his shoulders tells me what he's thinking before the words even leave his mouth.

"I'm done waiting on you."

And.

I.

Just.

Snap.

"I never asked you to!" I scream, the sound ripping from my throat in a guttural cry that bounces off the buildings, the street signs, and yanks both my heart and soul right from my body. They're both lying here on the sidewalk, mangled and broken, ready for River to take them forever. And he might as well. I don't want them anymore.

They'll never belong to anyone else.

River twists his body back toward mine with neck breaking speed. "Because you didn't have to ask! I could see it in your eyes. You were terrified to let me go." I watch, helpless, as tears begin to well in his eyes. "But fucking hell, Rain. You're even more terrified to let me in."

As if my heart could break any more, it does.

After everything we've been through, after all the pain I've caused him in the course of a few short months, he always remained strong. He bent, but he never broke.

He never let me see him tremble. Never let me see him cry.

Somehow, I know that is about to change.

"I'm sorry," I gasp, knowing it's falling on deaf ears. But it's

AFTER RAIN FALLS | 149

all I can get out with these emotions suffocating me.

I catch the slight sway of his head from side to side. "Sorry isn't good enough anymore. You can't keep stringing me along this way. I deserve more."

I know, mo grá. If only you could see not giving it to you will be the death of me.

Guilt consumes me. "I wish I could give it to you."

River strides toward me, taking my face in his hands, and looks deep into my eyes. "All you have to do is try. Please, just try, *goddammit.*"

Our eyes stay locked on each other, and I beg for him to see all that I'm not saying. That he owns every inch of me. That he deserves more than what I can give him.

Staring into the depths of what might as well be his soul, find all the emotions I'm feeling reflected directly back at me. Love. Heartbreak. Desperation…Fear.

"Tell me. Just one last time." My voice is filled with gravel as I close my eyes and lean my forehead against his, both my hands wrapping around the back of his neck. Breathing him in before I force myself to give this up. "What song?"

I hear him choke on a sob before his rough whisper breaks the air. "Breaking Benjamin. 'Give Me A Sign.'"

My body fractures, and I don't even know how I'm standing at this point; I've never felt so destroyed. Cracks start making their way through my armor as tears stream down my face.

How am I ever supposed to let him go?

"I can't fucking stand this, Abhainn. I can't do this anymore."

River grips my shirt in his fist, like he's drowning and I'm the only thing that will keep him afloat. Little does he know, he is the reason I have yet to sink into a bottomless pit of despair.

"You can't fucking stand this?" He snarls, pushing off me. "You want this to be over? Be careful what you wish for. Because that's asking fate to intervene. Letting her deal with it for you, like the coward you are. And mark my words Ciaráin Grady, you aren't going to like how she decides to do it."

My name, my real name, on his lips chills me to the bone, just like they do every time he says it like that, filled with anger and disgust. And I haven't been anything but Rain to him for so long, I never even realized how wrong it was for him to call me anything else.

My entire body goes numb. "It wouldn't be the first time fate decided to fuck me over. Or have you forgotten the hand I was dealt?"

Venom and despair battle for control in his voice. "That's the point. I don't know what it is. Not entirely. You give me a piece, the tiniest fucking glimpse, but then when push comes to shove you build your walls higher and tighter every time."

I say nothing.

He's right. We both know it.

Just like we both know he has the strength to knock them down, if only I'd let him try.

River's jaw clenches and the glassy haze returns to his eyes, brightening them to the color of the sea. "Are you going to be able to live with yourself after this? Because baby, as much as I hate this... I have to fucking quit you." His voice breaks and his fists clench, as if the pain of his words cause him to crumble. "This goes so much deeper than need and desire. The way I ache for you? It's fucking toxic."

I wipe my eyes, not realizing I'm still crying, before whispering out more lies. "It's toxic because it's not meant to be. Can't you see that? We were never going to make it."

"That's where you're wrong. I think we had a chance to make it, Rain. I really do." He glances away, and I can't stand that he won't look at me. "But I guess only one of us decided it was worth the risk to try."

"The cost outweighs the gain, River. It's not what you want to hear, but it's fucking true. It's not safe."

His lip trembles as it curls up into a grimace. "It wouldn't be called a risk if it was safe."

My head shakes at his words, even though, once again, he's right.

But I can see him still holding on, despite all his words. I know, to my core, that I have to be the one to end this. I have to convince him…and myself.

"You're the one who walked out of my apartment that day, mo grá. Not me. That's all on you. *You* are the one who gave up on *me*."

He steps away from me, lengthening the already monumental crater between us, and I watch as my words register in his brain.

They aren't true. But he doesn't know that.

This is the only way to keep you safe, River. I have to let you go.

I'm doing this because I love you.

I'm paralyzed, agony running rampant through my ruined body, as tears begin to stream down his face. Knowing I'm the reason they're there, it's a knife to the gut. It's at that moment, I know.

I broke him. Ruined him.

I ruined *us.*

His words are strangled, but I hear them all the same. "Walking out that day was the last thing I wanted. It only happened because you didn't give me another choice."

When he turns to leave, I sink to my knees right there on the lawn of my apartment, shattering, as River walks away with every single fragment of my severed heart.

TWELVE

River

The pill is bitter on my tongue as I swallow it dry before lying on my bed in hopes to get some sleep. Which doesn't come for more than a few hours at a time these days, especially since seeing Rain last week outside his apartment.

At this point, I'm getting desperate for it because it's the one place I can manage to find some semblance of peace.

The room is spinning slightly as I stare up at the ceiling from my bed, lost in my thoughts. Though, I figured getting stoned out of my mind, in addition to my Xanax, might manage to calm my mind—or better yet, force me to sleep—I'm finding out the hard way I was sadly mistaken.

I'm no pharmacist or doctor, but I have a feeling it's because of the Adderall I snuck from my sister. I've only taken a couple on the days where I felt like I'd pass out from exhaustion, needing to be more awake and alert for class or whatever I have going on during the day that my sleepless nights impact me most.

But then on those nights, it's hard to sleep again. A never-ending, vicious cycle leaving me with nothing to do but stew in my thoughts as the hours of darkness drag on for an eternity.

So that's exactly what I do, though I know I shouldn't. And to make it worse and as terrible as it is for my mental health, the thoughts that often come easiest are the ones I need to forget.

But I can't help but relive moments from the cabin as I stare at the ceiling and beg for sleep. The happy, the sad, whatever it might be. Anything to keep my mind from remembering where we are now. *What* we are.

An almost.

Not friends, not enemies. Not exes, not lovers. Can we even be called strangers anymore when we shared some of our deepest, most vulnerable moments with each other?

No, we can't. So in my mind, we're nothing but an *almost.*

I think that's what keeps me up more than the mixture of pills, knowing what we could have been compared to what we are.

Why would tonight be any different?

"Am I getting rewarded for all my hard work." I grin, pulling his *sweatshirt over his head before tossing it away. His lips find mine again before the material even has a chance to hit the ground.*

His kiss is bruising. And in the most addictive way. I want to feel it on every inch of my body as he worships it with his lips, tongue, and teeth.

"What makes you think you get rewarded? I'm the one who had to put up with your Christmas-loving ass. You're worse than Will Ferrell in Elf *with your fucking Christmas music."*

I laugh softly and pull my shirt over my head. "Haven't you heard, Rain? The best way to spread Christmas cheer is singing loud for all to hear."

He rolls his eyes. "I hate you."

A smirk crosses his face when he says it and I grab his arm to pull him back into me, kissing him fiercely.

"I hate you too," I say with a smile against his lips. His tongue wars with mine as a cloud of need settles over us, hands fumbling with each other's pants as desperation takes over.

"Get on the bed," he tells me as he manages to remove every last article of clothing from my body. I do as he says, watching as he slips out of his pants, leaving me with an unobstructed view of his rock-solid cock.

Is it possible to be in love with someone's dick?

I'm not sure, but if it is, I'm infatuated with everything about his. From the blunt head to the veins running down either side, and how soft it is against my tongue. Even the slight curve to the right it takes as it stands at attention is perfection.

Fuck, I must be in love with it. I'm basically waxing poetic about it while it stares at me from across the room.

There's a bead of pre-cum on the tip I'm begging to lick off, but I stay where I am, eyes flicking back up to lock with his. My heart beats a little faster when I find them staring back at me with the same amount of lust I feel coursing through my own body.

"You planning on just standing there?" I ask, gripping my length and giving it a few long strokes. "Or you gonna come over here and let me get my mouth on you?"

A slow grin creeps over his face as he crawls onto the bed, his body covering mine. Our mouths connect, tongues joining as our hips move together, seeking friction. I reach between us, gripping our lengths together in my palm.

Rain groans against my lips, and I smile. "You like that now, yeah, baby?"

His moan of approval comes when I squeeze on an upstroke. "Fuck. Yes."

I release our dicks, leaning over to the bedside table in search of the lube bottle. But it's really fucking difficult with Rain's mouth licking and biting a path down my neck.

"Shit." I breathe in sharply when he nips the skin where my neck and shoulder meet, still sensitive from the bite he gave me the first time in the shower. I feel him smile before pulling back to look at me.

"You like that now, yeah, babe?"

I try not to laugh because that morning is still a toxic cloud hanging over us at times, something we don't talk about. But it's impossible not to at least crack a smile when we've turned a complete one-eighty since that morning.

But when I look up at his eyes, I see a flash of vulnerability in them.

"I can handle it a little rough," I tell him in reassurance, holding his gaze, doing my best not to melt when I realize he called me babe again, for the second time today.

"Good to know," he whispers, ambers searching. "But I actually had something else in mind, if you're wanting to try it."

The way he says it, so unsure and hesitant, it squeezes at my heart. "You might not know this about me yet, but I'm willing to try anything once."

His smile grows as he plants a rough kiss on my lips before rolling off me. He positions himself on top of me to sixty-nine and I can't help but laugh because this *is what he wants to try?*

God, he's fucking adorable.

He doesn't waste any time, pulling me into his mouth with a deep suck and I groan, reaching up and grabbing his cock and jack it a few times, long and slow in rhythm with his mouth.

Replacing my hand with my mouth, I start with teasing his head, flicking my tongue against the underside, then along the slit, earning me a reflexive thrust of his hips.

Yes, just like that.

Grabbing his ass in both my palms, I pull him down into me, trying to tell him I need his help to take him in deeper. It only takes a couple of times of me trying to set a pace for him to get what I'm doing and he pops off to look back at me.

"I don't want to...choke you," he says, his brows furrowed.

I release him and give his tip a lick before smirking, meeting his eyes. "Fuck my face, baby. Like you mean it."

Still holding his eyes in challenge, I take him back in my mouth and start working the length in as deep as I can take. I watch him swallow and it doesn't take long for him to start meeting me with shallow thrusts of his hips, letting about half his length slide in and out past my lips.

That's it, baby. Keep going.

His eyes close and he returns to his task, sucking me like a goddamn Hoover until I feel like I'm going to explode. And from the sounds we're both making, he loves it just as much as I do. Not that I don't understand. Fucking him with my mouth gives me just as much pleasure as it gives him. He's just finally starting to learn it.

But learn it, he does. And quickly.

Before I know it, I'm taking his length balls deep into my throat as he fucks my face, rutting me into the mattress as he works me in the most delicious way with his mouth and tongue. A slight graze of his teeth every once in a while has me quaking, on the verge of release.

Fuck, yes.

I scrape my teeth lightly against his skin too as he pulls out on an upstroke, causing him to twitch in my mouth. A low groan escapes from him while his lips are still wrapped around my cock, and fuck if it's not the greatest thing I've ever felt. The vibration sends a shock straight to my balls and I feel them draw up and explode into his mouth.

He milks my cum from me like he was made for it and I reach up, kneading his balls in my hand until I have him shooting straight down the back of my throat too, another gravelly moan coming from him as he gives my dick one final lick.

Satisfied that I've swallowed every last drop in his body, I swirl my tongue around his head and release him so he can climb off me. Licking my lips, I let my head rest against the pillow and take in deep, steady breaths to calm my heart rate back to normal.

"Fuck, I never knew I could enjoy a blow job more than actual sex," he breathes, crawling up to me and planting a kiss on my lips. His cheeks are flushed and his eyes are happily sated, making me feel like a million fucking bucks.

Because I did that.

"You say that now, but once you let me fuck you, you'll be singing a different tune," I say with a smile as I roll to my side and meet his eyes. I hate the apprehension I find in them, knowing full well he isn't taking the joke all that lightly.

And that's what it is. A joke. Because as much as I'd love to sink deep inside him, the likelihood of it happening is slim to none. And I honestly am okay with it.

His reservations are his to have when it comes to sex and bottoming. I'm not blind or stupid, I know there's an underlying reason as to why he's so massively opposed, and I have a feeling it's much larger than his whole

I'm not gay *mantra he has rolling around his head and off his tongue. But it isn't for me to pry into, but for him to tell me if and when he's ready.*

Until then, I'll give him everything else I can.

"*Always so sure of yourself.*" *He chuckles after glancing over at me from the other side of the bed, his arm tucked under his head, mirroring my position.*

I arch a brow and smirk, reaching over and trailing my finger against the underside of his half-hard dick, noting the way it twitches again at my touch. "Care to test my theory, babe?"

His eyes narrow and before I have time to laugh, he's on me, pinning me down to the bed.

"*Making fun of me, are you, Lenny?*" *There's a wicked lilt to his voice as he rubs up against me already thickening for a second round.*

"*Not a chance,*" *I tell him, pausing for dramatic effect,* "Babe."

His smile is calculating as he leans forward, nipping my lip between his teeth. "You're gonna pay for that."

Before I have the chance to reply, he flips me to my stomach below him and pulls me up so my ass is in the air, his dick now completely fucking hard pressed right against my crease.

Reaching over to grab the bottle of lube, he squeezes some out directly onto me, using two fingers to trace and spread it around my hole. A single finger slips in, then a second, and I push into them, seeking more pressure against my prostate.

But then he pulls out of me right when he starts hitting the right spot and I groan.

"*Don't stop.*"

"*Are you gonna stop poking fun at me?*" *he whispers, teasing my rim.*

I smirk and glance over my shoulder at him because poking *and* wait silently for him to get it. When the lightbulb flicks on, he glares. "Goddammit, River."

I laugh and he shakes his head, a smile playing at the corner of his mouth as he lubes up his cock next.

"You can call me whatever you want, baby," I say as I watch him, my heart pounding in my chest with anticipation and excitement. "I really don't care what it is."

Tossing the bottle to the side and glancing up at me, he taunts my ass with his dick. "I'll think of something else," he says, pressing the head in, then another inch and another.

"Fuck, you're huge," I moan as he slides all the way inside, hitting the deepest part of me.

A laugh comes from him as I feel his forehead press between my shoulder blades. "You're just realizing this now?" He chuckles, flexing his hips forward as he says the word now.

Another moan slips free as I breathe out, "Apparently."

Rain pumps his hips again in two quick strokes that drive me fucking wild and have me pushing back as much as I can. His hands grab my waist, stilling me as he leans over my body.

"You said you're fine with it a little rough. Ever heard of the term pillow biter before, Riv?" he whispers hotly against the back of my neck, causing goosebumps to rise along my skin as his cock slides in deep and slow from this angle, stretching me so fucking perfectly. "Because I'm about to turn you into one."

My eyes snap open from the memory and I glance down to find my hand covered in cum.

Shit.

As shameful as it is to admit, it's not the first time this has happened either. On more than one occasion I've returned to reality with a mess on my hands. Literally.

I groan in frustration, filled with self-loathing, and roll to my side. Reaching to grab some tissues, my eyes flash to my bedside table to find the painting Rain gave me as a Christmas gift later on that same night I was just replaying in my head. The alpine lake he painted while he thought of me.

The color…it reminded me of your eyes.

And it's moments like those, remembering the way he looked at me or the slight way he'd let me in, whether it be by words or actions, that have me grasping at straws of hopes everything from the cabin was real. What I felt, he felt too. Because we were in sync and connected on a level even deeper than before.

So much, I *fell* for him.

But he doesn't want you.

After cleaning up, I reach over to grab the painting from its place and trace over the lines of the mountains, the trees, the lake itself, feeling the slightly bumpy texture beneath the tips of my fingers.

Throw it away, a voice inside me, the smartest part of myself, chants. Begging me to free myself from his clutches.

But I remember the look on his face when he gave me this. The raw vulnerability and honest to God fear in his eyes. It was the beginning of him opening up to me and letting me see the side of him that he, for whatever reason, keeps hidden from everyone else.

Which means I can't throw it away. I can't give up the small piece of him that cared about me enough to do something like this. Fuck, I refuse to believe he can separate and detach so easily to the point where *this* wasn't a monumental moment for both of us.

Doesn't mean I have to see it every single morning when I open my eyes, though.

So, I don't throw it away, but do the next best thing instead. Open the drawer and tuck it safely inside. Along with what remains of my heart.

Though, God knows it's useless for me to try to protect either anymore when they're both so easily shredded.

THIRTEEN
Rain

This is a really bad idea.

My feet cement in place outside the sorority house, the same Tri-Delta house River took me to at the beginning of the year. When we went to the first after-party of the season.

Also where Elliott told me River was bisexual, and I decided, in that moment, River couldn't be anything more than an enemy.

Oh, how wrong you were, Rain.

And I know he's here tonight too. But it's not because I was told by someone or heaven fucking forbid, he invited me. My teammate, Aiden, was the one who invited me seeing as it's his party, the girls are just the ones throwing it for his birthday.

No, I just *know* when River is around. I can *feel* his presence the moment I step onto the porch, like a vibration running through me. And it's not from the music pulsing inside.

"You good?" Roman asks, brow quirked with his hand on the

knob to the door. His eyes search my face, for what, I'm not sure.

Allowing the mask to slide in place, I shrug. "You know me, parties aren't my thing."

He smirks. "That didn't always used to be the case, man. I remember the days you were the life of the fucking party."

My skin heats, remembering the shit we got into near the end of high school. The way we would always egg each other on and push each other into doing something stupid. Never anything *too* stupid, because of who our families were. But enough to be considered somewhat juvenile delinquents.

Except even then, it was Roman who always drug me out in the first place. It wasn't ever my idea. Just like tonight wasn't my idea. *All fucking Roman* after he saw the text from Aiden on my phone.

You need to start living normal, Rain. Ted will still be here tomorrow to be dealt with. There's no reason we can't go out and have some fun tonight.

And like old times, like *every fucking time,* I cave.

Because he's right. I need some normalcy, even if it comes in the form of a party with a bunch of idiot college kids I don't really care for. It's better than sitting in my apartment, brooding over the guy I'm losing with each passing second.

"Coming from the guy who parties harder than Robert Downey Jr. in the nineties." I roll my eyes, shoving his shoulder as he opens the door into the house. The beat of the music pounds in my ears the second I step into the foyer, the scent of sweaty bodies and spilled alcohol overwhelming me.

Glancing around in a quick scan, my eyes search for River. It's stupid and toxic as hell, but I need to see him. I haven't since the day he came to my apartment and ripped my heart out and told me he was done with me. For good.

I look around, but I don't find him. The only sign he's actually here is the blood boiling in my veins, waiting for a hit of my addiction.

Where are you, mo grá?

In the process of my second sweep of the open floor plan, I spot a few guys from the team by the keg. Aiden waves me over the second he sees me looking in their direction and I give him a nod before meeting Roman's eyes beside me, letting him silently know to follow me across the room.

Aiden is already holding out two cups of beer to me before I even reach the group, so I take them, handing one off to Roman before clapping Aiden on the shoulder.

"What's up, man?" He grins, returning the gesture with his massive paw of a hand landing on my shoulder. "Haven't seen much of you around recently. Didn't think you still went here."

I smirk and shove him away, feeling surprisingly at ease in the moment. "Fuck off, Aide. You saw me a couple weeks ago in the hall outside the gym."

He lets out a gruff laugh, the sound booming through the house louder than the bass of Bad Wolves' "Killing Me Slowly" currently playing through the stereo system.

"Always so damn serious, Grady. For real though, glad you could make it."

I nod, taking a swig of my beer. It tastes like shit, which I guess is to be expected, but I can't complain. "'Course. Happy birthday, by the way."

He grins. "Thanks. Now we have to actually *celebrate!*" It's then he notices Roman beside me. "Hey, I'm Aiden. Guess you could say I'm the guest of honor."

He offers Roman his hand, which Ro takes, and the two start chatting like they've been friends their entire lives. Within thirty seconds.

Un-fucking-believable.

I stand there and shoot the shit with them as best I can, but frankly, between the two of them talking over each other and the pounding of the bass, I can't get a word in edge-wise. Guess that's what happens when you throw two extroverts together in a loud as hell environment.

It's not long before this shitty ass beer makes me need to break the seal, so without them even pausing their *riveting* conversation about sports cars, I head off to find a bathroom. Knowing the downstairs one is probably in use, I head to the stairs in search of one up there instead.

After the first couple rooms are either locked or...*in use,* as I unfortunately find out, I see a girl I know *has* to live here and decide to ask her.

How do I know she lives here? Well, she's clearly not dressed for a party, wearing one of those oversized long sleeve shirts with Tri-Delta written across the front, a pair of sweats, glasses, and her hair piled on top of her head with a clip.

"Hey," I say, holding my hand out to stop her from walking by. It has the desired effect because she halts in her tracks before looking up at me. She scans me up and down and rolls her eyes.

"Not interested. Go look elsewhere."

My eyebrows raise at her immediate assumption that I'm stopping her out of interest. "I was just gonna ask where the bathroom is..." I trail off, leaving an opening for her name.

At least she has the decency to look slightly embarrassed. "Oh, um. Sorry. It's Harper," she tells me, stating her name as she points over her shoulder down the hall. "And the bathroom is the second to last door on the right."

I give her a polite smile, even though I'm feeling anything but happy *or* friendly. "Thank you. Sorry to bother you."

She bites her lip and a smile teases on the edge of them. "Sorry for being kind of...a bitch." A soft, empty laugh escapes her and she shakes her head. "Not that you care, but the guy I'm kind of seeing and my best friend, who happens to be his brother, just got into a massive fight. And I never know what to do when this happens. Picking sides has never been my strong suit."

Damn, do I ever feel that. Might as well be me trying to decide between my friendship with Roman and having River's back. It's basically impossible.

"Not a situation I'd want to be in, but I hope you figure it out," I tell her.

"Thanks," she says, shifting her weight from foot to foot. "Anyway, I'll let you get back to...*it*." The words come out awkward as hell and honestly, it's kind of cute.

"Same." I laugh, stepping around her and heading down to the door she told me was the bathroom.

Grabbing the knob, I find it unlocked, but I'm startled when it turns and is pulled from my grip by the person on the other side.

Then my heart stops when River steps out through the door.

His attention darts up to my face, shock covering his features when he realizes it's me. But just as quickly, the shock disappears, a mask of indifference sliding over his face instead.

"Why are you here, Rain?" He says it with a snarl in his tone, but it's clear he doesn't expect an answer when he goes to push past me, heading back toward the stairs.

My hand is on his arm before he has the chance to make it more than a single step though, pulling him back to me.

I search his eyes for a sign, needing to know what he's thinking. But they're closed and guarded and all fucking wrong. And I hate, more than anything else, I'm the reason.

"Abhainn," I whisper softly and immediately, his hollow eyes start to show some life, melting before they sink closed.

"Stop," he pleads, his head coming to rest against my shoulder. He sounds like he's in agony, but I haven't said anything other than his name. I guess it was more than enough.

I can't stand it though.

I hate how he refuses to meet my eyes and when he does, all I see is the pain I'm desperate to take away from him.

But I can't…because I'm the reason it's there.

"I have no right to ask this…" I mutter as I trail off, not really knowing where I was heading with the sentence in the first place. Pulling his head up so he's forced to look at me, I search his face again. Needing something, anything from him. But he just licks his lips and inhales sharply at our closeness, the proximity of my face to his.

Fuck me.

All I want is to kiss away his pain and anger and resentment. Show him how I feel. It's basically killing me that I can't.

So I shouldn't be standing here, ready to ask him to do just that.

Just one more time.

"Why would you start now?" he says simply, a slight challenge in his tone.

And all it takes is one glance at my mouth for me to give in and latch my lips to his with desperation.

Something between a whimper and a groan escapes him and I take the opportunity to slip my tongue into his mouth, seeking its sparring partner.

My body crowds his and I push us back into the bathroom, letting the door swing closed behind us. Without looking or breathing or daring to break this moment, I turn the lock on the knob and press him against the wall.

The ball of his piercing rolls against my tongue, sending a bolt of desire rushing to my cock. And of course, he's quick to notice.

"So, that's why you're *really* here?"

"What? I was invited, same as you," I pant, once I find the strength to remove my mouth from his entirely.

"So, you *weren't* looking for me? Hoping to get one last quickie in before I file a restraining order against you?" The bite in his tone is new. It's full of bitterness and disgust, neither of which I'm used to coming from him. "And you know, I easily could. Between you decking me in the middle of a game with thousands of people watching then to what happened at the cabin…I think there's enough evidence for a judge. Don't you agree?"

His mouth spews the vile words, but his lips give him away in the next breath when they return to mine, molding against them in a needy frenzy. And it's his body that betrays him most when I grind my hips against his, both of us hard beneath our clothes.

"You wouldn't," I hedge, calling his bluff. Because I know

River. We forgave each other for the words and the anger and resentment from *before.*

My hand slides between us and I cup him over his pants while he anchors my mouth to his with his fists in my hair. I manage to work his pants open enough to slip my hand inside and take him in my palm.

Hot and rock fucking solid.

"You can tell me you hate me. Try to hurt me. Bare your teeth in defiance. Say we're toxic like your soul will let you believe it," I whisper against his mouth, jacking him slowly. "Tell me you're done with me. Wish it never happened, wish *we* never happened."

His head snaps back against the wall with a *thud,* and I watch as his eyes sink closed.

"You can glare at me with only ice left in your heart every time you see me. Freeze me out as if it can make you feel less. But just know, it doesn't stop my veins from boiling the minute *I* see *you*. Every thought of you burns my skin. And knowing my sleep is the only place I'm able to kiss you, touch you, and feel the fire you consume me in…makes me crave the nightmares."

Panting and thrusting into my palm, he groans, "And that's *not* toxic?"

"Nah, mo grá," I say, nipping his neck. "That's addiction."

"You know the best way to curb an addiction?" he asks, a snarl in his throat, bringing his hands up to my chest. "Cutting the habit cold turkey."

A hard shove against my pecs breaks the trance we fell into. And I watch, helpless, as River adjusts himself before pinning me with a glare. "You know why? Surviving withdrawals isn't nearly as agonizing as the constant ache in your chest from depending on something you know will eventually kill you."

His shoulder brushes mine when he steps toward the door, and my hand instinctively reaches out for his arm. Only the look on his face stops me from touching him again. The pure, unfiltered misery written on it, barely contained by a bitter mask.

"Do us both a favor and leave me to suffer in fucking peace."

An hour later, Roman's buzzing and I'm pissed at not only the world, but myself for once again not thinking.

Coming here was a terrible idea. I could feel it. But still, here we are.

Because I can't *stay away.*

Even when he's asked me to, I can't.

Even when I see how much it hurts him. I know, because it hurts me too. But it hurts so much less by being near him at the very least. So much less than the constant wondering, playing a game of *what-ifs* in my mind.

That's what has me heading down into the basement with a slightly swaying Roman. It's not enough to be drunk, but he's nowhere near the realm of sober either, using the wall to make it down the steps.

And while I've felt the familiar heat and vibration running through my body since we stepped into this house from River's presence, the second my feet land on the ground of the basement, it intensifies. To the point where it doesn't take me more than two seconds to find him.

But what I find…I'm not prepared for it in the slightest.

River slumped back against the couch, eyes staring blankly out in front of him. Zoning on absolutely nothing.

The instinct to go to him and see what's wrong is instant, but as I glance around, I notice a good portion of the party has moved down to this level. Anyone could see. And after the last two threats from Ted, I wouldn't put it past him to hire a college kid looking to scrape together a few hundred bucks to come in here and keep an eye on me and anyone I might talk to.

Roman, on the other hand, smirks at me the moment he notices River sitting on the couch all alone, and moseys over to him without a care in the goddamn world.

Plopping down in the seat beside River, Ro gives him a smile that, had I not known him since we were kids, would have been perceived as genuine.

To be clear, it's not. It's calculating and slightly vindictive.

His attention flashes from River to me and quickly back again when he turns on the couch, pulling his leg up and leaning his arm against the backrest. That same hand finds his head, and he watches River, absorbing every inch of him.

"River, right?" he says after a minute, surprisingly alert for how he just practically stumbled down the stairs. "I'm Roman."

River's glassy eyes, clearly incoherent to anyone with two brain cells to rub together, do their best to focus on Roman. "I know," I hear him reply, his voice hoarse. But then he just leans back against the couch and stares up at the ceiling, unblinking.

I can tell he's high, and while I shouldn't be surprised with the weed I found at his apartment, this is clearly something so much more than that. And while the cup of beer on the table might not be his, I have a feeling he's been drinking too.

Fuck.

"River," I greet him, clearing my throat as I take a seat on the couch parallel to the one they're on. The seat on the other side of River might be unoccupied, but I know my strengths and weaknesses.

Sitting beside him, being within touching distance…it's a bad idea. And for once, I manage to talk myself *out* of the bad idea.

Doesn't mean I'm able to stop myself from watching his every move. Which I have to say, isn't much at all. God, when he leans his head back against the cushion of the couch, I swear he doesn't so much as *breathe.*

Of course, when I do finally manage to pull my eyes from him a few minutes later, I catch Roman studying me, a gleam like I've never seen before in those hazel orbs. It's like the fun, party-hard fuckboy I knew him to be for years is just gone.

Replaced with a shark, his calculating and penetrating stare boring into me like he's dissecting my innermost thoughts with just his eyes.

"What, Ro?" I sigh, getting slightly irritated with the way he keeps his attention on me. The drinking and fun never even started for me and he sure as hell isn't doing a damn thing anymore, so why the hell are we even still here? "Do you want to leave? Because then let's just fucking go."

Roman shakes his head, licking his lips as he leans forward to finish off his beer. Tossing the cup on the table, his elbows come to rest on his knees as he continues to examine me.

"Do you think I'm stupid?"

What the..?

I gape at him. "What the fuck are you talking about?"

"Do you. Think. I'm. Stupid?" he enunciates in staccato, sending my temper into overdrive. Not that I exactly had my shit together in the first place, but we sure as fuck are reaching the point where I'll gladly rip him a new asshole if he doesn't stop this bullshit.

"No," I snap. "Why the fuck would you say that?"

"Because you're doing a fucking fantastic job of acting like it!" he shouts, but no one bothers to even look our way. The bass coming from upstairs drowns out half the noise and everyone down here is probably too drunk to give a shit either way. Crowds are only drawn when punches are thrown at places like this.

I gawk at him again and shake my head, not knowing if he's on something because I can tell, even with the amount of beer he's consumed tonight, his buzz is completely gone now.

"What is—"

"Do you really think I don't *know?*"

I'm gonna fucking kill him.

"Know *what?*" I growl through my teeth.

"You think I don't know it's *his name* you had inked on your skin the day I got here?"

His menacing stare flashes over to River, letting mine follow, and my heart instantly crawls into my throat.

Fuck, fuck, fuck a duck.

At my non-answer, he turns back to me. "You don't think I've realized by now there's another player in this game for your heart, Rain? Because I see it. *I know.*" He glances at River again before nodding his head in his direction with a scoff. "And if *this* is my competition?" He just smirks and shakes his head before meeting my eyes. "Babe, it's not even a contest."

Competition? What is he even —

Roman scoots over on the couch, slipping his finger into the collar of River's shirt, flicking open the button with ease, causing a knot to form in my throat at the sight. His hand moves down, unbuttoning two more buttons, revealing the valley between River's pecs.

"What are you doing?" I whisper, barely audible over the noise of the party around us. But I know Roman heard me. It's unmistakable from the wicked grin crossing his face.

Fucking stop this, my brain is screaming, knowing that River is literally so far gone he has no idea what it happening right now. Especially if the way his head is rolled back on the couch is any indication.

Fixating my glare on Roman, I grimace as he continues to unfasten each button slowly, his fingers visibly brushing against the smooth skin just beneath it.

"Get your fucking hands *off him,*" I hiss, but it does no good.

I need to stop him.

Except I can't move.

My eyes are glued to River's exposed skin, the amount of it growing larger by the second as Roman releases the last button on the shirt, flipping each side open to reveal his entire torso. Each muscle, perfectly defined and his smooth skin, save for the line of hair trailing down into his jeans…even in this crowded house, it has my mouth watering.

Roman trails his first two fingers from River's collarbone down to his belly button, dipping inside the shallow indent before directing his path over to one edge of his V.

And then I feel the snarl working its way from my throat as Roman gets close to the edge of River's jeans. The second they tease the edge of his underwear, I see fucking red.

"I'm just checking out the merchandise that's got you all up in this fit of rage. You know, the one you're clearly trying to tamp down right now," Roman says, a smile in his voice. When I manage to remove my eyes from his hand on River to meet his gaze, the grin he's still sporting only serves to infuriate me more.

"Why do you have to bother looking if you're so certain there's no competition to be had?" I snap, curling my lip back as I fight my anger.

Do not make a scene. Do. Not. Fucking. Lose it.

Licking my lips, I smirk at Roman with an ease I don't entirely feel while he's touching what belongs to me. "Doubting yourself, Ro?"

But that only makes Roman's grin widen more. "Not at all." He laughs as he presses his entire hand down on River's stomach, fingers teasing the waistband of his underwear again. "Just tell me, what is it that you want from him most? I mean, yeah, his body is damn near perfection," he tells me, leaning in and running his lips down River's throat before pulling away. Glancing back to me, he slides his hand back up and brings it to rest on Riv's left pec. "Or is it his heart? Perhaps his mind? Tell me, what is it that's ensnared you, Rain?"

All of the above. Fucking everything.

"Who said I even want him? Because I *don't*," I growl, the words tasting bitter. Like the lies they are.

Roman's brow quirks in amusement. "What did I say about bullshitting a bullshitter?"

"It's not bullshit, it's the fucking *truth*."

"You sure as hell want him a lot more than you wanted the girl in Portland."

All the hair on my body stands on end as I register the words and their implication. From the look of pure terror I'm sure is written across my face, he knows it too.

My nostrils flare and I grit my teeth, but *fuck* he's got me.

"That's right. I was there that night, Rain. At the club in Portland. In the bathroom while you fucked that slutty blonde who could barely stand." He smirks, letting his finger circle around one of River's nipples. "I watched you pound into her against the wall. Your face looked pained, and I could tell you weren't into it. You were just trying to convince yourself it's what you wanted when really...you can't turn yourself straight. No matter how many pussies you fuck."

My lips curl back, and I pin him with a glare. "Where the fuck do you get off, Ro?"

He shakes his head, glancing down at River's disoriented gaze, his shirt pulled open enough to reveal the edge of the ink on his ribs. Roman's hand trails over it, tracing the letters I can barely read from my spot across from them.

I know what it says though. I've memorized every inch of his body with my hands and lips and tongue.

River's head lolls to the side and his glazed eyes meet mine, barely aware of what's happening around him or *to him,* and I'm so confused as to what's going on with him.

What have you done with my *River?*

He licks his lips and his eyes sink closed when Roman continues to tease his fingers all across River's exposed skin. His abs, chest, neck. One finger dips into the waistband of his underwear a third time and I about lose my mind right there when the faint sound of River's moan reaches my ears.

"Baby."

It comes out as a strangled whisper, his eyes opening the moment he says it. They lock on me, a faint amount of clarity in them, though it's not much. And while he might not be completely aware or in control, I know he understands I'm here.

I'm here, Abhainn.

But what has me coming undone, ripping my soul in half as I continue to war with myself, is the second his expression softens. Then he does the unthinkable, turning his head toward Roman to let their lips meet in a slow, tortuous kiss.

My molars feel like they're about to crack under the pressure of my jaw clenching as their lips lock and all logic about not making a scene goes out the goddamn window. The only thought blaring like a siren through my brain is *mine, mine, mine, mine.*

And *no one* fucking touches what's mine.

I'm in the middle of rising to my feet to tear them away from each other when something else does it for me.

"What in the ever-loving *fuck* is going on in here?" a deep growl asks.

My attention snaps to the doorway along with Roman's,

where I find both of the Benson twins glaring daggers at us from across the room. That's when I realize River's head has lifted completely off the back of the couch. His lips are swollen and eyes filled with lust as he looks at me.

He licks his lips before glancing between Roman and I with confusion on his face. Then he mouths the word again. *Baby.*

And that's when I realize…he thinks it was *me* he just kissed. *My* hands roaming his body.

But it's not me.

And I lose it.

"Leave him the fuck *alone*, Roman," I seethe, pinning my best friend with a glare.

The corners of his mouth lift in a smirk. "Here I was thinking you might like to join us," he says, glancing at River. His thumb reaches out, brushing against Riv's bottom lip as I continue to watch in horror.

But Roman leaning in again, his eyes locked on mine, has me breaking free from my paralysis, my hand grasping his wrist and yanking him away.

"*Stop,*" I hiss, but it's overpowered by the death grip on my shoulder and I'm pulled away from both Roman and River.

"Haven't you done e-fucking-nough?" Elliott growls in my face, his anger radiating off him in waves strong enough to pull me under.

I blink in shock. "I'm just trying to keep him from making a—"

"A mistake?" Elliott finishes, blue eyes boring into mine. A laugh slips out, and he sneers at me. "Ironic how you want to look out for him now when you're the biggest mistake he ever made."

Ouch.

I bite my lips and close my eyes, letting the burn of that one sink in. Because I deserve it.

If I was questioning him talking to his friends about us, I don't have to anymore. The hatred and disdain they're leveling me with tells me more than enough.

They know everything.

"Everyone get the *fuck out,*" Drew yells, causing plenty of eyes to snap our way. Anyone who dares to make eye contact with me, I aim a scowl at. The room, which has long since fallen silent except for the music blaring from the system upstairs trickling down into the basement, feels like it's closing around me as every person gawks.

With a snarl, the words rip from my throat, a dash of venom mixed in. "Did he fucking *stutter?*"

That gets them moving quick enough, filing up the stairs as quickly as they can without drunkenly tripping and causing a domino effect on the way back down.

Once the last person is gone, leaving just River, Roman, and the twins, I shake my head and look at Elliott, who still has a vice grip on my arm.

"E—"

"You have no *fucking* right," he continues, releasing me to shove me in the chest towards the stairs. "I don't care what kinda hell you went through as a kid. It sucks and I have sympathy for you, but it doesn't give you a free pass to treat people like shit."

"El—" I try again, but he shoves me again, this time making me catch myself on one of the stairs.

"Don't fucking bother, Grady. We don't want to hear a goddamn word you have to say," Drew hisses, dragging Roman off the couch and over to us. Roman doesn't fight it though, just smiles with copious amounts of satisfaction.

Together, the twins lead us up the stairs and to the front door, pushing us through it before following us outside.

Roman just keeps walking, not bothering to look back; a maniacal laugh sounding from him as he heads to my Jeep parked down the road. But I turn around and face the twins. My teammates. *His* best friends.

"Nothing was—"

"Get the fuck out," Elliott snaps, something like anguish crossing his face as he glares at me. "Of this house, this city, of fucking Colorado, I don't give a shit which. Just *go.*" His grimace grows as he shakes his head, attention flashing back to the house as the words come out filled with gravel. "You have to. Before you destroy him even further."

I slam the door to my apartment closed the second both Roman and I are inside, still seething about what happened at the party.

Not just at Roman for touching River like that in front of me, knowing I was powerless to do anything about it. While that pissed me the fuck off, it was more the way River's friends—*our teammates*—were looking at me when they walked into the room, finding the three of us together like that.

I instantly knew River had told them everything that's

happened between us with one look, but their words only made it more obvious. They're his best friends, after all. And if I can be glad for anything in this fucked up situation, it's that he has people around him to pick him up and make sure he's okay.

Because I was awful to him.

Hateful. Rude. Toxic as fuck.

And nothing I can say or do will take away from that or maybe ever make up for it.

Knowing all this, it didn't make the situation easier when Elliott got in my face to defend River. But then to be called out in front of everyone? And then kicked to the curb like some unwanted puppy?

It was mortifying. Infuriating, even.

Not because of the possibility of being outed. I don't give a shit about that. If everything hadn't gone sideways the day we arrived back in Boulder from the cabin, I would have found myself coming out, anyway. Because I knew I'd at least have River to lean on and help me through it.

And I don't think it would've been too difficult. Not for the team, at the very least. Everyone fucking adores River. The only person who ever had a problem with his sexuality was me. Because I was too afraid of my own.

It was knowing I couldn't be the one to stand up for myself or make a scene or do fucking *anything* regarding River was the hardest part of all. All because I don't know who is watching. Ted could have eyes and ears just about anywhere.

I already know he's aware I'm in Colorado. I know he's watching and waiting. But at this point, I'm not sure what other information he has or who he's using to get it.

So, no matter what I do, he can't find out about River. Otherwise me cutting him off, saying all that awful shit to him? All the heartache I'm putting us both through right now? Fuck, it would be for nothing.

Even though I was willing to throw it all away to get Roman's lips off River.

The thought alone has me spiraling, desperate for reprieve.

With a glare in Roman's direction, because clearly he's to blame for part of this, I head into the kitchen, grabbing a bottle of Jameson I keep in the cabinets.

"We're still drinking?" Roman asks as I fill a tumbler halfway with the golden liquid.

"I am. I don't give a fuck what you do," I tell him, not meeting his eyes as I slam the bottle onto the counter, not bothering to put the cap back on. I'll be needing a refill soon enough as it is. Taking a swig, then another, I let the alcohol burn down my throat and coat my stomach in warmth.

"You might wanna take it easy there, man," he says, grabbing a glass and pouring himself some whiskey.

"Fuck off, Roman," I growl, grabbing the bottle the minute he places it back on the counter, heading over to the couch.

Of course, not knowing how to take the hint and, I don't know, *fucking off,* he follows me and takes a seat on the opposite end of the couch. And for some reason, it enrages me. Here's my best friend in the entire world, the person I trusted with my life from the age of eight, and I have nothing but animosity for him at this moment in time.

An uncomfortable silence settles over the room, hanging in the air like a poisonous fog I'd give anything to escape from. So, I drink.

To escape, to forget. To get through this night without making my way back to the party or worse, ending up back at River's apartment.

Neither of us are in the state to be around each other. We haven't been for a while now. And as much as I hate it, I know he's right when he says we're toxic and so fucking bad for one another. It's been evident for a while now and if we were smart, we'd stay the hell away from each other for good.

But that's the kicker of this whole situation. Sometimes the very thing you need to stay afloat is the same reason you're drowning. And it's relationships like those you have to cut off at the knees, before you become each other's downfall.

Yet no matter how many times I think it or try to convince myself it's for the best, I know deep inside my bones, I can't stay away. I can't just *give him up* like I thought I could. Like I *wish* I could. If only to make protecting him easier.

I continue to drink, letting my mind get lost in itself while Roman and I sit in silence. I'm on my third glass of whiskey and definitely feeling a bit drunk, but I haven't seen him refill his glass once since we sat down.

Or maybe I just didn't notice. Who knows, and more importantly, who fucking cares?

Anger is still bubbling inside me as I glower at Roman, who must feel my heated stare, because he chooses that moment to look up from his glass resting on his knee to meet my eyes.

"Fuck you, Ro."

He lets out a soft snort, shaking his head. "Fuck you too, Rain."

"No," I growl, shaking my head as I set my glass haphazardly on the table beside the couch. "*Fuck you* for that stunt you pulled at the house. What the hell were you even thinking?"

He cocks a brow. "You really wanna know? *Truly?*"

"I wouldn't be asking if I didn't," I hiss.

Roman slams his glass on the table and turns to me, his collected mask he seems to dawn these days slipping a fraction. "I was thinking I'm sick of seeing you look so fucking miserable over someone who, frankly, you can do better than. Because *River* is a damn mess of a man-child. I was *thinking* by doing what I did, you'd be forced to see the person who's been in front of you this entire time is the one you should be trying to make things work with. Because *he's* the one who has put *you* first. Since fucking *childhood.*"

My breath hitches and I work to swallow, my throat suddenly dry. *Shit.*

I mean, yeah, he referred to River as his competition at the party, but I honestly thought it was to get a rise out of me, the asshole he is. Because we both know he and I…it would never work between us. For so many reasons.

Right…?

I open my mouth, but whether it's my buzzed state not allowing me to speak or I actually can't formulate words because of his confession, I'm not sure. Whatever the case, it doesn't matter because Roman's grabbing the back of my neck, reeling my mouth to his.

And the second his lips meet mine, my body is on fire, remembering the one and only kiss we shared before this. But this…it's nothing like that one. That one was filled with hesitant exploration and the strength of years of friendship.

This is an explosion of pent up aggression and frustration coming to a head.

His tongue slips past my lips, and I groan into his mouth. It's hot and tastes of whiskey and a touch of mint. Immediately, I wrap my tongue around his, seeking the bar that now runs through it.

But it's not there.

Because he's not River.

I don't have time to process more than that though, because Roman's fingers on his free hand drift down to pull my shirt up and over my head. And I'm fucking helpless to stop it.

Fuck, right now, I don't *want* to stop it.

"Four fucking years," Roman growls against my lips when he comes in for more after removing his own shirt too. "Ever since the night in the pool, I've thought about this. Tasting you again. Your desire, your *need*." His hand slips down and caresses my cock behind my jeans and it twitches at the contact. I groan again and my hips rise of their own accord, seeking more friction to ease the ache. I feel him smile against my mouth before biting my lip and tugging hard enough it almost hurts. "And this time, Rain? I'm not fucking stopping."

His mouth starts trailing down my neck, carving a path down my shoulder to my chest as I think about him doing this to River only hours early.

How far would he have taken it? Would he have taken Riv home? Fucked him even?

The amount of jealousy at the mere idea of Roman touching River any further sends bouts of rage rushing through me as he keeps trailing his mouth and tongue down my body.

God, all I feel is angry anymore.

At Ted, my mom, Roman, River, Doctor Fulton, my-fucking-self.

I'm filled to the brim with hostility for every single person in my life and in this moment, I just need to release it. Let it go.

Be free, if only for a moment.

So, I don't stop this from where it's headed, though I have no clue if it's what I really want.

Roman slides off the couch, sinking to his knees between my parted legs as his fingers swiftly rid me of my belt. My eyes are locked on his as they move to the button of my jeans, then the zipper before tugging them down to my ankles.

And I let him.

I don't stop him when his fingers dip into my underwear, curling around the waistband and dragging those down too. I don't stop him when he takes me in his palm, jacking my length once, twice, a third time.

I don't stop him when he wraps his mouth around me.

I let it all happen, hoping the alcohol clouding my brain will help ease the throbbing in my chest that hasn't left, but has only grown from everything that happened at the party earlier.

Yet as Roman's mouth works, taking me into his throat to the point I'm thrusting up into his mouth greedily, I still feel the pain. When his hands slide under me and grab my ass to spur me on more, I still don't feel better.

Not in the way I need to. Not the way I fucking *crave* to feel whole again.

Because he's not River.

And that's just the fucking problem, isn't it?

The one thing I want—no, the one thing I *need* to not feel so goddamn miserable — is the thing I can't fucking have. No amount of pleasure is going to help me forget that.

So what's the point of trying?

"Ro, stop," I gasp as I tense, my fingers gripping his head.

But he doesn't stop, just continues to suck me as the tips of his fingers teasing against my crease, making bolts of lightning shoot through my body.

"Roman, I said *stop!*" I shout the words, my voice raw and animalistic in the face of fear. It's an emotion I'm all too familiar with, just never when it came to him. Not true fear, at least.

But for the first time in my life, that one word that signifies lack of consent is heard.

He stops.

"What's wrong?" he whispers against my skin after releasing my cock, though he still strokes it in his palm. His eyes flick up to my face as his hot breath tickles against my hip. "Don't you want me, baby?"

That single endearment, it's wrong coming from his lips. So fucking wrong.

My jaw aches as I bite back my initial response to his question. Which, to be clear, is a big, fat...*I don't know.*

Do I want him? It's a helluva lot more complicated than the simple yes or no response he's searching for. When it comes down to it, what I felt for Roman in the past doesn't begin to compare to the way my entire being is lit on fire when I'm simply in the same room as River.

Roman was friendship. And yeah, at one point, lust. But it's never been love.

That will always and only belong to River.

But this? *Sex* with Roman? Slipping back into the safety net of my vices? It would be so easy. To give in. To be with him. To let him try to take the pain away with every inch of his body against mine. It would be so fucking easy.

Four years ago, I was ready to jump at the chance.

But I just can't.

It's about more than want and need and desire. It's about... betrayal. And being with Roman would only ever be a betrayal to River. Knowing it was probably Abbi who sucked River's dick for a few meager minutes hurt me bad enough. And she's just a friend with an unrequited crush.

But this with *Roman?* The person who I flat out *told* River was one of the only people I've ever wanted in this way? It's so much worse.

This is...deplorable. Disgusting. It's the exact opposite of what I should be doing, knowing I'm in love with him. When I want to have another chance to be everything I know we can be.

Because we would never be able to come back from this.

Roman's mouth stops trailing against my abs when I tug on his hair again. He pulls back and at me with a lusty stare.

"What is it, Rain?" he asks softly, that fucking nickname so much worse than the *baby* he said before. I'm not the Rain he knew. To him, I might as well be Ciaráin again.

I don't respond right away, just look away from his heated hazel gaze. They're more green right now, heavy with desire, and it's making it hard to think.

"What do you want?"

I close my eyes, almost wanting to laugh out loud at that one as torment wreaks havoc on my mind.

I want you to be River.

I shake my head, wondering if at any point in my life, I'll manage to not be hurting someone at every goddamn turn.

"I just can't," I whisper brokenly, bringing my eyes back to his. "I can't fuck you. Or let you fuck me. Or let this go any further." A deep breath escapes me before I continue. "I can't be with you when I'll be thinking about him the entire time instead."

I don't say his name, but we both know who I'm talking about.

Roman leans back on his heels completely now, and I do my best not to look at the insane bulge behind his jeans. I watch as the sting of rejection crosses his face quickly before he hides it away.

"I see."

"I'm so fucking sorry," I groan, bringing my hands up to cover my face. "I just…"

I hear him rise from between my legs before uncovering my eyes. He grabs his shirt off the floor and slides it on with ease.

"I get it, Rain. Believe me." He lets out a wry laugh before running his fingers through his hair. "You can't stop yourself from wanting someone. Even if they don't want you back. I think I know that better than anyone."

His words singe my skin, as they're probably meant to.

My eyes follow him as he wordlessly slips into his jacket and shoes before walking over to the door and out my apartment without a backward glance.

And then I'm completely alone once again.

FOURTEEN
River

My head is pounding as I take a seat on the couch of my therapist's office. It's the same as I remember it from a few years ago, the last time I was here.

God, it's been fucking *years* since I felt the need to go to therapy. But after last night—the little bit I do remember of it—coming in for this appointment was the best thing I could do for myself.

I need to find a way out of this downward spiral. The path of self-destruction I'm barreling down is one I don't want to be on, but I can't find an escape. It might be the only way to cope right now, to numb the pain, but at what cost?

I've become someone I despise. My own worst enemy.

Being high out of your mind on Xanax and Adderall will do that to a person, I guess.

"What brings you in today, River?" Dr. Fulton asks from her chair, pulling me from my thoughts.

I glance up at her from the sofa, my eyes colliding with her soft blue ones that always put me at ease and help put things into perspective for me. "I just…" I sigh, shaking my head. "I need to get my head back on straight, I guess."

"I get that, and you know my door is always open," she tells me with a small smile. "So why don't we start with *why* you feel the need to get your head on straight."

Swallowing roughly, I mutter, "I'm becoming a person I don't recognize anymore."

She gives me a sympathetic look meant to set me at ease and urges me to continue.

Rolling my teeth over my bottom lip, I do my best to sort my thoughts and find a place to start. And like every visit I've had with Doctor Fulton in high school and my first year of college, once the words begin spilling from my mouth, they don't stop.

I tell her about Rain. The cabin. Coming back to find Roman here, waiting with open arms for the man I'm in love with. The fight with my parents, more fights with Rain. Skipping class and weight sessions. Slacking on my schoolwork. Every fucking thing, every demon is stripped bare and put out on display for her. Each thing that's happened since the beginning of this school year, I let spew from my lips in an endless stream of word vomit.

All except the drugs. Not that it matters much now, seeing as I got rid of them the moment I woke up this morning. I just can't bring myself to tell her about them. Because I can't stand the idea that I'd be a disappointment to yet another person.

When I'm done, I feel the rough patch in my throat as I hold back the tears threatening to make their appearance. Even though

I know this is a safe place for me to let out the emotions plaguing me, I don't want to. I'm tired of wallowing in misery for the people who don't care about me. All I want is to feel strong and self-assured again, the way I was before I ever laid eyes on Rain Grady.

I find the courage to look back up at Doctor Fulton, finding her scribbling into her notebook. Waiting silently, I tap my hand to my hand against my leg sporadically until she glances up at me.

"Tell me more about your feelings for Rain. Not the ones from a month ago or last week or even yesterday. Your feelings for and about him right now, in this moment."

Not where I was expecting her to start.

Rubbing the back of my neck, I settle back into my spot on the couch, bringing my hands together on my lap, wringing them while I wrack my brain with the best way to describe the level of emotion I feel for him.

"Have you ever hiked above the tree line on a mountain? Climbed a fourteener?"

Doctor Fulton raises a perfectly sculpted eyebrow. "Fourteener?"

I smirk, knowing I've got my answer right there. "A mountain with an elevation of fourteen-thousand feet or higher. Colorado is kinda known for having them."

Shaking her head, she replies, "I can't say I have."

"Yeah, I kind of got that," I say with a soft laugh. "Well, when you're up that high, there's a lot less oxygen, so it's difficult to breathe. The higher up you go, the harder and harder it gets. And if you aren't careful, altitude sickness can set in. You'll get nauseous. Off balance. Lightheaded. It's not life threatening or anything, but it makes you feel like complete trash. Sometimes the effects last for hours or even a couple days, depending on the person."

I know she must be confused, the way she lifts her pen from the paper and looks up at me again. And I've got to give her credit for trying because right now, I don't even know where I'm going with this.

"But the thing about climbing a mountain like a fourteener is you know going into it you're taking a calculated risk to get the reward. And for some, the reward is bragging rights or the pride to say you did it. But for me? I do it because, despite how much it drains my body to make it to the top…" I trail off, shaking my head before glancing out the window. "…the view is just worth it. And the feeling of being on top of the world? Nothing compares. So even though I know it's dangerous, that it might not be good for me…I don't think I'll ever be able to stop wanting to reach the summit."

Biting my lip in thought for a moment, I allow my gaze to collide with hers once more.

"That's the best way I can describe how I feel about Rain. He's a calculated risk. One I know both the consequence and the reward of."

"And if I'm following your logic," Doctor Fulton says slowly, leaning back in her chair, "even though you know it might be unhealthy for you, the feeling of wanting him, of getting to the top outweighs that?"

I smile, shaking my head. "Sort of. Except he's not the mountain in this scenario. They're the walls he hides behind. Rain himself, he's the oxygen. Not a want or a desire, but a *need*. And it feels like the higher I climb, the closer I get to the top of the mountainous walls around his heart and mind, the less of *him* I

have once I reach the top. It's like in an effort to get more of him—
from him – the more I lose in the process."

And lose yourself too.

Goddammit.

It's not like I don't know he's bad for me. I absolutely do. If
Rain and I had never met, I would, more than likely, be the exact
same person I was at the beginning of the year. The guy who
cracks pervy jokes and smiles because why the fuck not?

Not this shell of a person, bent on self-destruction.

But I also wouldn't know what it was like to give myself to a
person completely. To overcome what he and I did—the battle of
dominance and control—to find peace in each other's company.
And to have someone to just listen and *get me*, even when all the
odds were stacked against us.

"Is that a cycle you can see yourself being happy in? Like you
said, you don't feel yourself at the moment. Do you think this
relationship with Rain might have something to do with that?"

"I know it has everything to do with it." I laugh ironically.
"We're toxic together, yeah. Especially in the beginning when
all we did was fight and push each other to the breaking point.
And even when things were good for the few short weeks
we were in the cabin and not trying to kill each other, I was
consumed by him. I gave him everything I could possibly give,
and he wouldn't do the same. Not really, at least. I know it and
see it and I understand I could, and should, find someone else
to give my heart to.

"But at the same time, even when we hated each other and
have never been on an even playing field, I've never met someone

who balances me better. That was only proven when he started to open up more with me." My eyes move out the window again. "The parts he was willing to show me."

Setting her notepad and pen on the table beside her, Doctor Fulton waits until I meet her eyes again before asking the question I've been asking myself since the day Rain and I met.

"So does the reward outweigh the risk?

Swallowing roughly, I let out a long exhale. "I wish I knew. It's probably the biggest reason why I'm here in the first place."

Doctor Fulton nods, assessing me the way she always does when she's trying to read more than just the words coming from my mouth.

"There might be another question you need to ask yourself, River, when it comes to risk versus reward. One you might not know is even there. You absolutely need to decide if the risk of possibly losing Rain by pushing too hard is worth the chance that you could have him, as we've established. But you also need to determine if the reward of having him is worth the risk of losing *yourself* in the process."

Rubbing the back of my neck, I shake my head and smile ruefully. "I've been asking myself that every single day, Doc. Is feeling like shit about myself for a guy worth it? Turning into someone I'm not? If you would have asked me that before the cabin, you'd get a resounding *fuck no* in response." I bite my lips and shrug. "But at the end of the day, I can't choose who I love. Unfortunately for me, it's him. And loving him has made me self-destructive on a level I've never experienced before."

"Have you ever heard the saying, 'you can't expect someone

to love you if you can't love yourself' before?"

Rolling my eyes, I scoff. "Everyone and their uncle have heard that. And it's not that I don't *love myself*. I just don't know *who I am* anymore. Trying to find him *to* love him is the issue."

"And that's why you've turned to drinking and weed and skipping classes? As an attempt to find yourself again?"

Fuck.

It's not a question I'm prepared for and I honestly have no idea how to answer her.

I can lie to her, my friends and family. God, I can lie to *myself* all I want, but it doesn't erase the truth her words bring to the forefront of my mind.

I'm just trying to cope instead of facing the feelings head on. And then labeling it as some journey of self-discovery when all I'm doing is digging a hole to bury myself in when the reality of the situation is simple.

Pills and booze were easier to swallow than knowing the person I love will never love me back.

And though she doesn't say it, I know she sees right through me.

But can she blame me? Can I fucking blame *myself* for wanting to feel a little less, even if the way I went about it was wrong?

"I just don't want to feel the pain. Even though…I know I need it in order to heal," I sigh.

She nods her head, giving me a small reassuring smile. "River, right now it might seem dark and bleak. It's understandable, seeing as you're weathering a storm that feels catastrophic. But you *will* get through it."

I give her a smile back, not believing a single word.

The door behind me falls shut as the wind whips around me. I'm feeling slightly better after my session with Doctor Fulton and more than anything, I'm just glad to have someone objective looking in from the outside.

Flipping my hat backwards to keep it from blowing off in a wind gust, I begin to head over to my car.

Well, that is until a firm hand lands on my arm.

Even through the thick layer of my sweatshirt, I feel the heat from his hand and know…

Rain.

Teal meets amber as our gazes collide, and from the look on his face, I'm brought back to last night and the few flashes of things I do remember.

Every thought of you burns my skin. And knowing my sleep is the only place I'm able to kiss you, touch you, and feel the fire you consume me in…makes me crave the nightmares.

Shaking my thoughts free, I yank my arm from his grasp. "I thought I told you to stay away from me? You did a fucking fantastic job of it when I didn't want you to, but now you're everywhere I am."

His mouth flattens into a thin line as he bites his lips closed, and I watch the gears spin in his mind. Calculating how much he's willing to tell me.

Whatever it ends up being, it won't be enough. It never is.

"I'm keeping my distance because I have to, River." The words come out in a rough whisper as he steps forward, not more than a foot from me now. "Because I know I can't have you."

More bullshit, I'm sick of it. And the lies.

"But you *can* have me," I snarl. "You did before and still you do! Jesus Christ, Rain, I know you remember. You said the words back to me, *verbatim*." A knot works its way into my throat and I push it down, spitting the words at him. "Until every last star burns out. I fucking *meant* that."

I hate the truth behind the words and the power they still hold. Each and every promise I made to him at the cabin is etched into my mind. I'm not soon to forget them.

His silence speaks volumes like always as I watch him attempt to figure out what to say next. But if the answer isn't obvious, I don't want one at all.

"This has *nothing* to do with me, Rain. We both know this has everything to do with you and *Roman* and your inability to open up to me." I shake my head. "Are you really too proud to let someone actually give a shit about you?"

He scoffs. "You don't know shit about my pride."

"I think I know more about it better than anyone!" I shout, my temper flaring as my fists clench at my sides. "Finding a way to get you to swallow your *fucking* pride is constantly on my mind because *I know* I can't be so unwanted you would just toss me aside like a piece of garbage."

"*Constantly on your mind?*" He laughs. "Was I *on your mind* when someone else had their mouth wrapped around your cock? I'm betting it was Abbi, right? Or were you too high on a fucking speedball just like last night to even know who was touching you or sucking you off?" His mouth spews it with hatred that doesn't quite reach his eyes as he tints his voice with ice. "Did you think it was me?"

I wince, now realizing last night was clearly the tipping point for me and I'm thrilled I threw every one of those pills in the toilet this morning when I woke up.

"I wasn't *high,*" I snap, getting in his face. It's not a lie; I was just drunk when Abbi and I hooked up. "And you have no fucking right to even bring that up. We aren't together, *remember?* You made sure of that! And honestly? You don't get to judge me for how I try to fix myself when you're the reason I even broke in the first place!"

His jaw ticks and I see the vein throb in his forehead, as his eyes scald me with disdain. "Well, I hope Abbi's mouth did the job for you. Or whoever it was. It doesn't matter. It only proves, despite your claim, you haven't been thinking of me much at all."

"You're all I think about, Rain!" I roar, throwing my hands in the air. "Not because I want to. God, no. I wish I could erase you from my mind and forget you ever walked into my life."

Rain recoils slightly and a somber expression crosses over his face. The wince is so quick, I take a step back from him and take a deep breath as he watches me intently. And it's then I understand the gravity of what I just said and how it outweighs every good moment we've ever shared.

But it's too late. I used to live by the mantra of sticks and stones breaking bones, but words could never hurt. It's only now when I understand…it's a fucking lie. Words are weapons, and when used properly, they cut deep enough to kill.

His eyes hold a palpable amount of pain, and he lets the

words grind out of his throat on gravel, "Too bad that isn't the way the world works, mo grá. I carved my name into your heart and you branded your very essence into my soul. You can't just forget that."

I grimace because he's right. Everything we've done and said up to now, it's going to change us. Shape us into our future selves. How can a relationship this volatile not?

Shaking my head, I sigh. "Seems to me you forgot easy enough, what with *Roman* warming your bed at night." I bite my lip and let out a humorless laugh. "At least you got what you wanted in the end, I guess. The *person* you really wanted."

"I could say the same about you."

This time I actually do laugh because he has to be blind or straight-up fucking stupid. "Really, Rain? Because from where I'm standing, I didn't. All I wanted was to be with *you*. For us to be a goddamn team."

The fire reignites in his eyes as he scowls at me. "Teammates fight for each other."

Rubbing my lip, I attempt to hold my temper and control my tone. After all, he's alluded to this once before when he brought up me walking out on him. But I know what it's like to be abandoned. How it feels to have no one in your corner.

I didn't fucking do that to him. It's what *he* did to *me*.

"Are you kidding me?" I laugh when he doesn't respond, clasping my hands behind my head above the brim of my hat. "I shouldn't have to fight for you, not when I fought for *us* long before there ever *was* an us! Hell, I fought for us when you gave me every fucking reason not to at all!"

We both know I'm right. He has no leg to stand on here, not anymore. Hell, I can see the way he's trying to keep his story straight as it's shattering before us. But that doesn't stop him from digging himself an even deeper hole to bury what we had in it.

"How, River? Please, enlighten me."

Nodding, I step up to him, close enough for our chests to brush, and lick my lips. I don't miss the way his eyes track the movement.

Both my hands find their way to the back of his neck as I look into his eyes. I don't miss the way his own give away every ounce of the war waging inside him.

"I fought for us when you spewed hatred at me, refusing to let you win. I fought for us when you shut down on me time and time again, refusing to let you slip away." My fingers dance on the back of his neck, playing with his dark hair. "Every night I slept on the floor outside your room. Every nightmare I soothed you through. Every word you were hesitant to reveal. Every fucking torturous moment of your past that would sneak up to haunt you, I fought against them all. For *us*." I swallow the glass in my throat and press my forehead to his and close my eyes, inhaling him like it's the last chance I'll ever have to do so. "Every time you let me inside your body, and I let you in mine…I was fighting for us."

I feel the vibration of his body quaking as I speak, getting worse with every example I give him. But he doesn't touch me. Doesn't give in.

Doesn't swallow his pride.

"You fucking did this, Rain. *You*. Not me. So please, baby, just tell me this. Haven't we suffered enough for the sake of your pride? How much more damage can we endure?"

His forehead rolls against mine as he shakes his head before stepping away. He licks his lips, running his hand through his hair before motioning to me. "You're the all-American boy next door. The perfect one. The *happy* one. Fuck, Riv. I don't have the power to change that."

Shaking my head, I clench my teeth and feel my jaw tick. Because he doesn't see something as strong as a diamond can break if you press hard enough, and I'm nowhere near as durable. "Even a golden boy can break. Especially if he had chips and fractures beneath the surface all along."

He winces. "You hid them so well. Even when you told me, I never would have guessed how deep they ran."

His eyes meet mine, and in them, I see the questions he's too afraid to speak. They're the same ones running through my mind.

Can we ever recover from this? Or are we both standing here grasping for anything where there's nothing left for us to hold?

I rub my shoulder, playing off the need to ease the ache in my chest. "I can sit here and pretend. That we were just a way to pass time. That we've run our course. Of course I can, Rain. Or, I can stand here and tell you from the very beginning, I fucking *knew*. From the moment we met, something inside me said *you'll lose your heart to this one. After him, you'll never be the same.* And it was right."

I smile, but I don't feel it. I feel nothing but empty inside as I look into his eyes, the man who has the capability to be my greatest ally or my worst enemy. "A piece of me is missing, the piece of me that pumps the blood through my veins and allows me to fucking live. You cut my heart out that day on the tarmac and honestly?" I shake my head and swallow, a soft exhale leaving me. "Honestly, I don't have it in me to care. I don't even want it back."

Rain shakes his head profusely, as if rejecting my statement could make it untrue, that he could erase it and manage to forget. But he was right about one thing; that's not how it works.

Because he carved his name into my heart when he tore it from my chest.

I don't think there will ever be a day it doesn't beat for him.

FIFTEEN
Rain

I yank the door to Doctor Fulton's office open and storm inside, not bothering to wait for her to welcome me, let alone turn around from her desk before practically shouting at her.

"Is River Lennox your client?"

To her credit, she doesn't seem startled by my outburst or my barging in. She simply turns around cautiously and leans back against her desk, crossing her arms.

"I can't share that information with you, Ciaráin. HIPAA —"

"Oh, for fuck's sake, don't give me that bullshit. You didn't give two shits about HIPAA and their laws when you took *me* on as a client at the request of my mother and whatever weird ass relationship the two of you used to have."

She glares at me. "That situation is one of a kind and I *only* agreed because I owed her a favor. But even then, I treated you like a client to—"

"So, you gaslight the hell outta *all* your clients?" I growl, cutting her off. "Because that's sure as hell what you did to me."

She sighs and rubs her temple. "No, that's not how my sessions normally go. And you have to believe I had no intention of planting any seeds in your head when your mother contacted me or even when our sessions started. I wanted to be by the book." She pauses and meets my stare. "But I could see you struggling and I had a feeling if I pushed you to just *see*, you'd make immense progress. And you did. So while I might've gone outside the bounds with *you* specifically...I can't say I regret it because look where you are now," she says, motioning to me. "Storming in here to defend him isn't something you'd have done a few months ago. You've grown so much *because* of him, just like I thought you would."

"You didn't have the right."

She nods. "I know that. And I *am* sorry for any mistrust I've placed between us. I know it wasn't easy for you to even agree to be here again after all that's transpired."

I watch her move to her chair, bringing her usual pad and pen with, gesturing for me to sit on the couch across from her like we're about to start my appointment.

Which, to be fair, is why I'm here in the first place. Running into River outside was just the biggest coincidence of my life.

My brows furrow as I glance between her and the couch. "You still want to have a session? After everything I just said?" I ask skeptically.

She cocks her head. "Sounds to me like you need one. At this point, I'm done taking payment for any time we spend together,

Ciaráin. It doesn't feel right. But I do want to help you in whatever way I can. It just might not be in the strictly professional capacity the way it is for the rest of my *actual* clients."

I'm still confused. "So, I'll talk to you as if you're my…"

She shrugs. "A friend? One who can be objective, but also has your best interests at heart. That's what I'd like to prove to you more than anything. You can trust people, let them in even." She leans back and tosses the pad on the side table and crosses her legs at the knees. "So, tell me what's going on with you and River."

I sigh and take a seat, leaning back to stare at the ceiling. "I don't even know. He's not himself right now and I hate knowing I'm a massive part of it."

"From what you've told me, I'd say that's a safe bet. Have you told him the truth?"

"He knows what Ted did to me, yeah."

A raised brow. "Does he know *everything* though?"

"No." I rub the back of my neck. "Not even close."

She nods and purses her lips. "I know you don't want to, but I think you should tell him. Let him in even deeper, even if it scares you."

I give her an exasperated look. "I can't put him at risk. He's too important to me. I'd rather live the rest of my life with him hating me and knowing he's *alive* than let him in and *finally* get to love him only to lose him to Ted." My throat constricts on the last few words and I swallow down the knot best I can. "But I'm at a loss as to whether this is even the right thing to do anymore. I think he's falling down into this bottomless pit and doesn't even care if there isn't a ladder or rope or some sort of lifeline left to help him climb out. Because he's cutting every single one."

She gives me a sympathetic look. "You realize that's probably *why* he's lashing out, right? Because he feels alone and helpless and doesn't know what else to do?" She sighs, then adds, "It's a classic defense mechanism."

I narrow my eyes at her, attempting to read her expression. "He's absolutely your client. There's no way you peg him that well without ever meeting him or talking to him. And I *just* saw him leaving the building on my way in."

That perks her interest, but she reveals nothing. "Did you talk to him?"

Rolling my tongue across my teeth, I nod. "Yeah, though I don't know if any good came out of it. All we ever seem to do is fight when we're around one another anymore. It's just worse than before because we know each other's weaknesses. We've learned what to do or say that'll cut deepest."

"And do you *want* to hurt him?"

My eyes land on her blue ones and I shake my head, an overwhelming sadness hitting me. "I want to love him the way he deserves. I just don't know how to do that *and* keep him safe."

Another compassionate smile crosses her features. "Then as much as you don't want to hear this, I think you need to. He needs the truth, Ciaráin. The full story, not the snippets you feel like you're able to give in sporadic little bites. The entire story, front to end, needs to come from you."

Groaning, I put my head in my hands and mumble through them. "What if it's not enough?"

"Then it's not enough. But isn't the risk worth the possibility it might be? The only way you'll know for sure is by trying."

Sighing, I look up at her from my hands, knowing the information I have is something she absolutely needs to know if there's even a chance she's his therapist. Even if it breaks hundreds of rules.

"He's using. Weed for sure, but last night…" I trail off, sighing. "I don't know what it was. But it was bad enough that he was completely…incapacitated. He was there and awake, but not *aware.*"

Her expression gives nothing away and I'm starting to think either he isn't her client after all or I really was just the exception when it comes to how she conducts herself with clients. Regardless, she responds in a way I should have seen coming.

"You need to tell him about Deacon."

"He already knows—"

She raises a brow. "*All* of it, Ciaráin. Because the River you've described to me wouldn't be using any kind of drugs if he knew the whole story."

I know she's right. That's the worst part, feeling like I have some sort of power to help him. Because I fucking do. All of the power is in my hands and I don't know how to use it.

It's tearing me apart, this constant battle of not knowing what to do when it comes to him. I just need someone to tell me. Give me the answers. But life doesn't come with an instruction manual, and especially not for situations like this.

So when the good doctor gives me an out and makes a demand, holding the office phone from on the coffee table out to me, I could honestly jump for joy.

"Call him," she tells me. "Right now."

Knowing River wouldn't answer a call from *me* right now—something I'm sure she realizes—I take it from her hand.

And for once, I don't hesitate. I don't overthink all the ways this could go wrong or why I have to keep my distance. Because I'm not doing a good job at keeping him safe if he's turning to vices to cope with my absence.

Holding my breath, I wait as the phone rings and rings and rings again, only to release it when he answers the phone. "Doctor Fulton?"

"River."

Just the single word, his name, is all I can manage because the relief I feel from him even answering the phone is overwhelming.

"What do you want, Rain?" he sighs on the other end of the line. "I thought I made myself—"

"Riv," I cut him off. "I know you don't owe me a damn thing. But if you can just please...don't fight me right now and just listen." The plea in my voice is evident and thankfully, he remains quiet, allowing me to proceed.

A glance to Doctor Fulton and her reassuring smile is all I need to push forward.

"I...have so much to say to you. And it's getting to the point where I can't find a reason to keep lying to you. Secrets are consuming me, and while I don't want to drag you down and bring you into this, seeing you last night and then again today made me realize keeping it from you is drowning us both."

He's quiet for a moment before he responds slowly. "Where are you trying to go with this?"

"I want to tell you everything," I utter, desperate for my head and gut to get on board with my heart. "You told me you want me to share my life with you. Give me the chance to do it. Tomorrow."

The silence from his end is deafening. The only thing I hear is the faint sound of him tapping as I wait for a response. Begging for an inch of forgiveness and understanding, even if I don't deserve it.

"River, please," I whisper over the line, my chest physically aching at the thought I might be too late to offer an explanation for all of this. "Please come over tomorrow. Let me tell you everything."

More silence.

And after an eternity, a single word comes through before he hangs up the phone.

"Okay."

Doctor Fulton, who now insists I call her Erica, spent the rest of my so-called *session* talking through everything else that's been going on. Between the stuff with River, divulging the horrid details of what happened with Roman last night, and then updating her on anything Ted or FBI related, the remaining time goes by seemingly instantly.

It's not until we have a few minutes left she gives me a look that sends a shot of anxiety into my blood.

"Before you go…I have something for you," she says, pulling out an envelope from inside her notepad that's been sitting on the table this entire time. It's stark white, nothing written on it except my name in a neat print I'd recognize anywhere. She gives me a reassuring smile as she hands it to me, uttering the words I already knew to be true.

"It's from your mother."

And though I knew, hearing her say it doesn't keep my heart from stuttering in my chest the moment the words are spoken.

My hand takes the envelope on its own accord, shaking as I bring it back to rest in my lap.

I stare at my name. Just stare and get lost in thought about what could possibly be in this envelope. What merits her attention now instead of when I needed it most?

"Why did you have it?" I ask, looking up at her.

"She sent it to me to give to you. Probably because she knew you'd be back," she adds wryly.

I do my best to smile but I'm sure it's not very convincing, what with my entire body feeling like it was just thrown into a vat of acid and left to decompose the second she pulled this thing out.

"What do I do with it?"

She looks at me funny and I have to admit, it's a stupid fucking question. But holding it in my hand, seeing her handwriting on it, I feel as if all my intelligence just went out the window. Not even two brain cells left to rub together at this rate.

"You read it, Ciaráin," she says. "Not for her, but for yourself. For whatever closure you might need."

Read it. Right.

So, I open the damn thing and do just that.

SIXTEEN
Roman

You've gotta be fucking kidding me.

    I glare at Rain when the sound of an engine cutting outside signals what he just told me—he wants to tell River everything—is, unfortunately, the truth.

"I thought you were trying to keep him out of this," I growl as I try to fight the sting in my chest before turning to watch River slam the door of his car closed from the apartment window.

Of course this would be the situation I'm walking into after two days of not speaking to Rain, save for a single text yesterday morning to let him know my brothers would be here today. And we needed to meet with them, if only to give them an update on the situation.

And by *update*, I mean let them know why the hell I'm in Colorado on a solo mission when I should be back in Asia training.

Rain's fist slams down onto the island counter before he

groans, stepping closer to me.

"I did. Fuck, I still *do*." He runs his hand through his hair before clasping both hands on the back of his neck. He glances out the window as River starts up the sidewalk to Rain's building. "But at this point, it's doing more damage keeping him in the dark. He's spiraling and—"

"And that isn't your problem, Rain," I cut him off, not letting him take the blame for River's decisions since I've been here. "He's an adult. One perfectly capable of making his own choices."

A soft sigh escapes Rain as his hands drop down to his sides once more, attention still out the window. "That might be true, but you and I both know the amount of guilt that eats away at you when you know you're part of the reason for it happening in the first place."

The second River enters the building, Rain aims his penetrating stare back at me. It's the one he uses when he calls me out on my bullshit, not wanting to say the word *hypocrite.*

This is definitely one of those pot meet kettle situations.

That's when I know I've lost this battle. Because I felt that same guilt when I heard about what Rain went through after I left for the Enclave the summer after graduation.

The excessive drug use. The constant partying. Fucking anything that moved.

Watching Deacon die in front of him.

He was fighting a battle not only against Ted, but also against himself in his mind. All on his own, even when I'd promised to always be by his side, in his corner. Then I left. And I failed him. So much of what happened after I left is proof of that.

I'd have to be a damn sociopath not to understand his guilt. The irony of this situation isn't lost on me, not one fucking bit. But it doesn't mean I have to like the position I find myself in currently. Namely, between the guy I'm crazy about and the one person probably on this goddamn planet who has the power to claim his heart.

River knocking on Rain's door brings me back and I glare at my best friend.

My jaw ticks as I fight to keep my cool. But fuck me, I can't deny him a goddamn thing. I've never been able to, so why start now?

"Fine. He can come," I say slowly as Rain crosses the room towards the door. "But information needs to be kept at a minimum. You knowing as much as you do about the Enclave is bad enough, but they'll accept it when they hear the circumstances. Bringing him into this is a completely different story."

Rain just nods in agreement before turning to open the door for River. The second he steps into the apartment, the tension that was already present in the room damn near triples.

And when he removes his eyes from Rain to find me across the room, I want to crawl into a hole and die right there. Because the last time the three of us were in a room together was at the party the other night and…

Shit.

Even though the word *sorry* is one I don't use often, it's on the tip of my tongue to apologize for everything I did and said the other night. Hell, even I know I was so far out of line, using him while he was three sheets to the wind just to make Rain jealous. Or to, I don't know, make a fucking choice between us?

Except it backfired because he was jealous for all the reasons I didn't want him to be.

And he didn't choose you.

Shaking the thought free, I straighten my shoulders, allowing my gaze to harden on the two of them standing there.

"I take it you didn't tell him I was coming over?" River says quietly, glancing back at Rain.

"No, I told him. Because he has to take us to where you can get the full story. He might not agree with it, but at this point he doesn't really have much of a choice. I don't want you in the dark anymore, Abhainn."

Abhainn.

My mind latches onto the single word. The fact it's inked onto Rain's skin.

And I want to fucking hit something.

"Let's go," I growl, grabbing Rain's keys off the counter and heading to the door. "Before I change my fucking mind."

The ride up to the Jameson family estate in the mountains outside Boulder is quiet. Thankfully. I don't think I could have managed to keep my shit together with either of them for blindsiding me with this.

At this point, I'd have been better off never answering the goddamn phone when Rain called me back in January. Life would sure as hell be a lot simpler. But even still, I don't regret it. Which might be the stupidest part of this entire situation.

Apparently Rain still holds enough power to continue to

make me dumber than a box of rocks.

The second we pull through the security gates and the massive house built into the edge of the cliff comes into view, I hear a slight intake of breath from River in the back seat of Rain's Jeep.

Glancing into the rearview mirror, I smirk. "Welcome to the Jameson estate."

His eyes widen as they meet mine in the mirror. "As in William Jameson?"

My brows furrow and I'm about to ask him how he knows who William is when Rain turns around to look at him from the passenger seat. "Why do you sound like you're about to shit a brick?"

Throwing the car in park outside one of the five garages, I turn too. "More importantly, why do you say it like you know him personally?"

"I don't know *him*," River says, his eyes darting between us. "I haven't met him or anything. But I know he's from the Boulder area because I went to prep school at Summit with his son, Asher."

My eyes snap closed, and I sigh. *You've got to be fucking shitting me.*

"The Asher you and the twins and Taylor would hang out with?" Rain asks.

I open my eyes in time to catch River's nod before his gaze collides with mine. "How do you know Asher?"

I snort. *We're getting to that part.*

"I guess you could say our families have been friends for a long time. But we're more like brothers than anything."

He narrows his eyes on me slightly, studying my face as Rain opens the passenger door to get out. River and I follow suit and I swear I hear him mumble something about explaining Facebook pictures under his breath before he exits the vehicle.

Whatever.

Together the three of us head toward the front door inset between the two bays of garages. I go to grab the knob when River says, "Shouldn't you knock?"

I turn and smirk at him as I open the door. "Basically brothers, remember?"

We step into the opulent foyer, the main living area visible straight ahead, each wing of the house containing the bedrooms, bathrooms, and offices branching off to the right and left. I hear River's low whistle as he spins around, taking the whole place in.

And then I glance at Rain to find him watching River, an adoring look on his face that makes me want to simultaneously punch something and vomit all over Asher's pristine marble floor.

"I can't believe Ash grew up in this place," River says quietly.

Rain cocks his head. "You haven't been here before?" A shake of the head from River is his answer.

I'm honestly not surprised that's the case. We were taught as kids that the childhood and teenage friendships we form have no place being brought home to any of our estates. It's how the Enclave has remained one of the most elite and secret organizations in the country — and the world — for as long as it has.

The fact that Rain was constantly at my home as we grew up, let alone with Father's approval, was astounding. But as Grand Elector, I guess he was able to have a bit more sway over the other elders when it came to how he ran his household.

I watch as River and Rain share a silent look, like they're

communicating with just their eyes and thoughts alone, and my stomach rolls.

Oh, fuck *this shit.*

Not bothering to announce our arrival or take my damn shoes off, I start toward the living room, knowing one of the four should be around here somewhere.

Without a backward glance, I call them to follow. "C'mon, it's time you meet the guys."

I hear their footfalls behind me as I peek into the living area to see it's empty. Which is…odd.

Rounding the corner, I find Asher in the kitchen alone, his head bent over his laptop typing away at something. He glances up from his work — why he doesn't just work in his office, I'm not sure — and his brown eyes lock on mine.

"Where's everyone else?" I ask, glancing around. It comes out a little harsher than expected, but I'm on edge and can't help the bite in my tone.

He frowns. "It's bad enough you're pulling this fucking stunt to begin with, picking up a job you had no business getting us involved in. But now you want to walk in here demanding shit like you own the damn place?" His eyes flick over my shoulder as the word *place* leaves his mouth and a scowl takes over his face. "And apparently inviting *guests* too."

But I catch the moment recognition sets in because his scowl flips into something like incredulity. "River?"

A glance over my shoulder reveals both River and Rain standing near the glass wall of the sunken living room, which leads out to a deck suspended off the side of the house…and the mountain. Like I said, built into a cliff.

River's attention snaps our way at his name, Rain's quick to follow, and a smile overtakes his face. "Hey, Ash."

Asher lets out something between a scoff and a laugh and heads over to him, giving him one of those stupid dude-bro-hugs guys give each other when they haven't seen each other for a while. Which I guess makes sense, seeing as it's the circumstance we're in.

"I didn't realize you knew each other until we pulled up," I tell him curtly. "Turns out it's a small world."

And getting fucking smaller by the goddamn minute.

Asher shoots me a look at my sour demeanor, clearly reading my tone, perceptive as ever. He turns back to both of them, taking a moment to introduce himself to Rain while I just stand by and watch. Already feeling like an outsider.

"Go call for the guys," Asher says with a wicked grin after a minute or two, finally remembering my existence. "Seems like we're in need of a little *family* meeting."

Confusion crosses River's face. "How many of you are there?"

"Five," I growl before turning away from them. Walking out into the foyer, I cup my hands around my mouth and shout for the remaining three. "Kaede! Callum! Hollis!"

It earns me a glare from Asher when I return to the living room. "You don't have to be obnoxious. You could have used the intercom."

River turns to Rain and they share another *look*. This one is clearly about the amount of wealth that's present around them. Whatever, we have money. Judge us for it. But stop fucking looking at each other like you can read each other's minds. I'm getting real sick of that shit.

"Why would I do that when I live to piss you off?" I smirk.

Asher doesn't give a retort because Kaede and Hollis appear beside me, Callum's blonde head popping up close behind.

Kaede's silver eyes pin me with a glare. "You're gonna tell us why the fuck we're here?"

"C'mon now, K." Callum grins, wrapping his arms around his and my shoulders, hanging between us. "Let's not get in a tussle immediately after months apart."

Hollis rolls his eyes, slipping his inked fingers through his dark hair. "Can we get this over with?"

Jeez, they're fucking lively today.

Slipping out from Callum's embrace, I step into the living room, letting six sets of eyes linger on me. Some with intrigue, some with disappointment.

Well, that's mostly from Kaede.

"Gather 'round boys," I say with a smirk, motioning to the giant U-shaped sectional in the living room. "It's time to share some ghost stories."

River's eyes turn to saucers as he glances between me and my brothers. "You're serious? A *secret society*? Passed down through generations of five *noble* families? For almost a *thousand years*?" he asks in a mixture of awe, disbelief, and astonishment.

Okay, yeah, so *ghost stories* isn't an accurate description of what we're doing gathered together on the couch. But dropping a bomb like this one requires some amount of theatrics or the crowd just stares at you like you're from another planet.

Case in point, River right now. Even *with* my theatrics.

After I updated the guys about why I was here, letting Rain tell his story how he wanted, though none of them were surprised in the least once Senator Anders' name was mentioned, we were hit with the big question from River.

Who are we?

Bomb equals dropped.

Because the answer to that is…we're the wealthiest families in the country, born of noble blood, who run a goddamn secret society. And that brings us to where we are currently.

And even though I'm enjoying the dumbfounded expression on River's face right now, I try my best not to laugh too much. Because I know firsthand from explaining the bare details to Rain once upon a time when we were younger, it's a lot to take in. So, as much as I don't care for him, I can't blame a guy for needing a minute to catch up.

"Do I look like I'm joking?" Kaede retorts immediately, wearing his signature expression of boredom.

Rolling my eyes at his never ending level of dickishness, I nod. "We're serious, yeah."

River nods absently, but he doesn't seem convinced as skepticism crosses his features. "You mean like occult symbols and blood oaths and rituals? Illuminati and Knights Templar and Freemason type shit?"

Rain cracks a smile and I can't help but join because pop culture tends to oversell what secret societies entail in almost every circumstance. "Not exactly in the way you might be thinking, but along those lines."

Asher chooses that moment to pitch in, his smirk radiating as he adds to my comment. "Who do ya think taught them everything they know? We're a fuckton older than any of those assholes."

Of course, this spurs on about fifteen consecutive questions from River, Rain popping in once in a while with his own. So many and so quickly, Asher and I struggle to answer every single one of them.

But clearly Kaede is getting irritated with the little Q and A session we have going. Not to say I blame him, trade secrets and all that. So, being the Commander Douche he is, he takes hold of the reins, stopping Asher and I in our tracks.

"Look, it's simple," he growls, sitting up with his elbows on his knees, finally looking a little invested in this conversation. "Five families make up the Enclave. Each generation comes up as what we call legacies. That's what we are currently. We're then trained and become apprentices. Once we're all of age for initiation, we take on the roles as elders." He pauses, giving them both a chance to process the information before continuing. "One of the newest elders becomes the next Grand Elector, also known as the one 'in-charge' of the Enclave. And then they marry and the first male born to each family is the next heir to the key and the next generation of legacies, yada yada yada until the end of time." Kaede looks bored again as he finishes, regaining the emotionless tone to his voice, offering no remorse or sympathy to either River or Rain for the shitstorm of information being unloaded at a rapid fire pace.

Did I mention he's a fucking asshole?

"Your dad is Grand Elector, right?" Rain asks me. The

question earns me a glare from both Kaede and Hol because he definitely shouldn't know that, but I ignore them and nod.

"Okay..." River starts, his gaze darting between me and Asher. "Then how does it work? What's the purpose?"

Ah yes, we didn't get to address this one before Kaede so rudely interrupted.

Asher takes the reins this time. "Enclave is broken into five definitive *sectors* if you will, with one of each elder from the different families tasked and trained specifically in that area. There's law and politics, information, military and security, economics, and media. Though one of us is highly skilled in our assigned area, all of us have the basic knowledge required in each."

"Assigned? You don't...pick?"

Hollis gives River a look. "We're assigned based on aptitude and what we're already skilled or interested in prior to our official training. They weren't going to stick me on a computer trying to hack into the CIA database when I don't know a modem from a hard drive. And they sure as fuck wouldn't place Roman in a high profile political or media position when he can't keep his dick in his pants." He pins me with a glare, green eyes filled with venom. "Seeing as we tend to *avoid* scandal as much as possible."

River nods, his gaze meeting mine at *dick in his pants,* and I smirk when I see worry cross his features.

Good, let him wonder what Rain and I have been up to these past couple months.

"So, who is in charge of which portion?" This comes from Rain.

"It doesn't matter in this instance," Kaede glares, flashing me a look and dares me to challenge him, though we all could guess I

AFTER RAIN FALLS | 225

won't. Dickhead already knows I'm in enough shit as it is without giving them more information than necessary. Especially seeing as Rain already knew too much prior to this little information exchange.

"Then what do you do within each of those sectors?" This comes from River.

"*Jesus Christ*, enough with the questions already," Kaede hisses, his gray eyes a molten silver as he shoots laser beams at River and Rain.

Asher sighs, and takes over, ever the diplomat. "We infiltrate, basically. Whatever is needed within that sector, but as high up as we can possibly go in society as a whole." He smirks at River. "And no, none of us have ever been President or even Vice. Some cabinet members, though. Like my father. It's good to get someone up in the line of succession if we can."

Rain and River share a look I can only describe as overwhelmed. Which is fucking hilarious because the words *government conspiracy* is written all over their faces and they haven't heard the half of it.

"Currently," Asher begins, "our political role and the post of Grand Elector is being filled by Senator Mitchell, media is the Bennett's, economics is the Sinclair's, information is the Carlisle's, and my father is military. Though those will all change once we've been initiated."

River cocks his head. "Your dad is a lawyer? How is that military?"

Asher smirks. "*Military* lawyer. It's not always black and white, how things are divided. It's whatever we need, wherever we can sneak it. And it changes rapidly. My dad's now the US

Attorney General with the recent election, but that's not forever. Though it's actually a really fucking awesome position for us to snag. High up politically and heads up organizations like the FBI, still meeting the requirements of the *security* sector. "

River's head looks like it's about to explode and I look over to Callum, finding him enjoying this as much as I am.

"And the main goal of all this?" Rain asks.

"What do you get when you have money, information, security, and the knowledge of generations before you?" Kaede asks.

"Power and control," Hollis replies dryly, though the question wasn't meant for him.

I roll my eyes. *Glad these two are so fucking chipper today.*

"Basically," I say with a sigh, taking pity on them, "we want to be able to have a hand in the way this country is run. To make it better, smoother. It might sound bad when we use the word *infiltrate*, but all we're looking to do is good. It's more like..."

"The Justice League on steroids," Asher says with a grin.

"Except we don't have superpowers and we wear suits instead of spandex," Callum adds, the fucking dumbass he is.

"If you wanna water it down, sure. Let's go with that," I sigh, shaking my head in dismay at their idiocy.

And they call me the rogue one.

But after a minute, my lips quirk, realizing I have the money, the suits, and the Lambo. Only missing the tech to be a real-life Batman.

Kaede, ever the arrogant ass he is, interjects again. "Basically all you need to know is we have the power and clout to take care of this. And if you still don't believe me?" He shrugs, his eyes taking on a vicious glint. "Who do you think put men on the moon?

Started the American Revolution? Drafted the Constitution? None of those things happened by chance. *We* made them happen. So, if we can do all that without a damn person in the world knowing about our involvement, there's no reason we can't find Anders and have him detained by the end of the week. With all the resources we have at our fingertips, it's child's play. But we've already told you more than enough to trust us, so anything else is strictly need to know."

River and Rain both nod vehemently, which earns a low snicker from Cal.

Kaede shoots him a glare before his eyes latch onto mine in a warning. He stands then, signaling this little *meeting* is over. "And Roman, they *don't* need to know. Am I clear?"

My eyes flash over to River and Rain before moving back to Kaede. They might not see the anger radiating off him, but I do. I know him well enough to see his perfectly crafted façade is an inch away from cracking.

So I smirk and flip him off as he starts walking away. "Crystal."

SEVENTEEN
Rain

I settle into a seat on a patio chair, letting the cool breeze whip around me as I stare out at the mountains littering Asher's backyard. The wooden deck juts out slightly from the cliff face the house is perched on, giving me a one hundred eighty degree view, free of any obstructions.

It's stunning, the silence and serenity with a majority of the peaks still snow-capped.

A shiver runs through my spine, but not because of the weather or the wind. Mid-March is quite a bit warmer than I thought it would be, only cool enough to need a light jacket and a pair of jeans.

No, it's everything Roman and his guys just spewed at River and me. Each and every detail they could share about a goddamn secret society that's been around for centuries.

Things even I, who knew more than anyone outside the

Enclave is supposed to know, had no idea about or been close to thinking up. Yeah, I knew Roman's family held an insane amount of power thanks to the Enclave. I even knew it was some weird secret society his family has been members of long before America's birth.

But to be traced back as far as medieval monarchy? To be the highest of the elite?

Hell, to claim some of the greatest achievements America has made in the past three hundred years as *their doing?*

All I could sit there and think was...*what the actual* fuck *did I walk into?*

More importantly, what the hell did I bring *River* into?

As if summoned by my thoughts, the sliding of the glass door to the living room opens before gliding shut again. A glance over my shoulder reveals River on the outside with me.

Alone.

Really alone for the first time since the morning he kicked me out of his apartment. Yet even now, I don't think I can count this as completely alone, what with five sets of eager ears ready to dish up whatever dirt we might serve and devour it like starving animals.

One in particular...

His eyes lock onto mine and he lets out a soft sigh, his weight shifting from foot to foot.

I hate that he feels nervous or unsure around me now.

"I came out for some air. Do you mind if I join you?"

The thousands of words I want to say choose that moment to catch in my throat, so I lick my lips and nod towards the empty chair beside me.

After easing down in the chair, silence surrounds us again while we look out at the landscape before us. I can't help but sneak a glance or two at River, watching him as he takes in the mountains like they're the most fascinating thing in the world.

To him, they might be. His love for them is nothing short of obsession.

But the way his hand is twitching against his leg tells me he's also uneasy.

It takes everything in my power to not reach over and take his hand in mine and pull him to me to just…hold him. As if having his hand in mine or him in my arms has the power to erase everything from the past couple months. For the life of me, I wish it did.

"I fucking hate this," he says softly after what seems like an eternity of silence, still looking straight ahead.

"I know it's a lot," I tell him, keeping my eyes trained on the mountains as well. If I look at him…fuck, I'm just not strong enough to see I'm *this* close to him and not be touching him. "And I know you probably have a lot more questions than you do answers since coming out here with me today. But I felt like it was time for you to know…something."

I catch his nod out of my peripheral, but the second he turns his gaze on me, I cave and find myself drowning in two alpine eyes.

"While I agree with you…" he starts, his hand tapping as he searches my face, "…that's not exactly what I meant."

My hand reaches across the space between us without my permission, desperate to reach him. Except when I'm about to feel his skin under mine, he pulls away, casting his gaze back at the mountains.

And the pieces fall together.

He hates *this.* Being here with me.

Or at least, that's my only logical thought until the next words come out of his mouth.

"I miss you," he all but whispers before letting out a long sigh riddled with frustration. Helplessly, I watch as a grimace clouds his features. "And I hate how weak that makes me."

A baseball lodges itself in my throat at his comment and it's at that moment I decide…I'm done hiding. There's no point anymore.

Pulling my chair to sit directly in front of him, I get close enough so our knees are touching and reach for both his hands. I expect him to fight me, to pull away again, like he has been in every facet since we got back from Vail. But instead he surprises me, letting his fingers entwine with mine the second our skin connects.

It's the greatest feeling in the world. The spark that's sent through my body the second we make contact. An adrenaline rush I don't think could ever lessen with time.

Holding his eyes with mine, I rub the back of his hand with my thumb and give him a small smile, knowing he's so much more than what he sees himself as. "It's not weak to miss something. It's weak to be too proud to admit it."

His words from our fight outside Doctor Fulton's office ring in my ears. *Haven't we suffered enough for the sake of your pride?*

Yeah, Abhainn. We have.

"Just know I miss you too."

River shakes his head, leaning back in his chair, but he still keeps his hands in mine. "You say that now, but how am I supposed to believe you? You've been playing this game of hot and cold ever since we got back. I told you, Rain. I can't do it anymore."

His words hit me like a freight train because *of course* he can't. I hardly can blame him for wanting to walk away from me forever. Because what he's saying…it's the truth. How can I expect River to believe a damn word coming out of my mouth when I haven't exactly been consistent in expressing what I want from him?

I let out a sigh and pull our joined hands into my lap, forcing his body back up closer to me. "Abhainn, please believe me. I hate this too. I fucking *miss* you."

Something between a laugh and a scoff leaves his lips before they settle into a slight snarl. "Then why? Just fucking *why*, Rain? Why do you fight me? Why did you keep this from me?" His eyes implore me for honesty, for the truth, just once. "It doesn't have to be this way."

I roll my teeth over my bottom lip. "I know. And please trust me when I say I'm done with it. It's why I brought you here. I don't want to keep shit from you anymore."

I watch the words as they process through his mind, and when he's determined they're genuine, he nods a couple times. "Okay, then tell me."

"What do you mean?" I ask, my brows furrowing.

"You bring me here and have *Roman* share this massive bomb about the history of his family. All their families. Of fucking *Asher's* family, who by the way, I've known just as long as E and Drew and Taylor and I had no clue about any of this." He pauses and I watch his Adam's apple bob as he swallows. "But Roman trusted *you* with this information. You *knew* some of this shit. That's why you pushed to have me here, because you already know about the Enclave and their power."

"I knew some, yeah. But what they told us in there?" I motion to the house with my head where Roman, Asher, and the rest of them are. Probably watching us, discreetly. "Nah, I knew nothing about that shit. I only knew Roman's family has power. A lot of it. And were part of this...organization which held even more of it. What I knew...it was the tip of the iceberg compared to what they shared with us today."

River's lips actually purse as if he's ready to disagree, but thankfully he takes my words at face value. Which is a fuckton more than I deserve at this point. "That might be true, but you pushed him to tell information that isn't yours to share. You're sitting here, saying you don't want to keep shit from me? Instead of getting others to reveal their secrets, why don't you give me some of *yours?*"

I shake my head, biting my lips to keep from doing something stupid, like lashing out at him. Because it's not like I want to lash out. I really don't, least of all at River. Not when I'm trying my damnedest to win back any semblance of trust with him.

But being vulnerable, even with River, who has *never* judged me...it's fucking difficult to say the least. Yet at the same time, he's the person I trust most right now.

I feel River's fingers twitch inside my hands and for a moment, my mind grasps onto that movement and what it means.

And I have to know. What song is playing through his mind right now. What it means, what he's thinking. I won't ask though. Because that's not for me to know anymore. The right for me to ask left the moment I told him he was nothing to me but a place to stick my dick.

So instead, I meet his eyes and ask him something that leaves me open to whatever interrogation he has planned.

"What do you want to know, Abhainn?" I say slowly. Deliberately. Letting the words sink in and preparing myself for the onslaught of his questions.

He's quiet for a minute, just watching my face. For what, I don't know. But once he's decided on a question, his eyes soften into something like sadness. "I wanna know why you felt the need to call *him*? I mean, clearly he has connections and money and that can be helpful…" he trails off with a groan, pressing his forehead into mine. My blood pounds through my veins at the familiarity of the gesture and I swear to God, in this moment, it feels like he's still mine.

His hands squeeze mine as he continues, "I guess the question should be, what does Ted have on you that's made you so afraid? Because you can try to play it off, but I know. I can *see* your fear, baby. I feel it like it's my own."

Releasing River's hands, I run my fingers through my hair and lean back in my seat. I look up at the sky, begging some sort of higher being to help me even know where to fucking start.

At the beginning, dumbass.

So without looking away from the sky fading from yellow to a deep purple, I begin.

"Do you remember anything I told you about a friend of mine dying from drug use? I know I only mentioned it once to you at the cabin, but—"

"I remember," he says softly, and my gaze collides with his once again. "It was the morning I pulled out those joints."

Nodding, I continue. "His name was Deacon. We were friends. Not great, but good enough to enjoy hanging out and shit. It was mostly after Roman and Siena both had left school, our senior year and…"

"Look, man. I don't know what the fuck crawled up your ass, but you need to chill out," Deacon says, his silver eyes boring into mine from across the table. His pupils are already red and half blown to hell from the blunt he smoked in the car on the way here.

And he's pissed I wouldn't light up on the drive over. Which I never do.

I roll my eyes and nod to the coke on the table, thoroughly fucking annoyed with him. He's been a bitch all night, or at least more so than normal. And I'm over it already. "You start off, since you're so fucking impatient."

Truth be told, I'm not in the partying mood at all. But it's his fucking birthday, a whopping eighteen years old, and seeing as he's just about the only person I could call a friend these days, I feel like I owe him at least a couple hours of my time.

Not like anyone else is going to spend a moment or thought on him, even today.

He scoffs and grabs the baggie from the table, popping the ass of the girl firmly planted on his lap to move out of the way. Pouring the powder on the surface, he sets up three lines. Glancing up at me while he does this, he cocks his head.

"Got a bill?"

I scoff right back at him and pull out my wallet, grabbing whatever's on top, handing it over to him to roll. "Never fucking prepared for anything," I grumble under my breath.

Taking the bill from me, he looks at it and shakes his head. "Tossing out Benjamin's for this? Must be nice to be a rich fuck."

I'm not the rich fuck. My stepfather is. And this is his way of keeping me fucking quiet about the shit he did to me as a child. Paying me for my silence.

I don't know what's worse. That he does it or that it works.

But I guess either way, it's better than what Deacon has. The only reason he's even at Foxcroft or I know him is because of what they call the "outreach program," where they pull "inner-city" Philly kids and drop them into this pretentious as fuck environment and expect them to magically fit in.

Spoiler alert—it doesn't fucking work. Deacon here is a perfect example of it.

"Keep it," I tell him, pulling out two more and tossing them onto the table. "One for each line you got out there. And if you can snort 'em faster than I can line mine up, I'll double it."

His eyes widen, and I know he sees right through me. Deacon might be an addict, not unlike me, but he knows how to use money wisely. He has to, since he's the only one who takes care of his little sister, Britton.

So, while that money might be pocket change to me, that's over a month of groceries for the two of them.

"Six hundred?" he asks skeptically.

I glare at him, leaning forward and tossing three more hundreds on the table before grabbing the baggie and pulling it to my side. "Haven't you ever been told not to look a gift horse in the mouth? Call it a birthday present."

He shakes his head and laughs, rolling the original I'd given him. "Okay, okay. You got me." Once he's done rolling to his liking, he nods at the baggie and glances up at me. "Ready when you are."

It's kind of funny how in the zone he is, like I wouldn't blow this little contest on purpose just to make sure he went home with the money. Hell, I'll probably just make it an even grand and call it a day.

"Good luck," I tell him with a smirk. "You're gonna need it."

My throat is hoarse, filled with gravel as I continue. "He didn't even make it through the third line before he was just… gone. Right in front of my fucking eyes."

Scrubbing my hand over my face, I glance up at River to find him watching me. His brows furrow as his gaze tries to read me, his concern written all over his face. One, because I know he's realizing it could very well have been me who died that night.

But also…

"I was the one who tossed him the coke. Fuck, I was the one who *bought* it, though my first clue this was a bad batch was when my dealer dropped the price. It was because the shit was laced with fucking Fentanyl." Guilt washes over me, consuming me for what might be the thousandth time. "I'm the reason he's dead. He never stood a chance."

"You didn't know," River urges, grabbing my hands again, entwining our fingers, and pulling them to his lips. "It wasn't your fault, baby. You had no way of knowing."

I shake my head, unable to speak with all the emotion still clogging my throat.

Thankfully, he doesn't try to argue, just sits with me while I relive that fucking night yet again. The way he dropped to the floor in an instant. Powder flying across the room as I tried to get to him. Shouting for someone to call 911, only to have to do it myself when everyone else scattered.

I doubt there will ever be a day I don't fucking think of it.

After five minutes, the night fading from my mind, I finally gain the courage to speak again.

"The reason I'm telling you this in so much detail is not only because of how it pertains to Ted. It's because it was also my wake up call. Which, yeah, you already know because I had mentioned it in the cabin." I pause, measuring my words as I look him in the eye. "But Abhainn, I need it to be yours too."

His brows furrow for a minute before the recognition begins to sink in.

"I know you're using, Riv," I continue, holding his eyes. "I don't know *what* you're using, how long it's been since you've started, but I can tell. Especially the night at Aiden's party, it was more than obvious."

He bites his lip, guilt consuming his expression, and his eyes drop to our hands. It triggers my memory of the words he told me at the cabin, how we don't need to feel guilty about the way we try to repair ourselves. And he's right. But while coping mechanisms can help, at least in my experience, they also often come in the form of vices. Usually unhealthy in small doses, but in the face of grief or loss…they can cause irreparable damage.

So, at what point do you draw the line and look at the person you love most and finally tell them it's a problem?

"I'm not judging you. I'm the last fucking person to do that, given my past and everything I've told you. And this is gonna come out sounding a thousand percent hypocritical. But I want you to know there are other ways. To deal or cope or escape." I swallow hard and roll my tongue over my teeth. "I'm assuming I was right though? Pharma speedball? Xanax and...?" I trail off, letting him fill in the blanks.

"Adderall," he whispers, pulling his hands from mine to bury his head in them. "Xanax and Adderall. But it was only the one time." A soft groan escapes him, and I wrap my hands around his wrists. "I'm done with it all, though. I fucking swear. The morning after, I threw all of it into the toilet."

I pull, freeing his head so I can see his face. Neither one of us says anything for a minute, we just look at each other. I feel every bit of the shame and self-hatred he feels right now and all I want is to take that away from him.

"I'm not self-important enough to think I'm the only source of your pain and what you were trying to deal with," I murmur, "but I'm sorry for whatever part I played in this."

"It's not just you," he confirms quickly.

My stomach drops, knowing something else is eating him and I wasn't there to help him when he needed it most. If I know him as well as I think I do, only his father could cause the torment he's carrying around. To the point he thought using was the answer.

His teeth sink into his bottom lip and my eyes track the movement. It's written all over his face, the way he's grasping at straws to keep himself together.

"You can tell me when you're ready, Abhainn. *If* you're ever ready. Just know I'm sorry for keeping the truth from you and for saying all the awful shit. For making this worse. You have to know I was just trying to protect you."

"But why do you feel this need to protect me? Why couldn't you just tell me and we could figure it out? That's what I don't get."

I smirk. "Have you met you? You're probably the most

stubborn person I've ever met. And on top of that, the most selfless. Neither of which is necessarily a bad thing. But if I told you everything that was going on, the truth behind it all, you wouldn't be willing to leave my side."

"And that's a bad thing?"

"No." I chuckle. "But we both know you'd be willing to take the bullet for someone else. And I was terrified it could come to that. Because I know that's something Ted would be capable of doing."

"And circling back to him…" he says, his eyes searching mine, "where does he fit in with what happened to Deacon?"

Right. Ted and Deacon.

Gathering my thoughts, I sigh. "After I called the police, I made the idiotic decision to stay with Deacon. So, I was there when they arrived, sitting next to a dead body with what used to be a bag full of blow pretty much everywhere due to the commotion when people scrambled to leave. And between the coke and the weed he had in my car, there was easily enough there to get me on possession and paraphernalia charges. And then there was the whole…dead body situation."

River's eyes widen as the wheels turn in his mind. "So, he paid off the cops and you weren't arrested."

"If only." I laugh. "I was arrested and spent the night in jail. Released the next day, thanks to Ted, of course, with a court date set to handle the possession and paraphernalia charges. But Pennsylvania also has a charge relating to drug-induced homicide, and they were slapping me with that too. Since I was the one who supplied the cocaine. With all of that together, there could have been a prison sentence for up to forty years.

242 | CE RICCI

"So, we went through the arraignment and all the legal shit to get court dates set. But then it all just disappeared. The charges were dismissed and the case tabled, probably indefinitely. And my life went back to normal like it never fucking happened."

"He paid off the *judge?*" River asks, clearly in disbelief.

"Yeah, along with a bunch of other people, I'm sure. How this shit never made the paper or the news, I'm not sure. I don't know all the details, only that Ted was up for reelection and was willing to do whatever it took to save face." I smirk and roll my eyes. "Can't exactly portray the happy family man to the voters if his eighteen-year-old stepson is sent to prison, right?"

River blinks a few times and shakes his head, still processing. "And he just got away with it. Like he's getting away with what he did to you." It's a statement, not a question.

Biting the inside of my cheek, I nod. "Yes, but that's because of the deal we made."

He shoots me a look. "What kind of deal, and more importantly, *why?*"

"I didn't really have a choice in the matter." I sigh, scrubbing my hand over my face. "He paid off whoever to keep the whole mess quiet and in repayment for *his generosity,* I needed to keep my mouth shut about what happened between the two of us while I was younger. And if I refused, he wouldn't stop them from locking me up for life."

"So you're telling me, and correct me if I'm wrong…" he says, "…he blackmailed you into staying quiet about the fact he raped you? Repeatedly? For *years?*"

I nod. "Yup."

"And you just *went along with it?*"

"It was that or spend my life behind bars, Riv. Obviously it was the least desirable option. Because even though I feel a shit ton of guilt for what happened, I'm not the one who actually killed Deacon. So, what was I supposed to do?"

River sighs, raking his hand through his hair. "I don't know. That's just…fucked."

"You're telling me." Leaning back in my chair, I look up at the darkening sky. "That's why I was so afraid. Now since this all has come out about what a sick, twisted bastard he is, I'm worried he's going to make good on his threats. Find a way to send me to prison for what happened years ago."

"Isn't there a law against that sort of thing? You can't be tried for the same crime twice?"

"Yeah, but I was never tried. The case was never closed, the charges against me just dismissed."

"Shit," he mumbles under his breath, his head hanging. "So you could still get put away for this?"

"Maybe? I'm not sure, honestly. I'm sure he would find a way. He always manages to make shit work for him, always getting what he wants from whoever might be standing in his path. Not giving a fuck about the collateral he creates." I sigh, rolling my head against the back of the chair. "He's ruthless in his attempt to crawl his way to power when the people who deserve to be there, deserve *good* things in life, are the ones he crushes in his palm on the way up."

"*Some rise by sin and some by virtue fall,*" he repeats the words inked into my skin, his eyes search mine. "You were just trying to protect me."

I nod solemnly. "It's all I ever wanted, River. You have to believe I never planned for it to come this far. For the way I hurt you — and I know I have — whether you deny it or not. I just hope you can forgive me one day. Start over and actually manage to…" I trail off, the words catching in my throat.

"I want that too," he whispers softly, knowing my thoughts I can't speak. "But how do we come back from this? Is it even possible?"

"I don't know," I tell him honestly. "I hope we can. Because back in the cabin? Where no one could touch us? Fuck, Abhainn, we were everything."

He nods in agreement, glancing up at the stars now shining brightly in the deep blue night sky. "We just royally fucked it up somewhere along the way."

He says we, but in reality, I'll take all the blame here. Every bit of it belongs on my shoulders. My cross to bear.

We're silent for a while after that, and I can tell by the way his hand is tapping, he's got a song. But I won't ask. Not when I told him I wouldn't anymore.

"'My Heart I Surrender,' I Prevail," he whispers, reading my mind.

And the words make *my* heart ache.

"For what it's worth, I wish I could take it all back. Everything that happened these past couple months." A sad laugh slips out and I shake my head. "I wish we never left the cabin. Because I can't remember a time I've ever been that happy."

He bites his lip and nods again, his eyes shining as he clears his throat. "Me either, baby. Me either."

EIGHTEEN
Rain

Slamming my door closed, I immediately head over to the couch and flop onto the cushions. This entire week since going up to Asher's estate has been complete and utter shit, packed full of midterms. Studying and college is the furthest thing on my goddamn mind right now, seeing as my crazy step-father is trying to flip my life upside down and even with enlisting the Enclave's help, it doesn't feel like we've made much progress at all.

It seems Kaede was wrong to assume it'd be easy to lure Ted out of the shadows because this week has passed and they've come up with absolutely *nothing*. They followed me around themselves discreetly as a secondary surveillance, but didn't catch anyone lurking around. The only person they'd see regularly is the FBI agent assigned to me to keep an eye out, which isn't abnormal at this point. I've grown accustomed to his presence.

But having no leads as to where he is or what his plans are, even with how much power is in the Enclave…it's frustrating.

I don't understand how the only new information we have didn't come through our own efforts but was delivered by Ted himself. Well, or someone he hired. But from the note my mother sent to Doctor Fulton, all his bank accounts and stocks have been frozen pending investigation.

I know you probably don't want to hear a thing I have to say, but just know this. He's getting desperate, Ciaráin. He sees you as the source of all his problems, with the law, and for losing his money. But he also sees you as the solution.

As she went on to explain to me in detail what she thinks he's after, I realize my family has so many more secrets than I knew. Because this was the first time I was hearing about a trust, my father set up for me as a kid, one my grandparents handled after he died.

And most importantly, neither my mother nor Ted could touch the funds. Which probably pissed them both the fuck off when they found out about it.

My mother sent the account information in her letter, everything I needed to access it.

My bet is Ted knows about my trust and is going to do everything in his power to extort money out of me. Enough to flee the country and live the rest of his life comfortably on some fucking island in the Caribbean. Hell, even my mother alluded to it in her letter.

I'd never dream of telling you what to do with this money. But darling, if he does come looking for you for a payday, I hope you consider handing over as much as he wants. In the end, I think it would beat the alternative.

Honestly, I'd give him the entire thing if I knew it would keep his mouth shut and he would disappear from my life forever. The problem is…I know he won't believe me if I tell him that's all I want.

He won't stop until I'm silenced for good. I can just *feel* it.

The door being pushed open brings me back from my thoughts, not at all surprised to find Roman walking into the apartment. Even after all the shit, I can only be grateful he convinced his brothers and fellow legacies to share more information on the Enclave with us than probably anyone outside the organization knows.

But when I glance up at his face, I know immediately he doesn't have good news.

Tossing a manila envelope on my chest, he heads into the kitchen and immediately pours himself a glass of whiskey, downing it faster than I've ever seen him drink a glass of water. Grabbing it off my chest, I flip it around and start opening the damn thing, speaking as I do.

"I take it this isn't any intel you've gathered," I state dryly.

"It was taped to the door when I got here," he tells me, pouring himself another glass of whiskey.

I pull out a stack of those massive photos, the same kind Ted sent previously, tension and unease settling throughout my body. And for good reason, because when I turn them over and begin flipping through them, I realize they're so much worse than the others.

First, an image of River and I outside in the quad at school. From the look on my face, it's clearly the day River was asking why I felt the need to bring Roman here. I can tell from the light snow dusting the grass. It's concerning that Ted was walking around on campus but it's not the end of the world. I could just be talking to a friend, right?

The second one is an image of the two of us again, this time outside Doctor Fulton's office in the middle of the argument we had there that morning. I remember it vividly. Analyzing the photo, I spot my hand on River's arm. Which is slightly more concerning, yes. But again, I can't say I'm surprised he's been tailing me over the past few months. And friends can grab each other's arms to stop them from walking.

The moment I flip to the third, panic begins to set in. Again, the image is of two of us. This time we're in front of my apartment building and my palms are cupping his cheeks, our foreheads pressed together in a way that screams of intimacy. It's the day River finally spoke up for himself, saying he was done for good. And the way we're holding onto each other...there's no way Ted didn't know right then and there he'd hit the fucking jackpot.

Fuck.

I must've said it aloud because Roman is by my side in an instant, his hands wordlessly reaching for the stack. I give him the first two and let him look at the third before flipping to the next one.

At this point, I don't know why I bother to keep going, except I'm a damn masochist. Because it's the fourth one that makes me want to vomit. It's just me this time, but it's from the morning after I went to River's apartment. After I spent the night and he kicked me out. I'm walking down the steps outside his building, heading to my Jeep parked on the street.

He followed me to River's apartment.

Flipping to the last one, I find a zoomed in shot of the previous photo, focusing on a window of the apartment building. It takes me a second to realize River is standing in it, watching me leave.

And the amount of anguish on his face, I can feel it even through the grainy photograph.

My chest vibrates as I realize Ted's purpose for sending me these.

He knows where River lives. I lead the goddamn way.

And now he wants me to know he has the leverage he needs to get whatever he wants.

He sure as fuck does too, because I'd do anything for River. *Give* anything up for him. It's why I was so adamant about staying away from him until all this bullshit is behind us.

Except I failed. Meaning…I put us through all this shit for no fucking reason. Ted found my weakness anyway. More than that, I basically handed River over to him on a silver platter by not realizing the pull between the two of us is more powerful than sheer will. We're magnetic, two opposites pulling at one another until we cave and snap together.

Glancing over at Roman, I can see he's put the pieces together too from the somber expression on his face.

We sit there together in silence for I don't know how long, this new revelation weighing heavily in the air.

"What do we do now?" I finally ask him, the words catching slightly in my throat. I'm raw with emotion, knowing Ted could be outside River's apartment right now.

Fuck.

I rise to my feet and immediately Roman is grabbing my arm. My eyes snap to his and I feel like a caged animal.

"Whatever you're thinking of doing, which I know is going to River's," he says slowly, releasing my arm. "Don't do it. You'll only play into his hand, feeding him your panic."

"He's got my fucking panic," I hiss, stepping toward the door. Only Roman catches my arm again and I'm a second away from ripping the damn thing off his body.

"I understand, but you need to calm down and think. He doesn't know without a doubt River means anything to you. But you going over there right now on the edge of hysteria?" Roman shakes his head and sighs. "It shows every card you have in your hand, Rain. Which is exactly what he wants."

Biting my lip, I curse under my breath. He's right. This is why I have him here. In addition to his training and connections, he's got a knack for thinking clearly when I'm not.

"Fine," I mutter, digging my phone from the pocket of my sweatshirt, finding River's contact and pressing the call button.

Unlike the last time I was in this position, River answers on the second ring and I immediately breathe a sigh of relief.

He's safe.

"Rain?" he asks when I don't say anything at first.

Clearing my throat, I try to figure out what to say because *hey* seems like the wrong move in a situation like this. Far too calm and collected. That's what I end up going with though, before I sit here in silence with him on the line long enough he might think I accidentally pocket-dialed him.

"What's going on?" he asks.

Sighing, I walk toward my bedroom to talk to him in private. A quick glance over at Roman and I find him dialing someone on his own phone, pacing the length of my kitchen island with his whiskey glass in hand.

"Do you trust me?" I ask, ignoring his question altogether.

There's a long silence on the other end of the line while I wait for him to respond. And I'd be lying if every second he let pass wasn't a stab to my heart.

"Sometimes," he finally says, and at this point, I'll take it as a win.

Sitting down on my bed, I rest my elbows on my knees and sigh into the phone. "Ted contacted me again tonight. Pictures, like last time."

I hear River's soft intake of breath from the other line. "Of what this time?"

"Recent pictures. Of us. Fighting, mostly. At school in the quad, outside Fulton's office," I tell him, my voice hoarse. "The day outside my apartment."

I focus on his breathing in the other line. "Okay, more pictures. I don't see the big deal."

"There's more," I groan, pinching the bridge of my nose.

Goddamn, I wish I could have managed to keep him out of this. Nothing happening right now has a fucking thing to do with him other than he and I having this obsession with each other neither of us can seem to break free from.

"There was one of me leaving your apartment, the morning after we…" I trail off, not wanting to think about the last time we had sex. "It was right when you kicked me out. Which yeah, he was following me. But he knows it's *your apartment.*"

"How?"

"Because he sent one zoomed in on your window. Of you watching me leave."

River goes quiet again, processing the information I'm giving him.

"He knows where you are, mo grá. It's not safe for you to stay there anymore."

A soft laugh escapes him. "And where do you suggest I go? My mom's? I'm sure that'd go over really well when she asks *why* I need to stay there."

"Stay here."

Apprehension is present in his voice when he asks, "With Roman there too?"

Well, when he puts it like that...

"Then I'll come stay there with you," I plead, needing him to give me something here. "Just for the night, and then once your last midterm is over tomorrow you can go wherever you were planning to go for spring break."

I hear a light knock come from my bedroom door and my eyes snap to the door, finding Roman stepping through it into my room.

"Yeah?" I ask him, moving the phone away from my mouth.

"I called Kaede, just to give him an update. He thinks…" he trails off, glancing at the phone in my hand, "…you and River and I all need to stay up at Asher's estate. At least for the next week. It should be enough time for us to get a real protection game plan together for when you get back for the last bit of the semester since Ted is being a lot more slippery than anticipated."

My jaw ticks, knowing the likelihood of River agreeing to this are slim to none. Giving Roman a quick nod, he goes to leave the room. Presumably to get his shit, because the look on his face tells me he wants to get up there as soon as we can.

Moving the phone back, I sigh into the receiver. "Did you catch any of that?"

A groan. "Yes. The real question is do I have a choice in this matter?"

I laugh a little because he wouldn't be River if he didn't put up some sort of a fight. "Normally, I'd say yes. But this is the furthest thing from normal circumstances, Abhainn." I swallow, slightly nervous he still won't care enough to listen. "Please come stay up there with me next week."

"Because five weeks in the mountains already this year wasn't enough?" he grumbles, but there's a slightly playful tone in his voice.

No, mo grá. It would never have been enough. I'd have been happy staying in the cabin for the rest of our lives.

And somehow, even in this fucking situation, I manage a smile. "Clearly not. I think we need one more, don't you?"

More silence, but thank God, he relents. "Okay. I'll text Asher for the address and meet you up there tomorrow after my test."

Ice runs through my veins. "But what about tonight? And tomorrow during the day? You can't be alone. *River,*" I say his name on a plea.

"Relax. I'll call Elliott or Drew to come stay here tonight. And Elliott has a final at the same time in the same building." He pauses and I hear the slight smile in his voice. "I'll leave straight from there. I won't be alone except for the drive up."

Even knowing that still has me on edge. I'd rather be the one with him the entire time, so I can see for myself he's not in harm's way. But I'm afraid if I push, he'll pull back again and refuse to come at all.

"Okay, but you're on the phone with someone all the way up to the estate."

"Yes, Mom," he says sarcastically, making me chuckle as he says goodbye and disconnects the call.

And then I'm stuck sitting here, amidst all this chaos and insanity, with only one thought on my mind.

Fuck, I love him.

NINETEEN
River

"Even after all these years, I still can't believe you like pineapple on pizza."

My eyes flash up to Elliott sitting on the other side of the couch, my slice of heaven paused right in front of my mouth. "Are you planning to make fun of my choice of toppings until one of us dies?"

He grins, grabbing another slice of his plain-ass pepperoni pizza and biting into it. "Way to make it fucking morbid, jackass."

I laugh and flip him off. "You asked for it when you dissed me for being higher evolved."

"Sure if that's what you wanna call it," he shakes his head, still grinning when I shove my pizza in my mouth, chewing to my heart's content. And it feels great to just exist again, knowing everything with Rain, while it's not perfect by any stretch of the imagination...it feels like it might be mending.

I know I don't need Rain to be happy. I'd find it again after I managed to crawl out of the hole I was digging for myself when not only my relationship with him, but also my parents, came crashing down around me. There's not a doubt in my mind I wouldn't eventually bounce back, just with a few years taken off the lifespan of my liver.

And as miserable as he's made me, he's also given me the happiest moments in my life. Like I told Doctor Fulton, the view at the top of the mountain is worth it, even if it's hard to breathe.

Elliott relaxes back into the couch after he finishes off the rest of his pizza, cocking his head, he gives me an analytical look I'm not too sure I want to try to deduce.

"What made you call me to come over?"

I furrow my brow. "I can't ask you to come over for pizza and to study for a final?"

"Yeah, you can. But you usually invite both of us," he says, meaning both him and Drew. He pauses, narrowing his eyes at me again. "And honestly? You haven't really *been here*. Not really, I mean. Ever since you came back from Vail."

I sigh, leaning back against the cushion. "I know. I was going through some shit."

Understatement of the century.

"Understandable. And I don't blame you for dealing with it in your own way. But fuck, man. You scared the hell out of us. When I walked into the basement at Aiden's party…" he trails off, flashing me with a sympathetic stare. "I don't know what I thought. I just hated seeing you like that so I had to do something."

"I don't remember much about the entire night," I say

honestly. The only thing I remember for certain was kissing Rain in the bathroom upstairs after I'd taken the pills.

"It's probably better for you that you don't."

The truth is written all over his face too. I don't want to know or remember a goddamn thing after going back downstairs from my run-in with Rain. Whatever I got myself into, it's probably best left unsaid.

Elliott continues to eye me as I finish eating. "Have you seen him at all since?"

Biting my lip, I decide to go for honesty. "Yeah. I saw him this weekend."

He flashes me a disappointed glare and I don't know why I let it make me feel guilty. Probably just because he wants what's best for me. Taylor is the same way, sometimes even Drew. "*Why? River, why would you do that to yourself when you know he's with Roman?*"

Realizing what he thinks by the word *saw,* my eyes widen and I shake my head. "No, no. Not like that. We just talked." But I wince and rub the back of my neck, knowing how that one sounds too.

He continues to study me with furrowed brows, wearing a look that says *really?*

"I swear, E. We haven't…" I trail off, shaking my head. *Do not start lying to your best friends.* "It hasn't been like that for a while."

"So, you haven't fucked him since you've been back from Vail." He says it as a statement, not a question, and I have to keep myself from laughing that he'd automatically assume I top only.

"Only his face," I reply on instinct, which earns me a sour

look and an eye roll.

But hey, at least it's not a lie. Technically speaking, Rain fucked *me* at my apartment.

"Damnit, Riv," he groans, but there's a smile on the edge of his lips. "You're such a fucking child sometimes. Always in the middle of serious moments."

"I can be serious, asshole." I toss a balled-up napkin at him. "Life's just too short to be filled with heavy bullshit."

Elliott nods, but I can tell he's just placating me. Frankly, I'm a little glad he is. I've had enough of the heavy. Enough heartache and misery in twenty-one short years to last a lifetime. And I'm done drowning in it, letting it pull me under into a depressing cycle of sadness and despair.

It's not who I am, and it's not who I want to be. I wanna be me again. Happy. Carefree. Wild.

I wanna fucking live. And I sure as hell deserve those things just like everyone else.

So, I don't care if Elliott or Taylor or anyone else judges me for it. I'm going after what makes me happy. Digging in and getting what I want. What makes me glad to be living each day.

And Rain… he's all that for me. No matter how sideways things have gone for us in the past and no matter how we seem to hurt each other.

He's the oxygen.

And he makes me feel alive.

The next morning Elliott and I head to our last exams before break and I have to admit, even though midterms are here, I have so much catching up to do to make sure I pass some of my classes with cumulative finals at the end of next month.

Which…is all of them.

In short, I'm really regretting fucking around the first couple months of this semester.

That's not the only thing putting my anxiety on full alert today as we walk across campus though. I'm also just paranoid. Ever since I got off the phone with Rain yesterday, I feel it. And while I don't think Ted would make a move against me with other people around or in public, I'm still uneasy.

But then again, why would Ted see me as a target at all?

The only decent conversation Rain and I have had was at Asher's house this past weekend, where I finally learned the truth about Ted and Rain and Roman and just…why this entire situation is even happening in the first place.

We haven't spoken much, other than fighting, that is, since we were at the cabin.

I almost want to laugh when I think about it. Both of us used to hate it when we were so in sync with each other at all times. On the field and off. It made hating each other nearly impossible and falling for him…instant.

But now the only place we can seem to be on the same wavelength anymore is when we're surrounded by the wilderness. Like the mountains are a sort of cathartic communication tool for us or something.

Those are the thoughts rolling through my mind as I sit through my exam instead of the damn material I studied for the past week in hopes to cram enough information into my brain to squeak by with a passing grade.

It doesn't bode well for me passing the damn thing, but at this rate, how can I focus on anything other than secret societies and rampaging rapists and Ciaráin fucking Grady?

Groaning, I speed through the rest of the test because I've wasted most of the time daydreaming. At least some of the answers were completely obvious to me and I had a one in four chance of guessing the correct answer on the stuff I didn't know.

Thank God for multiple choice.

My focus is nowhere to be found when I step out of the classroom again, almost walking right past Elliott leaning against the wall talking to a girl I think I've seen before. She's cute, dark hair and glasses wearing a Tri-Delta shirt and I realize that's probably how I've seen her before if she lives in the sorority house.

"You ready to head out? I've got places I need to be," I tell him, cocking my head.

He rolls his eyes and gives the girl a smile before kissing her on the cheek. "I'll see you later," he whispers before returning his attention to me. "Yes, Captain Buzzkill. I'm ready to escort your spoiled ass to your chariot."

My forehead creases. "Captains have ships, not chariots."

Lips form into a thin line as he glares. "Remember when I said I missed the old you? Yeah, I lied."

I grin. "You love it and you know it."

"No, I truly hate you sometimes."

"Two sides, same coin," I singsong, pushing open the door into the warming late-March air and heading toward my car.

"You're really going up into the mountains with him again for another ten days?" Elliott asks skeptically, raising his brow as he stops at my vehicle. "Don't you think it sounds like a terrible fucking idea?"`

I laugh and shake my head, not bothering to explain the truth behind the situation. It's not my truth to tell, after all. So instead I give him a shrug. "What's the worst that can happen? It's not like I can fall in love with him a second time."

His eyes flash with a hint of sadness. "You're setting yourself up for failure, Len."

I lean back against my car door and tilt my head to study him. "If you go into something with that thought process, sure. But I'm not gonna do that."

"Then what are you gonna do?"

Sighing, I adjust my hat. "Honestly? I just have to go into this reminding myself of what he and I are to each other. It's the easiest way for me to be around him now without feeling like I'm being ripped apart."

"But isn't it a sign you should just…not be around him? Why put yourself through it?"

"Because I'm a fucking masochist?" I laugh, though it's not really all that funny.

He gives me a look. "Just be careful, okay? Let me know when you get there."

I can't help but roll my eyes. Jesus, when did he become so protective? "Yes, *Taylor.*"

He smirks, his blue eyes dancing. "We all know I'm much better looking than that shithead."

Biting my lip, I grin harder, knowing it's always a competition with Elliott. Must come with being a twin or sibling so close in age. He just wants to compete against all of us.

Yanking open the door to my car, I'm halfway inside the vehicle when Elliott grabs the door to keep me from closing it.

"What are you and Grady to each other? Now, I mean?"

Tapping my hand on the steering wheel, I roll the options around in my mind before settling on the closest thing to the truth. The only conclusion I can arrive at that seems accurate.

"At this point?" I shrug, gripping the handle of the door. "We're the greatest almost."

TWENTY

River

DAY ONE: FRIDAY

Pulling my bag from the back seat, I slam the door to my Rover and glance up at Asher's mansion on the cliff side. I still can't believe *this* is his house. After knowing him for ten years, I guess I never knew him at all. The real him. He lived a double life none of us had any clue about.

Stepping up to the front door, I pause with my fist raised and debate on knocking, seeing as I don't live here. But they know I'm coming to stay here so…

The choice is taken from me when the door opens and Asher stands on the other side, smirking at me when he sees my raised fist. "I win," he calls over his shoulder, to which I hear one of the other guys curse.

A second later, Callum comes rounding the corner. He smooths back his blond hair and studies me. Still with my fist raised in the air like an idiot.

I drop it immediately.

"What did you win?"

"A bet." Asher smirks again before glancing to Cal. "He thought you'd walk in like the rest of them do. But I know you well enough to know you'd stop and knock."

Okay. Seems like a ridiculous thing to make a bet for.

"What'd you win?"

Asher's grin grows. "A yacht."

My eyes widen. "A *yacht?*"

Callum rolls his eyes. "*My* yacht, specifically. Because the dickface apparently can't go buy his own."

I blink a couple times to wrap my head around this, but honestly, I wouldn't know what it's like to be able to bet yachts for something as stupid as me knocking on a door.

Must be nice to have more money than Bill Gates.

Asher chuckles and lets me through as Callum heads back toward the living room, grumbling something about fair wagers under his breath, which only makes Asher laugh harder.

"It wasn't really fair, you know," I tell him as I follow him to what I'm assuming is the room I'll be staying in.

"I know." He shrugs, leaving it at that.

Asher continues down the hall of the east wing and opens one of the many doors to a bedroom that's apparently mine for the course of the next ten days. At least it looks that way because the massive king bed is freshly made up in this insanely opulent room. It's hard to believe he grew up in a place like this, filled with furniture and decor and all this *shit* that costs more than probably a thousand of Roman's stupid fucking Lamborghinis.

It's all fine and dandy, but I don't really notice much else because I'm already on edge. I can feel Rain's presence, even in this massive house with what could be thousands of square feet between us.

Hopefully this room is on the opposite side of the place from his and not, say, directly next to it. But I'm not about to ask where it is. I don't need a reason to go looking for it.

"Thanks, man," I tell him as I set my bag on the bed.

"'Course, Len," he says, using my old nickname. "That's what friends are for, right?"

I nod, feeling the sincerity in his tone.

"I'm gonna let you get settled," he tells me with a glance over his shoulder as he heads to the door. "But I'll be back in the living room getting the title of my new yacht signed over if you need anything."

I laugh and shake my head. "Sounds good, Ash."

He grins and walks away and I'm glad to have someone so chill on my side and helping with this entire fucking mess that is Senator Ted Anders. Not that it's even *my* mess. But at least he's someone I trust. Definitely a fuckton more than the rest of them, Roman most of all.

A knock on the open bedroom door pulls my attention and my eyes raise to meet Roman's deep hazel green.

Think of the devil and he shall appear, it seems.

He stares at me for a moment, his eyes dancing over me, and I try not to flinch under his scrutiny.

"Roman," I grind out, taking in his probably three thousand dollar suit he's wearing just because he can. "What can I do for you?"

He shakes his head, a deep chuckle leaving him as he practically sneers at me. "Not much, River. There's not a damn thing you can do for me. Or anyone else here, it seems."

Ouch.

Rolling my shoulders, I take a deep, calming breath so I don't lose my shit within the first ten minutes of being here. "What do you *want* then? Is that the better question?"

Running his tongue across his teeth, he steps into the room. He stalks toward me like an animal hunting their prey, looking for the perfect opportunity to attack. "It's all about asking the right questions. Something you'll learn quickly during the short amount of time you're here."

So we're playing mind games. Awesome.

"Why don't you just tell me whatever you came here to tell me and leave me in peace, yeah? Because you clearly don't want to be around me, so why waste more time in my presence than you have to?"

Roman grins wickedly, a sick gleam to his eyes as he continues to study me. "Figuring it out so quickly already. I must admit I'm impressed. Slightly, that is."

I bite my tongue, letting the taste of blood keep me calm.

But it seems my silence only serves to infuriate him more.

"Let me make this perfectly fucking clear by spelling it out for you," he hisses, eyes hard and cold. "You're right, I don't want you here. The only reason it's even being *considered* is because Rain is the most important person to me outside the Enclave and you happen to be one of Asher's former...*friends.* So make no mistake, you're here out of obligation, not out of want or need.

I'm simply here to remind you of your place."

I glare at him, cocking my head because I see right through this bullshit just like I did with Rain. "Feeling threatened, are we Roman?"

He smirks, shaking his head. "You know what I do with threats, little *Abhainn?*" he says, emphasizing my nickname from Rain. He steps closer to me, raising his hand to my face and trails the back of his knuckles over my cheek.

And as much as I don't want to, I shudder under the touch. Because it's cold and manipulative. Fitting for him, I suppose.

I straighten, doing my best to portray a level of confidence I just don't feel. "I have a feeling you're gonna tell me."

He bares his teeth, and paired with his wicked tongue sharp enough to kill, the hunter goes for the jugular.

"I *eliminate* them."

Staring at the ceiling, I debate and war with myself. To get up and leave. Go back to Boulder, maybe stay with Mom for the rest of the semester. Only, I don't want to endanger her or Willow if Ted is really following me too. Which he is, according to the images Rain showed me.

They're the only reason I agreed to come here in the first place, paired with Rain's level of concern for me being unusually high. It's why I let myself be convinced this was a good idea.

I can firmly say I was deadass wrong because I'm more miserable right now than I've been the past few months. I toss and turn, my mind running a million miles an hour despite the exhaustion overwhelming the rest of me. To the point where I have to will my body to stay in this damn bed and just *go to sleep.*

But for the life of me, I can't.

All I can think about is *him*, just on the opposite side of the house where we tip-toed around each other today. Not out of necessity, but because the dynamic is different now. It's not just the two of us alone in a cabin. It's seven in a mansion.

But it doesn't keep my mind from latching onto him being in his bed, warding off nightmares for another night.

The protective side, the side that cares too much for people... he hurts for Rain. It's why I spent countless nights on the floor of the cabin in Vail. Because I fucking care. I *care* about him.

No, you love *him.*

A laugh escapes me.

Yeah, that too.

Groaning, I slide out of bed and find a pair of athletic shorts, slipping them on before padding out of my room, down the hall of the East wing and through the foyer. I'm almost to the hallway of the West wing where Rain is staying when I notice a dim light coming from the living room.

Curiosity peaked, I turn and head in that direction, momentarily forgetting the destination I originally had in mind. Honestly, it might be best to see who it is. Last thing I want is to be caught sneaking around the other side of the house in the middle of the night, trying to figure out which room is Rain's.

The second I step into the kitchen, I find Asher sitting at the massive island, a bowl of cereal in front of him. Such a strange, human thing to see someone who holds as much power and control as he does, only to have more in a few years.

Then again, until recently, I only ever saw him as a regular guy like Elliott and Drew and T.

Glancing up from his bowl, he spots me and nods once in a way of greeting. "Couldn't sleep?"

"Something like that," I mutter, walking over and sliding into one of the bar stools beside him. My fingers tap against the smooth stone of the countertop and I hear Asher chuckle from beside me.

"Still doing that?" he asks, motioning to my hand.

I give him a wry grin, feeling a little better now that the ice seems to have been broken between us. "Some things never change."

His expression sobers slightly, but he still has a smile on his face. "True. But plenty of things do too."

He's got a point, of course. Just look at the friendship he and I had back as kids versus now. Sure, he was never *as* close or integrated with the group, but he was a year older and from our view, a lot "cooler" than us. It didn't help that his parents were strict as hell about who he could see, when he could hang out, and literally *never* let his friends come over.

Clearing my throat, I glance over at him as he continues to eat, wondering how fucking lonely it must've been for him, growing up in this giant house, just him and his parents. No friends over, no siblings to hang out with.

It's surprising he's not socially inept, to be honest.

"I guess you get it now," he says, meeting my eyes. "Why I never fit with the rest of you."

I shrug because, yeah, it's obvious. "We wouldn't have

thought any differently of you for having this much money, Ash. You know none of us care about your money, power, or whatever."

His brows furrow as he pushes his bowl away from him. "I couldn't have told you, Riv. It's called a *secret society* for a reason, though most of us loathe the term all together."

Wait, but…

"I don't understand," I say slowly, my face showing my confusion. "Roman told Rain about—"

"Roman is an idiot who doesn't know how to follow a fucking rule to save his goddamn life," Ash snaps. "But that's what happens when your father is the Grand Elector. I'm just glad Roman isn't going to be ours. Another Mitchell in charge would be a damn shitshow."

A smile plays at my lips seeing him share a little bit of animosity for the guy who is supposed to be like a brother to him. "You'd be good at it," I tell him, remembering the way he would always lead the four of us around as kids, like a pack of puppies following a parent.

He lets a low chuckle out and shakes his head. "Nah, man. I'll leave that shit for Kaede. He's made for it. It's bad enough I'm being groomed for *politics* for fuck's sake. There's no way in hell I'd wanna be in charge of the Enclave too."

"Then why do it at all?"

He frowns at me. "The politics?"

"No," I shake my head. "*This.* The Enclave. All of it. If you're so unhappy, why not just…" I trail off, searching for the right word. "…quit? Leave?"

A smirk crosses his face like I've said the funniest thing in the world. "You say it as if we have a choice. As if each of us haven't thought about that exact thing more than once." He pauses and bobs his head back and forth in thought. "Except Kaede. He's old school Enclave through and through, family and country above all else. But the rest of us?" He shakes his head and sighs. "We might be built and trained and taught to live this lifestyle, but we're still human at the end of the day. We have wants and dreams outside the life we've been forced into by birthright."

"But leaving isn't an option," I repeat, raising a brow. "Even if all of you want it? I don't get it. Disband, dismantle, whatever you wanna call it. You guys should be able to live the life you want like everyone else."

Another laugh. "Spoken like a true idealist, Len. If it were that simple, I'd like to think we'd come to an agreement. I know for certain Roman and I are on the same page and honestly, Hollis probably wouldn't give a fuck either way because that's just who he is. Callum will do whatever anyone else does because heaven forbid he make a decision on his own. And yeah, while Kaede might be by the book and shit, there are days I think even he second guesses this entire thing."

He picks up his spoon and twirls it around in the milk remaining in the bowl, clearly lost in his thoughts. "It doesn't matter though, because it's not enough to break the cycle, even though it should be from the outside. Nothing is ever as easy as it seems. As effortless as you might wish it to be." He bites his lip and sighs again before rising from his seat to dump his bowl. "It's the life we were dealt. Hoping for anything different would just be wishing on a starless sky."

My chest tightens for him, hearing the sound of defeat in his voice. "Sometimes it really is that simple though, Ash."

He shrugs. "It's almost a millennia of history you're talking about just tossing away. And for what? A few selfish, entitled rich kids to go off and *yolo* the hell out of their lives? Attempt to find happiness when, let's face it, do any of us even know what that looks like?" His eyes latch onto mine, trying to get me to understand. "At the end of the day, no matter how much we hate it, how much we don't want this life, if we don't do it, who will? If we don't stand for the people who don't have a voice and try to make this country, this *world,* a better and safer place, who will?"

When you put it like that…

"Sacrificing your own happiness for the sake of power and control seems like a lonely way to live the only life you're given."

"Would you put *his*," he says, pointing toward the West wing of the house, "happiness above your own? Do anything in the world to give it to him, even if it meant sacrificing your own?"

In a heartbeat.

My answer must be written all over my face because Ash just nods. "This is just like that, Riv. Only on a much larger scale."

"And for billions of people you don't owe *shit* to, Ash. It's different than doing it for someone you love."

I clamp my lips shut the second the word slips free, but he just laughs.

"You're not fooling anyone here, man. Roman included, though I'm starting to wonder if he's just fucking delusional, thinking he has a chance in hell at getting Rain. It's obvious from the way you two look at each other…" He chuckles and shakes his head, letting his thought trail off. "Shit, if I believed in a thing like true love, I'd say you and him are the real fucking deal. If you can manage to figure your shit out."

I smirk because while he puts up a good front, I know there's gotta be a piece of him that's able to love and be loved like everyone deserves. "If it's coming from your mouth, it must be true."

Grinning, he laughs before filling up a glass of water. "Romance isn't my area of expertise. Clearly. But when two people are as in tune with each other as you two are? And that I've noticed from just a few encounters?" His eyes lock on mine and he raises his shoulder. "I dunno, man. To me, it's dangerous. The idea that someone can have so much control over you. But for whatever reason, people want that in their lives."

I snort. "God help the poor girl who ends up hitched to your sorry ass wagon."

He smirks. "Ever the romantic."

We're quiet after that, but I don't feel the need to fill the silence. Just being in the same room with someone I can trust feels good. Because I have no idea where I stand with anyone else here. Including Rain.

But eventually we both seem to tire and he moves, presumably heading off to bed. I'm grateful for the distraction he provided for the time being. Because at least running into him prevented me from seeking Rain out, even if it's what I wanted to do in the first place. And kinda still do.

"Hey, Riv?"

I turn, glancing over to Ash without a word. His brown eyes

hold mine for a moment, searching them for the answer to an unspoken question.

It takes a minute, but he speaks again. "Third door on the right," he tells me, nodding to the West wing and grabbing the glass of water from the counter and heading toward the direction of his bedroom back in the East wing. But he stops and looks over his shoulder at me again for a brief second, a flash of sympathy on his face. "I hope you know what you're doing."

I nod, swallowing as I rise from my spot at the island to watch him disappear down the hall, warring with myself.

But it's not much of a war at all as my feet carry me in the direction Asher instructed, stopping outside the third door on the right-hand side of the West wing.

This is such a bad idea.

I press my forehead against the door of his bedroom, I fucking beg and plead to whatever God might listen for him to be in here and more importantly, *alone.*

Holding my breath, I twist the handle and push the door open, thankful for silent hinges.

But it doesn't matter, because the second I step into the room, I hear a groan from the bed, followed by a shadowed figure rising to a seated position.

"Abhainn?" Rain's voice comes out deep and raspy. It's sexy as hell and I vividly remember waking up to it each morning for the last portion of our stay in Vail. And combined with him using my name in Gaelic, my chest physically aches.

"Yeah," I whisper, closing the door behind me, feeling a lot better once the soft *click* of the lock engages.

"Are you okay? Why are you in here?"

If only I knew the answer myself, baby.

Instead of responding, I quietly cross the room to his bed, pulling the sheets back on the side I sleep on.

Though it's difficult to see in the dark, nothing but a faint sliver of moonlight creeping through the closed curtains covering the windows, I can feel his eyes on mine. Attempting to search them for answers.

Whatever he gauges in our silence must be what he was looking for because he scoots over to one half of the bed, allowing me to climb in the empty space beside him.

With my head resting against the pillow, I stare at *his* ceiling. Or at least, what I manage to make out in the darkness.

"River?" my name comes softly in his sleepy timber after a few minutes.

"Yeah?"

"Are you okay?" he asks again.

God, why does that have to be such a complicated and loaded fucking question?

Swallowing, I let out a sigh. "I guess, yeah."

More silence.

"Why did you come here?"

"I don't know," I tell him honestly. "I just felt like I...should."

I hear the telltale sign of Rain's hair brushing against his pillow, probably in a nod. "I'm glad you did. I might've been dozing when you came in, but I'd rather stay up if you're looking for company."

Rolling my teeth over my lip, I resist the urge to drag him across the bed and into my arms. The need to hold him and take away his demons and just...

Sigh.

Love him. It's all I fucking want.

"Do you still have the nightmares?" I whisper, chancing a glance in his direction in the dark.

I feel movement from him, probably running his hands through his hair the way he does when he's frustrated or unsure of what to say. Which, with me, happens a lot.

So, I'm surprised when he seemingly tells the truth. "Most nights, I do."

"And the one...it's about Deacon, yeah? About the night he died?"

I know I'm hedging my bets, but if he's in a sharing mood tonight, I'd rather get the most of it that I can.

But when Rain exhales deeply, I can't help but wince, hating myself for prying into a subject I know can only cause him pain. "I haven't had that one in a while. Since we were in the cabin. Most of the ones these days center around..."

Ted.

He doesn't say the name. He doesn't have to.

So, when he says *you*, I'm taken aback, to the point where I don't even know what to say.

Instead we stop speaking, letting the sound of our breathing fill the silence between us until his hand reaches out in search of mine. I grab hold of it, letting the skin of his palm bring me the tiniest amount of solace.

This. This is what I've needed for the past couple months. Just a hand to fucking hold.

And I know he must need it too, when he entwines our fingers together.

Pulling me closer, our bare shoulders touching, sends my nerve endings into a frenzy and I'm immediately hyper aware of every inch of my skin against his. It's on fire. Rolling to my side to face him and ease the burn, he mirrors me, and wraps an arm around my waist and tugs me flush to his chest.

Not exactly what I was going for, but at this point, I'll take it. Anything he has to give me, I'll greedily lap up like a man dying of thirst.

Resting my forehead against the smooth skin of his pecs, I force myself to keep my hands to myself. I didn't come here for sex, only to make sure he was okay. I focus on the faint sound of his heartbeat and his steady breathing until I'm finally lulled to sleep.

And that's exactly how I wake up around six the next morning, wrapped in his arms and my body pressed to his.

It was the most perfect and restful few hours of sleep I've had since the cabin.

I only give myself five more minutes before wordlessly I slip out from his hold and head back to my cold, empty bed on the other side of the mansion.

TWENTY-ONE

Rain

DAY TWO: SATURDAY

I use the back of my hand to wipe the steam fogging up the bathroom mirror before running my towel though my hair, drying it best I can before wrapping it around my waist. The condensation in the air clings to my body like a thick blanket, wrapping me up tighter in my thoughts with each breath I take.

It's only been one night sleeping under the same roof as River again and I have to say, it didn't go the way I expected. I imagined we would keep separate from each other, what with us staying at opposite ends of the house. Sure, we'd see each other during the day and interact and do our very fucking best not to let awkwardness hang between us. But it wouldn't be like it was last time, spending every waking minute curled up together. Naked or not.

So, him crawling into bed with me in the middle of the night was honestly the *last* thing I thought would happen.

I can't lie and say I didn't enjoy every fucking minute of being with him. Just existing. I don't think I've slept so well since the night I showed up at his apartment over a month ago now.

And that's just the thing. The way River consumes me is so much more than *just sex*. The most vile thing I could ever do would be to dumb it down to just a physical reaction and need for release with him.

Last night, nothing happened. And while I'm addicted to touching and tasting and treasuring every inch of his body with my own, being able to simply feel the heat of his skin against mine and hear the deep, steady breaths as he slept was everything I didn't realize I needed.

Not only for last night, but for every night to come.

So I couldn't help the ache in my chest when I woke up alone this morning. The only indication he even slept in the bed with me was the indent on the pillow beside me and the tossed back sheets. Otherwise, I'd have thought I dreamed the whole thing. Even a dream of River in my arms would be a step up from another nightmare about something terrible happening to him at Ted's hands.

Or worse, my own.

I do my best to lock down those thoughts as I yank open the bathroom door, stepping into the hall and quickly moving down to the door to the room I'll be staying in for the next week or so.

Letting the door swing shut behind me, I'm startled to find River sitting on the end of the bed, head in his hands. The position is familiar, reminding me of the way I found him when I came back to our hotel room in Portland after going out to the clubs and getting fucked in every literal sense of the word.

His eyes snap up to mine, but he quickly does a double take when he sees the state of undress I'm in. A slight blush tints his cheeks and the tips of his ears and he glances away.

A smile finds its way on my lips and I move over to my bag on the dresser, rifling through it to find a clean pair of boxers and jeans.

"You know you don't have to look away, right?" I say over my shoulder. "You've seen me in a towel how many times by now? A hundred, easily?"

"I've seen you in a lot less than that too," he mumbles just loud enough for me to catch.

My grin grows as I turn around and lean against the dresser. "What was that, Riv?"

His eyes widen, and the tint on his ears deepens. It's a cute fucking look on him, embarrassment. It's not one I've seen very often.

"Nothing," he says quickly. "Just being a smartass."

Oh mo grá, you think I'll let you off that easily?

"If that's the case, you know I want to hear it. So tell me, Abhainn. What did you say?"

Rather than answering, he just stares at me, careful to keep his eyes locked on my face. With great amounts of effort, if the way his fingers are dancing against his thigh is any indication.

His silence only spurs me on more though, my blood racing as I leave my clothes on top of my bag and drop my towel.

Eyes still locked on mine, his nostrils flare as he does everything in his power not to look down where my cock is already at half-mast from his insinuation alone. I cross the room in two long strides, standing before him stark fucking naked, and wait for an answer.

It still doesn't come.

"You've seen me in a lot less, hmm?" I say, tilting his chin up toward my face. Looking down at him below me has my length growing thicker and longer by the nanosecond, to the point where I might actually break down and beg for him to touch me.

"Yeah," he whispers, licking his lips then rolling the ball of his piercing between his teeth. "Something like that."

His right hand connects with the outside of my thigh, just above my knee, before skimming up until it reaches my ass. Then his left hand follows the same path on the opposite leg, all while holding my eyes.

Anticipation rushes through me, bubbling up and filling me to the brim. And the second his tongue flicks across the head of my cock, his piercing rolling against the sensitive skin there, a soft groan escapes me.

"Fuck," I mutter, slipping my hands in the hair at the base of his skull. His tongue licks up my full length, teasing the underside of the head and immediately driving me insane.

Every time he touches me, it's more addictive than anything else. Drugs, alcohol, whatever it might be. He seeps into every cell of my being and all that matters is him.

But I can't continue to let him think all I want from him is his body. Nothing short of every piece of him will satisfy me anymore. So when he moves to my hip, biting down on my tattoo in the way he loves to do, I'm brought back to my senses.

Slightly.

"Riv," I breathe, pulling back on his hair to make him look at me. "As much as I love where this is going, I know it's not why you were here waiting for me."

He smirks at me and shakes his head. "It's not. But I don't mind taking a rain check for an hour." One of his hands moves around to grip me, slowly jacking my length. A slight hiss escapes me, which causes those dimples to pop in his cheeks. "Or maybe two."

He pulls from my hold on his hair, bringing his mouth back to my aching cock and working me in a way only he can. His mouth, it's fucking magic and *godmotherfuckingdamnit,* how did I manage not to fall at his feet the very first night I saw him back at the bar?

How did I ever think I could live without this?

River sucks me in deeper, fucking me with his mouth and throat. The sensation of his tongue ring rubbing against the underside of my cock a foreign, but welcome feeling. One I'm desperate to have as my new normal. After all, waking up every morning with his mouth on me sounds like a good way to spend the next sixty or so years.

"Abhainn," I rumble when a few fingers roam around to tease my crack, my voice thick with lust. "I fucking want you. I *need* you. Right now."

River pops off my dick and immediately whips his shirt over his head. "Far be it from me to deny you anything," he pants, standing to work his belt with frantic urgency.

His enthusiasm has me grinning, but I don't want to rush this. God only knows the next time this will happen, so I need it to last. I need it to *count* as something more than a meaningless hookup.

And more than fucking anything, I need it to be a step in the right direction. For him to trust me again, the way he did before my past came crashing in to screw everything up.

I reach out and stop his movements, using my own hands to work the zipper on his jeans. Taking my time to undress him instead.

Then I sink to my knees in front of him, pulling down the rest of his clothing with me.

Not thinking twice, I take him in my mouth, working his length in long, leisurely strokes of my tongue until it hits the back of my throat. Riv's hands fly to my hair, gripping tightly and for a second, I think it's going to be like it was at school in the broom closet. Hard and rough and *using.* And if that's what he wants, I won't stop it. We might be in a slightly better place than we were then, but I still deserve every goddamn ounce of his rage.

Yet instead of fucking my face like a madman, he just uses his hold on me to guide me at a smooth, steady pace, helping me take him to the place he needs to be. The two of us working *together.*

I moan around his cock and the vibration causes his grip to tighten on my head.

"Don't do that again, baby," he groans out the warning, "or this show will be over a lot sooner than either of us want."

Yeah, not happening.

I release him without a word and step away, going over to my bag to grab the bottle of lube I had stashed in one of the pockets. When I turn to him again, he has this expression on his face as he looks at the bottle in my hand.

Something like…pain, maybe? Regret?

Whatever it is, it's gone in a flash when he schools his features.

No, no, no.

"What's with the face?" I say in a panic, desperate for him not to shut down on me like he has the last few times our dicks have taken over for our brains.

"Nothing, I'm good," he says, holding his hand out for the lube. But like the open book he is, it's not convincing to say the least. I still see the crease in his forehead and his playful, sinfully addictive side has left the fucking building.

"Don't lie to me, mo grá."

River bites his lip and shrugs, not meeting my eyes. "Look, it's honestly nothing, okay? I know what this is, Rain." His eyes flick up to mine and I see the barrier building in them. "We don't have to pretend this is anything more than getting off. Mutual pleasure or whatever. I understand and I'm fine with it."

I raise my brow because *what the fuck?* "You're telling me there's nothing here besides fucking? Just a good romp between the sheets?"

He nods once, but there's a slight hesitation to it. And to be clear, I don't fucking like it.

"Bullshit."

"I'm serious," he urges. "No attachments, no feelings."

I scoff and shake my head. "Who do you think you're kidding? We both know it's not fucking possible with us." Stepping up directly in front of him, I cup the back of his neck and force him to look at me directly.

Eyes, darkened to a deep green, stare back at me. I watch as they map my face in infinite detail. Memorizing. Searching.

After a minute, he swallows. "It's possible. It has to be. It's the only way this will work." His gaze is begging. Pleading, even, to believe the words coming from his lips.

And though he's trying to hide it, to protect himself from me and the pain I've caused him, it's right then I know I'm right.

"It's not," I whisper softly. "You look me in the eyes a little too long to feel nothing for me."

He winces, the somber look in his eyes taking over as a grimace crosses his face. "I only wish I could say the same for you."

"River..." I sigh, pressing my forehead against his, closing my eyes. "Let me show you you're wrong. Because I feel *everything*."

Not giving him a chance to respond, I pull his mouth to mine and kiss him fiercely, urging him to see he isn't alone in this. Hell, I'd say the words, those three words I'm terrified of, right here and now if we weren't already naked and both hard as hell. But that's not how I want to tell him I love him, when we're horny and ready to fuck. I want it to be clear it has nothing to do with sex and everything to do with *him*.

I want him to know I mean it.

Running my tongue along the seam of his lips, I seek entrance, needing to wrap my tongue around that goddamn bar capable of bringing me to my fucking knees. I love it, it's just so *River*.

"Abhainn," I groan against his lips when his hand starts jacking me, long and slow. "Let me show you," I plead again without breaking away from his mouth.

I need him to let me prove to him...he's everything. All I want, all I need.

And suddenly I have an idea. Something I can do. *Give him* what I've never given anyone.

"Bed." It comes out a growled demand as adrenaline courses through me, pushing out any anxiety. He doesn't seem to mind the tone though, just bites my bottom lip and tugs it between his teeth.

"You could ask nicely instead of grunting like a caveman." He grins after he says it, flicking his tongue out against my lips in a wicked caress before moving to the bed, lying on his back. His fist automatically wraps around his shaft and he begins pumping himself, his attention locked on me while he does.

I study him, every line and plane of muscle I want to worship. Every piece of who he is—his dimples, smile, eyes, you name it—I adore.

"On your stomach, Abhainn. I wanna see the ass I've been missing so much."

He smirks before rolling to his belly, propping himself up on his elbows to look over his shoulder at me. This time I'm the one ogling his body, my hand cupping my aching cock as I stare at his ass. Right there for the taking.

And I'm done hesitating.

Covering his body with mine, I plant my hands on either side of his shoulders and brush my lips against the spot behind his ear. A shiver runs through him and I notice the hairs on his arms rise to stand. I let them settle before trailing a finger down the indentation of his spine, smiling when the goosebumps come back yet again.

I love the way he reacts to me, the way our bodies give our thoughts away now that we know how to reach each other. I'm just hopeful this will be enough to convince him.

My mouth lands on his shoulder, then it carves a pathway over one blade to the next. I take my time nipping and sucking down the skin of his back, exploring each and every indentation along the way. When I reach his ass, I flick my tongue against the top of his crease, his body tensing beneath me.

"What are you doing?" He sounds winded, like he just ran suicides during practice, and I look up to find him watching me over his shoulder.

Instead of answering, I sink my teeth into the taut muscle of his left cheek, pulling back to look at the marks my teeth leave behind. Two white crescents I lick and soothe seconds later.

Mine.

The word runs through my head on repeat as I kiss and suck one cheek before moving to the other, letting my hands knead the opposite. And he must like it with the way he starts slowly rocking his body into the mattress.

But when I grip one cheek in either hand and pull them apart, letting my tongue lick his taint, he tenses again.

"Baby, what're you—"

My eyes lock on his just as the tip of my tongue dances over his tight ring and I smirk. "Shut the fuck up and let me make you feel good, mo grá."

Pressing the flat of my tongue against his rim, I lap at his hole, letting just the tip slip in on every pass. River lets out a sound, something between a moan and a sigh and it spurs me on more. Emboldening me.

Gripping his hips, I pull him up into a better position on his knees, spreading his legs and cheeks wider. My tongue circles the rim of his ass, tracing it as I reach between his legs to grip his cock. All it takes is two strokes while I lick around his balls, letting my mouth tease them just enough to feel them tighten in desperation for release.

"Jesus Christ," he curses, a shudder trembling through him at the dual sensation. "You're fucking killing me."

I smile against his skin, pressing a kiss to one cheek before diving back, finally letting my tongue breach the puckered hole leading to my own personal paradise. River's body lurches forward in surprise as he groans softly. But then he presses back into me, allowing me to take advantage of the motion and slide my tongue in deeper, fucking himself on it.

"Goddammit, what are you doing to me?" The words come out in a rushed mumble as he moves against me. It's not something that was actually a question for me to answer, but more a mindless slip of the tongue as he loses himself in pleasure.

And I love watching him let go.

I continue for a while longer, teasing his balls, taint, and ass with my mouth and lips and teeth and tongue until he's unable to hold himself up on knees and elbows anymore. He's a sweating, panting, needy mess when he pulls himself away from me and flips over, his eyes wild and hazy with lust.

"*Fuck me,*" he growls, grabbing the back of my neck and reeling his mouth to mine. Our tongues meet and I start fucking his mouth with it the way it was just fucking his ass. Taunting and teasing and playing with his sanity until he takes control of the situation himself.

His hand grips my shaft, pumping me a few times as a wicked glint takes over his face. "You wanna edge, yeah, baby? Because two can play that game."

I smirk. "Do whatever you want to me."

His hands move to cup either side of my neck as he pulls us down into a lying position, my body covering his again.

"What I want is for *you* to put that beautiful cock to good use."

My lips quirk at his slight agitation, but I don't blame him. If I had my ass eaten for a solid fifteen minutes without coming, I'd be ready to blow too.

Grabbing the lube again, I lather my cock in the liquid and I grip both of us in hand to start stroking, letting our lengths glide together with ease.

It's easily one of the most satisfying feelings in the world.

I capture his mouth again, grinding down against him to let our dicks rub against each other. One of his hands wrap around the back of my neck, holding me while the other skims lightly down my side, sending bolts of lightning shooting through my body from the simple touch.

He feels it too. He fucking has to feel this.

"You can have whatever you want, mo grá," I whisper against his lips. "Top, bottom. Hard, soft, fast or slow, I'll give it to you. Just give me a chance."

Both of his hands slide into my hair and pin my face to his as we meld together in a pool of simmering heat and lust. My hand continues to give us leisurely strokes, loving the way he groans into my mouth as I do. Every breath and moan and whispered curse leaving his lips is the sexiest sound I've ever heard as I bring him towards his release.

"One chance," he grunts, pushing against my chest to roll us over, him leaning over my body as he kisses a path down my neck. A few strategically placed bites and sucks are given on his way to my chest before he takes my nipple between his teeth and tugs.

The sharp bite of pain is eased the second he releases it and traces his tongue around the bud, meeting my eyes.

"One more chance," he repeats as he climbs on top of me, his knees on either side of my ribs. Leaning forward to take my mouth again in soft kisses, his fingers slip into my hair and I run my hand down his back in a gentle caress. "Because I'm not about to be played for a fool for a third time."

I just nod before kissing him fiercely, nipping at his lips.

I won't fuck this up. Not again. There's not a chance in hell.

River releases my mouth, arching his back as my hands snake around to lube his crease. The blunt head of his cock is inches from my mouth as he straddles my torso and I flick my tongue out on instinct. The taste of pre-cum spurs me on, lapping at his dick while I taunt him more with my fingers.

"Fuck, baby. Your mouth on me is magic," he whispers, his voice filled with gravel and lust.

I pull more of him in, swirling my tongue around the tip and he starts making shallow thrusts forward, helping me set a pace. One hand moves to his hip, the other still trailing down his crack. Tracing circles around his rim, I let one finger slip barely inside, just to the first knuckle.

"Fuck, fuck, *fuck*," he says on an exhale, pushing his hips forward and back again, seeking me from both directions. He fucks himself on my finger, clenching tightly around it in a way that has me wishing it was my cock he was riding instead.

Shit, I need to be inside him. More than I need air or food or sleep or literally anything else in this world.

But this isn't about me.

It's him. It's *us.*

I add a second finger, pumping it in and out of him slowly, curling up in just the right spot to get him groaning and bearing down on my hand as hard as he can. Desperately seeking more of what he craves while his cock fucks my mouth.

" I need more. *Rain,*" he says my name like a prayer. A plea.

Letting him slip from my mouth, I take over with my hand, stroking him hard and fast in time with my fingers. "Take what you need, Abhainn. I'm yours."

His eyes snap open and find mine the instant the words are out, probably in disbelief he heard them correctly.

"I'm *yours,*" I say again, removing my fingers from him as he slides down my body, positioning himself over my cock. Teasing his hole for barely a minute, I take extra pleasure in sliding the head inside him. The exquisitely tight fit has my balls squeezing already and it only gets worse when I look back up and see him still staring down at me.

Shifting his weight back, he sinks down further on my dick, letting the entire length fill him to the hilt.

But it's not deep enough. It's not *enough.* I won't be fucking satisfied until it's impossible to tell where I stop and he begins. Until we're *one.*

"Damn fucking right you're mine," he pants, building speed as he grinds into me on every downstroke. My fingers dig in, holding him in place as I take my turn to thrust up into him in hard, greedy pumps.

"Always, completely yours, mo grá."

A low groan of pleasure slips from him and I sit up, bringing us chest to chest as he slowly starts to fuck himself on my cock again.

"Tell me you understand," I murmur against his collarbone as he rides me like he was made for it. Because he fucking was. He takes every inch of me, bearing down on my dick in search of what he needs to get himself there.

And as I watch him through love and lust drunk eyes, I realize something I should've known all along.

The universe designed him to be my own personal downfall.

But fuck if I'm not going to enjoy every second I have with him as I barrel towards the Earth.

"You're everything. Fucking *everything*," I whisper against his mouth. "*Chuisle mo chroí.*"

"What does it mean?" he asks, dragging his tongue across the seam of my lips.

My stomach convulses, anxiety making me second guess my answer. But he needs to know. I made a promise. I'll never keep anything from him ever again. I'll give him all of me. Now that I have him back in my arms, I'm not about to break it.

No more second chances.

"Pulse of my heart."

I feel his smile against my lips as a soft laugh leaves him. "And the air you breathe?"

He says it as a joke, a lilt of laughter in his tone I don't quite understand, but the reality of it rings true all the same.

Still, I chuckle as I pull back to look into his eyes. "You're both, Abhainn. You're always both," I tell him, not thinking twice about the amount of cheese coming out of my mouth. It doesn't matter when it comes to him.

He kisses me fiercely, sliding up and down on my cock in tandem with my heartbeat. And he kisses and fucks and just *loves* with so much fervor and passion, my entire world ignites, and I briefly wonder if it will always be like this.

Fucking transcendent.

"What song?" I ask, pulling back to look in his eyes. My hands move from his hips to trace down his spine and he shivers under my touch, his eyes lighting up in hunger.

"'Power Over Me.' Dermot Kennedy," he answers, his husky voice laced with desire as his hand slides over his dick while he rides mine in slow, steady movements. "Because that's what you have. What you'll always have."

My stomach clenches and my heart twists, knowing exactly what he means. Because I feel it too.

I love you, Abhainn.

Again, the words look to slip out, but I keep it in. It's too soon. He doesn't fully trust me yet, and if I'm being honest, *I* don't trust myself.

I don't want to, and I don't feel like I will, but I'm still terrified I'm going to fuck this up.

But if I can't say it, I sure as hell plan to show him.

"I'm right there," he tells me, jacking himself as he continues to grind down on my cock. I'm right there with him, seconds from exploding inside him.

And when I feel the hot spurt of cum spill from him onto my stomach and chest, I lose it entirely. My release shoots from me so powerfully, my eyes go blurry for a minute. His ass milks my cock, pulsing around it as I continue to rub against his prostate with every thrust.

Fuck.

We're both panting and sweating, his cum sticky between us as it covers both of our stomachs. Once I manage to catch my breath enough to get my vision back to normal, I let my eyes lock on him.

He gives me a dopey, sated smile I learned well those weeks at the cabin and before I can smile back, he's cupping my face in his hands and kissing me gently.

It steals my breath all over again. Even after he pulls away.

My God, you're perfect.

He lets out a low laugh, rich and husky, his smile growing as he presses his forehead to mine.

"Hardly," he whispers, answering the statement I must've let slip. "I think that's just the orgasm high talking."

I smile, knowing how wrong he is. But I'll let him think that for now.

"If you say so, Abhainn."

River smirks as he trails his fingers up my stomach, gently tracing each indentation of my abs. It turns into a soft smile as he watches the path they take, sliding through his cum and smearing all over my skin.

I can see the possessive look in his eye as he does it too. It screams a single word.

Mine.

It's already got my dick thickening again, still deep inside him.

And that's when I realize what he's doing.

He's marking me. Claiming me.

A grin forms on my lips, knowing he doesn't need to mark my skin because I already did it for him by inking his name where I'd see it every single day.

Forever yours, Abhainn.

"What are you thinking?" I ask, shifting my hips to let him feel my cock getting ready to go again. Grabbing his hand, I stop his teasing, licking the cum off each of his fingers.

It tastes like him. Salty, yet somehow sweet. Deliciously addictive.

I'll never get enough.

"I think…" he says, rolling his hips with a sly smile as he lifts his eyes to meet mine. "I'm starting to believe you."

TWENTY-TWO
Rain

DAY SIX: WEDNESDAY

Wanter hile sex doesn't solve problems on every occasion, it certainly doesn't hurt us in this one. Because after another round of the most acrobatic shower sex we've attempted yet, River agreed to let me back in.

"It won't be easy, but I want to trust you. I hate fighting what I feel for you."

Honestly, that's all I could hope to have from him. All I asked for. A chance.

Him being willing to give it to me is nothing short of a miracle, but I'll take all the luck where I can get it.

It doesn't hurt that the past few days have been nothing short of amazing, even if Ted's insane ass is still on the loose looking for ways to bring me down. I just don't have it in me to care.

I'm happier than I've been in months and I can tell River is too. And I don't think it's just from all the sex we've been having.

I smile at the thought as I'm lying on the couch watching TV, River across from me in the armchair reading his textbook. Every once in a while I'll tap the cover with my foot, breaking his concentration and earning a playful scowl aimed my way.

But at least I can say the word *playful* now instead of straight up filled with sorrow, anger, or contempt.

Only our flirtatious exchange is cut short when Asher walks into the living room, a solemn look on his face. Clicking mute on the remote, I frown.

"What happened?"

River glances up from his book, seeing Asher for the first time just as he goes to speak.

Rolling his tongue over his teeth, he sighs. "Can you guys follow me?"

I share a look with River as we both rise and start down the hall behind Asher. He leads us to the East wing and into one of the many offices and over to a bookcase, pulling out a hardback and pressing a button on the shelf behind it. And to no surprise, part of the paneling on one pops open, revealing a door.

River arches a brow. "Really? Secret room behind a bookcase?"

Asher laughs, but I can tell he doesn't feel it. "Didn't we already explain Hollywood stole all the good shit?"

He doesn't wait for an answer, just motions us through to a dimly lit hallway that feels eerily like it's leading us to a dungeon. Because it's definitely the vibe the giant oak door gives off, complete with a giant iron lock, one of those old-fashioned skeleton keys would open.

But I guess *secret chamber* works too, seeing as that's what the door opens to. A massive circular room with a round oak table placed in the center, emblazoned with a dark gray skeleton key wrapped in vines in the center. Two cursive maroon E's, one forward, one backward, make up the handle with a keyhole peeping through the center from behind one of the vine leaves.

And etched into the bottom of the key in script is a single word. *Enclave.*

One look at this room would have made me a believer in secret societies if I wasn't already. It screams of old world power, the kind monarchs would fight for back in the medieval ages. The walls are lined with bookshelves filled with what looks to be some form of archives, old worn texts and scrolls neatly arranged on each of them. I'm assuming some sort of history of America, Enclave, or both, is within their pages.

River's eyes widen as he takes in the space and when he glances over at Asher, who's now at the table with the rest of the legacies, I think it's starting to really hit him that one of his best friends growing up was living a double life their entire friendship.

"I don't think you're understanding what—" Roman is saying into a phone set between the guys, just off to the side of the key at the center of the table. But he's cut off by a disembodied voice from the other line.

It's a voice I recognize to be Roman's father. And from his tone? Let's just say my heart plummets at hearing it.

"Roman Francis, you will *hear me* when I tell you this little shenanigan ends *now.* It's high time you think of something other than your own selfish wants, especially when you've put everything we've spent generations protecting at risk!"

My eyes find Roman's from across the table and I give him a sad smile, mouthing the words *I'm sorry* to him. Because I know he's currently getting his ass chewed. Probably for coming here to help me without permission, even though he told me repeatedly it would all be fine.

Maybe it would have been, had he not needed to get the rest of these guys involved.

"No, *you listen*," he yells back and I can tell from the reaction of everyone else in the room, things are about to get ugly. Because I might not be a member of the Enclave, but I can guarantee no one is supposed to talk to the Grand Elector like that. Not even his son.

But Roman's fuse has been lit, and when that happens, there's no stopping him.

"Ted Anders is a vile, sadistic piece of shit. I don't give a fuck about what kind of working relationship you used to have with him. He's a *monster* and he needs to be taken out."

The words rip from his throat in a snarl, menacing enough to surprise me it came from him at all. I've never seen Roman anything close to unhinged, but from the looks of it, he's two seconds away from snapping.

There's silence from the other line for a good while, no one on our end daring to speak after Roman. And just when I think the line has disconnected, Senator Mitchell speaks.

"You will leave by the end of the week. The only one permitted to stay at the Jameson Estate is Asher. Each of you will return to your respective training by Monday."

"Fath—"

"This is not up for *discussion*."

"Just hear me out," Roman insists, and my heart drops to my stomach when I hear the defeat in his voice. "Why can't we just keep an eye out to make sure nothing happens? At least until the authorities find Anders? What's the harm in my trying to help my best friend?"

I hear his father scoff from the other end of the line and my eyes flash between the rest of the present Enclave members. Each of them, even Kaede, has a solemn expression on their face. So does River, the most optimistic one of us all.

It's then I start to lose all the hope remaining in my body.

"The world is much bigger than any one person, Roman. You've been taught better than this. You're Enclave. Ciaráin Grady doesn't need your protection or your help. And God only knows if he's even speaking the truth about what Anders is being accused of. For heaven's sake, his mother didn't even take him at face value."

Those words have me seeing red, storming over to the table and slamming my hand down on the smoothly polished surface next to the phone.

"I know what happened to me," I hiss, my voice filled with venom. "I remember what he did to me when I was nine and ten. What he continued to do to me for *five fucking years*. She might not believe me, *no one* could believe me, but it. Fucking. Happened. The entire world could be against me but *I know* the truth about what a sick asshole he is beneath his shiny exterior."

A long sigh sounds from the other end of the phone. "Why hello, Ciaráin. So nice to hear from you again. I'm glad to see my son continues to enable this little *friendship* by breaking more rules."

"Rules are made to be broken, Father. Something you've taught me more than anyone," Roman seethes, his shoulders tense against mine.

"You might be right," his father replies dryly, "But I never put this organization at risk. Inviting outsiders into sacred spaces, allowing your heart to cloud your judgement." Another scoff. "Your service is to your brothers and this country. That is *it*. Do I make myself clear, son?"

My molars grind together in order to keep silent because *fuck him* and the damn unicorn his Grand Elector ass probably rode in on.

My eyes flash to River, doing my best to give him a reassuring look from across the room as Roman hisses out his response. "I don't think you do, *Father*. Because I'm having a hard time understanding how a man who is involved in a national scandal of this degree is fit to remain in office in the first place."

"I hardly think it's any of your concern. None of you have been initiated. You aren't in charge. So it's time you stop questioning those who are and *do as you're told*."

Roman opens his mouth to speak again, but Kaede grabs his arm and shakes his head, signaling him it's time to wave the white flag in surrender.

"Let it go," he mutters. "It's over, Rome. Don't go down with a sinking ship."

Taking a deep breath, I look over at River, hoping to God he doesn't feel as discouraged as I feel. But of course, he does. It's written all over his face.

We're well and truly fucked.

"Have I made my demands clear?" the senator asks, still on

speaker.

"Yes, sir. We'll be gone come the weekend," Kaede replies, ending the call.

He glances up from the phone, tilting his head as he studies me with his penetrating silver eyes. "For what it's worth, I'm sorry. This situation isn't ideal—"

"*Ideal?*" Roman seethes. "You're kidding, right?"

Asher places a hand on Roman's shoulder, but Roman brushes him off, to which Asher lets out a relenting sigh before heading to the door. Hollis and Callum are quick to follow, Kaede bringing the rear.

"Lock up," Asher calls back, I'm assuming to Roman.

My eyes catch River waiting by the door and I give him a sympathetic half smile, hating myself for involving him in all this. It's nothing but a damn soap opera at this point, someone or something constantly getting in the way.

I tilt my chin to go ahead, letting him know I'd follow him out before turning to my best friend.

"C'mon, Ro. What's done is done," I tell him, only a small hint of bitterness in my voice. It's not for him, but for his father for being such a condescending asshole. It has absolutely nothing to do with him. Just like River or me. How we turned out as well as we did with such poor excuses as father figures, I'll never quite understand.

Guess apples can fall far from the tree after all.

I leave the secret meeting room—chamber or whatever you want to call it—hearing Roman closing the door behind us. He sticks his hand in his pocket, pulling out a skeleton key. It looks just like the one carved into the table from what I can tell, minus the ivy vines wrapping around it.

Roman catches me watching him and shakes his head with a small smirk. "We all have one."

I raise my brow. "An old key or a dungeon it opens?"

He snorts. "Both, I suppose. But the key we each have opens any of them."

Together we walk back through the bookcase doorway and into the office where Roman catches my arm just as I'm about to leave and head down the hall back to my room and pack up my shit. Because if they're all leaving, there's not really a point for us to stay here either. Asher will more than likely leave also, even if he doesn't necessarily have to.

"Do you have a minute?" Roman asks, the sound of disappointment evident in his voice.

Quickly looking at the door, I realize everyone's already left to go about their business. River included.

"Yeah," I sigh as I turn my back to the exit and face him, not having the slightest clue about what he could possibly want. "What's up, man?"

Ro leans back against the desk in the room, hands gripping the edge of the wooden surface as he stares at me. Not saying a word.

The temperature in the room spikes slightly when he continues to look at me like he was a blind man seeing for the first time. And I sure as hell don't like it.

"I'm so fucking sorry, Rain. I thought..." he groans, running his hand through his hair. "I guess I thought I could make this shit work. I'd be able to help you and then things could be normal between us again and—"

I hold my hand up, cutting him off as my forehead creases in confusion. "You thought you had to come here to make shit be normal between us?"

"Not in so many words."

That's a yes.

"Really? So you *didn't* think you needed to basically *buy* back our friendship by doing me a favor? Instead of just talking to me and explaining why you went dark on me?" I scoff and shake my head. "Jesus, all you had to do was say you were sorry. That's it. Which you did, and I fucking forgave you. And all of it would've easily been managed over the phone. Four years ago."

Biting his lip, he nods absently. "That's the issue though. I wasn't sorry. Not really." His dark hazel eyes find mine, filled with heat. "I'm still not sorry for what happened in the pool."

Pushing off the desk, he comes to stand in front of me, searching my face as he does. There's palpable amounts of emotion visible on his own, everything ranging from anger to sorrow. Like he's being torn apart from the inside out.

"I wish I could be sorry, but I'm not. I wanted you so fucking bad. I *still* do, Rain. And now I have to leave again. But this time? I'm not going to be stupid and leave without at least asking you to come with me." He swallows harshly and reaches up, his hand pressing against the side of my face. "Let's get the fuck out of here. Go anywhere. Train and work to find Ted and—"

My head starts shaking before I realize it, dislodging his hand. My eyes widen and I take a step back. "I can't leave. Not now, Ro. Not when Ted knows about Ri—"

Roman rolls his eyes. "*River,* of course. We can't forget about precious fucking River being the center of the goddamn universe." Pinching the bridge of his nose, he starts pacing the length of the desk. "I just don't get it. You keep these giant secrets from him until he practically forces them from you, yet you're still standing here in his defense?"

"He's *innocent* in this, Roman. You have to realize that. You have to see through your anger and understand he's exactly the person you supposedly swear to protect from people like Ted. What makes him any different than me?"

"He's not my best friend. I haven't known him for over half my life. I don't fucking *love him.* Are those reasons enough?"

I bit the inside of my cheek to the point of pain when he says the word *love.* Because I love him, just not the same. It'll never be the same.

"You don't know ninety-nine percent of the people in this country, yet you live to serve them," I point out.

Roman shakes his head, his jaw clenching. "That's not the point."

"Then what is? Because I'm at a loss as to what the hell it is you're trying to get at. Other than asking me to abandon the person *I* brought into this mess in the first place. Leaving him damn near defenseless."

He remains silent, eyes filled with anger aimed at me and we stay there, locked in a mental battle of wills. But I'm not backing down on this. I won't dare compromise River. Not anymore. Never again.

So it's no surprise Roman's the one to break first.

His voice is thick, the words coming out strangled as he grimaces. "What is it about me that you can't give me a damn chance?"

"You're my best friend, man. That's always going to be true. But we aren't…" I trail off, not knowing how to tell him he's not *it*. He's not who I want. And even if he was, would it really work?

"We aren't *what?*" he snaps. "Because from where I'm standing, we're a fuckton more than you and River are. We're history and friendship and memories and the people who held each other during the worst moments of our lives. And I refuse to believe you don't *see* that and don't *feel something* for me because of it."

Starting to pace again, he shakes his head repeatedly while I watch, helpless. Because what can I say right now other than I'm sorry?

"I don't get it," he growls, pinning me in place with a glare after a while. "We have this insane friendship. An unbreakable bond. For fucking *years*. It was built to withstand *anything*. And then it blew up because of one fucking kiss?"

I tilt my head and look at him because is he *serious?* "We both know it was so much more than the kiss that ruined us, Roman. You're delusional if you manage to convince yourself otherwise."

He winces, a grimace overtaking his features. "Would you rather I hadn't told you the truth?"

Biting my lip, I try not to burst. It's not worth it at this point when we can't change the course of history.

But something inside me lets the words slip out, giving him my honesty.

"I would've rather you hadn't made the fucking move in the first place, knowing it would have been nothing more than a single night if you'd kept silent." I scoff and shake my head. "Fuck, I wouldn't have been anything more than a goddamn one-night-stand to you if you hadn't said something. So no, I'm glad you told me and saved me from more pain in the end."

Roman's eyes carry all the pain his mouth isn't willing to share, the deep hazel pleading with me to understand. "The Enclave's rules are crystal fucking clear, Rain. The five families find a suitable companion, marry, have kids, raise them as brothers, and when the next generation comes of age, they're groomed to take over. That's it. Wash, rinse, repeat. So please, explain to me how my being with a *man* guarantees an heir to continue the legacy that's been alive for almost a *millennia*."

His words bring back the night in the pool, his body against mine, his hand around my dick and his tongue in my mouth.

Roman's body presses me back against the edge of the pool, the tile biting into the skin of my back as he continues to jack my cock. "And I have to have you this one time, even if it's the only time I can."

My mouth pauses against his and I pull away, breathing hard as I look into his lust-filled stare. "What are you talking about, the only time you can?"

Roman swallows hard, his hand coming up to cup my cheek and his hand around my dick begins to slow into long, leisurely strokes. "Enclave forbids me from being able to…" he trails off, his forehead sinking against mine. "I have to follow their rules. Their regulations. The way things have been done since the beginning."

I shake my head, causing the pressure of his forehead to slip away from mine when I push against his chest. His hand releases my length and I'm quick to tuck it back into my shorts, painfully aware how fucking hard I am right now.

For him. My best friend.

The guy who might as well be stomping all over my heart this very moment.

"And what are their rules?" I ask, though the ache in my chest is already telling me everything I need to know.

Roman tongues his cheek, his eyes locking on the water before meeting mine again. "Part of my duty is to produce an heir. A next generation after mine. And in order to do that...one day, I'll have to find a wife."

I shake my head, trying to make sense of the words. But they're... nonsense, right? This is the twenty-first century. People aren't forced into marriages anymore.

Right?

"But Rain," he whispers, reaching for me again. His hand lands on my arm, the warmth of it heating my skin that's long since gone ice cold. "We can figure it out. Make it work. And at the very least, we have tonight."

His eyes plead with me. For understanding. Forgiveness.

For anything, really.

But all I can do is stare at him, the painful truth sliding over my body and wrapping around me like barbed wire, cutting into my flesh with every word and what they mean.

He and I... we have no future.

Shaking my head, I bring myself back to the present and meet Roman's eyes from across the room. "We were never going to work. It was a fucking pipe dream, the last night in the pool."

He licks his lips and goes to adjust the cufflinks on his suit jacket, only to realize he must've taken it off before the conference call with his father. His anxious tick, not unlike River's incessant tapping, and one of the only ones I've ever picked up on from him.

"It wasn't a dream, Rain. I was ready to figure it out. Find a way to make it work, just like I am now." He swallows and shakes his head, directing his gaze out the window at the mountainous horizon glowing in the sunset. "If I had a choice in the matter, I would have flown you out to me the minute you graduated from Foxcroft."

From the gravel in his voice, I have no choice but to believe him. Roman might be a lot of things, but the strength of his word might be the thing he honors as much as his duty to family and country.

The very thing engraved into him since he was a child.

"But instead you cut off all communication because I *shut you down?*"

He swallows. "It wasn't because of that. Everyone told me it would be for the best."

"The best for you, maybe. But leaving me *there?* In that house, under the same fucking roof as him with *no one* in my corner?" I hiss, my fingers curling into tight fists. "You broke every promise you ever made me by listening to *everyone* instead of your gut."

"Would it make a difference if I told you it was an order?" he shouts, throwing his hands out. "That all five of us were demanded to cut communication with anyone from our pasts while beginning our training?"

Not one goddamn bit.

"No, it wouldn't. Because you follow blindly instead of having a tiny piece of human fucking decency to at least *tell me.*"

"You want to talk about decency?" His lip curls back and he scoffs. "I've been raised from the time I could walk to serve my country and then my family. That's our code. And it's a lot more than just decency, Rain. All I ever did was make a fucking choice to honor it."

"Yet you said for years *I* was your family," I counter.

"And you were. God, you were. And you still *can be*." The plea inches its way back into his voice, a small speck of hope, but he tamps it down. "We'll talk to my dad and figure out a way."

I bite my lip. "No, Roman. You and I are never going to happen."

The dash of hope is gone in an instant. "What, so it's because of *him?*" he sneers, his eyes dashing over my shoulder to the door. I immediately know he means River.

"This isn't just about him. It has to do with you, me, and the code you just said you spent your entire *life* being trained to live by. One that, as you mentioned, has been passed down for *centuries*. What makes you think now, after all this time, they're going to allow one of the five get by without producing an heir?"

Roman shakes his head, looking over my shoulder again. "I can produce an heir."

I give him a look. "Last time I checked, I can't have babies, Ro."

He shakes his head again, stepping up to me, a wild look in his eyes. "I can find a girl, marry her, produce an heir, and then—"

I rub my temple, desperate for this conversation to be over. "You think I'd idly sit by and watch all of it go down? Nah, fuck that. I don't share the person I love. Not even for some secret society legacy bullshit you have going on. And if you think I *would*, you really don't know me—"

My words are cut off when Roman slams his mouth to mine in what I would describe as pure rage. The way his lips move over mine is angry, yet pleading. Like this is it, his last resort, and maybe if I can just feel what he does, I'll agree.

But I don't want him. I don't want to hide in the shadows

312 | CE RICCI

anymore as someone's *mistress.* For once, I want to be true to myself, my mind, and my heart.

All of those things lead me straight back to River.

My spine stiffens on reflex when his hands cup my face as his tongue seeks entry to tangle with mine.

And I'm so fucking torn.

Not because there's a choice to make, but because I know this final rejection might very well be the nail in the coffin for whatever is left of our relationship. No one wants to love someone who doesn't love them back. A person can only handle being friend zoned so many times before they decide the effort isn't worth it anymore. I wouldn't blame him for never speaking to me again after this.

So, as fucking shitty and stupid and idiotic as I might be for doing it, I let the guilt consume me. I relax in his grip. Let my hands release the death grip I have on his shirt.

I kiss him back.

Just enough to let him have this one damn moment before I come in with a wrecking ball to destroy our friendship. But me kissing him back is all it takes for him to come to his senses.

He pulls back slightly, panting before he speaks. And when he does, it chills me to the bone. Holding enough animosity, he might as well be a tornado, hell-bent on destruction, making me terrified to find out what carnage he's leaving in his wake.

"Good luck explaining that one," he mutters, his lips still brushing mine before shoving against my chest. It forces me to step back and out of his way, but he doesn't make a move to walk out. Just sits on the edge of the desk and glances over my shoulder toward the door.

The way my stomach is churning and the fire I feel in my core tells me what's happening before I even look. But it doesn't stop the bile from rising in my throat when I turn to find River leaning against the open doorway. Arms crossed over his chest. An expressionless mask on his face.

Fuck.

TWENTY-THREE
River

DAY SIX: WEDNESDAY

My blood boils as I do my best to keep my shit together. But it's difficult. *Really* fucking difficult as I watch Rain turn toward me, guilt written all over his goddamn face. Add in the gloating look on Roman's, and I'm about to toss some hands.

But that's not me and it never will be.

Even when the words, "*What, so it's because of* him?" caught my attention as I passed in the hall, spitting from Roman's mouth like a vile insult, I was fine. Even when I stepped into the room to watch how this would play out between them, I didn't wanna hit him.

Now, all I can sit here and think is...*how fucking* dare *he?*

I know Roman and Rain have had unfinished business, but for fuck's sake, he had to pull that shit right in front of me? Put his fucking lips on Rain's like it's his goddamn right? I don't know when he realized I was watching from the doorway, but when his eyes flicked to mine, I knew he was doing it to be a dick.

And if that's all it was, I could live with it. Be pissed for a bit and move past it.

But the worst part of all is Rain didn't pull away. He stood there and he fucking took it. I saw the tension leave his back and him *accept* what Roman was doing. Like it didn't matter I could walk in at any second or that we've been sleeping in the same bed for the past five nights or that he's been screwing me a good portion of the time we've been up here.

He didn't fucking care Roman was kissing him.

Rain opens his mouth to say something, but I hold my hand up, not letting him start.

"I don't want to hear it."

"But Ri—"

"I said," I growl through clenched teeth, "I don't want to *fucking hear it.*"

He shuts up at that, clamping his lips closed as my attention flicks to Roman. There's not a single look of remorse on his face for playing dirty and offering up some half-assed attempt to get Rain to run away with him. He looked in my eyes before he kissed Rain and said all that horseshit about, for all intents and purposes, *giving him another chance.* So they can *be together.*

Fuck that.

Yet at this rate, I wouldn't be surprised if it worked.

God, I knew it was stupid to come here with both of them, yet I did it anyway. I let my heart lead over my brain. And look where it brought me. Into the crossfire of two guys who clearly can't figure out what the hell they mean to each other. Even when my gut was telling me to deal with this on my own.

But the idiot I am, I let Rain in. *Again.*

Into my body, my mind, and my fucking heart.

I hate that once again, we've proven we're nothing but an almost.

Almost…everything.

And knowing this tears me apart.

Eyes still trained on Roman, I shake my head and let out a soft laugh. "I don't know why I'm even surprised at this point. You made it perfectly clear you had only ill will towards me from the moment I stepped foot in this house."

Roman says nothing, just shrugs and smiles, and it lights a fire inside me.

This has been a game to him from the beginning. It's been filled with heartache and agony and he's been a puppet master behind such a large majority of it. Feeding into my insecurities, letting me assume the worst.

And all for what? To have Rain be his *kept man* or *mistress* or whatever the fuck you wanna call it?

It's hilarious to the point where I want to laugh, but I can't. Because this is *my life* and the person *I love* being thrown into the equation. The person I've battled for, gone to war for, and it still manages to feel as if I'm the only one fighting.

If I don't manage to give him up, I'm never getting out of this shit alive or resembling any form of the person I used to be.

"You want him?" I ask Roman, a calm to my voice I don't feel. The next words come out tasting like lies on my tongue. "Fucking have him. I'm done fighting."

Rain's eyes widen in panic. "Riv, I don't—"

I pin him with a glare that has him stopping in his tracks. "I've heard enough lies out of your mouth to last a lifetime." Looking back to Roman, I scoff. "And you? You're no better. Deception is the name of the game for you, for *all* of you in this secret society that hasn't managed to do jack shit to help with this mess we're in."

Rain steps toward me and I scowl, not daring to let him get within touching distance. My mind was made up the moment I saw him give into Roman. But I know my willpower has no chance against him if he manages to touch me.

"All either of you do is bring chaos into the lives of everyone around you. You're a match made in hell and you fucking deserve each other."

Neither of them says anything. How can they? We all know I'm right.

Rolling my teeth over my lip, I let a wry laugh slip with another shake of my head to mask the mass of emotions flooding me as I address Roman once more. "Consider the threat eliminated."

I don't bother giving either of them a chance to say a thing, storming from the office and making a beeline to my bedroom and to where my bag is on the floor. I grab it and start shoving my shit inside as quickly as I can. Because I can't stay here another damn minute.

There's being played for a fool for a second time because of this stupid little thing called hope and then there's the straight up idiocy of asking fate to fuck you up the ass for a third time. I'm not about to stick around for that shit.

As I'm zipping my bag closed, I hear the sound of the door to my room being opened, a set of heavy footfalls following.

I know it's Rain, like always. I just do, even before he speaks. Hell, I'm not surprised he followed me in here.

But when I hear the lock engage on the door, I snap.

"What the fuck do you think you're doing?"

Rain raises his brow. "Me? What the fuck are *you* do—" His words cut off when he notices the bag in my hand. "Put the bag down and let me explain, River."

"I'm leaving. Now," I hiss. "Coming up here was a dumbass move on my part. Hell, being stuck in a cabin with you for five weeks was already a shit storm. I don't know why I agreed to another week when I've seen this show before. It always ends in disappointment."

And also fuck you for thinking you deserve any sort of chance to explain when I've given you fucking everything.

My fingers tighten around the bag when I realize I have no way out. Rain has locked, and is standing against the only door out of this room.

"You're not fucking leaving. It's not safe," Rain says, crossing his arms over his chest. "Ted is *here.* So sorry, not sorry, mo grá, but you aren't leaving my sight until this situation is handled. With or without the Enclave's help. Because at this point, he's getting desperate and I'm not allowing you to put yourself in danger."

My jaw ticks as I throw the bag across the room and stalk up to him.

"And what makes you think you have a say in what I do or where I go? You're not my keeper, Rain. I'm an adult, capable of making my own goddamn decisions, so stop treating me like a fucking child."

Rain slams his fist back against the door again and I watch as fury lights up his eyes. "Then maybe you should stop *acting* like one, River. Like right now and instead just listen to me while I try to ex—"

I scoff. "You're kidding. This is actually a joke, right?"

His eyes flick between mine as his nostrils flare. "Dead serious. Because contrary to what you seem to think of me, I care about you—"

My eyes roll without permission. "You looked like you cared a whole lot about me five minutes ago while *Roman's* tongue was in your mouth," I snarl, pushing him in the chest.

That's all I need to say to stop him dead in his tracks. Because neither of us can be fooled into thinking this isn't a big deal. *One chance* means *one. Fucking. Chance.*

He just stares at me, searching my face for any clue or sign as to what I might be thinking because words are clearly failing *him* the moment they mean the most.

"Just let me go. Please," I utter softly, allowing myself this vulnerability with him for the briefest second. "I gave you a second chance and we had it. So, let me make this decision for the both of us, because you clearly can't. And I can't ask you to choose me over someone else."

Rolling his tongue over his teeth, he continues to watch me, measuring my words and the sincerity of my tone. And I honestly mean them. Every damn word. I'll step out of the way and let him figure his shit out with Roman without interference on my part. I meant it when I said I was done fighting. It's obvious this is what needs to happen, so I'll do it. Even if it kills me.

"Arguing with you isn't going to change anything, so just tell me this. Is that really what you want? Because if it is, I won't stop you again," Rain whispers after a minute and it takes every ounce of willpower not to laugh at him.

No, it's the complete opposite of what I want.

There are about a million things I could want or ask for at this very moment but him letting me leave and ending this thing between us is dead last on the list.

Those very thoughts must be written all over my damn face because Rain's expression softens and he takes a step closer to me. Then another and another until he's directly in front of me. His hand reaches up and cups the side of my face, fingers sinking into my hair and I try my damnedest not to nuzzle into his touch.

"It's not what you want, is it? You're just trying to play the martyr."

I hate him for reading me like an open book, but I can't blame anyone but myself at this rate. I've never had a good poker face. But what I can do is keep my damn mouth shut and get the hell out of here.

He'll let me go, he'll figure the shit out regarding Ted with the help from Roman at the very least. Because I saw the look in his eyes, he's not going anywhere. His father's orders be damned.

Roman's right; Rain doesn't need me here for any of it.

Rain closes his eyes, letting his forehead drop against mine and rubbing his nose against mine. "I need you to speak words."

I don't listen. Not just due to my stubbornness, but because all I can do is focus on the way his skin feels against mine, drinking it in and memorizing this moment.

A frustrated sigh, almost like a growl, slips from deep within his throat and he rips his entire body away from me. His eyes settle on mine, pinning me with his fiery stare. One that immediately tells me I'm about to get reamed out.

"You need to open your mouth and talk. *Right now,*" he hisses, a dangerous lilt to his voice as it starts to rise with his anger. "What do you want, River? I'm not a mind reader. If you want something, say it. Please, just tell me."

I let out a huff, biting the inside of my cheek to keep from screaming in his goddamn face for being so blind. It doesn't work.

You asked for it, baby.

"What do I want? Shouldn't it be fucking obvious by now? Shouldn't you know? I've so much as *told you,*" I seethe, ice dripping in my tone. "I want something more than some high altitude fucks for a week or two at a time with absolutely no word from you in between. I want to know I'm not being played like a goddamn fool by feeling more than I should."

A sardonic laugh slips from my lips and I scowl at him. "I wanna be able to claim you and mark you as mine and not look like an idiot for it. I want the words from your goddamn mouth to mean something. To be confident, knowing when this shit is all over and we go back to Boulder, we still *have something* instead of being terrified everything will come crashing down again."

"Mo grá—" Rain starts, his eyes wide, but I'm on a fucking roll and in no state to stop now.

"Shut the fuck up, I'm not finished." I cut him off, glaring at him. "I wanna know you aren't going to leave. Because everyone fucking does and I'm sick and tired of waiting for the other shoe to drop with every single person in my life. I wanna know I mean something to you. Know I don't have to worry about another Roman coming in here and taking you again because for fuck's sake, Rain, *I just want you!*"

My chest is heaving as the last words break from my throat in a growl so vicious, I'm surprised I was able to make the sound in the first place. But something about him makes me unhinged. To the point where I become the worst version of myself.

Or when he lets me, the best.

Rain's eyes are a liquid gold, scalding me as they stay firmly fixated on my face. Crossing his arms over his chest again, I see the veins flex beneath the ink covering almost every available inch of skin on them.

"Are you done?"

I shrug slightly, not sure what to do with the emotionless state of his tone. "Sure."

But it's short-lived since that little act sets him right off.

"Good, because it's your turn to shut up and listen," he hisses in a low gravel, so deep I can almost feel it touching my soul. It actually makes me take a step back from him because even in the worst fights we've had, I've never heard *this* in his voice.

The only way I can describe it is he's lost hold on the only string of sanity he had left.

"For someone who loves to talk, you sure know how to keep the most important shit bottled up inside you, never letting it see the light of day. And for someone so smart, how can you be so blind?"

"What—"

"No fucking *what* anything!" he roars, his cheeks and neck tinting a slight pink. "Everything I've done and said for the past two fucking months has been for you! With you in mind and no one *but you!* And I've been hanging on by a goddamn thread myself. But then having to stand back and watch from the sidelines as you struggled and fought to stay afloat? It killed me. Because I don't want to be the reason you fucking *drown*, Abhainn." His throat catches on his nickname for me and I catch the flash of panic in his features change to regret. "So, the night in your apartment when you told me I destroyed you… I know you couldn't see it or feel it, but just know you destroyed me too."

My chest aches. *I highly doubt it, baby.*

I turn to the bed, not able to look at him as I let out a gruff laugh. "You have a funny way of showing it sometimes."

But I wince the moment the words slip out because all it's going to do is fan the already scorching flames.

"Because me standing here and practically begging you to give me your thoughts and your words isn't showing you, right?" He scoffs, and I glance over my shoulder to see him tossing his hands out and letting them fall to his sides. "I don't know what else I can do other than sit here and scream at you until you listen. Because it should be clear by now I'm not the kind of person to put in *this* amount of effort for just anyone. Fuck, Riv. How don't you get it? I'll give you anything you want. *Any-fucking-thing.* Say the goddamn word and it's yours."

I groan and walk over to the window, shaking my head. I need to get out of here before he makes me more promises he can't keep. Not when all he's ever done is break them. Today was the perfect example of that.

But the masochist in me keeps my feet firmly planted in place and allows the single word to pass my lips in a question.

"Anything?"

"Yes." He sighs, his temper dissipating slightly but I still hear the frustration in his words. The desperation and ferocity. "Anything. You want to even the playing field? Fine. You want to cuff me to a bed and take me by force? Do it. You want me to relive one of the worst moments of my life to prove it to you? Because I will. Swear it on my fucking life, I will. Because *I love you*. And making sure you understand that is more important to me than anything else."

My breath hitches as my entire chest damn near caves in.

He just…

I turn slowly, letting my back sink against the windowpane and my eyes collide with his. There's nothing but honesty glowing in them.

"What?" I whisper, sounding like I just swallowed glass.

"You fucking heard me," he says, his voice just as hoarse as he walks up to me. "But in case it was somehow lost in translation, I'll say it again. I love you. And all I want is you too."

Holy shit.

My jaw must be on the floor because a smirk crosses his gorgeous lips as his gaze floats between my eyes and my mouth.

For the first time in my entire life, I'm speechless.

But who needs words? I sure as hell don't when I just want to fucking kiss him.

So that's what I do.

Fingers snaking into his hair, I pull his mouth to mine, molding our lips together. I slip my tongue into his mouth and his wraps around the bar running through it, pulling and tugging at it.

Breaking away, I pant against his mouth. "I swear to God if this is some fucking ga—"

He smiles, nipping at my lip. "It's not. I love you."

That's three times now he's told me and my heart honestly can't take it.

But in the back of my mind, the little tiny piece of worry creeps in. I know the doubt won't easily be erased with the amount of damage we've done to each other. Yet at this point, I don't even think I care. Even if it's all a fucking lie, I need these stolen moments with him to be something more than a beautiful tragedy.

So, as stupid as it might be, and no matter how much my brain tells me to shield my heart, I allow myself to take him at his word. Again. I let myself believe him.

Rain's body is plastered to mine, pressing me into the glass as he takes my mouth, claiming it as his and his alone. My cock is aching in my jeans and I'm ready to beg him for some sort of release, and he's quick to notice. He snakes his hand between us, palming me over my jeans, and I moan into his mouth and my hips rock to meet his touch.

"Insatiable as ever," he quips, licking my bottom lip.

Fuck, you have no idea. I honestly don't think I'll ever tire of this. Of his touch, the way his body affects mine at every turn.

It's need and desire and ownership.

I'm his. I think I have been from the moment we met on the field that first day of practice; I just didn't know it yet. And for the life of me, I hope this finally means he's mine too. For real this time. No more Roman or Abbi or anything fucking it up.

Just him. To claim and to own. To touch and love and fuck and worship.

Mine.

I move my mouth to his neck as I fumble with my belt buckle. "Just because I'm hard doesn't mean I'm not mad at you."

"I know. It just makes you a little bit of an *I love you* slut."

I almost laugh because he's right. I'll do anything to hear those words from his mouth again and again.

His harsh breath in my ear sets my nerve endings on fire as I lick and suck and bite at his throat. My fingers work down the zipper of my pants while his hands slide under my shirt, grazing down my sides so softly, goosebumps rise on my skin.

"We're gonna talk about all this," I remind him—and myself. "Later."

"I know," he repeats, pulling me back towards the bed.

"And Rain?" I say, swallowing roughly. Pulling back for a second, I hold his eyes as I put my heart on the line for him. Hopefully, for the last time, as the words come out barely more than a whisper. "I love you too."

A slow smile creeps onto his face, one I swear he created just for me. "I know," he tells me as he yanks my shirt over my head before mouths and hands roam each other's bodies.

"You. Naked. In my bed," I demand, a challenge to my tone as I nip at the sensitive spot below his ear. Then I repeat his words from the other day. And from the night at my apartment. "Let me show you."

Because I know now that's what he was telling me all those times. What he was trying to prove to me.

Rain groans as he wrenches his body away from me, stepping back and slowly — torturously fucking slowly — starts stripping out of his clothes. First his shirt, then his belt. The muscles of his arms beneath the layers and swirls of ink flex and bulge at his movements. His jeans go next and finally, the underwear until he's gloriously naked and standing in front of me.

And I smile as I strip the rest of the way too, seeing for the first time, we're finally on the same field. The same page. The same team, where we give as much as we take.

Equals.

I realize now, I'm the only one he's willing to relinquish control to.

If that isn't love, I don't know what is.

Grabbing my wallet from my bag, I search until I find a small packet of lube.

"Ever the boy scout," I hear in an amused tone from the bed.

My lips lift slightly as I turn to Rain, finding him now lying on his back, his cock in hand. His eyes are glued to my face as he strokes himself, and an overwhelming amount of emotion surges through me, circulating around one thought.

He's really mine.

I smirk as I rip the package with my teeth before coating my cock with the lubricant and cover his body with mine. Gripping both of us in my hand, I start jacking us together.

"River," he gasps, against my lips while I kiss him more, moving against me as I stroke our lengths in tandem. It's the greatest thing I've ever felt apart from being inside him.

"Rain," I whisper. Gripping the back of his neck, I separate us enough to be able to take in his face completely. Mussed hair and swollen lips and amber eyes filled with love and lust; I've never seen anything more perfect in my goddamn life.

Of course, he has to slam the breaks on by asking the stupidest questions I've ever heard.

"Are you sure? About this? Us? There's so much—"

Oh, no, you don't.

I cut him off by crashing my mouth to his again, not letting him ruin this moment with self-doubt or insecurity. It might be running through my mind too, but I'm not letting it derail us. Because we fucking deserve this. After all the pain and the heartache and the bullshit, we deserve this one goddamn moment to be nothing but *happy.*

"I'm fucking sure," I pant against his mouth when we're finally forced to come up for air. "This is gonna come out sounding stupid and fucking corny, but my world begins and ends with you. I see you, the real you. The *you* kept hidden from everyone else. I know who you are, baby. And despite the shit we went through and all the shit we still have to overcome, I'm undeniably in love with you."

He smiles and places soft kisses on my lips, my nose, all over my face before moving back to my mouth as I say the words, ones I've felt but held in, because I was fucking terrified. He does it like he's completely lost control, needing to lick and kiss and touch and love every piece of me.

I get it. I need it too.

"Fuck, fuck, *fuck, Abhainn*," he mutters, his eyes shut as he gets lost in his desire as I bring the two of us closer to release.

But I don't want him to finish till I'm buried deep inside him, feeling his ass milk me as he comes.

Wetting my lips, my chest heaves as I lean back, coating my erection with more lube before settling on my knees between his legs. My fingers tease his crease, slipping and sliding around the puckered rim of his asshole before easing a finger inside, then a second to follow.

And from the look in his eyes, he's enjoying it.

"That's it, baby," I whisper, watching his face as it begins to tint pink with heat. He meets my hand with every pump of my fingers and soon, I'm wrapping my other fist around his shaft, desperate to give him everything he needs.

His moans are the only sound in the room as I work his cock over, bringing him closer to the edge. But he grips the wrist of the hand that's stroking him and manages a husky *Riv* that pulls me from my task.

I glance up, his gaze colliding with mine and he reaches out, grabbing the back of my neck to pull my mouth up to meet his.

"Inside me," he pants against my lips and I can't help but smile. There was a time when he was adamant this would never happen. He fought it at every turn. Now he's asking for it. Needing it.

Begging, like I told him he would.

"Soon," I exhale, my breathing coming out sporadic as I work a third finger into him, stretching him in preparation. It's been months since I've topped him and I have to make sure he's ready for me. The last thing I want to do is hurt him.

But Rain has other ideas, reaching down and grabbing my cock. "*Inside me. Now,*" he demands, stroking my slick length.

"So greedy." I laugh hoarsely, loving how demanding he's becoming in bed.

Not that he wasn't *demanding* before, this is just more...open. Free.

Pulling my fingers from him, I waste no time to align my cock with his ass and start working myself inside him. He's tight — so fucking tight — and I think I've died and gone to heaven, it's been so long since I've felt so consumed.

It doesn't take long for me to be able to slide in completely with one smooth thrust, bottoming out with my hips flush against him. My lips come crashing down to his as I hold my weight on my forearms beside his head, covering his body with mine. I groan into his mouth as our tongues move together in their erotic dance, warring with who's in charge.

Pumping my hips in long, slow strokes, I drive Rain crazy with each pass I make over his prostate. Each and every time I hit it, a little grunt of pleasure slips from his lips and I swallow it whole.

His mouth continues to devour mine until I physically have to come up for air, satisfaction rolling through me at the sight of those swollen lips.

It doesn't stop me from tasting the rest of him though. I kiss his jaw, his neck, his chest until my tongue teases his nipple, tugging and sucking the bud into my mouth when he lets out a strangled sigh. My hips piston into him hard and slow, letting him feel me hit the deepest part of him imaginable.

And then straighten to look down into his love-drunk expression, smiling.

"Bottom is a good look on you, baby," I whisper, gripping his hips and yanking him toward me, impaling him further on my cock. I shift his legs over my forearms and pull him even deeper. The new angle sets off a chain of expletives from Rain's mouth in a gasp as I slide in so deep, so far, we might as well be one. His heated gaze flicks to mine and I smile wider, reaching down to grasp his shaft, jacking it slowly while I roll my hips into him. "Watching you take my cock is the hottest thing I've ever seen."

Another groan sounds from him. "Give me more, Abhainn." I know he's not talking about my dick, either.

I honestly don't know how much more I *can* give him. It doesn't seem like enough. Nothing I do or say will ever express how far he's rooted himself into my very being.

But fuck, nothing has ever felt greater than this moment with me buried inside him and our hearts filled with so much love, they might burst at the seams. I can't imagine anything ever topping this.

"Gladly," I whisper, picking up speed as sweat drips from my forehead. I wipe it away and squeeze his shaft on the upstroke, feeling the pre-cum slipping over my fingers. "I'll give you everything, baby."

"You already have," he breathes, his hips bucking as he seeks more and more from me.

And my grin now feels like it might split my face in two.

My palm continues to spread the leaking evidence of his arousal all down his cock and I thrust into him, one hand still clutching his hip in place. "You take my cock like you were designed for it. But that's because you were, yeah, baby? The reason you never willingly gave this to someone else is because it was only ever meant to be mine?"

His throat works to swallow, his gaze searing into my soul as he nods in agreement, his face flushed with lust and pleasure. When he goes to open his mouth to speak, nothing more than another moan manages to come out as my dick makes swipe after swipe over his prostate.

Soon he's clenching around me, the most impassioned sounds slipping from his lips as I stare down at him. He's the most beautiful thing I've ever seen.

That is, until he rolls us, slipping off my aching shaft before sinking back down on it, straddling my lap. And this position, him riding me, it brings me full circle once again. To the cabin. The paint. The floor.

Him owning his pleasure, finding it, and letting it consume him.

The passion and love between us was palpable then.

Now it's incendiary.

"You own me," he utters, swallowing hard as the blunt ends of my fingers dig into his hips as I thrust up into him. "I might have you, but you *own* me. Every inch. Every thought. Every moment of every day, Abhainn. *You own me.*"

The words are filled with emotion and I know them to be true. I know now more than ever, he won't ever lie to me again.

We're past the bullshit. The games. The heartache.

While our story might've started months ago, this is the true beginning.

Of something real, tangible. Mind-altering perfection.

Because the love flowing through us is something only achieved by fate swooping in and giving you the piece of the puzzle you never knew was missing. The other half of a whole.

He's mine. Only mine.

Just like I'm his.

And I know now, we're no longer an almost. We're everything.

"You know I'm telling you the truth, right?" he asks later as we lie in bed, still naked and wrapped in each other. The only thing covering us is half a bedsheet and the mixed scent of sex and sweat. And I'm feeling...content. Happy, even.

In love? Definitely.

My gaze darts up to his face to find his forehead creased in worry. "About what?"

"I don't want Roman. I *never* wanted him," he insists, my eyes searching his face. "You're the one I want, mo grá."

I see it in his eyes, I can believe him. Trust him.

"I know," I whisper.

My eyes leave his face, watching as I trail my hand over his arm, tracing the ink covering his skin. An extensive collection of Celtic symbols and knots all intricately pieced together like the artwork it is.

"You designed this, didn't you?" I ask softly, my fingers making their way to his wrist.

"Yeah, I did all of them. Makes them a little more special, I guess. Worth the pain."

I nod in understanding, flipping his hand wrist up. And it's then I notice the new piece of ink that didn't used to be there when we were in the cabin.

Running the pad of my thumb over the single word, noting it isn't raised the way it would be if it was extremely fresh. Meaning he got it sometime in January or February. My eyes stare at the word as I try to read it, knowing full well it's Gaelic.

"A-b-h-a-i-n-n," I mutter, spelling out the word and looking up into his eyes. "How do you say it? What's it mean?"

Rain leans forward and presses a kiss to my lips, smiling against them before he whispers, "Abhainn."

Nuzzling my nose against his, I respond with a quiet, "Yeah?"

He chuckles then, pulling back to look at me. "No, that's what it says. Abhainn. River. Your name."

I cock my head and look at him, and my mind starts to spin. And somehow, the first thing to come out of my mouth is probably the most ridiculous thing of all.

"That's not how I thought it would be spelled. It sounds completely different."

A throaty laugh leaves him, and he presses his forehead into my shoulder, hiding his smile. "That's Gaelic for you."

I smile too when he looks back at me, it only grows when he traces the dimple on one of my cheeks, intently focused on the task.

"You really got my name tattooed on you?"

He nods, his finger still playing with the dimple.

I grin more, amused by his fascination with them. "That's like the biggest no-go in the history of tattoos. When did you decide that would be a good idea?"

He shrugs, his eyes colliding with mine. "On the way back home from picking Roman up at the airport."

My heart squeezes because…why would he do it when we were nothing but…*nothing* at that point? How did he have so much faith that we'd make it through? He was willing to risk having my name marking his body for the rest of his life, even if we never reconciled?

I swallow roughly and bring my hand up to lace my fingers through his. "Even though we weren't together? Even though you said…"

"Even though, Abhainn," he mutters, his thumb brushing the back of my hand, and I enjoy the way he constantly feels the need to touch me now. It feels like everything I've ever wanted.

Happiness. Contentment. Joy.

Love.

And if this doesn't give me the confidence to know he's in this for the fucking long haul, nothing will. Because you don't brand yourself with just anyone's name.

"It didn't matter to me, us not being together. I didn't care if we were never going to be together again. I just had to do it." He pauses and searches my face, his eyes expressing just as much as his words. "Your name was already inscribed on my heart and etched in my soul. The only place it was missing was inked on my skin."

And that's all it takes for emotion to clog my throat, stealing my ability to speak. Instead I pull his hand out again to study the ink, the perfect script of my name forever written on his body. Marking him as mine for the world to see.

"I want one too," I say when I finally find my voice again.

He cocks his head. "Your name tattooed on your skin?"

I smirk. "No, jackass. *Yours.* What's Gaelic for Rain?"

His brows furrow. "Báisteach, I think?" he says, but he doesn't sound too convinced.

"Never mind." I laugh, pulling him closer. "I'll figure something else out."

I feel his grin against my forehead before he gives me a soft kiss there. "Whatever it is, we'll both get it. Anything you want."

I quirk a brow and decide to test his meaning of *anything.* "I want matching dick tattoos. On our asses."

Of course, I'm not surprised when he shoots the idea down with a deep laugh.

"Not in this fucking lifetime, mo grá."

TWENTY-FOUR
River

DAY SEVEN: THURSDAY

The next morning, my chin is tucked into my pillow as I sprawl across the bed on my stomach, covered by just my boxers and the thin white sheet. I flip through the pages of my textbook, absorbing as much information as I can over the remainder of break to make up for all the class I've missed recently.

Who would've thought skipping class would be a bad idea in the long run, right?

Movement from Rain slipping back into my room from the corner of my eye has me pausing. He sets his bag down beside mine, grabbing a plastic bag from inside it and carrying it over to the bed.

"What's that?" I ask him, rolling to my side.

"Don't know. It was sitting on my bed when I went to grab my stuff," he says, taking a seat beside me. He's in only a pair of athletic shorts, leaving his chest and stomach on display for my perusal. My fingers tap against the book and I struggle to keep my hands to myself because I *need* to study. Not jump my boyfriend.

Fuck, it feels good to think. Probably much better to *say,* though neither of us have used the word aloud. Maybe because the word seems really fucking inaccurate to describe what we are to each other.

He sets the bag on the bed between us and I attempt to keep a neutral expression while Rain starts pulling small tubes of acrylic paint, one of those palette things artists use, a few paint brushes, and a roll of canvas from the bag.

"Did you do this?" he asks, glancing up at me as he sets a tube of white paint on the bed.

"Nope," I reply carefully.

But I have a feeling I know who did.

His brows furrow as he looks down into the bag again, pulling out a folded piece of notebook paper. Without flipping it open, I watch his eyes flash from me to the paper, his expression softening slightly.

"Roman?" I ask, voicing my suspicions.

Rain clears his throat, holding out the note for me to see. "You tell me."

I shake my head, not needing nor wanting to know what it says. "It's fine."

His brows furrow, tossing the note onto the bed beside me. "I don't want secrets between us. And I know how you feel about Roman. So read it."

Sighing, I put my weight on one elbow, pick up the note and flip it open, finding three words written on the inside. My face must be priceless because Rain chuckles as I read the words aloud.

"'I'm sorry. Roman.'" My head cocks to the side and I flip it over, looking for any other words that might be there. But I find none. "That's it?"

Rain laughs, grabbing it from me and reading it himself before placing it back in the bag. "Yeah, I guess so."

"If that's all it said then why did you feel the need to show me?"

The corner of his mouth lifts and he leans over, giving me a soft kiss. "Because *you* didn't know that's all it said. It could have been him professing his undying love for me or something for all you knew. Yeah, it wasn't, but regardless I wanted to prove to you I mean it when I say I don't want secrets. So, I let you see it first."

I roll his logic around in my mind for a second and laugh. "Okay, I'll give it to you."

His smirk grows as he crawls up beside me, situating the paints to one side of himself, setting the palette in his lap, and quickly adding a bit of white and blue and black to it.

"You can keep studying. Don't let me stop you," he says without looking up from what he's doing.

Rolling back to my stomach beneath the sheet, I find where I stopped reading and pick up from there. Well, I attempt to, but it doesn't exactly work because the second I start to get back into my kinesiology book, I feel something cold and wet brush against my back.

I let out a low hiss, my spine stiffening. "What the fuck are you doing?"

Glancing over at Rain, I find him sitting cross-legged beside me, mixing a couple colors together on his palette. I see him trying to keep a straight face, but the beginning of a smile on the edge of his mouth gives him away. "Painting. What are you doing?"

I'm about to open my mouth to answer, but he lifts the brush with the light gray paint on it and swipes it against my back again.

I suck in a breath at the chill and glare at him, but Rain doesn't seem to notice as he uses the brush to move it across my skin. "You're painting me?"

That makes him chuckle. "Technically, I'm painting *on you.*"

"Can I ask why?"

Another cool bit of paint slides over my skin, this time directly on my spine.

"Because I've painted something for you, drawn a sketchbook filled *of* you, had paint sex *with* you, but I've never painted *on you.*" He says it in such a way, as if his thought process should be completely obvious to me.

Spoiler alert…it's not.

But honestly, that's kind of half the fun. For being on the same wavelength a lot of the time, at least before all this bullshit the last two months, the moments when we have to actually work to understand each other are some of my favorites.

When I don't respond, he looks up and meets my eyes. "You might be the muse, but there's no reason you can't also be the canvas."

He dips his brush back in the paint, bringing it to my skin again, but stops just before it touches me, meeting my gaze. "I can stop. If you aren't comfortable or I'm distracting you or whatever."

I shake my head, letting my cheek fall to the pillow as I keep my eyes on him. "No, you're fine. Just surprised, mostly."

He smirks before turning back to his task at hand.

I try to go back to reading, but he was right. Each pass of paint, while it's not a shock or uncomfortable, it's definitely distracting me from being able to comprehend anything I'm reading. So instead, I turn my head on the pillow again to look at him beside me, concentrating intently on whatever he's painting.

Letting my curiosity get the best of me, I hedge slightly with the question that's been sitting in my mind since I read the note. "What is he apologizing for?"

Rain shrugs. "Could be a few things. His father wanting him and the guys to leave, maybe? For the fight we got in after the rest of you left the office? For kissing me?" He laughs softly. "Fuck, maybe all the above? Him actually apologizing for any of it, though? That's what's strange. He's never been the type to apologize for much. Not that he's an asshole or anything, it's just the way he is."

I watch his face as he works, taking in his expression as he thinks about Roman and how much he's changed from the guy Rain used to know. "Do you miss him?"

"Sometimes, yeah. What we had back in prep school was fun and easy. He and Siena both gave me legs to stand on during some of the worst times in my life and for that, I'm always going to feel a little indebted to them. But now…" he trails off, glancing away. "I don't know. I can't see us ever getting back to that kind of friendship."

Biting my lip, I try to hold the question in. But I just can't stop the masochist inside me from letting them break free.

"Did you sleep with him? When we weren't together? Or…ever?"

"Riv—" he starts, his features strained.

"No secrets," I remind him.

His eyes close and I swear my heart crawls up into my throat. "Rain, if you did—"

"We didn't," he says firmly, his eyes opening. "We didn't have sex. The night of Aiden's party, we went home and I got fucking plastered because I was pissed off. And we made out a bit, he blew me for a minute or two maybe."

My throat constricts, wanting every fucking detail but none at the same time. Because it hurts, it really fucking does.

"But the *second* he tried to…I just couldn't do it." His Adam's apple bobs as he swallows harshly. "I wanted to, I think, at least. If only to make myself feel better for a little bit. The probelm was, I just fucking couldn't stand the idea of betraying you. So I told him I couldn't because the entire time I'd be thinking about you. Wishing it was you. And I would've been."

I see the sincerity in his eyes, hear the plea in his voice. And no matter how much it might kill me to think about Roman's mouth touching any part of him, I know I can't be mad.

"I believe you, I promise. We both know I have no right to be mad at you for something that happened when we weren't together," I tell him, repeating the sentiment he once told me.

After all, his statement was accurate. And if he wasn't mad about Abbi, even when I threw it in his face as a form of punishment, how can I be angry with him and Roman doing basically the exact same thing?

"I just hate seeing that look on your face. Like I kicked your puppy or something."

A soft laugh bubbles out of me. I appreciate his attempt to lighten the mood again. "I mean, I'd rather you *actually* fuck

Roman than kick a puppy."

He snorts, shaking his head. "Well let's just say I have no intention of doing either, so you never have to look at me like that again." Smirking slightly, he meets my eyes. "You can only look at me like one of those heart-eye emojis from now on."

I laugh and shoot him a dirty look, the ache in my chest easing. "Fuck off, that's not gonna happen. You're lucky there is paint all over me or I'd kick your ass for even saying it."

"Sure, you would, Abhainn. Sure you would." He says it with a straight face, but I hear the amusement in his tone more than anything.

We settle back into silence; him painting my back, and before I know it, I find my eyes closing. It's like that for a long time, nothing but the sound of his brush scraping against the palette or sliding over my skin, slowly lulling me into a content state of happiness.

A low humming comes from the back of my throat, making Rain pause.

"What song?"

I smile, keeping my eyes closed. "I swear you told me the day outside your apartment it was the last time you'd ask me that."

"In a shocking turn of events," he states, sarcasm lacing his tone, "I lied. You can expect this question every damn day for the foreseeable future. So spill."

I chuckle softly, eyes still shut, and sigh from the back of my throat. "'Follow You' by Bring Me The Horizon."

The smile in his voice is evident when he says, "Good choice," and carries on with his task.

That's when I take the chance to open my eyes and look at him.

And I absolutely know, he could and has put me through hell, but none of it could ever make me want him any less.

"I love you," I tell him softly. And nothing in the world has felt better coming from my lips or the freedom to say them in the first place.

He glances down and meets my eyes. "You have no idea how amazing it is to hear you say it."

I quirk a brow because *really?* But he just laughs and shakes his head. "No I mean, you *do* know. But it's just..." He trails off, adding more paint to his brush. "I don't know. I'm not good at being vulnerable or honest. And most of the time with you, it just sort of happens without me having to think about it. Which is terrifying, but at the same time, I've never felt...safer, I guess?"

"I get it," I tell him. Because I feel the same damn way.

While my home life was a lot better than Rain's, both of us struggle when it comes to love. Giving it to people who don't deserve it and never receiving enough of it in return. And yeah, it fucking sucks, but it also makes me appreciate the feeling that much more. So I have no doubt Rain feels the same way.

"Hell," he says, an ironic laugh in his voice. "If I'd known those three little words would get this kind of response, I wouldn't have been nearly as afraid to say them."

That grabs my attention. "When did you know?"

He starts moving the brush against my back again in light strokes, staying silent for a minute before speaking. "In the cabin. The last night we were there." He pauses and licks his lips, causing my gaze to track the movement. "I actually did say it. But you were sleeping. And I said it in Gaelic."

I let out a soft laugh. "I think that's cheating."

"Kinda the point." He chuckles, resuming once he mixes a light blue before applying it to my skin. "But I still said it. Which in itself was a miracle. So, to tell you while you were awake *and* in a language you could understand?"

I let out a sigh and close my eyes again. "Well, I'm glad you did."

Rain goes quiet once more as he keeps working, letting me get lost in the comfortable silence between us. So lost, I don't know if it's been a few minutes or hours since we spoke. But it doesn't really matter.

It's still hard to believe this is actually happening. After the way the past few months have gone, I would've never expected this turn of events, even if I'd hoped for them every day we were apart.

As if reading my thoughts, Rain clears his throat. "I know it feels like it will be right now, but this won't always be easy."

"I know."

"But do you? We're gonna fight. Knowing us, probably a lot."

Leaning up on my forearms and opening my eyes, I furrow my brows to give him a *what the fuck* look. "I know, baby. But I don't care. I know what I'm signing up for. We'll fight and we'll make up. That's what couples, what *partners,* do." I move to sit up completely, careful to keep my back from touching the sheets and scoot over directly in front of him. "Don't try talking me or yourself out of this. I fucking meant it when I said forever."

His eyes track mine. "We're only twenty-one," he whispers. "How can we know what forever is supposed to look like when we've barely lived?"

I think back to what Taylor said the day we were all up in Vail together and take a second to appreciate my best friend's insane Yoda-esque advice.

"When the person you're meant to be with is tossed in your path, you grab them and hold on for dear life. And I don't care how old we are. You hear it all the time about some people meeting their soulmate at the age of five or whatever. Who's to say we can't at twenty-one?"

Rain's eyebrows rise. "Are you saying I'm your soulmate?"

I roll my eyes. "Poke fun all you want. But if we were, we'd be together forever, right? That's not me being sappy. It's logic."

He shakes his head in mock innocence. "Nope. Not logic. Sounds like something completely different to me."

Jesus Christ, I'm gonna kill him.

I sigh. "Well, don't keep me on the edge of my seat. Please, Rain, share with the rest of the class."

He leans forward, his face humorless, and he locks his eyes with mine. "Sounds and looks a lot like," he pauses for dramatic effect and the fucker actually bats his lashes at me. "Heart-eye emojis."

I blink at him, the poster child of indifference as a grin slowly creeps up on his face.

"Oh, c'mon. It's funny and you know it."

Blink.

"It's okay if you have heart-eyes for me, Riv. You know that, right?"

Blink.

"Look, I'm not gonna judge you for it. After all, I am your soul—"

He doesn't get to finish the word because I launch myself at him, pushing him onto the mattress, straddling his lap, and pinning his arms above his head in one quick move.

His paint palette gets flipped onto the white sheets and the tubes of paint, most of them closed but a select few, are scattered across the bed. Paint is everywhere including his chest and hair, splatter and smeared across it. The mess only gets worse the second he flips me on my back, his artwork still wet on my skin.

"Soulmate," he finishes, his devious smirk still sitting on his lips. "But now look at the mess you made, Abhainn. There's paint everywhere," he whispers roughly as he grinds his hips into mine. "Were you looking to get another paint sex session in? You should know all you have to do is ask."

I shoot him another glare, not letting my dick do the thinking. "No, I was looking to get you to shut up about the soulmate bullshit. Forget I ever said it, *please.*"

He smirks. "You know the best way to get me to shut up would be to stick your—"

I cover his mouth with my palm, effectively cutting him off. Except the asshole licks my palm, and the shock causes me to yank my hand away.

I wipe my hand, coated with his saliva, across his face. "I hate you."

"I hate you too," he says, bringing his mouth to mine for a slow kiss. When he pulls back and meets my gaze, he's wearing my favorite smile. The one that lets me know he's mine and I can't help my own grin breaking out across my face. Dimples and all.

"Yeah?" I laugh.

"Yeah," he agrees, kissing me again. "So fucking much."

TWENTY-FIVE

River

DAY EIGHT: FRIDAY

A crash from the foyer has me running in that direction from the living room. When I get there, I find a giant Ming vase toppled over, the broken shards scattered all over the ground. And then there's Callum standing there, two bags in hand and a shit-eating grin on his face as he looks at the mess, not noticing I'm there.

"Oops," he whispers and starts to glance around.

I take a step back around the corner, hoping to get out of sight in time before he catches me watching. Thankfully, it works.

Asher chooses the next moment to step back into the foyer from the open front doors and sighs at the mess. "Goddammit Cal, my mom's gonna be fucking pissed."

"Why?" He laughs, tossing one of the bags over his shoulders. "The thing was hideous anyway."

Asher rolls his eyes and heads past me to the kitchen, finding me hidden behind the corner the second he passes by. I raise my finger to my lips, the universal signal for *shut the fuck up and say nothing,* to which he just smirks and shakes his head before heading in the kitchen to grab a broom.

"Roman!" Kaede yells from the front door, looking pissed. At first I thought he was just mad about something, but starting to realize it's just his natural state.

A minute later, just as Asher passes me again to clean up Callum's mess, Roman comes from down the hall. He's wearing a bored expression on his face as he gives Kaede his attention.

"You called?"

"We're leaving, Ro. Now."

He shakes his head, grabbing the dustpan from Ash's hand and leaning down to help him pick up the shattered pieces. "The fuck I am. You guys go, but I'm staying."

Kaede's jaw visibly ticks. His fingers twitch on his hand, a clear signal of frustration overtaking him. "I might not hold the key to the Enclave yet, but I'm still the one with the power here. So, do as you're told and go grab your *shit*."

Roman glances up at Asher as he sweeps the last bit of broken pieces into the dustpan. "Don't look at me, Ro. You heard your dad. This is my house, so I don't have to go if I don't want to."

"Well, *are* you?" Roman pushes.

Asher glances in my direction and meets my eyes for a brief moment before casually going back to his task. "No, I'm not. I figure I'd take some *me time* away from all you asshats. You know, before my life becomes a goddamn shit show after initiation and I'm fucking stuck with you all the time?"

"You're already with us all the time," Callum points out, heading past Kaede out to the Mercedes G-Wagon parked out front, one of the six cars Asher's family have parked in their garages. I just barely see Hollis loading some other bags into the car too, presumably his and Kaede's.

Roman crosses his arms over his chest and glares at Kaede. "I'm not leaving until this is figured out. Anders is still fucking out there."

"You heard the order," Kaede growls fiercely, his fist clenching. "*Your father* is the one who gave them. As son of the Grand Elector, you think you'd know to listen to an order when it's given."

Roman shakes his head. "I don't give a fuck what my father has to say about this." The words come out in a snarl so vicious, I flinch even though it's not being aimed at me. "You and I and everyone in the goddamn Enclave know this is much bigger than just Ted Anders and Rain. I might not know *how* but clearly I'm the only one willing to *figure it out.*"

Kaede lets out a short exhale and even I can tell he's mere moments from snapping. "Why do you feel the need to rebel at every turn? And for *what?* Someone who you could *never* have, even if he wanted you?" His jaw ticks again and he smirks. "You're willing to put *him* above everything our families have worked towards for *generations?* It's idiotic, Roman. Especially when he doesn't love you."

I hold my breath at the comment, knowing it could very well be enough to set Roman off entirely. Because while Roman might've egged both Rain and I on while we've been here, neither of us want to sit here and play *couple in love* in front of him.

That's just a dick move.

Roman shakes his head and chuckles, though it sounds hollow and empty to my ears. "You speak as if you know anything about human emotion when we all know you're the most heartless of us all."

Fuck.

The words are harsh and ruthless, though not completely without merit. Like I said, Kaede is…well, a lot of an asshole and doesn't really have another setting other than angry or annoyed.

But as I watch them interact, I notice a flash of something on Kaede's face. Something like regret, maybe? Whatever it is, it's gone almost instantly before he quirks his brows.

"Love isn't in the damn cards for us, Roman. We aren't meant for it, we weren't made for it, and no sane person would survive us anyway." He says the words harshly, his piercing gray eyes locking Roman in place. "We've been taught this from the beginning. No attachments. It's not my fault you can't fucking listen."

Kaede pauses, his eyes flicking to Asher for backup. When Ash remains silent, Kaede shakes his head, letting his voice lower. "I'm not trying to be a dick, man. But it's been *years* and you're still this hung up? It's time you learn to accept your fate and let him go."

"Because trying to do that worked so well for you, right, Kaede?" Roman spits.

Kaede rolls his shoulders, setting them hard, and I catch a venomous glint in them. "I've learned from my mistakes. You might want to do yourself a favor and learn from them too."

Roman shakes his head, stepping back toward the hallway.

"Caring about others? Putting someone else's needs before your own? It isn't a *mistake.* It's being fucking human."

Asher's eyes flick to where I am and he gives me a subtle signal with his eyes to move. Probably before I hear something I might not want to. But I stay.

"Fuck, you should try it sometime. Being human," Roman continues. "It'd be nice to see you be taken down a goddamn notch."

"*Roman,*" Kaede hisses, a clear signal his fuse has been lit. "This isn't about *me.* It's about you and your inability to see past this…*infatuation* you have with someone who clearly is in love with someone else! Let it *go.*"

I watch as Roman nods his head, but whether he's accepting Kaede's words or not, I can't tell. What I do notice, though, is each and every one of the shutters being pulled closed as he stares at one of the guys who is *supposed* to be one of his most trusted allies.

"I'm here until he tells me to leave," he finally says, his voice now detached. "That's what you do for the people you love."

My blood boils, knowing fully well what he means. He won't let Rain go. Fuck, he might *never* let Rain go as long as Rain doesn't say the words himself.

And as much as I know what Rain has said to me is the truth. That this thing between us is the real deal, knowing Roman loves him too still sets me on edge.

It should be a good thing, knowing there's more than just me who wants to help Rain get past this drama with his step-father and finally be able to live free from the demons he brings. I should be *grateful* for Roman's presence.

But I still harbor so much resentment and I think I hate that more than anything else. Because I don't have it in me to bring this up to Rain. Ask him to make Roman go too.

Even if all I want is for each of us to just move on.

Rain and I, together.

And Roman with his brothers in the Enclave.

It's what would be best for everyone and I think Asher and even Kaede see that. It's why they're pressing him to follow orders and get him to leave with them.

Yet I get it. I wouldn't leave Rain in this situation if someone asked. And especially if I had the capabilities to do something about it. So I can't fault him for his disobedience.

Kaede continues to stare at Roman, eventually letting his attention drift to Asher, then back again. I faintly hear Hollis call his name and the three of them continue to silently work through this impasse they find themselves in.

And to my surprise and disappointment, Kaede steps back and walks out the front door without a backwards glance.

"Fucking douche," Roman mutters, storming toward the entry to the living room.

Where I'm currently eavesdropping.

Asher calls his name, knowing I'm here, but it doesn't matter. It's too late. Roman rounds the corner before I have time to hide and our eyes lock instantly.

And while I expect them to be full of anger or resentment at the sight of me, all I find in them is loss and defeat.

It's a punch to the gut, seeing him look anything less than completely composed.

He's quiet, just stares at me for a minute in the calculating way he does. It's penetrating and troubling all at once, like he can see straight into my soul. Then he says something I know to be the truth because it's exactly what I feel too.

"I just want what's best for him."

And I can't believe I'm even thinking this, but part of me has sympathy for the guy—for all of them, really—knowing their chances of finding what Rain and I have are practically non-existent with the lifestyle they're forced to lead. While I might not have been searching the ends of the Earth to find someone to love me, I also can't imagine living without this feeling either.

Not anymore.

All the power or money in the world wouldn't tempt me to give it up.

TWENTY-SIX
Rain

DAY NINE: SATURDAY

ain is pouring down outside as I stand beside the wall of glass that leads out to the deck from the living room. It's surprising because from what River's told me, Colorado doesn't get much rain, let alone at the end of March. But it's fitting in a way. It matches the mood that's been surrounding the entire estate since Kaede, Hollis, and Callum left yesterday.

Roman's been holed up in his room or one of the offices since the moment the three of them left and Asher is more irritable too, not having spoken to any of us.

Fuck, *River* is even in a bit of a mood, doing his best to lose himself in his textbooks while we just stew and…wait.

For what, I don't know. Something, anything, would be fantastic at this point.

The only person in this mansion who seems to be content is me, which is kinda hilarious considering the circumstances involve *my life* as the one being fucked with and flipped upside down.

Two arms wrap around my waist from behind and a chin rests on my shoulder as I continue to look out at the mountains, letting the downpour soothe the anxiety that's surrounding the four of us left here.

"You would love the rain," River whispers, placing a soft kiss on the side of my neck before burrowing his face there.

I let out a low laugh. "I've always loved the rain. Far before you or anyone else gave me the nickname."

And it's true. It's always calmed me in a way nothing else managed to do, especially in the darkest days of my childhood. I never quite understood it as a kid, but now that I'm older, I do. There's a cleansing that comes after rain falls. This sense of peace that blankets your surroundings. That brings more possibilities and gives way to new beginnings.

In a way, it's hope.

He smiles against my skin and squeezes me. "It fits you."

One of my hands reaches up and grabs both of his that are locked around me and together we watch the rain fall, letting the peace settle around us as we do.

"What're you thinking?" he asks after a while, breaking the silence.

"Just that I want this to be over. I want things to go back to normal. Or as normal as they can be after what's happened." I shrug, feeling his chin rise up and down on my shoulder with the gesture. "I miss being able to go somewhere without feeling like I'm being watched or having to second guess each and every decision I make on an hourly basis. I wanna get back to classes and football and spending time with you and—"

His soft, warm laughter slides over me, making me smile. "Baby, life is never gonna be normal again."

"What do you mean?"

"I mean if we're gonna be like…" he trails off looking for the words.

I turn in his arms and raise my brow. "Be like…"

He rolls the bar in his tongue in the new way I fucking love as he thinks. "Dating?"

A laugh slips out. "Why do you say it like a question?"

Shrugging, he smiles. "I don't know. It just feels weird, doesn't it? I mean, to get to this point in such a messed-up, round-a-bout way? I feel like it's so much more than *dating*."

I kiss him softly and smirk against his lips, whispering, "*Soulmate*."

"God, I'm never talking to you ever again," he says, kissing me back, his hand sliding behind my neck. My tongue slips into his mouth, playing with the bar running through it until I force myself to pull away.

I'm not against letting Asher or Roman or the entire world know he's mine and I'm his. I don't care about coming out or whatever repercussions might come from it. And I sure as fuck don't care what the twins, Elliott especially, have to say about our relationship.

This is it. *He's* it. I'm done letting a bunch of bullshit stand in the way of us.

But it also doesn't mean I need to stand here and flaunt it in front of Roman's face either. I know I hurt him, rejecting every advance he's made up 'til this point. And he's still here, despite it all.

So, the least I can do is respect him enough to be courteous of his feelings.

"I hope you know you can, though," I murmur, kissing him softly before stepping out of River's hold.

His brows furrow. "Can what?"

"Talk to me," I say, cocking my head. "About anything, Abhainn. We're a team now. And you were right, it's what we always should've been from the beginning."

"I know I can," he says, but I can tell he's still not picking up on what I'm trying to say.

Because I've seen him at his absolute lowest multiple times now and even now that we're in a good place, he still hasn't tried to talk to me about any of it. And it doesn't sit well with me, even though being open with my own feelings is something I've always struggled with.

River's always been different.

Fuck, when we were still enemies he told me about his dad and all the shit that happened between them. He trusted me when we were *nothing* to each other. It should be easier now more than ever, right?

He watches me for a minute, his eyes a little more green than blue today. I can see the wheels spinning in his head as well as the lightbulb flickering on when he finally gets it.

"Sometimes," he starts running his hand through his hair, looking slightly anxious, "you have to hit rock bottom. Just to know what it feels like. To know *how bad* it can be and still be alive. I mean, I *know* you know what I'm saying," he sighs, his eyes flicking out the window.

"I can't say I've ever hit that kind of low before, the kind you've gone through. But I *do* know I've always had someone's hand to hold to get me through it. Whether it be my mom or my therapist or Taylor or *whoever.* But I've never stood on my own two feet and figured it out by myself. Figured out how to *cope* with my issues without needing a shoulder to lean on. And I felt like I needed to go through it. To know how difficult it can be to climb out on my own." He scoffs and laughs, a wry smile on his face and I can tell he hears just how insane it is, trying to take on the world all alone.

I shake my head. "You don't have to do it alone, though. Never again."

"Yeah, well, I know that *now.*" He laughs again. "I just wanted independence. To not need anyone, but especially not to need *you.* But you're the one person who just gets it."

"Your stubbornness was showing," I grin, knowing we both have hard heads. It's honestly half the fun in the time we were together at the cabin and again now. Seeing who will bend first. "Even if none of this shit happened with Ted and Roman, you would've tried to deal on your own regardless. I know you would've."

He's tempted to disagree, I can see it. But thankfully he doesn't, just nods. "You've already had so much pain," he whispers. "You don't need mine too."

"I want it though. The same way I know you want mine."

His eyes dart between mine, and he nods again. "Then it's yours."

Okay, fuck this whole non-PDA for Roman's sake thing.

I reel him back in, pulling his bottom lip between my teeth

and tugging softly before molding my mouth against his. Kissing him, feeling the skin of his cheek or the light scratch of his stubble against my palm. I don't think I'll ever get over it.

I can't imagine a day I'll ever get used to having him. Part of me hopes I never do.

My phone rings in my pocket and I groan against his lips, dragging my mouth away from his as I pull the stupid thing from my pocket. A quick glance down reveals an unknown number and my entire body tenses, even as River places soft kisses on my jaw.

But when he realizes my agitation, he glances down at the screen.

"Is that...?" he whispers, eyes latching onto mine.

I nod, my jaw ticking before shouting for both Roman and Asher, pulling River into the foyer.

They both appear from opposite wings of the house just in time to accept the call on the final ring.

The conversation with Ted was relatively short, considering. Not anything unexpected either.

"I know you're hiding out at that mansion in the mountains. I see your Jeep from outside the gate," he hisses through the speaker for all of us to hear before a dark chuckle fills the foyer. *"With both of your little boyfriends, no doubt."*

But I wasn't about to feed into his bullshit. Not anymore. Not now, when I'm content with where I am despite the chaos he's caused.

"What do you want? Spell it the fuck out, Ted."

I wish I could say I was surprised when he brought my trust into this. My mother's warning in her letter was all the heads up I needed to know where this conversation was heading.

"Ten million dollars. It's the least of what you owe me."

I laughed, knowing how convenient he knew the exact amount there was in it too. But the money, it doesn't mean jack shit to me. If handing it over to him was the easiest way to get him the fuck out of the country and my life, I'd happily fork it over.

So I did the only logical thing for anyone in my situation to do. I agreed. Immediately and without second thoughts. He gave me the address and time to meet him tomorrow and I hung up not more than ten seconds later to call the agent with the FBI and tell him everything.

And I felt good.

This was it. The end of the line.

We'd devised a plan where Roman would come with to the meet-up, the FBI would show in the middle of the exchange, and Ted would be arrested. Game over.

It sounds simple because *it is* simple.

But an eerie sense of foreboding sits in the front of my mind, keeping me from being able to fall asleep. All I can do is stare at the ceiling, replaying exactly what the agent told us to do over and over and over to the point where it starts to become a jumbled mess of nothingness in my brain that doesn't make sense at all anymore.

"You're thinking too loud," River murmurs into my neck, his breath and lips warm as they brush against my skin.

He's curled into my side in his bed since it's the farthest away from both Asher—and more importantly, Roman—when he shifts and grumbles it in his sleep. Or at least, I think he's asleep.

Every once in a while he'll have a full out conversation with me completely unconscious only to not remember it the next morning.

I smirk. "I didn't know thoughts could be loud."

"Yours always are," he groans, blinking his eyes open to look at me through a sleepy haze.

I curl the arm that's under his head around his neck and snuggle in impossibly closer, letting his presence seep into me. Enjoying the calm he manages to radiate.

His hand that was resting on my chest dances over stomach, trailing down in sporadic taps to where my tattoo follows the line of my hip. I think he's as obsessed with the bit of ink as I am with his damn tongue ring.

"What song?" I whisper, glancing down at him.

He smirks, meeting my eyes. "That Hoobastank song everyone and their mom knows."

I quirk a brow. "'The Reason'?"

He nods, still smirking, but I see the crease in his forehead as his fingers move back up, tracing the ink on my arms all the way down to where his name is written on my wrist. His eyes follow the path like it's the most interesting thing in the world, though he's done this a hundred times by now. He knows the meaning behind each one—if there is one—where I got it done, how old I was. All the silly details people always ask.

That's how I know he's stalling. Or holding something in he's desperate to say or ask, just doesn't know how.

It doesn't last long though, because only a minute later he lifts his eyes back to mine.

"I'm coming with you tomorrow," River tells me, shifting to

prop up on his elbow. The determination in his eyes dares me to challenge him.

And I sure as hell will. For fuck's sake, isn't this exactly what I wanted to avoid? Him rushing into action?

"Mo grá—"

"Don't even think about it." He glares. "You know we're going to be worried sick about the other if we aren't both there. It makes sense for us to go *together*. Handle this as a team, the way we should've the whole time. Isn't that what you just told me this morning?"

Groaning, I roll to my side and grab his hand in mine. "I fucking hate when you make sense."

A whisper of a laugh escapes him, but it sounds exhausted. I get it; my entire body feels like it could sleep for a week, even if my brain doesn't want to let me.

"You don't hate it. You just hate when it's the opposite of what you want."

"Same fucking thing," I growl, wrapping my arm around him and slide in so every possible inch of skin is touching his.

"I love you," he exhales the three words I'll never tire of hearing, burrowing his head under my chin, his cheek pressed against my pec, right next to my heart. "I don't want to fight with you. And if you *really* think I should stay in the car, I will. I'm just not comfortable staying behind completely."

I nod, his hair tickling my chin before I kiss the top of his head. "I know, Abhainn. I just want to keep you safe."

"We're safest together."

I nod again, wishing I felt as confident as he sounds. "You've made your point. And you can come. Because, I love you too. Apparently enough to go along with this stupid idea."

I feel him smile and he kisses my skin above my heart before murmuring something unintelligible, already half asleep again.

But I lay awake all night holding him in my arms wondering if not being able to deny him a goddamn thing will end up being a terrible fucking mistake.

TWENTY-SEVEN
River

DAY TEN: SUNDAY

My eyes take in the mountains as Rain, Roman, and I head back down toward Boulder to the warehouse address Ted gave us last night. The meeting place where Rain is to make the exchange of ten *million* dollars for his freedom.

It seems like a simple enough task, make the trade and get the hell outta dodge. But I have a gut feeling shit's about to go sideways in the worst way. It's got my anxiety on high alert, my hand tapping instinctively against my knee until Rain reaches over from the driver's seat and stops me.

The back of my neck tingles as I feel Roman's penetrating stare on me the minute Rain makes contact and it sets me more on edge. To the point where I have to remind myself of what I know to be true. The one thing I can hold onto.

He chose me.

Against all odds, he *loves* me and I love him, and we're making this work, no matter how fucking hard it gets.

It helps assuage the jitters inside me a bit, but not entirely. The anxiety is heavy in the air as we travel closer to the man who's made all our lives—most of all Rain's—a living hell.

Rain squeezes my hand in his, glancing over at me every so often. Asking me a question with his eyes.

Are you okay?

I give him a smile, doing my best to be convincing.

He smirks and shakes his head, reading me through the bullshit and gives my hand another squeeze before resting it on the gearshift again. It's a gesture so loving and intimate, I kind of want to pinch myself.

Or reel him in and kiss the fucking daylight out of him. But unfortunately, we don't have time for that…nor the privacy with Roman in the back seat.

We still haven't spoken much since everything went down between him and Rain. Frankly, I don't have any desire to have to speak to the guy again. He's been nothing but rude and volatile to me from the moment he laid eyes on me, all because I have what he wants.

But he's still the person who got Rain through the hardest part of his life. He's still *here* trying to help us take care of this situation, no matter the cost to the Enclave. For that, I have to give him credit.

As if he knew I was thinking about him, Roman asks, "So, we're clear on the plan, yeah?" I turn slightly to meet his eyes over the seat.

The plan is to have the local FBI agents show up and meet

Roman outside the warehouse while Rain and I are inside, keeping Ted distracted. Roman's to call the agent when we get out of the car after doing a quick scope of the building to make sure Ted did indeed come alone, just as Rain was requested to.

But we obviously didn't listen to the memo, so chances are he didn't either.

Part of me wishes we would have brought some sort of weapon, but Roman was certain it wouldn't come to that, as was Rain. They both are under the impression Ted is going to show up looking haggard, like he's barely scraping by after months of being on the run and lying low. No way would he have a bunch of goonies with him, following his every order.

And he on his own is no match for all three of us if it came down to a physical altercation.

Even still, the plan is less than appealing to my tastes, but I kept my mouth shut. This isn't my fight, it's Rain's. I just want to be here for him while he finally manages to take the bastard down for good.

I study Roman for a second before replying. "Yeah, crystal clear."

He nods, running his tongue along his teeth like he wants to say more before he just sighs, looking out the window again. I catch Rain's eyes as I turn back around, seeing his brows raised in question, but they quickly return to normal as his attention refocuses on the road.

Not much later, we pull up to the abandoned warehouse Ted gave us the address to meet at. The Jeep comes to a stop atop the gravel right beside the massive garage door of the loading area and Rain turns off the car.

A shaky breath escapes me as I glance between Roman and Rain.

"Ready? Rain asks, reaching for my hand again and squeezing to offer some comfort. But it doesn't work, my anxiety is on high alert and every part of me feels like this is a bad fucking idea. Too many variables, too much could go wrong.

But I nod anyway and he releases me, all three of us hopping out of the vehicle and set to work on *the plan*.

Rain and I enter the warehouse, the bag full of *ten million fucking dollars* from Rain's trust inside. I try not to think about how insane the amount of money is, or the fact Roman offered to give him the cash so Rain wouldn't have to use his inheritance.

Yet another thing the guy can do for my boyfriend I can't.

I don't let those thoughts linger though, because the second we walk through the open garage door into the warehouse, my skin goes ice cold. It's like the feeling when you're in a haunted house or watching a horror movie and you just *know* you're about to get jump scared and piss yourself. It's the adrenaline beginning to pump through your veins.

And mine is flooded with it.

The interior of the building is lit by stark fluorescent lights glaring down on the concrete floor, casting shadows against the walls. My eyes scan the inside perimeter of the building and that's when I notice an outline on the opposite side of the warehouse.

It's him. Senator Theodore Anders.

Child molester, rapist, and now extortionist. A shining list of accomplishments for this one.

Rage fills me at the sight of him leaning against the wall of the warehouse in what's possibly a thousand dollar suit. As he steps into the light and strides toward us, even from this far away, I realize he doesn't look any worse for wear than a stockbroker on Wall Street, well fed and impeccably dressed.

If I was right beside the man, there'd be no bags under his eyes from lack of sleep or exhaustion from staking us out every available minute of the day. He may as well be staying at the goddamn Ritz.

"Ciaráin." Ted smiles. His voice slides over me from across the open space like a poisonous fog, and I feel suffocated by it immediately. And also enraged.

Because this is him. The man who turned Rain into who he is today.

Blond-haired, brown-eyed *politician* with a striking smile, who loves to play the family man.

Fuck, I hate him.

He stops about thirty yards from us and I'm grateful for it. I don't want myself or Rain any closer to this fucker than we have to be.

"Let's toss the cash and just go," I tell Rain. I don't want to back out—I'm actually dying for Rain to get revenge on this guy—but right now, the timing feels off. Like we're only going to lose more if we try now.

"It's our only chance," Rain whispers, dropping the bag of money at our feet between us.

Nodding once, I let it slide, reminding myself this isn't my fight.

Ted's attention darts between us before landing on the bag at our feet. "Glad to see you came prepared. I must admit, I had my doubts, knowing the way you always liked to defy orders after a certain age."

Rain grimaces and I see the actual, physical pain he is in from being in this man's presence. He's trying to come off as strong, but I can tell. I can feel it. And it makes me want to scream.

So, I do the next best thing and probably equally as stupid. I spew venom.

"We're not here to chit-chat, Anders," I snarl, glaring at him from where we stand. "We have your money. If you want it, do us all a favor and kindly shut the fuck up."

He cocks his head and studies me. "You must be River."

My skin crawls at the way he says my name.

"Don't talk to him," Rain hisses, his protective side coming out in spades. "It's bad enough you were stalking me, but to send images of him? Trying to use him to get to me? Fuck, Ted. I'm not surprised, but it doesn't mean I'm not *disgusted* with how low you're willing to sink."

Ted chuckles darkly and shakes his head. "You're right, you shouldn't be surprised. Not when you, my good boy, led me right to him."

Rain's face tenses as he glances at me.

I try to tell him it's okay, I don't hold anything against him. It's not like it was news to me. It's why Rain wanted me at Asher's house these past ten days, to be kept out of Ted's reach. But I see the anguish he's in, realizing all he's done to keep me safe was in vain. Ted was still able to lord me over his head in the end.

We were just pawns in his game.

"How were you always so many steps ahead of us?" Rain growls, frustration growing in his features.

Calm down, baby, I want to tell him. I can't let him snap, at me or anyone, right now. But telling him that might be the very thing to set him off.

"Are you really so dense to not realize?" He scoffs. "Everything you know, all the information you've been given about me, my location was fabricated. You had it because I *wanted* you to have it. That's how I was always a step ahead. I only let you know what I wanted and when. A game of calculated risks." He pauses and gives me a look that could melt Satan himself. "In fact, I've known about River for *months.* Since your little rendezvous up in Vail with the Mitchell girl."

The first set of pictures Rain was sent comes to mind. Pictures of us at the resort with Siena and Taylor. My stomach lurches at the thought of him watching us at the cabin too, not knowing there's been someone this wicked lurking in the shadows this whole time.

"And it doesn't just stop at the calls and the photos." Ted gives us an evil grin. "The FBI agent assigned to your case? Also mine."

My heart is in my throat at his words, attempting to process the implications of his claims.

Eyes darting over at Rain, I see him working through the puzzle pieces slightly faster than I am. But the minute he goes to speak, it all clicks in place.

"The Enclave infiltrates the FBI," he mutters with a curse. "That's what you meant by you had the ones with real power. You had the fucking *Grand Elector* helping you make deals and call the shots. Got someone under their thumb assigned to my cases so any information I gave them was just fed right back to you."

My mind is reeling as I recall what we were told up at the

Jameson Estate. How the Enclave works.

Infiltrate to the highest level possible.

It shouldn't be a surprise the FBI is one of the organizations they've stuck their hands in, not one bit. Hell, Asher's dad *controls* the FBI. But it doesn't stop my stomach from churning, knowing the agent who Rain and Roman were calling and giving information to all these months was going straight back to Ted and Senator Mitchell, probably laughing about it over drinks.

Senator Mitchell...

"It's why Roman's dad was so quick to call the legacies off without any real answers," I say, glancing at him. "Whatever deals were made, he was trying to fulfill those obligations." My eyes land on Ted and I squint at him, cocking my head.

Ted shakes his head and starts pacing in a line back and forth. "You're starting to get it, boys. Yes. But you're still missing the big picture. What started this entire mess in the first place."

Biting my tongue, I glance at Rain for help in understanding what the fuck is actually happening right now. Because I'm hardly keeping up at this point.

Why is Ted playing this guessing game with us? Why not just take the money and run? Why bother giving us all the pieces of this puzzle *now* when he's about to be out of our hair, hopefully for good?

And most importantly, where the *fuck* is Roman?

He should be outside waiting for the FBI, but if they aren't coming... *Fuck,* what if Roman was even in on this? What if —

"The ring," Rain murmurs, cutting off my thoughts to catch his eyes widening. "The drug and sex trafficking ring they raided Doctor Shelton's office for. When they got my file and learned about the missing tapes. You actually *are* involved in it."

Ted nods. "Unfortunately for me, there are a few agents who do abide by the laws and aren't under the Enclave's pull. Those are the ones who took it upon themselves to get information to the media, and even the Enclave couldn't stop the spread of information once it was out."

Ted stops walking and scoffs, cocking his head. "And are you really so naive? Who do you think laced the cocaine that killed that friend of yours in the first place?"

Ice runs through my veins as Rain stiffens beside me and the puzzle pieces fall into place even more.

Ted is part of the ring. He played a role in Deacon's death. He had help with the Enclave to cover it up. All of it.

But if the Enclave is meant to get rid of the corrupt people running this country...

"The real question is why? Why would arguably the oldest and most influential secret society in history want to help *you* get away with this?" I pause and let my mind wander.

Why would Roman's father allow Ted to have this much power and information in the Enclave when it's meant to be kept secret? When it's supposed to be the five families and nothing else?

That's how secrets *stay* secrets. By limiting the amount of people with the insider knowledge.

Rain voices my thoughts in the next second, irritation in his tone. "This makes no sense. You're running the kind of underground operation the Enclave looks to exterminate and *rid* the world of. Why would—"

And then it clicks.

"You know something," I breathe, glancing over to Rain, then up at the piece of shit. "Something big. Massive even. It has to be in order for you to be able to use it as a bargaining chip. Another source of blackmail."

Ted just smiles. Though the longer I look at it, the more it seems to morph into a vicious sneer. "You're getting warmer."

My mind spins as I try to grab all the puzzle pieces and put them together one by one, moving and rotating them in desperation to make them fit.

What would he have on them? No one knows they exist. He couldn't have any intel on them unless…

"They're part of the ring too."

My head snaps to Rain as he speaks the conclusion I just reached. Because it's the only explanation I can come up with that makes any amount of sense.

They wouldn't turn Ted over if they were involved themselves. It would only implicate them as well. And possibly jeopardize everything they've built over a millennium.

But the Enclave, the secret society meant to protect America's interests…is part of a drug and sex trafficking ring? It makes no sense. They have everything they need. Money, power, weapons.

Why would they want to be part of something so vile?

Ted nods his head. "I'm impressed boys, you put it together rather quickly. Guess the new generation of legacies have looser lips than a Vegas whore." He paces a few steps from side to side, letting the information sink in before speaking again. "But you're wrong too. They're the ones *in charge*."

They aren't in the ring…they run *it.*

My stomach clenches as my head starts spinning. There's no way any of the guys we met know about this, right? There's no way Roman knew the drugs Rain handed Deacon on that fateful night were part of not only an elaborate plot to force Rain's hand under blackmail—a contingency plan if he ever decided to tell anyone else about what happened to him as a child—but also a darker, hidden part of a ruse lead by the Enclave themselves.

Shaking my head, I let out a breath and look at Ted.

"Why are you wasting your time telling us all this?" I ask, my brow creasing. "You could have gotten away with it and no one would be any wiser. And for all you know, we could've called the cops before we stepped out of the car. They could be here any second."

Ted gives a casual shrug. "I know you didn't, so why not waste the time?" he asks, cocking his head. "The ten million dollars was the *least* of what you owed me. If I want to take your time like you took mine, I damn sure will. But Ciaráin," he says with a wry, sadistic smile, "you also took my *life*. How do you suppose we square that one up?"

That's when I notice him reach around his back and pull out the pistol, aiming it directly at Rain's chest.

TWENTY-EIGHT
River

"Toss the bag, Ciaráin," Ted demands, motioning towards himself with the weapon before retraining it on Rain, my heart pounding in my chest with every movement of the gun.

I watch as Rain's jaw ticks and he rolls his shoulders. Glancing at me out of his peripheral, he follows the command, throwing the bag filled with cash.

"Go," he murmurs under his breath as he does it, pinning me with a glare that lets me know his request isn't up for debate.

I shake my head. "Rain—"

"River, *go*," he says, a plea in his voice and desperation in his eyes.

"Neither of you are going anywhere," Ted says, a vindictive laugh escaping him as he sets the gun on the ground and rifles through the bag, pulling out a few stacks of hundreds.

"It's all there, Ted. Every fucking penny. So, just let us go,"

Rain seethes, a ruthlessness in his tone I've never heard before.

I chance a second to look in the direction of the garage door we came though, hoping Roman will be coming in with the FBI at any minute.

Fuck, where is he?

"I believe you," Ted says, running his thumb along one of the stacks before stashing it back in the bag. Zipping it up, he rises to his feet, gun once again in hand.

At least this time it's not aimed at Rain, just hanging in his hand, the duffel in the other.

"Then we're free to leave. The deal is done. You go your way, we'll go ours," Rain tells him. And that's just it. He's *telling* this man we're leaving. A man with a *gun* in his hand, ten million dollars in cash, and absolutely nothing left to lose.

Ted gives us a puzzled look before raising the hand holding the pistol, flinging it back and forth between us like a fucking choir director. The action spikes my anxiety and I'm painfully, *painfully* aware of Roman's absence, the silence outside when there should be car doors slamming, and the way the gun once again stays aimed at Rain.

"Did either of you really think you'd make it out of here alive?" Ted says with a scoff. "Both of you and the Mitchell boy are nothing more than collateral."

I swallow roughly and glance to Rain only to find him whiter than a ghost.

As I go to open my mouth, movement from behind Ted catches my attention. Rain's too, because he visibly regains about ten shades of color to his face again when we find Roman sneaking through the door and around the perimeter of the building as stealthily as he can manage.

The unease in my stomach and the panic in my chest eases slightly, a least knowing he's alive and the outside of the building must be secure.

Which means Ted's alone. No back-up, even with the Enclave in his pocket.

Fantastic news, really, if he didn't have a gun trained on us.

I meet Roman's eyes behind Ted and he raises a finger to his lips, the universal signal to shut the fuck up. And I do, I keep quiet and just fucking...pray.

Pray to a God I haven't believed in for a long, long time to make this work out.

Let Roman get the gun. Let him have heard the truth about the FBI and call the cops instead.

Let Ted go down in brimstone and fire.

Let us fucking make it out of here alive.

"Ted," Rain says slowly, seeming far calmer than he should in this circumstance because my palms are sweating, pulse is flying at a thousand miles an hour, and the oxygen is getting a lot thinner as I watch Ted click the safety off on the side of the gun.

My hand instinctively reaches out to Rain, though he's not more than two feet from my side, and I feel his fingers brush against mine.

His skin is warm. Red hot, even, and I notice the way they shake out of pure anger.

Because if I know anything about Ciaráin Grady's emotions, it's when he's mad.

"Put the fucking gun *down,* Ted, and be on your way," Rain demands slowly, deliberately enunciating his words. "No blood needs to be shed in order to get what you want."

Ted's mouth lifts in a sneer and he cocks his head.

"My dear, good boy. Haven't you learned by now it's more about getting what I *deserve?*"

The wicked glint in his brown eyes tells me he has no qualms about doing what he deems necessary. To get what he wants. Or as he just said, what he *deserves.*

From where I'm standing, a trait like that should be enough to send him straight to the worst places imaginable. Yet for some reason, they've landed him in positions of power. Wealth. *Influence.*

Some rise by sin, and some by virtue fall.

The quote inked on Rain's skin rings through my mind and in this moment, I know Ted Anders deserves nothing worse than to rot in hell for all of eternity. I want nothing more than that for him, though I know he'd have it so much worse being bent over in the showers in prison for the rest of his miserable life.

I just want him gone. Out of this world, out of the way. Unable to wreak havoc on another soul.

This man…he'll never cause Rain another fucking *ounce* of pain again if I have anything to say about it.

So, I don't know how it happens. I don't even know if or when I make the conscious decision to push Rain as hard as I can while the gun is still trained on his chest.

All I know is he's on the ground beside me. I know I hear a shot, then a second, ring out in quick succession. I know there's the faint sound of metal clattering to concrete. I think I hear the sound of my name being shouted by Rain too, but I couldn't be sure with the adrenaline pounding in my ears.

All of it just happens…instantly. Less than a blink of an eye is all it takes for the entire world to shift.

And shift, it does, when the impact of the bullets knocks the wind out of me unexpectedly.

Gasping for air, I clutch my stomach only for it to come back blood red immediately, my knees feeling weak the moment I catch sight of it.

Two firm hands grip my arms and I look up, finding Rain on his feet again, a panicked expression on his face I'm sure mirrors my own. My gaze collides with Rain's when we both see the blood and I hear him say my name again, but I can't process it.

Looking over his shoulder, I find Roman practically wrestling with Ted, holding his own against the asshole. And thank God, the gun is halfway across the warehouse, far away from Ted's reach.

The concrete is cold against the skin of my palms and even through the denim of my jeans and cotton of my shirt as Rain eases us both to the ground as gently as he can manage. It must be tough with the way his hands are trembling as he stares at the blood already soaking through the fabric of my shirt.

Rain cups the back of my head, staring at me with a mixture of awe and terror. "You just took a bullet for me."

I let out a short wheeze, which quickly turns into a cough as I wince in pain. I swear I can feel the pieces of metal shift inside me at the movement. "Two, actually."

Fuck, it's hard to breathe.

A constricted laugh slips past his lips, before he leans forward and presses his forehead to mine. "You were just shot and you want to bicker with me about how many times? Jesus Christ, Riv."

I feel his hand press against my stomach where the wounds are, applying enough pressure it's painful. Not as painful as the shots themselves, but painful enough to have stars cloud my vision.

"I wouldn't be me if I didn't fight you a little bit, would I?" I smile, working to swallow.

His face starts to blur, the darkness eating away at my view of him slowly from the edges of my sight. But I hold his whiskey eyes; I stay locked on them in hopes they can ground me to Earth instead of floating away into the black abyss.

"Abhainn. Mo grá. Just hold on, okay? We'll get help." His voice cracks on every word, as if he knows it's pointless. That there's no use in attempting to get help because I'm already too far gone.

Hell, I even know it.

"Baby," I gasp, the words a knife in the gut as I feel those bullets moving around inside me some more beneath his hands. Each and every breath I take causes more agony to shoot through my stomach. "It's okay."

My hand shakes as I raise it to his face. His eyes catch my movement, the unsteadiness, and one of his hands grasps it. It's warm and wet as he covers the back of my hand with his palm, bringing them both to his cheek. Blood slips over his fingers as well as my own and suddenly I realize…

It's mine.

My blood is coating his hands, my hands, *our hands*. It's dripping over our wrists and smearing slightly against his cheek while he presses his other palm against my gunshot wounds even harder.

Fuck. I was shot twice.

"River, look at me. Not at the blood, at *me*," Rain urges. There's a slight panic to his tone, but he's doing his best to keep it in check.

The reality of the situation sets in, the shock wearing off as the black keeps creeping toward his face, more and more of it becoming distorted. The tunnel continues to form, and panic hits my chest.

I don't want to die. That wasn't my plan when I pushed in front of Rain to let those bullets pierce my skin instead of his. My only goal was to keep him safe from any more harm at the hands of Ted motherfucking Anders. He's caused him enough misery to last a thousand lifetimes.

So, no, I don't want to die. Of course I don't.

I want to spend the rest of my life with Rain. Every fucking day. Poking fun at his uncanny ability to leave himself open for dirty jokes and making him breakfast burritos every Sunday. Laughing with him at a stupid movie or some dumb thing I said. Smiling at him, and only him, because he loves my dimples and I fucking love *him*.

Loving him with my entire heart, because he owns it.

Until the end of time.

"I can't—" I choke on the words, the weight of a train sitting directly on my diaphragm, "—feel my legs."

Rain's jaw ticks under my palm, pulsing almost. From the movement alone I can tell he's trying to keep his anger in check.

Anger at what? I couldn't tell you.

Me, for getting shot. Ted, for doing the shooting. The world, for this fucked up mess we've found ourselves in.

Rain shifts his position from where he was kneeling beside me, moving to sit before sliding my head onto his thighs in a way that he can still hold pressure to my wound. It's starting to not hurt anymore. Just like my legs, I can't feel much of my lower abdomen either.

"You're going to be fine, babe. It's okay," he soothes, but the words are still broken. Ground out and filled with gravel and lies.

I cough once. Twice. Blood fills my mouth on the third and a tear slips from my eyes. "I don't want to die," I whisper, the waiver in my voice giving away my fear.

Rain shakes his head, which is completely surrounded by the darkness now, his blurry, blurry face almost completely out of focus.

I don't want to die.

"You're not going to, River. Don't fucking say that. Help will be here any minute."

More lies. They would be here already.

I shake my head, or at least I think I do, but the numbness has crawled up past my chest and into my neck, freezing me in place like an ice sculpture.

"Don't lie to me," I tell him. I can't handle it if the last things he says to me are more lies stacked on each other. "We said" —I wheeze—"no more lies."

Grimacing at my words, Rain's tears let loose and slide down his face as he bows his head over me. The salty drops slip off his face one by one, mixing with the blood still on his cheek. "But this isn't it, mo grá. This isn't fucking it. We can't end like this. We didn't have enough time." A choked sound slips past his lips. Lips that I'd give anything to kiss right now. All I want is to kiss his pain away, to assure him that we have a lifetime past this.

That this is just a blip. A small bump in the road.

But we promised.

And I'm done lying to him too.

"River, please. *Please.* You don't get to leave me. Goddammit, don't you dare fucking leave me, Abhainn. We said forever. We made each other that promise. And this? It isn't forever. Not even close. "

His jaw clenches as he leans his forehead against mine, letting wet tears drip down onto my cheeks where they mix with my own.

"Sometimes," I heave with effort. My lips are starting to feel cold and numb, my words feeling slurred. "Sometimes forever... is shorter than you think."

His lips trembling are a whisper against my own. I barely feel it at all, even though his mouth hovers mere inches away.

"No. River, *no.* You made me fall *in love* with you. I fought so hard not to, but I never stood a chance. It was always you, Abhainn. So you don't get to leave me here alone."

His mouth is on mine then, kissing me with desperation, his lips warm and wet and alive.

Everything mine isn't.

I try to kiss him back. Take all the love and warmth he offers me and soak it into my core, but it's pointless. I can hardly move my lips, seeing as I can barely feel them.

When he pulls back, his forehead against mine, his shudder jars an ache inside me that isn't from the bullet wound. "I love you. Jesus *fuck*, I love you. You can't leave me."

My hand, the one that is still cupped inside his, tremors as I attempt to tap my finger against his palm three times.

One. Two. Three.

I. Love. You.

I hope I did it so he can feel it. So he can know. That I love him, too.

Because I do. I love him with every inch of my being. He's everything I could have asked for, everything I didn't know *to* ask for.

He's the forever I didn't know I wanted, even if we won't get it now.

He has to know that.

"I love you. I love you. *I fucking love you*," he cries, cradling my head in his arm.

His words, the three I never thought I'd hear from his lips, play over and over in my head. *I love you.*

Forever, Rain.

Then the black abyss consumes me entirely.

TWENTY-NINE
Rain

My barely composed facade shatters the moment River's eyes slide closed for what might be the last time. Every part of my body and soul are screaming and cursing the world, refusing to believe that this is actually happening. Because it's not happening.

I just got him back. I can't lose him again.

Not for good.

I'll lose my fucking mind.

"Goddammit, no! River, look at me!" I shout at him, tapping his face with my bloody fingers. Shaking his shoulders with my palm. Anything to see those aqua eyes again. "Look at me, mo grá. Stay here. I *need you* to stay!"

But he doesn't fucking hear me. He doesn't fucking listen.

His eyes stay closed and I'm so lost already.

I don't know what to do.

I don't know what to do.

What do I do?

Pulling his body up, I hug him tightly to me and sob into his neck, the tears streaking down my face, mixing with his blood that's covering my face.

Desperation claws at my skin as my regrets consume me. Every decision I made, every moment we spent both together and apart since returning from the cabin...they all flood my mind at once while question after question is thrown in my direction from my subconscious.

Why did I bring him into this when I knew it wasn't safe? Why wasn't I strong enough to keep away from him when I knew it was the only way to keep him safe?

How the fuck am I supposed to survive in a world where he doesn't exist?

What we have…it's once in a lifetime. There is not one other person on this Earth more perfectly matched for me. No fucking way.

So why didn't I do everything to protect him? Why couldn't I just let him go?

I rub my nose against his neck, needing to memorize the smell of his skin and the feel of it on mine. Each piece of him I didn't learn well enough, the ones I didn't have enough time with. Because *forever* wouldn't have been long enough to spend with River. To learn him and *love him.*

The sensation of his blood, a deep burgundy, seeps through his shirt and onto my clothes and instantly I'm hit with the gravity of what is happening.

He took a bullet for me.

No. *Two* bullets for me.

The panic starts gaining traction, overtaking the shock of the situation.

He was shot.

Twice.

Because. Of. Me.

And now he's dying in my fucking arms and I can't do anything to stop it.

"I'm sorry, mo grá. I'm so fucking sorry. For the lies and the secrets. For bringing this into your life. I'm sorry for all of it," I tell him, the words suffocating me because saying them out loud...it feels like goodbye.

The forever kind. And I'm not equipped to handle that right now.

Grief and desolation swim through my veins, pooling in my eyes and spilling over in a continuous stream of emotion that fractures me at my core.

In my entire life, I've never felt this helpless.

And so I do the only thing I can think of.

I hold his body in my arms, begging for God to take me instead. I scream at Him, plead with Him. I bargain my fucking soul, letting those in heaven and hell decide where it belongs.

Because he isn't fucking dying. Not today.

Not until we're one hundred and five. Not until we've had a goddamn *lifetime* together.

Like we *promised.*

"You die, I die too," I murmur gruffly into his hair, barely more than a whisper tearing itself from my throat. "I go where you go, River. That's what forever means."

And I know in that moment, I mean every word.

I'd walk through hell just to find him and pull him back out the other side. Barter my soul to a God I don't believe in to keep him safe.

"I love you."

The words, three miniscule fucking words, that pack so much meaning behind them, they feel useless now. But that doesn't stop me from saying them. From telling him. Because what else can I do now except let him know that my entire world begins and ends with him?

And so I rock back and forth, clutching his limp body to my chest, whispering those three words on a loop.

Wishing like hell I'd said them sooner.

THIRTY
Roman

He's losing it. No, losing it is the understatement of the century.

What is more than wrecked? Destroyed? Obliterated?

Fucking annihilated.

Whatever is more than all of those combined, it's what Rain is while he rocks River's body in his arms, desperation and anguish causing him to produce the most guttural howl I've ever heard come from a human.

And it just about kills me.

Seeing him like this, knowing I can't do shit to ease his pain, take the burden of his sorrow and put it on my shoulders instead. It's what you do when you care about someone. When they mean the world to you and you would do just about anything for them.

Which is what I just did.

Because I fucking love him.

And he loves River.

River, who just proved the same goddamn thing as me by jumping in front of a bullet for the man we both love. River, who is currently bleeding onto the pavement, Rain's own body, just...fuck.

Everywhere. There is blood everywhere.

I'm no stranger to blood. I've spilled plenty of it in my life, but not to this extent. Never killed someone.

Except you just fucking did.

But I don't have time to process the implications of killing Ted Anders—snapping his neck with my bare hands—will have right now.

Right now, I have more important shit to deal with. Another move to make.

Namely helping River. The man the love of my life loves most in the world.

Because Rain *has* to love him. Because those three words aren't ones you yell and shout to someone when they are dying in your arms while you helplessly watch. Because I'm listening to him beg and plead and bargain with God to save River and take himself instead.

Because it's what Rain was willing to do mere minutes ago for River. Die to save him.

But River took those bullets instead. To save Rain.

It's what I would've done myself, had I been standing close enough.

Hell, my feet were moving in their direction the second Ted flicked his aim to Rain, but I just wasn't fast enough. I couldn't get there in time. I could only get to Ted and stop him from firing a third shot.

But River *did* make it.

And hell, while this might be the biggest mess in the goddamn world, I've never been more grateful to be in the most fucked up love triangle in existence. I'm starting to see now it's not even a triangle. It never was. Just a circle surrounding the two of them with me desperately trying to barge in.

But it doesn't matter, not now. Regardless of what the three of us are to each other, it doesn't change the fact that it could've been *Rain* on the pavement, blood pooling around him at astronomical speeds.

Then *I* would be the one who is shattered beyond repair.

And goddammit, as much as it tears me apart inside to see Rain like this, powerless in the face of fate and chance and destiny, a piece of me, however fucked it might be, selfishly feels hope.

Hope for *us.*

Because, while he might take the time to mourn River, he'll eventually find a way to move on. And I'd wait. For the pain of his loss to fade. For him to be ready to open his heart again. For him to be able to love again.

I've already waited four years. And for him, I'd wait a lifetime.

So like the jackass I am, I stand here. A fucking statue. Watching Rain press his palms over River's abdomen in an attempt to curb the bleeding, agony wracking his body in the process.

And I question my ethics. My morals. My values.

It's for only a minute. In this case, a minute could mean death. Yet I war with myself for a good sixty seconds about choosing between my happiness and Rain's.

But if that isn't the damn kicker. It's not even a choice, is it?

If I don't do everything in my power to get River to a hospital, I'll live with regret for the rest of my life. Even if I got Rain in the end. It would eat away at me, consume me from the inside out. And as much as I love him, I don't want to be his second choice. I don't want to be his consolation prize.

So, after sixty long seconds, I move. No, I run. To pick up the love of my life's shattered heart, hoping we have enough time to put it back together.

"Rain," I say softly, placing my hand on his shoulder. He flinches at the contact, but isn't put off long. Just continues rocking back and forth, one hand plastered to River's stomach, the other moving to hold his head to his chest.

Whispering those three fucking words. Over and over and over again.

The three words I covet from those lips more than air to breathe. *I love you.*

I say his name again, this time with more force. But still no answer.

So I grab his shoulder and shake him, jarring him from his stupor. "Rain, come on. We have to go. He needs to get to the hospital."

His eyes, a vivid gold as they tears spill over to streak his face, finally meet mine and everything I thought I knew about love starts to splinter. My heart drops to my stomach before they both quickly rise to my throat, forming a blockage so large I can't fucking breathe.

Breathe, Roman. He needs you.

My hand slips under his at River's throat, searching for a pulse. It takes a second to find it, but it's there. Faint. Weak. But there.

I snap my gaze back to Rain. "He's still alive. We have to move."

I quickly rise and glance around, a thousand things running through my brain as I attempt to formulate a plan. Getting to the hospital is my first priority, but there's also the dead body to deal with and an extra car and *fuck.*

Jogging to Rain's Jeep, I click Asher's name on my speed dial, praying he'll answer because I definitely need some backup.

"Yeah?" he says on the second ring as I hop in the driver's seat.

"I know I'm in deep shit, but I need you to come take care of something for me at this warehouse," I tell him, spewing off the address quickly, though he knows where we are. He tried to convince us not to come here in the first place. "There's a town car outside—" I swallow, pushing out the rest of the words, "—and a body inside."

I hear Ash's sharp exhale on the other line as I wait for him to lay into me, but he just asks one simple question. "Who?"

"The senator," I grind out through clenched teeth. "But if I don't hurry, there's bound to be another."

"Rain?" Asher asks immediately and I shake my head, though he can't see me.

"River." The name of one of his closest friends before the Enclave took every one of our life choices comes from my lips on a whisper. And from the silence of Ash on the other line, he's not taking the news well.

"I'll be there soon. To take care of things." Ash tells me after a moment, letting a beat of silence rest between us. He's more than capable of disposing the body and making it look like Ted skipped town. One of the many facets we're trained in.

"There's a bag of cash also," I tell him as I pull through the garage door opening and up beside Rain and River. "Don't forget it."

Asher is silent for a moment. "I won't say shit to anyone about this. It's between you and me. Just don't you dare let him die."

It takes everything in me not to roll my eyes at everyone obsessing over River Lennox's presence on this Earth.

So I don't bother answering, just hang up the phone so I can save his fucking life.

My chest aches as I watch Rain pace back and forth in the ER waiting room like a caged animal in front of me.

They took River up for surgery the second they put him on the stretcher outside, seeing as I had enough foresight to call and let them know we were coming. I got a good ass-chewing by the nurse who I spoke to about the importance of not moving a gunshot victim because the bullet could still be inside, but I'll just put a pin in that tidbit, seeing as I don't plan to rescue anyone else soon.

Rain's been a fucking wreck ever since River left his sight, snapping at anyone who asks him if he needs anything. Myself included. But I still try, because when the people you love are hurting, you do anything to help them through it. Even if it shatters your own heart in the process.

My hand reaches out and grabs his arm as he makes another pass in front of me and he glares at me.

"What?"

I raise my brow, letting my eyes sweep over him before going back up to his face. "Sit down. You look like shit and I'm worried you're going to pass out any second."

"No," he says dryly.

I sigh. "Then can we go grab a shower and change our clothes? We're both covered in—"

"I'm fucking fine, Roman. If you want to leave, be my guest. But I'm staying right here," he growls, yanking his arm free to continue pacing. At this rate, he'll probably wear through the linoleum before we get a word on River's condition.

He stays like that for another half an hour before a nurse finally takes pity on us, pulling us to a private room where we can wait without the stares of everyone else. Because *every* eye in the damn place was on him while he stormed around with a toxic cloud hovering over his head.

But at least in the private room, he managed to slump down against the wall enough to attempt to relax.

I watch as he runs his hands through his hair over and over again, and I get it. He needs a part of his body moving at all times, to feel like he's not stuck. Frozen. To know time is, in fact, still moving. Even when it feels like time and space have collapsed entirely.

And while they haven't, the reality is, he might.

Walking over and sliding down the wall next to him, I reach out and grab his hand in mine, needing to comfort him in some fucking way, even though I know he probably doesn't want it.

So when he turns and pulls me in for a hug, I'm rendered speechless.

His fists dig into the material of my dress shirt and I don't have it in me to give a fuck that he's covered in dried blood or that we're on a dirty hospital floor. We just cling to each other and for the first time since we were kids and he told me about what Ted did to him, I hold him while he sobs.

And while he cries, I pray to whatever higher being there might be to save River. Fuck, I pray to River himself to get through this.

He needs you. More than he's ever needed me.

But the sinking feeling in my chest makes the words spill from my lips like word vomit.

"Rain, I think you need to prepare yourself for the possibility—"

"Don't you dare fucking say it," he snaps, pulling away from me roughly. His nostrils flare as his eyes burn me with intensity. And for the first time since I've known him, I might actually be afraid of him instead of for him.

But instead of heeding his warning, I harden my tone and march on. "You need to fucking hear this. There is a chance he won't wake up. And even if he does, he's never going to be the same."

He pushes up off the floor and I'm quick to follow, but he's quick to put space between us again. And the gap, it feels insurmountable.

"So, what, Roman? You think if he doesn't make it, if he fucking *dies,* I'll somehow magically choose you?"

Grinding my teeth, I inhale deeply.

He's just hurting and lashing out. Don't react poorly.

"I never said that. But I think you need to understand—"

"I understand perfectly," he hisses, getting in my face. "From the beginning, this has never been more than a fucking love triangle to you. Thinking you can win me like I'm some sort of prize. A pissing contest. When in reality, you were right. Between you and River, *there is no contest.* It's him, a thousand percent.

Every day of every week of the rest of my fucking life, it's him."

Biting the inside of my cheek, I do my best to keep my cool. But it's hard when the person you're in love with compares you to the person they'd always pick first.

Or worse, sees you as a lesser version of them.

"Don't put this all on me." I shake my head. "What happened the night after the party was on both of us. I wasn't there alone. I know you felt what I felt, even if you deny it at every turn."

"I was angry and lonely. And even then, I didn't go through with it because I knew you were only a substitute for who I really wanted! It's the same thing as when you asked me to leave with you! *You're not it for me.* Do you really think that's fair to either of us to just settle?"

I scoff, my temper rising dangerously. Because fuck him. "You want to talk about fair? I gave up everything! I chose you over my legacy, my fucking *brothers.* Put my entire life on the line for this! For you! And you're telling me *now* I never stood a fucking chance?"

"You told me it was fine! Why would I believe anything other than what you told me was true?" He runs his hands through his hair again before tossing his arms out to his side. "And had I known your intentions when I called, I would have hung up the second I heard you answer."

The words hit me hard enough, I wish I would've taken the bullets instead. Because this...hurts so much worse.

"Rain—" I start, but he won't have it.

"Go, Roman. Just leave."

I think my lungs might collapse when he says it. Because I

said I'd only stay as long as he didn't want me to leave. I'd only go when he told me to.

All the oxygen is sucked out of the room and I feel like I'm gasping for air when I finally fucking realize...

He doesn't want you. He doesn't need *you.*

I search his face, desperation clawing at me to find some piece of him that's just saying it out of anger or sadness or guilt or *anything* other than honesty.

But all I find there is the cold, hard truth.

I fought the war.

And I lost.

But I don't even have it in me to be angry with him. We don't choose who we love.

So as I step through the door and into the hallway without a glance back in his direction, I pray I'm the only one who has to walk out of this hospital heartbroken.

THIRTY-ONE
Rain

I'm shaken awake a few hours later by a nurse coming to give me another update about River's status. I know his parents have to be here by now, but I'm grateful the nurse is still updating me too, even though I'm not considered family. I can tell she feels bad for me, being the person who brought him in and clearly distraught about the entire situation.

That's the entire reason she put us in this room in the first place. I couldn't sit the fuck down or stop moving for more than a few seconds without wanting to explode.

After Roman left, I called Elliott to let him know what happened, saying he needed to get ahold of River's family because I didn't have the first fucking clue how to reach them. He cussed me out for about ten minutes for putting River in danger, but then calmed down enough to call River's mom and let her know River is in surgery for two gunshot wounds.

I can only imagine how well that conversation went over.

She leaves after letting me know he's still in surgery, which honestly, is still good news to me. If the surgeons are still working, it means he's still alive. And alive is good.

My phone vibrates in the pocket of my jeans and I tense, not knowing if I should pull it out or not.

The chances of it being Ted? I don't know how high they are. Roman told the cops who took our statements when we arrived at the hospital that Ted was gone by the time we got River in the car to get him here. No one has seen or heard from him since, let alone been able to track him down.

The anxiety of not knowing wins out in the end and letting out a deep breath, I pull the device from my pocket. But all I can do is stare at the screen when I see who it is.

My chest aches at the sight of the name showing on it and with unsteady fingers, I hit accept.

"Hello?" I whisper, my voice thick with emotion, not believing my eyes.

"Ciaráin." She sighs, her voice cracking too.

My lip trembles and my entire body quakes at the sound of her voice, something I haven't heard in *years* now. Because there's so much I have to say, so many things that need to be heard between her and I. All of the pain and the resentment I've been holding onto starts boiling to the surface, fighting to break free from their confines.

But somehow, right now, it doesn't seem to matter.

So I finally release every single emotional chain, freeing myself of their hold with one anguish filled word.

"Mom?"

Mom and I talk on the phone for almost an hour. Most of the time it was spent with either one or both of us crying. Her, somewhat hysterically, while my tears were mostly silent.

And it was cathartic, even through the pain. Like ripping off the bandage and letting the wound heal with open air.

She repeated so many of the things she said in her letter to me. Mostly that she loved me and was so sorry for all the mistakes she made between when my father died and now. Much of it revolved around Ted.

"I can never take these things back, Ciaráin. Not believing you when you were only a child. Letting him control both of us. No matter how much I want to try, I can't rewrite history. But if you'll let me, I'd like the chance to make it up to you."

The sincerity in her voice is what broke me. And while I couldn't promise it would be easy to repair the damage our relationship suffered at her hands, I told her I was willing to try as soon as she wanted. My being able to say it — and actually *mean it* — was a miracle in itself.

But if I've learned anything in the past eight months, it's that I need to allow myself to trust again. Even if it's painful. Even if rebuilding the bridge takes years. And even if the person might not be worthy.

Holding onto the pain only hurts me more in the end.

It sparked enough hope in her to book a flight right there on the phone with me to come out to Colorado in the coming few weeks. She wanted to come immediately, but with the investigation into

Ted still ongoing and River being in the hospital, I thought it best she wait. And as I tell her about River too—while it physically pains me knowing he's in an OR fighting for his life as I speak to her—I hear in her tone that she already loves him almost as much as I do.

The emotion was thick in her voice when I came out to her, not that she necessarily deserved the honesty from me so soon. But to tell her, one of the people who it should have been hardest to, was liberating. Her reaction was nothing but loving and supportive, not that I should be surprised. Our family, pre-Ted, was always accepting from what I can remember as a young kid.

In the end, I can't ask for more than that.

The nurse comes in another hour after getting off the phone with my mother, only peeking her head in the door this time.

"He's out of surgery and up on the ICU floor," she tells me with a smile. She doesn't offer anything more, just like each time she's come back to tell me the smallest details she can, what with those fucking laws prohibiting her from doing more.

But then she enters the room and pats me on the hand, giving me a look of sympathy. "You need to eat. Shower and change. You can't do anything for him right now but take care of yourself."

She's right and we both know it, so I offer a small half smile and nod before she exits the room.

But I don't leave to do any of those things. I bolt up from my seat and out the door, skidding to a stop as I glance up at the wall near the nurses' station to look at a directory.

ICU - Floor Three.

Saying fuck the elevator, I barrel my way up two flights of stairs and burst through the doors. I make a beeline to the nurses station on the floor, panting and out of breath as I skid to a stop at the desk.

I barely have a chance to say River's name on a rough exhale to the nurse when a venomous voice rings out from down one of the hallways.

"What the hell are you doing here? Haven't you caused enough damage?"

My jaw ticks when I look up to see River's father closing a door near the end of the hall. The one, I'm assuming, River is behind. Stepping away from the nurses' station, I stride toward him quickly, but he meets me halfway.

"Is that River's room?" I nod toward the door he just came from.

"I don't see how it's any of your concern," Roland sneers, acid in his tone.

My brows shoot to my hairline. Is he fucking serious? "Why wouldn't it be my concern?"

A scoff leaves his arrogant, condescending mouth, and I'm instantly itching to deck him. Again. "As if the fact you're the reason he's even here in the first place wasn't enough?"

"I'm not—" But I stop myself.

I am the reason he's here. Fighting for his life like I should have been fighting for him from the very beginning.

"The fuck you aren't. Ever since you set foot in my home on Thanksgiving, you've left nothing but chaos and destruction behind you. You've pulled my son down whatever perverse hole you've dug for yourself and now you want to fucking bury him in it, too."

My nostrils flare. "That's not—"

"Shut your mouth right now, boy. Before I shut it for you."

I'd like to see you try, motherfucker.

I bite my lip hard, using the blood on my tongue to reel myself back from snapping his neck.

Except the fucker digs his heels in deeper, pinning me with a glare of hatred that would scare the purest soul into falling down the pits of hell.

But I've been to hell. Lived there for years with a man far more wicked than he.

Men like him don't frighten me anymore.

A snarl mars his face as he speaks, "I don't need some faggot involved with a national sex scandal being seen with my son."

You fucking didn't...

"Your son," I growl, steam radiating off me in waves, "happens to be the love of my fucking life! I would give up everything for him, just like he willingly did for me. I'm not some piece of trash slipping into his bed from off the street. I love him with every inch of my eternally fucked-up soul!" The words tumble from my mouth in a battle cry, causing the circulating staff to give pause.

Roland takes notice, casting his hatred their way for a moment. "You can continue with your work," he states calmly before bringing his icy eyes back to me. "There's nothing to see here."

I scoff, holding out my arms, aware the people surrounding us are rapidly disappearing. "What, Roland? Afraid someone might hear your son is bisexual? That he is in love with another man? That he is the person he's supposed to be, rather than the person you tried to shape him into?" I stalk close to him, my chest bumping against his. "I don't give a shit who knows about the two of us. I.

Love. Him. And I couldn't care less about what you think of any of it. So, I'm going to see him. Because he fucking needs me."

He grimaces, mixing pain and anger together on his face. "That's enough. I will not tolerate this kind of bullshit when it comes to River. You're an embarrassment to your own family, so please don't drag mine into your mess."

I bare my teeth at him because fuck this homophobic asshole. "You don't know jack shit about my so-called mess or my so-called family. I don't give a shit about any of that. Because my real family? He's lying in a hospital bed right now, probably scared out of his fucking mind! So do us all a favor and let. Me. See. Him."

Roland grits his teeth, his face contorted in a rabid snarl. "I will not allow you to see him, Mr. Grady. After today, you will not be allowed to see him ever again, as my lawyers will be contacted to file a restraining order."

Panic sends a bolt of rage zapping through my spine. Before I can even stop myself, a roar bursts from me, fueled by fire and anxiety.

"You don't have the right to tell me who I'm allowed to love!"

"He is my family," he hisses, his voice low and venomous. "And I am his. I have every right. I suggest you remove yourself from the premises before I have security escort you out. Or better yet, the police."

His words cause me to wince, knowing the threat isn't an idle one. *Fuck.*

Changing tactics, I step away from him and take a calming breath. Count back from ten. Use every goddamn coping mechanism I've learned in therapy over the years.

Sixty long seconds pass before I allow myself to speak. "I

need to see him. Please, sir," I beg. I beg the piece of shit. "I know that we didn't exactly leave off on—"

Roland holds a hand up to stop me, but for a second, his eyes softening slightly.

And then I feel it.

Hope.

But the thing about hope? She is fate's most lethal weapon, and we all know neither of them have ever been on my side.

Exhaling sharply, Roland speaks. "You can stop right there, Ciaráin. What you want in this situation doesn't matter. You. Can't. See. Him."

Goddammit.

My heart drops to my stomach at his father's words register, for real this time. They're a knife to the gut, twisted in deep, allowing all my blood to rush out of my body. Seep onto the tile beneath my feet.

He really won't let me see him...

No, no, no. But I have to see him, to know he's okay. He has to be okay.

Fuck, he has to be okay.

"Can you at least tell me how he is?" I rasp, a knot the size of a football lodged in my throat. I can't breathe around it, not knowing what his answer will be.

Because the blood. So much fucking blood.

I'd completely forgotten about it in my race to get up here once the nurse came down to tell me River was out of surgery. Glancing down, my stomach rolls at the sight of it.

His blood. Still covering my clothes, my hands. It's ground

under my nails and dried onto every free inch of my skin.

So much blood there's a very real possibility...

No.

He isn't dead.

Roland wouldn't be this composed if he was.

He fucking can't be.

Fate wouldn't be that cruel. I refuse to believe she'd shove River onto my path through life, one I was ready to walk alone, only to snatch him away when an ounce of happiness managed to crack the foundations of every wall I've ever built.

She's a bitch, but she fucking wouldn't.

"He's in critical condition, the doctors say it'll be touch and go for the next few days." Roland lets out a gruff cough. "His chances of survival are slim."

And just like that, all the air is stolen from my lungs from the anvil landing on my chest, the force bringing me to my knees, cracking against the floor.

They say your life flashes before your eyes when you're close to death.

But they don't tell you it also happens when the reason for you to live starts slipping through your grasp.

And as every memory, every laugh and kiss and smile and goddamn moment of fucking bliss with River flies through my mind, I shatter.

Emotions flood my soul, filling it to the brim with one in particular.

Regret.

For every vile word, every glance of disdain I aimed his way.

For every second I wasted, trying in vain to fight the intoxicating desire I felt—feel—for him. For refusing to give him every inch of my soul when that's all he ever asked of me.

For not seeing he's worth the risk, the heartbreak, the chance of being completely consumed by another person to the point that when you're apart, you risk disappearing entirely.

Because without him?

Fuck, it doesn't even matter.

I won't survive in this world without him. Not anymore. I wouldn't even want to try.

Without him, I cease to exist.

My hands claw at my hair, despair waging a war within me. Tears fill my eyes and stream down my face, coating my cheeks and slipping over my lips as a gut-wrenching sob rips from deep inside my chest. The guttural cries bounce off the walls of the near empty hallway, echoing around me. Forcing me to face just how alone I am.

My life as I knew it is over. One way or another.

I'll follow you anywhere, River. Even into death.

I feel a hand on my shoulder, causing me to jerk, anguish still wracking my body. Through the tears, I see Roland squatting before me.

"*Please.*"

I'll beg. I'll plead. I'll give my own fucking soul. Whatever it takes. I need to get into that room with him.

"I'm sorry, Ciaráin. But no."

"Why?" My voice cracks on the single word, along with whatever remains of my heart.

If I thought I was heartbroken before, during every moment we fought once I ended things, I was fucking wrong.

Nothing compares to this.

Bowing his head, one of his hands lifts to his face, where he pinches the bridge of his nose between his thumb and forefinger for a good minute. Letting out a drawn-out sigh, Roland raises his gaze to mine. His voice, it comes out so fucking soft, I could swear it was an older version of River's. "Because, son. We both know he'd be better off without you."

My intestines tangle themselves together, hating the truth and the lie in his statement.

Yes, River would be better off without me. He's been through so much suffering since we've met, a majority of it at my own hands. And through that, he's proven he can bounce back. His resilience knows no bounds. He's strong, he'd get through the pain and come out the other side to find someone who actually deserves his love. I know it.

But seeing what our separation did to him? I *have* to believe he needs me as much as I need him.

That he could survive without me, but it would be just that... surviving instead of truly living.

Before I can open my mouth, an alarm pierces from down the hall, from the direction of River's room. Roland bolts up and rushes down the hall, scrambling into the room with a set of nurses quick on his heels.

I find my way to my feet, unsteady and shaky, and follow behind them as quickly as I can manage. And when I reach the doorway, still slightly ajar from the commotion, I wish I never looked inside.

Nothing could prepare me for what lies beyond it.

Tubes. Wires. IVs and blood bags.

River, covered in them, his broken and battered body looking nothing like him.

Ventilators.

Monitors.

Beeping.

Shouting.

My feet propel me backwards. Which is wrong. I need to be in there. I need to be with him.

My back hits the wall just before my knees give out, nausea rolling through me.

And then.

The most dreadful sounds of all paralyze me in place.

A mother's wail. A sister's cry. A father's sob.

The decimation of my heart. My mind. My *soul*.

And

worst

of

all.

A flatline.

One Week Later

THIRTY-TWO
River

My throat feels like Death Valley and my entire body might as well have been run over by a truck; I'm so exhausted when I stir back into consciousness. My eyes ache too, I swear someone decided to super glue them shut and when I finally manage to open them, it takes a minute or so before I can adjust to the brightness of my surroundings.

It's only then I realize I'm in a hospital room. In a bed. In one of those awful gowns.

Alone.

What the...

And then it rushes back.

Ted. Rain. The gun. Being *shot*.

And then...nothing.

Glancing around, I can't help but think, *how the fuck am I alive?*

I don't have long to contemplate the thought or even take stock of my injuries because the door opens and in walks a nurse, probably in her forties, with what I'd assume is my chart in her hand.

My shifting to sit up alerts her I'm awake and she gives me a friendly smile. "I was hoping you'd be waking up soon. How are you feeling, River?"

"Like I've been shot twice in the stomach," I groan, trying my best to sit up completely. She rushes over to assist me, pushing the rail down and adjusting the bed so I can comfortably sit up without the sharp pain in my torso.

"You need to be careful about those stitches. There's more than just the top layer you can see and we don't want to risk you rupturing them. Just do your best not to move too fast or bend and do things in ways that cause a tugging sensation." I nod and she continues to chatter on about how long I'll take to heal and what I can expect while fluffing the pillow behind my head, but I zone out, lost in my thoughts.

The most forefront being, *where is everyone?*

As if reading my mind, this nurse gives me a smile. "Your family stepped out to get something to eat about thirty minutes ago. No one expected you to wake up already. But they should be back—"

The door opens just then, Willow the first person to walk though. She looks tired, her eyes red and swollen like she's been crying too. But the second she notices I'm awake, a giant smile takes over her face and she literally jumps into my bed and crawls into my lap.

"Miss—" the nurse starts, jumping back. I can tell she's about to reprimand Willow for probably a million things, one of which

I'm sure is jostling me to the point of pain. At least if the way she scowls when I wince is any indication.

But I really don't care about the rules or the pain right now.

"It's fine," I tell the nurse as Willow flings her arms around me and buries her face into my neck. "I won't tell if you won't."

The nurse gives me a stern look but I see a hint of compassion in her eyes before she nods and exits the room.

"Oh my God," Willow breathes. "Please don't ever pull a stunt like this again, Riv."

And then my little sister, one of the fiercest girls I know, breaks down before my very eyes.

Short bursts of tears escape her, slipping down and coating the skin of my neck. I wrap my arms around her, my palms running up and down her back, needing to soothe her.

"Will, it's okay. I'm right here," I whisper, pressing my cheek into her hair.

Glancing over her shoulder, I see my mom enter the room looking just as worse for wear. She smiles the second she notices Willow and I, coming over to the bed and sitting beside us.

I grimace as I lean towards her, inviting her into our hug, which she gladly accepts by folding her arms around both of us with care.

"I love you, sweetie," she whispers, her voice soft and trembling. It makes my heart ache in my chest. And it only worsens when Willow sniffles and burrows her face deeper into my neck, adding, "So much."

The sound of the door closing has me glancing up from between their heads and who I find standing in the doorway is a surprise, though it shouldn't be.

Of course he'd want to be here to see what latest mess his son has gotten himself into. Another box to tick off on the never-ending list of ways I disappoint him.

"Willow, get off your brother's lap. It's hardly appropriate," he hisses.

Same old asshole father, it seems.

No *glad you're okay* or *I was worried about you.* And heaven forbid he utter a single word about loving me like my other family members did.

It shouldn't come as a shock, but it doesn't keep the hurt from my chest that hits harder than either of these bullets did.

My mother and Willow withdraw themselves, my sister scrambling off my lap as quickly as she made it up here in the first place at Dad's harsh tone. My mother, on the other hand, gives me a smile and a kiss on the cheek, lingering a while longer before she joins Willow in a chair by the window.

"Glad to see you're awake," he says, though his voice is seemingly detached yet again.

And I don't understand why I keep giving him the power to hurt me.

Everything about his posture is relaxed as he leans back against the door, but somehow it's still threatening. I guess because I'm naked save for this stupid gown and lying in a hospital bed.

But it's him leaning against the door, as if unwilling to let anyone else in the room out...or *in* that has me slightly on edge.

At first I think it's because Ted might still be at large, but I have no idea if my parents even know how any of this happened.

Shit, I have no idea about *anything.*

How did I get to the hospital? Who took me here? Did Ted manage to escape? What is the extent of my injuries?

Where in God's name is Rain?

My brain focuses on the last one and I look around the room at my family. But he's missing...and he should *be here.* The only one I want to know is safe and well and fucking *alive.*

Dread floods through me as I look to my father. "Where's Rain?"

And for a split second, the worst thoughts imaginable fill my mind, taking control and attempting to root themselves.

Please be alive. I don't want to have taken these bullets for nothing.

Confusion mars my father's face. "Who?"

Swallowing hard, my throat still scratchy, I say his full name. "Ciaráin. Ciaráin Grady."

A hard expression replaces the confusion. "River—"

"I need to see him, Dad," I cut him off. "Where is he?"

Clearing his throat, he glances to my mother and sister, both of whom have fallen silent.

The roots begin to grow and blossom as an intense amount of dread fills my stomach, bile rising to my throat.

Oh, God.

"He's not..." I start, the words feeling heavy in my chest. My stomach aches, and it's not entirely for the two bullet wounds. My eyes start to water as I look at my mom. "Please tell me he's not—"

"He's alive, sweetie. He's being kept in a separate waiting room."

Relief washes over me in waves, and I let out a deep breath.

Okay, this is good. He's alive and in the other room.

Giving my mom a weak smile, I whisper, "Can you go get

him for me?"

"Right now is visiting hours for family o−"

Fuck hospitals and their asinine rules.

"He *is* my family. And I think being *shot twice* should get me some *leniency* when it comes to who is allowed inside this room and when."

My father clicks his tongue. "That's not how this works."

"Roland," Mom seethes, her eyes shooting daggers at him, and I can tell it surprises everyone in the room. Including Mom herself.

She quickly schools her features though, conveying the appearance of full confidence. I watch the silent battle waged between my parents for a moment and I have to admit, I'm floored at the way my mother is standing up to him right now. And while my father doesn't concede to her in words, she gives him a stern look and makes it known she doesn't give a damn when she turns and exits the room, my sister following right behind her.

Good for you, Mom.

Flicking my scrutiny to my father, he gives me a look I can only describe as pleading.

"River, listen to me," he starts, but I pin him with a glare.

"No, Dad, *you listen,"* I hiss, more bite in my tone than I thought myself capable of, especially in my current condition. "I'm done letting you tell me how I should be living my life. *Fucking. Done."*

I pause and give him a moment, waiting for him to interrupt with a rebuttal. To my surprise, it doesn't come, so I carry on.

"You've belittled me and made me feel inferior for *far* too long. And I'm tired of it. I'm sick of feeling like I need to back down and respect you because you're my father. It might be how I was raised, but respect isn't something everyone deserves. It's *earned*."

I growl the words out, letting all the words I've never said flow from me freely for the first time in my life.

"So, please tell me when it was you earned it from me? When you asked me to just *be straight* because you couldn't handle me being my own person? Or maybe when you divorced Mom and left our family because I wouldn't dare conform to the rules you were setting?"

He remains silent, and I scoff. "Right, of course you have nothing to say now. When it really fucking matters." I shake my head, rolling my eyes. "You don't *deserve* my respect. Not after the way you've treated me since I was a freshman in high school. Like less than the dirt on your shoes. And what? All because there's a possibility you might have a *son*-in-law instead of a daughter? Do you understand how fucking insane that is?"

"It's not insane when it goes against everything I believe in, River. Your passionate ramblings aren't going to change anything," he tells me, detachment evident in his voice.

And just when I thought he couldn't break my heart any further, he proves me wrong.

"Fine," I say. "Then you can go. Leave. I don't need your love or acceptance. I'll have Mom and Willow and Rain—"

Something between a grunt and a snort leaves him as I say Rain's name. "That boy almost got you killed," he retorts, ice in his tone.

I grit my teeth. "That *boy* happens to be the love of my fucking life. And while love isn't something deemed important to you, it is to me. And I'm not letting you sit here and tell me I can't love him."

His hard stare cuts holes through me, but I stand my ground, waiting for whatever verbal lashing will come next. But it never comes. He just continues to stare at me, a void in his eyes and detachment radiating from him in waves.

The ultimate sting of rejection hits me and I have to force my voice to remain even.

"He is the person I plan to spend the rest of my life with. *He* is the person I can't live without. And *he* is the person I willingly took two bullets for. So accept it or don't, Dad. At this point, it doesn't matter to me." Swallowing roughly, I let out a shaking breath. "But if you can't, I want nothing to do with you. I never want to see you — ever again. Because I don't need to be reminded of what a *disappointment* my father truly is."

He clicks his tongue again, nodding his head slowly before he glances over to the window. I remain silent, watching him, and when his attention lands back on me, I see a faint glaze over his eyes.

Nodding again, he turns and grabs the door handle and opens it to the hall. The ache in my chest magnifies as he steps into the threshold. But it completely shatters the second he glances at me over his shoulder and utters something I haven't heard from him in years.

"Know I love you, River. And I'm very proud of you."

Tears well in my eyes as he continues out the door, pulling it closed behind him.

It's only when I'm completely alone again I allow them to break free, letting myself feel this pain one final time before releasing its hold on me for good.

I'm half asleep when the door to my room closes again with a soft click. I don't know how much time has passed since I closed my eyes. Maybe only a few minutes or even a couple hours. I'm just so tired. Exhausted and drained doesn't begin to describe.

And I slept for the past week.

Getting shot and having a massive blood transfusion will do that, according to my doctor at least. When he came in with my nurse a few minutes after my father left to check on me, he filled in all the blanks as to what happened.

Two gunshot wounds to the abdomen, both of which the doctors had to fish out in surgery. Extensive blood loss due to a nicked artery, which required additional hours of surgery to repair. And then the stitches failed to hold after they got me into a room causing so much internal bleeding I needed the blood transfusion.

At one point, after I coded for the third time in the OR, they thought I was gone for.

The doctor explained all this, but I barely heard a thing with my mind wandering a million different places. To the point where I had to have the nurse tell me it all over again while she stood outside the bathroom, as I showered and cleaned up, just in case I needed help or began feeling uneasy. Which I was grateful for, because at one point I felt like I was going to pass out from the heat.

Then she walked me back to my bed, getting me settled back in and left me once again to stew in my thoughts.

I don't know how long ago that was.

A low groan escapes me as I stretch slightly. The tugging on my stitches makes my hand fly to the bandage covering them and I wince in pain.

Fuck.

428 | CE RICCI

The pain is sharp enough I don't even realize there was a hand resting on mine until I open my eyes.

Blinking profusely, I focus enough through the haze to see the room is empty once again of my mother and sister. The only person in here is the one with a head of dark brown hair and two tattooed arms resting on the bed directly next to me.

His back rises and falls gently as he takes long, slow breaths, and I immediately know he's asleep. My hand finds its way to his head, needing to touch him, feel him. Know he's real.

Rain.

And as much as I want to let him sleep, I just can't wait another second to see those amber eyes.

"Baby," I whisper, running my fingers through his hair. It's soft and still slightly damp, as if he's recently taken a shower and I run my hand through it again and again, forcing my brain to recognize this is real.

I'm alive. He's alive.

And right now, nothing else besides that matters.

"Baby, wake up," I say a little louder this time, but it still doesn't have the desired effect.

A knock on his skull sure does though, because he shoots up in a sitting position and looks around wildly and incoherently.

"It was just me," I say, grabbing his hand and his attention.

The second his eyes lock on mine, I can't seem to breathe. Like all the oxygen was just sucked out of the room the moment our gazes collided.

Or maybe it's because his mouth is on mine in a furious kiss that curls my toes and sears my heart. He's hovering over me, one hand against my pillow, the other cupping my face, and I'm so damn grateful I asked the nurse to let me clean up before I saw him.

He's seen me wrecked. A complete fucking disaster. And for once, I want him to see me whole again.

"I love you," he whispers against my lips before kissing me harder. I feel a few errant tears trickle down and join our lips, the salt from them hitting my taste buds when his tongue enters my mouth. It wraps around mine, and I groan when he pauses and pulls away.

"It's gone," he whispers, looking at me. His eyes search my face and he looks as tired as I feel. Immediately I wonder if he's managed to get any sleep in the week since I've been in the hospital.

I doubt it, seeing as this is the first time he's been allowed to see me.

"What's gone?" I ask, wiping his cheek with my thumb.

"The piercing."

I roll my tongue against the roof of my mouth and smirk. I found out myself when I brushed my teeth earlier and the nurse explained it was removed so they could intubate me for surgery. Of course it would be one of the first things he'd notice, knowing how obsessed he is with it.

"I can get it redone," I chuckle softly, sliding my fingers into his hair.

He brings his forehead back to rest against mine, and I breathe him in, finally feeling like the ground is steady beneath us again.

"It doesn't matter," he says gruffly in a harsh whisper. "It's just that…you were dead. You fucking died. For ten minutes, River." I hear the anguish in his voice and it cuts me, knowing what he must've gone through for an entire week without seeing me with his own eyes. Without *knowing* for certain. "And I couldn't...they wouldn't...I—"

"Hey, hey, hey," I soothe. "I'm here. I'm right here, baby."

He shakes his head, rolling it along my forehead as his hands tremble against my cheek and against my pillow. "You aren't allowed to leave me." It sounds as if he's swallowing shards of glass. "I swear to fucking God, River. And if you try to die on me again, I'm gonna find a way to bring you back to life just to kill you myself."

I hear him take a deep breath and feel more teardrops fall on my face. They keep coming and the urge to wipe them away and take his pain overwhelms me.

But the thing about pain is...you have to let yourself feel it. Otherwise you would never know the wound is healing.

His tears are his pain finally breaking free. I just never would have thought the guy who decked me that day on the field would be able to cry tears, let alone cry them for me.

It turns out I was wrong.

His mask was made for deception. It fooled me—fooled *everyone*—for so long, I was beginning to think he really was as heartless as he portrayed himself to be. Especially as he continued to push me away.

But Rain, while he's rough around the edges and so guarded and broken...he softened those edges eventually. *For me.* And he lets himself feel.

So as tears slide silently down his face, I stop wiping them away. Letting them mend his soul of all the pain and heartache recent months have brought. And all the misery his life was wracked with before we ever even met.

I let them heal him. Give him a fresh start. The new beginning we're both desperate for.

A smile plays at the edge of my lips at the thought, and I pull him down to kiss him. Letting him know he can break and I'll still be here while he repairs himself.

Pulling his hand, I try to scoot over and give him room to climb in the bed with me. It's difficult to manage, seeing as I have all these wires attached to me and of course, can't forget the bandages and stitches already making it hard to move around without wincing in pain.

But he just sits back in his seat beside the bed, sliding his hand in mine. "I'm fine right here. Don't keep moving around or you'll bust your stitches. Again."

I roll my eyes and continue adjusting. "I took a shower just fine. I think I can handle—"

"River," he says, glaring at me. "Don't fucking move another muscle."

His tone is threatening enough to give me pause, knowing it's his way of letting me know he'll make good on his threat to kill me himself.

"I love you too, by the way." I tell him gently. "I'm sorry my dad didn't let you in. When he wasn't going to do it, I snapped on him and—"

"You told your dad off for me?"

I try not to laugh at the shock in his tone, but it's difficult not to, even knowing I need to do my best to not rupture the stitches. "I'm a little insulted you think I wouldn't." I cock my head and stare into his eyes. "Baby, I'll always fight for you, right by your side. Don't ever doubt I'd go to war for you."

"You don't need to fight your family," he says, rubbing his thumb over my knuckles.

"You're my family. And I have my mom and Willow, they're more than enough." I shrug, accepting that my father will no longer be a part of my life. But like Rain, I'm using the pain of him leaving to heal the parts of myself he broke in the first place.

"They've been great," he says, watching me carefully. "They haven't done or said anything to make me think I wasn't welcome here. If it weren't for the two of them today or the twins and Taylor the past few da—"

"Taylor?" I ask. "He's here?"

He nods. "All three of them. Taylor flew back when he heard. I called Siena and it was a whole thing. But even Asher and Abbi and Garrett are here. They're in the waiting room I was in when your mom came to find me earlier." A soft chuckle comes from him. "She made me shower and eat something before I could come see you, said I looked like I was running on fumes and smelled like a barn."

I smile, knowing she was mothering him. And I can see it written all over his face how much it meant to him for her to do that.

"But then you fell asleep again before I could get in here," he continues. "It's only been like six hours, but I haven't left your side since. Texted everyone a few updates before I fell asleep myself."

"Why didn't they just come see me?"

He sighs. "Hospital is only letting the family in for now since you were asleep. Your mom lied and told the nurses I was your fiancé just to get me in here, but even that was a stretch to actually work."

I smirk and wink at him. "Fiancé, huh?"

He shakes his head and laughs. "Fuck off."

But he smiles when he says it, a little hint of mischief in his eyes that tells me he doesn't exactly hate the idea. Something to put a pin in for later. For now I change the subject back.

"Since I'm up, can I see them?"

Nodding, he gives me a half smile. "I think so? We'll have to check with the nurses first." I don't miss the way his eyes flash with disappointment though. And I get it.

He's waited a week. They can wait a little longer.

"Maybe tomorrow?" I ask and he nods again, the disappointment fading immediately and I almost laugh at how easy it's becoming to read him.

We sit in a comfortable silence for a while, staring and smiling at each other like we can't believe we fucking made it. But against all odds, we did.

At least, I think we did.

"Is it over? Can we finally…" I take a deep breath, wincing at the stitches tugging against my skin.

Fuck, this is gonna be a long recovery.

"We can finally," he confirms, bringing our hands to his lips. "Roman's gone for good, and so is Ted."

"Did he…?" I trail off, not wanting to know if he actually managed to get away with the millions of dollars that rightfully belong to Rain.

Rain makes a face I can't quite place. "I'm not sure what happened. I told the police everything I knew but once you passed out I was kind of a mess, to say the least." He laughs, but it's strained. And my stomach churns at what he must've gone through.

"Roman was the one who got us here. I don't remember anything. But when the police arrived and took our statements, he said Ted's car and the bag of money were gone before he could even get the Jeep pulled up to get you to the hospital. They found the car in the long-term parking lot of the Denver airport a few days ago and I haven't heard anything from him since the warehouse. So all signs point to…he's gone. It's over."

The immediate sense of relief I feel is short-lived though, because I'm worried he's going to come back once he's out of money or worse, decides he wants to finish the job altogether.

Rain's brows furrow as he looks at me. "I see the wheels spinning. And yeah, it's not ideal. But we can cross any bridges in the future. For now, let's just be."

I want to laugh since the statement coming from him is kinda hilarious, seeing as he's not the type to *just be.* Especially when it comes to Ted Anders and whatever power he holds over us.

"Is that really what you want? We can keep looking —"

"It's what I want." He says it like a promise. "I don't wanna live waiting around for the shoe to drop. I just wanna live."

I study him for a second, letting the words float between us as I gauge his sincerity.

"Okay," I concede.

He smiles and kisses my knuckles. "The real question is what do *you* want, mo grá? You're the one who took two bullets. So, whatever you want, I'll give it to you. Anything, fucking everything. Say the word, baby, and it's yours." He pauses and eyes me for a second. "Just no ass tattoos."

I grin and shake my head because that's the last thing I want from him right now.

"How 'bout something better."

"All ears."

"I want all of your secrets," I say, my brow raised. "Nothing is hidden between us ever again."

"Done." Not a hint of hesitation.

Nodding, I add, "I want you to move in with me."

This time he does hesitate, his forehead creasing. "You don't think it's too soon?"

I shake my head and smirk, pulling on his shirt so he'll lean in and kiss me. "How can it be too soon when we already had a thirty-five-day trial run?"

He lets out a soft chuckle, his nose brushing against mine lightly. "Fair point."

"And I want *you*," I swallow harshly, my grip on his hair tightening. "I want you for the rest of my life."

"Is that a proposal, River Lennox?" he asks with a lilt of amusement in his voice.

"I mean, you're *already* my fiancé, so—"

He glares daggers at me and I can't help but grin like a damn idiot.

Playing with the hair at the base of his skull, my eyes dance between his. "Trust me, baby. You'd know it if it was."

A smirk crosses his lips. "All right, then. Anything else you'd like to request?"

I pull back and give myself a moment to think about it. About what else I could possibly want from him. To share *with him.* He's already given me so much so what else could there possibly…

And then I know.

"A dog."

His eyes narrow. "A dog?"

I give him a wry smile. "Well, since ass tattoos are apparently off the table indefinitely, yeah. A dog. Or better yet, a puppy."

He stares at me in disbelief, and I shrug, popping my dimples.

"What? You said *anything.*"

EPILOGUE

Rain

ALMOST TWO YEARS LATER

The tires of the 4Runner crunch under the snow as River and I drive up the winding mountain road about thirty minutes from Vail. We've finally got some time to spend together with our busy schedules, so we're heading towards the cabin where we'll be staying for the next couple weeks to kick off the new year.

No, not the same cabin belonging to the Scotts. But one close by, at least by mountain traveling standards. It's only about a four-mile hike to the lake by Coach's cabin, just the opposite side, which is exactly why I chose it.

It felt right to come back out here for a few weeks of downtime we have before life picks up again.

Two years ago, after the fiasco with Ted settled down and River was released from the hospital, things went back to relatively normal. Our new normal, that is.

I moved in with River the day he went home, per his request, though it was no trouble on my end and I didn't bother putting up a fight. He still needed someone to help him during his healing process at home and his place was bigger, so it made the most sense. After the scare of a lifetime, I didn't want to be apart from him ever again.

I still don't.

River healed in time to play the first game of our final season in college. And we fucking dominated the field together, having a near undefeated season. We wound up going to battle for the National Championship, only to lose in overtime to Michigan.

Taylor still won't let River live it down. Even this morning, a year later, when he picked us up from the airport and lent us his vehicle while we stay up in Vail for a few weeks.

But I am pleased to announce after three nominations, I finally won the fucking Heisman. Thanks in part to the stellar arm of my boyfriend, that is.

In addition to the Heisman, I had an unbelievable performance at the combine, and I was drafted in the first round to the Patriots. This past season with them was rough, and while I played, it wasn't as much as I'd hoped. Regardless, I'm just glad to have made it this far, knowing how proud it would've made my dad.

My mom, though, she's been great. Our relationship is still a bit rocky but we're getting there. She even came to spend some time with us around Christmas and I swear she might be as in love with River as I am.

Riv ended up getting into a really great graduate program for physical therapy at a school in Boston, too, and I'm more grateful for that than anything else. After the long, grueling practices or trips out of town where I'd give anything to not be in the NFL, at least I get to come back to the brownstone we bought with the trust that somehow *magically* returned to my bank account.

How it happened, I don't care all that much. I'm just glad to come home to River.

And Vale, our now two-year-old gray and white husky mix.

Yeah, I caved and took River to a shelter to find a goddamn puppy the minute he was healed enough to be able to walk one. I wasn't lying when I said I'd give him anything. So if a puppy is what he wanted, a puppy he would get.

In all honesty, adopting Vale was the best decision I ever made and helped River immensely when it came to his recovery. Doctor Fulton—who we both continued to see regularly in our last year of college, though it was only River who saw her in a professional capacity—even signed some paperwork making Vale River's support animal for his mental health after being shot.

I know it has to still take a toll on him, though he doesn't talk about it often. But those days that are the worst, I'll catch him holding onto Vale a little tighter and burrow into my side a little deeper, letting us take away some of his pain.

And the smile on his face everytime Vale does something stupidly cute or coming home to find them snuggling on the couch while River does homework...it makes all the dog hair worth it.

Barely.

"Are you telling me where we're going yet?" River laughs from the passenger seat of the car, glancing over at me with mischief in his eyes. "Because if you're trying to get to the Scott's cabin, you were supposed to turn right a long time ago."

"That's not where we're going," I grin, glancing over at him, which makes him narrow his eyes at me.

He turns to the back seat to look at Vale, whose head perks up at River's attention.

"Do you know where he's taking us?" he asks the dog.

I glance in the rear view mirror to see Vale tilt his head and blink those big brown eyes, the same shade as mine, at him and I let out a throaty laugh. "Did you really think he'd respond?"

River shrugs, turning back to me. "You know as well as I do he's a talker."

I chuckle because he's not wrong. Go figure River would pick the one fucking dog on the planet that likes to talk back as much as he does.

River lets out a sigh, clearly taking my avoidance in stride and settles into the leather seat. Every so often I flash my eyes his way, catching him tapping his hand to the Beartooth song playing through the speakers.

As I move to grab his hand, my newest tattoo peeks out from under my sleeve. The one I got under his name. *You keep me safe.*

It matches the one on his own inner wrist. *You keep me wild.*

His palm in mine, I squeeze it three times, keeping my eyes on him as I do.

It's something we've been doing for the past couple years. Since the day he did it to me that first time while I held him in my arms, begging to whoever would listen to save him. He didn't know I felt it at the time, but now it's become my favorite way to tell him those three words.

His mouth lifts in a half smile, squeezing back before catching my eyes. "I love you too."

My heart stutters in my chest, just like every fucking time I've heard those words from his lips. Which is every single day since he first spoke them out loud. I still haven't gotten used to them. Part of me thinks I never will. But I do know that I'll never grow tired of hearing them, especially with how gut-wrenching it is to think I might've never heard them again because of Ted.

That's one piece of even better news: Ted's gone. Long gone from our lives, and in my theory, this world. The media came out with a story that Ted was spotted fleeing the country less than two days after River was shot, and he's vanished since, never to be heard from again.

The only issue is I know Ted and he wouldn't let this go that easily and I'd be lying if I wasn't concerned with the possibility of his return.

But one day, right around the time River was released from the hospital, I received a text from an unknown number. It was nothing specific, just a simple request.

Don't live the rest of your lives looking over your shoulder. You don't have to worry anymore.

My stomach dropped at the sight of it and I immediately attempted to call the number, but no one answered. But even still, I know it was Roman who sent the text.

Roman.

Who I hadn't heard from since that day in the hospital when I pushed him away for good. And who I haven't seen or spoken to since that single text.

I don't know what it means exactly, except Ted has been dealt with. In what capacity, I don't think I'll ever know for sure. My gut tells me he's dead, and I know from experience if that were the case, the Enclave could easily cover it up.

Regardless, it's a gift I'll never be able to repay Roman for, knowing Ted will never have power over me ever again.

The only person I'll ever let have that is sitting right beside me.

Turning onto a slight driveway, I pull up in front of the black and dark brown A frame cabin where we will be staying for the next couple weeks. I started planning this trip months ago, before my season officially started, and when I saw the design for this cabin online, I just knew. It was exactly what I was looking for when it came to our postseason get-a-way before River's classes resume. A place for the two of us to take the time to just *be* again.

It's simpler and smaller than Coach Scott's on the outside, but it's perfect for just the two of us and Vale.

River's grin grows exponentially as he takes in the cabin, complete with a wall of glass behind a deck with a hot tub on it that you can bet your ass we're going to christen as soon as possible.

I hop out of the car and grab our bags, letting Vale loose in the fresh snow the mountains got this morning, watching him act like a fucking idiot rolling around in the powder before zooming around the open area to the side of the cabin.

A quick glimpse in River's direction reveals a smile bigger than any I've seen in a while as he watches Vale run around. He takes a deep breath, filling his lungs with cool mountain air, and sighs in contentment.

"You love it here, yeah, babe?" I ask. "Feels like home?"

He laughs softly, his breath causing a puff of steam to rise in the air. "Yeah. With the three of us here, it definitely does."

I smile, knowing he always feels at home as long as we're all together. "Good, now let's get inside before we freeze our asses off." Making a quick hand-off of his bag, I unlock the door with the key from beneath the mat, exactly where I was told it would be.

"Damn," River breathes as he steps inside the front door, dropping his duffel just inside the door and removing his jacket and boots. "This looks like Coach's, just smaller."

It really fucking does. Rustic, yet modern, complete with a fireplace and wood stove just like the Scott cabin was. And it should be very close, seeing as it was done by the same builder who did Taylor's family's. That's my favorite part about it. It's just maybe half the scale. And the master suite is upstairs in a loft, the two extra rooms and a bathroom down the hall at the back instead.

Anxiety begins creeping up my chest as I watch River walk around, taking it all in while Vale sniffs every corner of the cabin before hopping up on the brown leather couch, making himself right at home.

"Do you like it?" I set down the rest of our stuff by the door and shrug out of my outerwear as well.

Fuck, why am I so nervous? It's River. He's just happy to be back in the mountains.

"It's perfect." He smiles, coming over to place a kiss on my lips. "I already see a lot of surfaces for us to—"

"Really? You're insatiable." I laugh, cutting him off.

"Sorry that you're not taking care of me during the season like you should be." He laughs though, letting me know he's just trying to poke the bear.

In reality, our sex life is nothing short of combustible.

Shit, I'm glad I've never said that out loud. He would have a field day with it.

River moves back into the open space, taking in each and every inch of the cabin as he does, before he halts in front of the fireplace. His attention locks on the artwork hung there.

It's an abstract piece, not really fitting of the rustic vibe the rest of the cabin gives off, but I personally think it belongs there.

It's a swirl of blue and green and teal, smeared and mixed together, coating a large, white canvas.

It's my favorite piece I've ever created.

Because he and I made it together.

"This looks kind of like..."

My heart falters in my chest when I hear River's sharp intake of breath before he whirls around to look at me. His eyes, matching that painting perfectly, search my face in disbelief.

I do my best not to smile. "Looks like what, mo grá?"

He glances back up at the painting, then to me again before licking his lips. "We're not *renting* this cabin, are we?" he asks slowly.

I shake my head. "No, Abhainn. We're not renting this cabin."

River blinks a couple times, processing this new information. "But that's..." he sputters, motioning to the painting, then to the rest of the cabin. "But how?"

I let myself smile now, stepping towards him and slipping my hand around the back of his neck. "Well, I had made an offer to Coach Scott to buy *his* cabin the minute we graduated school, but he wouldn't budge on it. Said he wanted to keep it, in case he needed to pull another stunt like he did with us. So, I had this one built instead."

River's eyes practically bulge out of his head. "You built it?"

I chuckle, leaning my forehead to rest against his. "Do you ever listen? I *had it built.*"

A noise, something like a choked laugh, comes from his throat. "No, I know what you meant. I'm just…" he drags in a lungful of air before sighing. "I can't believe you did this and didn't tell me. We said no more secrets."

I smirk. "Surprises are the good kind of secrets."

He pulls back to glare at me. "You hate surprises. You withheld sex for two days because I threw that surprise party after you got drafted."

I snort out a laugh. "You got me there. But I like surprising you."

He rolls his eyes, but the smile on his face lets me know he's not actually upset. "As if you haven't given me enough surprises to last a lifetime already? Besides, why did this need to be a surprise? You know I would have loved to help, I don't know, pick out shit."

I quirk a brow because *really, Riv?* We both suck at the whole decorating thing. That's why I had Siena take care of it instead, both at our brownstone and here. Just gave her a couple ideas and my credit card and it was done a fuckton better than either of us would have accomplished.

"Because I like doing nice things for you," I tell him, kissing his jaw, nibbling at the neatly trimmed scruff he keeps there now. "Because I wanted to see the look on your face when you put it together." My lips move up to his cheek, brushing against it where his dimples pop. "Because putting a smile on your face is my favorite thing to do every day." Licking the seam of his lips, I mold my mouth to his in a rough kiss I never want to end. "Because I wanted to give us a place here, where we fell in love, to be ours," I whisper against his mouth, barely able to breathe, I'm so consumed by him. "Because I love you more than anyone in the entire world."

Sliding my hand from his neck, I drop down to my knee in front of him. My heart pounds in my chest rapidly, beating a thousand miles a minute as I look up at him. Swallowing roughly, I slip my hand into my pocket to pull out a black ring.

One I've been keeping on me since we moved to Boston, trying to figure out how to do this the right way. But that's the thing. There's never a right way or a right time to put yourself on the line for someone else. It's vulnerable, it's uncomfortable. It's fucking terrifying.

Yet with River, I know that my heart is safer than it would be with anyone else.

Holding the ring up for him to see, I push my anxiety to the side and offer everything I have to give. "Because you fought for us at every turn, even when you had no reason to. Gave me hope for a better future. Held my hand and had my back and supported me through whatever life threw my way. And I want to do those things for you too. I want to spend the rest of my life making you as happy as you make me, if you'll let me."

The unease leaves my chest the moment his dimples appear in his cheeks. River grabs my hand and hauls me back to my feet, covering my mouth with his in a kiss so filled with love and passion, my heart feels like it might burst.

Of course, my mind latches onto the fact that this isn't a yes.

But it's certainly not a no either.

"If I remember correctly, I told you there would be a day I'd bring you to your knees," he mumbles against my mouth, biting at my lip. "But I guess I can live with just the one."

I choke out a laugh, pulling back to see his face. "Is that a yes?"

His fingers tease the back of my neck, playing with the hair there as his smile grows even larger. "Baby, you really don't know? It would never have been anything other than yes." He rubs his nose against mine before chuckling. "I was actually starting to wonder if you had changed your mind, it took you long enough."

My brows furrow as I lean back to look at him. "What do you mean?"

He licks his lips and moves to grab the ring I'm still holding in my hand, bringing it up between us. "I had actually found it. Months ago, not long after the season started." He shakes his head and laughs. "I guess that's what happens when you ask me to find your wallet from your pants you wore the day before and a ring falls out of the pocket."

I remember the day he's talking about, vividly. I was running late for practice and the headcase I can be, couldn't find my wallet or keys. I was too busy the night before getting fucked by my boyfriend the second after I walked in the door to make a conscious effort to remember where I put either of those things the next morning.

And when River came out of the bedroom with my wallet, he looked weird. Nervous even? I couldn't say for sure. I even recall laughing at him because the tips of his ears were red and that

448 | CE RICCI

only happens when he's really anxious or embarrassed.

But I never would have put it together that he found the ring.

"Why didn't you say something?"

He shrugs, sliding the tiny symbol of my love for him on the ring finger of his left hand. "Because I didn't want to ruin anything for you. So much was taken from you in your life and…" he sighs, his eyes flashing between mine. "I just didn't want to take this away from you. I'm actually glad I found it when I did because I had planned to ask you—"

"You were gonna ask me?" I ask, cutting him off.

He smiles that full-dimpled smile I can't fucking help but fall more in love with every single day. "Yeah, baby. I told you two years ago I wanted forever with you. Or did you take too many hits this last season to remember?"

"Jackass, I remember everything," I chide, but I don't care. He can take his little jabs all he wants at me because he's mine at the end of the day.

"Bet," he tells me, kissing me again. This time, there's more urgency behind it as his hand slips under the fabric of my shirt, playing with the muscles of my abs. "But we can put a little rain check on it if you need time to think. Besides, I wanna fuck my fiancé. *Hard*. And maybe my cock buried deep inside you will help jog your memory."

I groan because *dammit* he would have to challenge me when all I want is for him to be inside me in the next two-point-five seconds or I might go insane. But I can never let myself back down from his challenges.

"I can prove it. Remember what coach asked when he came

back to get us on our last day out here?" I murmur into him, licking at the steam of his lips.

River bites my bottom lip, tugging at it before laughing lightly against my mouth. "He asked if we worked our shit out or lost our minds. Like I'm about to lose mine if you don't start stripping."

A grin breaks out on my face, loving how impatient he is. "And do you remember what I said?" I ask, pulling his shirt over his head. My fingers trail along the two lines of ink on his ribs. The words I'm referring to.

He nods, ripping my shirt off me in a smooth tug and dropping it to the floor beside us. His fingers work their way to cup the base of my skull, pulling me in for another kiss as we stumble back into the hallway towards a bedroom.

"I wasn't kidding when I said I lost my mind while we were forced together for those five weeks. You made sure of that," I chuckle softly, molding my mouth to his for light kisses between words. "But Abhainn, I truly did find my soul in that cabin too. Thanks to you. Because *it's* you. Fuck, even when I didn't realize it, it's always been you."

River smiles against my mouth before pressing me into the wall and slipping his tongue into my mouth to tangle with mine. His hand, the one with my ring on his finger, cups the side of my face.

A rumble of possessiveness works its way from my chest at the feel of the cool metal against my cheek as he takes control from me.

Forcing me to follow his lead.

Pulling back, I smirk at him. "And you remember what Coach said the first day at the cabin when he dropped us off?"

His eyes, more green today and darkened with lust, meet

mine. Brows drawn together as his fingers rake through my hair, I watch as he works through my question.

And the moment recognition sets in, a smile lights up his face before he reels me back in for a kiss.

If you think you're lost, just follow the river.

"I need you to remember this if nothing else," I mumble against his lips while I work the button of his jeans, desperation and need clawing at me, ripping me open. After shoving them down his legs, my fingers brush against the two slightly raised scars on his abdomen. The ones left behind by two near fatal gunshot wounds.

Ones he took for no other reason than his love for me.

And while I might never be able to repay my debt to him, I'm so thankful he's going to let me spend the rest of my life trying.

Still teasing his scars that have long since healed, I release his mouth and lock my eyes with his. "You're all I want. All I'll ever need," I tell him, my voice rough and filled with gravel. "And I swear to you, River. No matter what, I'll follow you anywhere."

EXTENDED EPILOGUE
Roman

I watch through the giant cabin windows, hidden in the shadows of the winter forest surrounding me, as the love of my life asks another man to marry him.

A man who isn't me.

It's been two years since I've seen Rain this close in person, and the sight of him on his knee before River...it still fucking hurts. I've been keeping an eye on them all this time, just in case. But I've never had to witness anything like this.

Public kisses or holding hands, sure. Never this.

Still, the ache in my chest is insurmountable, even after the time we've had apart. Even when he told me it would never happen, that his heart would only ever belong to River, the throbbing pain won't go away.

I haven't found a way to get over it. *Him.*

After the time apart before our reunion nearly two years

ago, he still called *me*. *I* was the one he trusted above all others when help was needed to deal with Ted. The man who hurt him. Abused him. Treated him like an object rather than a person.

And like a horse to water, I came running, desperate for the mere scraps of attention and affection he might give me. I was on that plane before I had a chance to blink, desperate to see and feel him for the first time since I made the choice to leave him behind.

Still in that house, with that man.

That vile, wicked man.

I see now, that was my first mistake. Leaving him.

Truth be told, I had planned on ending Ted eventually, once my training was completed. When Rain had told me the truth about what he did to him as a mere child, I knew I would be the one to seek vengeance.

Retribution.

All for Rain.

I have to believe Ted is partially to blame for Rain not loving me back, being too afraid to be together when we stood a chance. I'm almost sure of it. It's the most bitter pill I have to swallow when it comes to the history he and I share.

I loved him for years. For as long as I can remember. From the moment I met him when I was nine, before I knew what *love* or *sexuality* even entailed. I felt something different for him. More than friendship.

I always knew that.

So I fought for him. A losing battle, as it turns out. Even when I killed for him, the first of what is now many, I still lost him.

All it did was divide me further from my brothers.

No one in the Enclave can know about how Ted came to meet such an early and untimely death. Asher assured me when he took care of Ted's body and redeposited the money from Rain's trust back into his account that everything from the warehouse would remain between us. Our little secret. And Asher, when he makes a vow, he takes it seriously.

I trust him. With what I need to, that is.

He doesn't know the things I overheard Ted say, the blanks that were filled from each of his confessions about the Enclave's involvement in the trafficking ring before I took his life. And all the answers to my many questions died with him.

This tiny piece of information, I've kept from all four of my brothers. I'll take it to my grave, if need be. Add it to the list of things that will end up buried, never to be spoken of.

The life I must lead is one filled with unspeakable acts that cause the soul to fracture.

Murder. Conspiracy. Deception.

Secrets, even from each other, are par for the course at this point.

The only thing that isn't a secret is the love I still hold in my heart for the person who will never feel the same. A love that will, more than likely, be there until my last day on Earth. Another thing taken to the death.

But none of it matters in the end.

I see now, Rain was right. We never would have made it. Not because love isn't enough, but because of the obligations that've been ingrained in me about my heritage to create a better future. Not for myself, but for everyone.

Those are the cards I was dealt, the hand destiny gave me as a birthright. And all the money in the world, all the power and resources I have at my disposal, are no match for fate when she decides to intervene.

Rain found a life I could never provide. But River can.

So, I just stand here, watching as they kiss. It's filled with love and passion as they quickly remove articles of clothing from each other's bodies, making their way out of view.

I know I have to let him go. To be happy.

When I told River all I wanted was what's best for Rain, I meant it.

After everything, it's the least he deserves.

Doesn't mean I don't wish it was me.

Shaking my head with that final thought, I make the choice. The one I have to do to survive. I turn my back on my past. There's no room for me to dwell there anymore.

From this day forward, my only goal is to protect myself, my heart, and all these vile secrets.

THE END

Acknowledgments

Wow. It's hard to believe River and Rain's journey has come to a close. It's been 235,000 words and six months in the making and now that it's over, I don't know how to feel. It's bittersweet, knowing these two are no longer going to actively run around in my brain, desperate for me to tell their story. There was a point there where I wasn't sure how they'd make it back to each other. Yet knowing they got the ending they deserve, it makes me insanely happy.

First, I want to thank everyone who made it to this point. I know it wasn't easy, but I'm grateful you chose to stick it out and see these two through until the end. There was a lot of heartache, but their pain was worth it to me, and I'm hoping it was to you as well.

To my alphas, Rita and Abby, for starting this journey with me and never letting me give up. I know I can be a pain in your ass, constantly running ideas by you and coming up with the most idiotic shit, but you guys are my bitches. I love you for it. And for pushing me to be the best I can be, talking me off ledges, and loving these boys just as much as I do. You two are everything. This book and these boys hold pieces of both of you in it.

To my betas, Sam, Neli, and Elle. You guys are fucking amazing and I hope you know how much each of you mean to me. Taking a chance on a new author is hard, but it's gotta be even harder when they're a friend. Thank you for not being afraid to be honest with me because I know everything you have to say is only coming from a place of love for me and my characters.

To Ella and Kristi, for taking me under your wings and giving me guidance in this community. The two of you have been invaluable to me with your knowledge and your friendships. I don't think I could've made it to this point without either of you. You both are amazing humans and I am so happy to have met you.

To all the incredible authors who sprint write with me, check in on me, pump me up, send me motivational Tiktoks, give me love, and make my imposter syndrome lessen each and every day. You guys make me feel so at home in the indie community that can be a dog eat dog world. Having y'all in my corner means everything to me.

To Amy, my kick ass editor. Thank you for helping me shape these boys into everything I want them to be and giving me your unbiased opinions. And for putting up with my literally insane changes I make between rounds. You're the real MVP dude.

To Zainab, for making sure this baby was cleaned up and ready to see the world in it's best form!

To Kate, for yet again, slaying this cover design for these boys. I can't thank you enough.

To my Street Team, my Enclave, for sticking by my side, hyping me up, and most importantly...for the GIFs. You guys remind me that this is meant to be fun, not just work. Thank you for being so freaking chill.

And last of all, to my readers. Thank you for taking a chance on me. For your messages, edits, reviews, and your love. This started as a journey to write just for me. To put words on a page and prove to everyone that I can do this if I put my mind to it. But now I'm writing for all of you too. Know nothing and no one is going to change that.

— CE Ricci

About the Author

CE Ricci is an international best-selling author who enjoys plenty of things in her free time, but writing about herself in the third person isn't one of them. She believes home isn't a place, but a feeling, and it's one she gets when she's chilling lakeside or on hiking trails with her dogs, camera in hand. She's addicted to all things photography, plants, peaks, puppies, and paperbacks, though not necessarily in that order. Music is her love language, and traveling the country (and world) is the way she chooses to find most of her inspiration for whatever epic love story she will tell next!

CE Ricci is represented by Two Daisy Media.
For all subsidiary rights, please contact:
Savannah Greenwell — info@twodaisy.com

Milton Keynes UK
Ingram Content Group UK Ltd.
UKHW022137251124
451529UK00013B/898

9 781960 81805